CW00551721

claire contreras

Elastic Hearts
Published by Claire Contreras, 2016

ISBN: 978-0-9994448-1-8

Cover Design by Okay Creations
Photographer: Perrywinkle Photographer
Formatting by: Champagne Formats
Edited by Marion Making Manuscripts and Karen Lawson

Copyright © 2016 by Claire Contreras

All rights reserved. No part of this book may be reproduced in any form or by any electronic or mechanical means including information storage and retrieval systems-except in the case of brief quotations embodied in critical articles or reviews-without permission in writing from its publisher, Claire Contreras.

This is a work of fiction. Names, characters, places, and incidents either are the product of the author's awesome imagination or are used fictitiously and any resemblance to actual persons.

Other Books

Kaleidoscope Hearts
Paper Hearts

The Wilde One

The Darkness Series
There is No Light in Darkness
Darkness Before Dawn

The Contracts & Deceptions Series
The Devil's Contract
The Sinner's Bargain

For anybody who thinks love only exists in fairy tales—

Love is limitless.

Believe.

"Give a little time to me or burn this out,
We'll play hide and seek to turn this around,
All I want is the taste that your lips allow . . ."

-Ed Sheeran

Prologue

"WE CAN'T DO this anymore," he said.

Those were not the words I'd expected to come out of his mouth given the last time I'd been here, he'd growled my name against my throat, telling me to be quiet so nobody would hear us. I blinked, swallowed, and blinked again, trying to focus on his intense hazel eyes as they studied my face, as if to make sure I understood him.

"Okay," I whispered. I wanted to ask why, but held my tongue. I knew why. Or at least I felt like I knew why. Instead I gave myself a pep talk. We'd become friendly. We'd hooked up a couple times. It was no big deal for things to be over. No big deal at all. But if that were the case, why did I feel like he was ripping out my heart?

"It's not . . ." He paused, sighing and running a hand through his hair. The hair I'd run my hands through a couple weeks ago. "I was going to say it's not you, but that sounds lame. You know why we can't do this anymore."

"Because you're scared of what would happen if my dad found out," I said. He nodded. I figured as much. It wouldn't look right if the new add-on to the firm was caught hooking up with the boss's daughter, never mind the fact that we hadn't even met here.

"It's in bad form," he said. "If we hadn't met at the bar that night I would have never let it get this far."

"No, I get it," I said, not wanting to hear the predictable excuses he was sure to fire off.

"I need to focus on my career."

I swallowed. My eyes drifted over his features taking mental snapshots, which was all they'd become. In twenty-four hours they'd be grainy in my memory. In twenty-four days they'd be faded; I'd have to squint my eyes and rummage through boxes in order to remember how he looked, what he wore, where we'd been. The only things I'd remember would be his scent and how I felt when I was with him. Important, and sexy, and smart. Victor was only four or five years older than me, but those were things boys my age didn't have a clue about.

"You're just now finishing college. You have an entire life ahead of you," he said.

"I know." I paused. "You don't have to sit here and give me a pep talk. I totally get it."

He let out a long, relieved breath, closing his beautiful eyes, eyes I wouldn't look into again on the brink of passion. I wondered if he'd even considered asking me how *I* felt about telling my dad. Probably not. Vic was too driven. Too much of a rule follower, and deep down I knew he hadn't wanted more. I knew he'd just wanted to have fun with me. He didn't want to settle down until he'd built his empire over the lies he construed in order to win cases.

Just like my father.

I always swore I wouldn't fall for a guy like him. Like *them*. I always said I'd end up with a guy who fit my lifestyle. One who didn't over plan or over calculate. One who followed his dreams, regardless of how crazy they were. Guys like Victor weren't like that. They became consumed by work—real work—not creative, fun dreams like the ones I had. We'd never work. That's right.

We'd never work. Maybe if I said that enough times I'd believe it.

"Well, it's been . . . nice." I stood up and walked toward the door. He stood as well, but stayed behind his desk, looking like he had no idea what to do. I let out a breath. "Remember to water your plants," I said, looking at the little bonsai on top of his desk that he never remembered to water.

"I will. Remember to try out those tennis lessons again just in case," he replied.

I smiled at the mention of that. I'd sprained my ankle a few months back when I went to play tennis with a friend of mine. He'd teased me relentlessly, not because I sprained my ankle playing tennis, but because I sprained it on a water break, when I stepped on the box for the water fountain. *Total* freak accident.

I closed the door and stood outside for a second, taking a deep breath to welcome air back into my lungs, wondering if I'd played it cool enough. When I felt settled, I left and drove to the set of a new sitcom where I'd been hired as a stand-in for a costume designer away on maternity leave.

By the time I got there, I'd replayed Victor and my short-lived history in my mind nothing short of forty times. I tried to think back and figure out at what point he knew things wouldn't work. Had it been when we went to the coffee shop downtown and ran into a friend of his? He'd introduced us as friends, which we were, but the tone in which he'd said it implied that it was all we could be. Was it because of my age? Or was it just him? We'd discussed marriage and relationships and our aversion to both. One of us had been dead serious; the other had made up lies along the way, because *I* wanted a relationship with real attachments and long-term goals.

I parked my car and waved at the lot attendee on my way in, and in those seconds where I was looking back as I walked in, I bumped into the person walking out.

"I am so sorry," he drawled, a slight southern accent I hadn't heard anywhere aside from movies. My eyes made their way up his body slowly until they landed on his face and caught on striking blue eyes. Holy wow. He was the definition of Hollywood.

"It's okay. I wasn't paying attention." We tried to sidestep each other three times, failed, and laughed. "Sorry," I said again, my cheeks blazing.

"The universe must really want to throw us together," he said, turning up his charming smile. "I'm Gabriel," he said, now blocking the door completely.

"Nicole," I responded, heart pitter-pattering.

"Are you an actress?" he asked. I shook my head.

"Costume design."

He nodded slowly, his eyes still on mine. "New?"

"First day."

"Nervous?"

"Very," I said, but smiled. He opened the door wider.

"I promise we don't bite," he said, his grin widening. "Well, some of us don't."

I laughed as I stepped inside. For the remainder of the day and week, Gabriel looked for ways to find me all around set, and just like that all thoughts of Victor began to vanish. As they should. Victor and Nicole were done. I needed to accept that, and Gabriel's charm was just enough to make me.

Chapter One

Victor

NICOLE ALESSI RARELY visited the law firm these days. I could count on two hands the amount of times she'd come, and six of those were before she'd gotten engaged. One of the last few times was after the ring graced her finger. I saw her in passing and she made sure to steer clear of me. As if I was going to pull her into my office and have my way with her while that thing was glaring at me, reminding me she belonged to somebody else. It was fine by me. It wasn't like I felt hurt by the engagement, I was more caught off guard. One day we were talking about how crazy people were to want to get married, and the next she'd become one of those crazy people. She'd given me no inkling, no sign that she'd wanted more, out of me, out of life . . . out of anything.

Even though that ship had sailed five years ago, or more accurately had never taken off to begin with, the buzz of her name around the office put me on alert. Everybody from my secretary to the receptionist was whispering about the beautiful Nicole, wife to the handsome Gabriel Lane, coming for a visit as if she herself were Hollywood royalty. Maybe she was. I made it my job not to keep up with her whereabouts. What was the point, anyway? And because I knew she was coming in, I busied myself in researching Sam Weaver, a star running back I was representing in a high-profile divorce. I'd asked him more questions than the SAT, and the guy still hadn't been one hundred percent honest with me.

How people expected me to represent them in court without all the information I asked for and win was beyond my understanding. My focus was cut by the loud knock on my office door. It was pushed open before I gave permission, and I didn't have to look away from my screen to know it was William. He was the only one with enough balls to do that. It also helped that he was my boss and owned the building.

"What can I do for you?" I asked as my eyes scanned the latest TMZ post about Sam and his encounter with not one, but two prostitutes. I looked away from the screen when I heard Will walk toward me without saying a word. He had *the* look on his face, the one that told me he was about to ask me to do something he knew I didn't want any part of. Like the time he asked me to take on the case of a porn-star divorce, which my sixteen-year-old self would have literally come all over, but the thirty-one-year-old me was too busy using disinfectant every time I went near any of my client's "work spaces."

"Fuck. Just spit it out."

Will chuckled, unbuttoning his suit with one hand as he took a seat across from me. The fact he didn't just come out with it and actually sat down to discuss it made me develop a little ringing noise in my ears. I gave him my full attention.

"You know you're the best damn attorney on my team," he said. I stayed quiet. I knew he wasn't going to fire me, but starting a conversation out like that could only mean . . . my heart skipped a beat at the mere suggestion in my thoughts. "Your worth ethic is enviable. You're driven, you're a cocky son of a bitch, but somehow you maintain a level of humanity with clients."

"Unless you're about to drop down on one knee and propose to me, I think you should just ask for what will clearly be a massive, Victor-please-don't-leave-my-firm-after-I-say-these-words favor," I said, mainly because I was starting to feel uncomfortable with the way his blue eyes leveled on mine. He smiled.

"I want to make you partner," he said.

My mouth dropped.

Those six words.

My reason for everything.

I reeled in my emotions before they let me get ahead of myself and sat back in my seat a little. "Just like that? What about Bobby?" Bobby, whose parents were old family friends of Will's, had been hired a year before I was. Even if I was a much better lawyer, I couldn't imagine him not giving Bobby the opportunity first.

"I've spoken to him about this at length. He knows where I'm coming from, and he agrees that you're better suited."

"Better suited . . . to make partner," I said, needing to clarify.

"To make partner, and for the job I need you to do in order to make partner." He delivered that with a wide grin. My heart sank. What the fuck was this man going to ask me to do?

"What is it this time? An actor needs representation because his wife slapped him with a divorce after he was caught cheating with their nanny?"

"Not quite, but good guess," he said, his smile turning somewhat serious. "I need you to represent Nicole in her divorce."

I blinked. *What? No.* I shook my head and swallowed loudly. It wasn't often I was at a loss for words, but this was just . . .

"She's getting a divorce?"

"Yes, and obviously I can't be her attorney, so I wanted her to get the next best thing."

Me. The next best thing. That in itself was high praise from William.

I closed my eyes momentarily, but the only thing I could visualize was the day she'd come in here and Will had introduced her as his daughter. Suddenly, I wanted the world to swallow me whole. It might as well have since I already felt like my career was beginning to sink as the memories of her and me in a bathroom stall at one of LA's most popular nightclubs choked me, and I barely got an audible nice to meet you out. She'd smiled, like it was no big deal, but the blush that crept over her face and neck had said differently. The way her eyes widened at the sight of me, as if her vision had to adjust to what I looked like in real life, outside of the dark club and dimly lit bathroom. And how that memory rushed through my body and to my cock when she came back the following week and started to flirt with me.

I'd promised myself I wouldn't get involved with her then, but from one second to another, Nicole's tanned legs were spread open in front of me on this very desk, and I became addicted to the way she threw her head back and said my name with that slight Spanish accent, regardless of what I did to her body. I swallowed, cleared my throat, and took a deep breath.

"I can't do it," I managed to say.

"Is this about the Sam Weaver case? If you want to take on less, you can give that one to Bobby. I want you for Nicole."

I want you for Nicole.

Nicole, who I knew the first time I laid eyes on her could be my downfall. Nicole, whose blue eyes held wicked promise every time she looked at me. Nicole, who had sworn she was completely against marriage, an oath I disputed when the tabloids dropped the bomb of her engagement. Nicole, who weaved some powerful shit with her wild streak and funny comments, rivaling anything that came out of my mouth. Nicole, whose fucking mouth was made by the gods for the gods and hadn't been anywhere near me for at least five years. I breathed out a heavy breath, trying to rid myself of all things Nicole. He had no idea what he was asking of me.

"Did she request me?"

"No. She doesn't know yet. She should be here shortly. I wanted to give you a heads-up first. But, Victor, you do this, you do right by her, and then I'll make you partner."

Fuck. My. Life. That *word* was too tantalizing to fuck around with. *Partner.* It was the sole reason I was billing so many damn hours.

"Okay."

"You'll do it?"

"Yes."

Now I just had to make sure I didn't do *her* and lose my goddamn license in the process.

Chapter Two

Nicole

"DIVORCE SUCKS," I said for what seemed like the millionth time since this whole ordeal started. Not that I needed to reiterate that for anybody. People didn't get married thinking they'd ever divorce. Being the product of a divorced household, and a father as a divorce attorney, I never saw myself getting a divorce. I always swore that if I got married it would be forever, but that was before the promise of forever became dreary and cold. It was before the word itself made me want to curl up into a ball whenever I thought of my estranged husband hitting the bottle or those pills he'd been partial to for the past two years. It was before shit went down the drain, basically. And that's how I found myself talking to the hot new security detail my soon-to-be ex-husband assigned me.

"Are you ready?" Marcus asked. Marcus. Even his name was fucking hot. The first time I saw him I wondered if Gabe's manager had picked him out on purpose, maybe to see if I'd cozy up to him and leave Gabe alone. Or cozy up to him and have something to hold over my head in this divorce.

"He's so full of himself, you know?" I said in response. Marcus's brown eyes flickered to mine in the rearview mirror, holding absolutely no amusement.

"Pardon?"

"Gabriel. He's full of himself. He thinks hiring a hot bodyguard is going to lessen the blow of the divorce. Let me tell you something, Marcus. I'm the one dealing with all this divorce crap. *Me*. I'm the one visiting lawyers and trying to sort things out quietly *for his sake*. You know why? Not because I'm a great human being, but because I still have feelings and he's a grade-A prick. Having a hot driver isn't going to make me forget that."

Marcus's light-blond eyebrows shot up in surprise momentarily. I wasn't sure if I was glad for his silence as he let me get that off my chest or pissed off that he had absolutely nothing to add to my rant. I hated when people didn't rant with me.

"I don't know him personally, and he's paying me, so I'm not sure what to say to that," he said. "Knock on the window when you're ready to get out." He opened his door and stepped into the swarm of paparazzi awaiting my arrival.

I was sure they were hoping they'd catch a glimpse of me crying. They would have to set up a tent outside my bedroom window in order to get that shot. I gathered my thoughts as I watched Marcus round the front of the car. As promised, he stood beside my door with his back toward me. I smoothed my hair and took a deep breath as I looked out into the crowd of photographers.

Of all the things Gabe had to endure on a daily basis, this was the one I'd never been able to fathom. When I was by myself they rarely followed me around, but if they caught wind that he was around it was no holds barred. They gunned for us, even if we were with my godchildren, who would cry because they hated the flash of the cameras and the nonstop questions.

A couple seconds passed before I knocked on the window three times. He held his hand out to help me exit the car and sidestepped a photographer who rushed toward me.

"*Nicole! How do you feel about the rumors that Gabriel is dating his new co-star, Lina?*"

"*Nicole! Over here! You look lovely today. Are you filing for divorce?*"

"*Are you going to press charges against Fey Winters for destruction of property?*"

"*Do you think Gabriel deserves a second chance?*"

"*Is it true he's screwing your best friend's nanny?*"

I never, ever showed emotion when being photographed under these circumstances, but that last question made me frown. *My best friend didn't even have a nanny.* I was sure they'd manipulate that frown to mean I looked like a mess when I went to visit a divorce lawyer, but who cares? Obviously Gabe's people, most likely his manager, called the paparazzi to tip them off about my whereabouts. Make me look like the bad guy, of course. Classic Hollywood tale, the less popular person was always at fault.

I was glad when Marcus opened the door of the building, and we were able to drown out their incessant questions, though the receptionist's voice replaced theirs immediately.

"My dad said you were coming by but I didn't believe him. Is what they're saying in the gossip blogs true? About Gabriel and you splitting up?" she asked.

I tried to swallow my pain and smile sadly, but my lips wouldn't tilt up, and the pain wouldn't stop grating against my throat. I nodded instead, a slow, small nod, and looked down. I'd always been sure of myself. Sure of my body, my career choice, my thoughts, my intelligence. Even after Gabe started going out more and not including me in his plans, and after he'd become so cold and distant, preferring to hit the bottle or stay on location longer than necessary, I was sure of myself. It wasn't until the rumors of infidelity began circulating that I began to feel the motions—my heart being chopped up. When the paparazzi started following me, putting their cameras in my face and their loud questions in my ears, I'd felt it going through the blender.

But that was then. Now I was back to my self-assured self. Or at least more than I had been last year. We'd kept it mum on the divorce filing, but when the papers were leaked, we were suddenly forced to confront the media, which was a nightmare in itself. I was coached weekly on what to say, or more accurately, what not to say. Gabe's publicist put out a statement saying we were working on our marriage. Gabe himself, whenever he was on camera, spoke highly of me and his commitment to our marriage. All the while I watched with a shocked expression on my face. At first, I believed it. I bought into it, because when it was all said and done, the guy was a hell of an actor. But that was before. And this was now. And I was tired of it.

"I'm sorry," Grace said, lowering her voice, her smile dropping. "You guys looked so happy together."

"Thanks," I said. It seemed like the wrong word for this, but I was used to girls like Grace, who were young with hearts in their eyes. I'd been that girl once. I was that girl five years ago. "Is my dad in the conference room?"

She looked startled for a moment before she began to move her feet in that direction. "Oh. Yes. Sorry. They moved it. Let me show you where it is."

Once the large wooden doors opened, I didn't have time to glance around and take in whatever décor my stepmother had most probably organized, because as soon as I stepped into the room my gaze froze on Victor Reuben. Victor, in a sharp navy suit that screamed sophistication. The way it fit him hinted at broad shoulders and hard planes I knew were beneath it. His expression was closed off, but the fact he was looking at me still made my heart hammer a little harder. I hadn't seen him in years, but my body remembered him well. His long hands and the way they'd gripped me. His deep chuckle and the way it had made my heart skip a beat the few times I'd heard it. The way he'd said my name, in a low, muttered, damnation that said he shouldn't be wanting, let alone doing what we'd done, but couldn't resist the temptation.

I swallowed to rid myself of the memories. I would've loved to say that having been married to one of the world's most sought-after celebrities had dimmed my lust for this man, but I'd be lying. I might have been the one who'd married, but to me, Victor would always be the one that got away. And even though I knew deep down we wouldn't have worked out, and it had been a long time since I'd seen him, the way his eyes caressed over me made me feel like I was slowly burning up. Like it was just this morning that he'd had me up against a wall. I shivered at the memory. His eyes heated in response.

"Nic. I didn't hear you come in," Dad said, standing from his seat beside Victor.

He came over and put his arms around me, and I reverted back to my seven-year-old self, leaning into his embrace. Dad wasn't much taller than I was, but he was tall enough that I could lay my head on his shoulder comfortably. I left my cheek there for a couple beats—inhaling the familiar smell of cigarettes and aftershave—my gaze on Victor's, his on mine, unmoving, unyielding, and completely unsettling.

"You remember Victor," he said, placing a kiss on my cheek as he moved slightly away from me. I almost laughed at that. Did I remember Victor? God. How could I forget? Victor stood, but didn't come around to greet me and I was glad for the space left between us. After the week, month, and year I'd had, I didn't think I could handle touching him even if it was just a handshake.

"Of course," I said, offering him a smile.

He was taller than I remembered, his shoulders wider, his hair a little longer, a little lighter, with scruff on his face I didn't remember him having. But those hazel eyes still hinted at wicked pleasures and wild sex, and the memory of all of the above made me flush and look away. I'd been with a Hollywood heartthrob for the last four and a half years, and I could still honestly say that I'd never met a man surer of himself than Victor Reuben.

"Nice to see you again," Victor said dutifully.

"Likewise," I replied, clearing my voice to rid myself of the scratch in it.

"Come, sit," Dad said, ushering me to the other side of the room.

He sat at the head of the table, Victor to his left, and I sank down in the seat across. I kept my face tilted to look at my dad, hoping to get out of this meeting without succumbing to the distraction of the man across from me. I didn't even question what he was doing in there. Dad liked to have people on hand to bounce opinions off during meetings with his clients, and I was just happy to be getting the best representation I could when it came to this divorce.

"We have more papers to fill out," Dad said.

I nodded, swallowing the small lump that threatened to form in my throat at the sound of the word. I hated so many things about this, but the failure I felt—as a wife, as a woman— was the worst.

"Have you spoken to Gabriel? After the papers were leaked to the media?"

I nodded again. "I spoke to him yesterday."

"And what did he say? Is he ready to proceed?" Dad asked. Gabe acted like my filing came as a shock to him. It wasn't a shock to anybody else, though, so I wasn't sure if he was really shocked or just wanted to treat it as an *out of sight, out of mind* kind of thing. Dad put his hand over mine when I dropped my gaze to the table. "Honey, it's okay. We need to talk about it."

I took a deep breath and wiped my eyes before I spoke. I was hyper aware of Victor's presence. I didn't want him to see me cry, hurt, or weak. I wasn't that girl. I'd never been that girl, but talking about this while my dad soothed me was more difficult than I could bear.

"He agreed on the motion and said he said he knew I would bail. That he knew when things got tough I'd leave him," I whispered. "That I couldn't deal with the reality of life."

I flinched when Dad slapped his free hand on the wooden table and stood suddenly.

"This is why I can't do it. I'll choke the bastard if I see him in court. I'd choke him if I'd see him right now."

I blinked, confused, looked at Victor, who was watching me closely and looked back at my dad. "What do you mean you can't do this?"

"Victor's taking this case. He's the best I got, love," Dad said. "It's like having me represent you. Promise."

Promise. I closed my eyes. He only said that when he was positive he wouldn't let me down. When I opened my eyes, I glanced at Victor, at his chiseled jaw and hypnotizing eyes, and that soft hair I'd loved running my fingers through. I tried so hard not to recall it, not to picture our back-and-forth banter before I'd locked the door of his office, and walked around his desk, possessed with lust—*with need*—with a hunger that wouldn't stop until I had him.

He must not have told my dad about us, because if he had he'd probably be looking for another firm, representing this divorce. Dad was weird about mixing work and personal life. Despite that, I knew Victor was a damn good attorney, the best, even. I had friends who'd hired him for their divorces and swore up and down by Victor Reuben. I didn't doubt his abilities in anything. I just doubted mine in being able to get through this without messing things up for the two of us, because when it came to *us*, things went up in flames. Or at least they used to. Perhaps he'd moved on, judging by his indifference.

"How long will it take to get this over with?" I asked Victor.

"The process has begun and it usually takes six months. So assuming he's on board and doesn't give us any trouble, and if he's not as . . . stubborn as you are, it shouldn't be too bad."

Dad chuckled at the mention of my stubbornness, and Victor's eyes flickered over there, smiling briefly before meeting mine again.

"Either way, I will do everything to make sure this is as painless for you as it can be. I'll be at your beck and call. Whatever you need, whenever you need it, I'm here," he said, his eyes dipping to my mouth briefly, to the low-cut dress I wore, and back to my eyes in a way that made goosebumps rake over my flesh.

What would it be like to have this man be *my* beck and call? I was sure he didn't do that often. He didn't seem like the type. Dad's cell phone rang, and he stood and excused himself. I looked over my shoulder to watch Dad walk out before turning back to Victor.

"What's your deal?"

"What do you mean?" he asked, pushing off the table slightly to cross his ankle over his knee. Totally casual, as if we were about to discuss sports.

"Why'd you agree to do this?"

"Why did I agree to do my job?" he asked, looking amused. "Let's see, there's the fact that I like it, and then there's the bit about those three years of law school I went through, and well, yeah, the most important part, it's what I get paid to do."

If I didn't know him, or know him as much as I thought I did, I would have been upset. Instead, I sighed. "Did you tell my dad about us?"

"Us?"

"Yeah, us. You know," I said, shooting him a look.

"There is no us, Nicole. There never was. We were friends, we had sex, but that was it. I thought that was clear."

There was no bite to his tone or the words he used. He said it soothingly, as if he were talking to a child or trying to calm down an ex-girlfriend after a breakup. Clearly I was in an overly emotional state. Had I not been, his words would have just rolled off me, but they didn't. They actually hurt a little. *I had gone off and gotten married.* It's not like I expected him to care. I looked at him momentarily. He didn't seem like he did, and at this point, what did it matter?

"You're right," I said once I collected my thoughts and looked at Victor again. "So, what do we do now?"

"The question of the hour is: did you sign a prenup?"

"Of course."

My father was a divorce attorney. Did Victor really think he'd let me marry with no prenuptial? Seemingly reading my mind correctly, Victor nodded.

"I'll have Corinne get it for me," he said, opening up the folder in front of him and jotting something down before picking it up and coming around the table.

"This will make it easier for me to explain," he said as he sat down beside me. The smell of his cologne enveloped me and

14

I did my best to take it in small doses, taking small and quick shallow breaths as I focused on the papers in front of me.

"Nic?" he asked, his voice low and near my ear. My stomach did a flip-flop.

"Yeah?" I whispered.

"You're going to have to learn to breathe when you're near me. We'll be doing this a lot."

My head whipped toward him, and he reared back slightly to put a little distance between our faces.

"You're unbelievable," I said.

"So I've been told."

"Let's get on with this," I replied, trying my best not to roll my eyes.

And then Victor went over the process and explained each page. I didn't care to know all the details, and I knew he had my best interest and wouldn't screw me over, but I listened anyway. He leaned over me and pointed at the spots I needed to sign and I wondered how many women had felt the warmth of his chest against their shoulder. When we finished, he backed away and picked up the papers to go back to the spot he'd been sitting earlier.

"So now that part is over," he said, sitting across from me and taking a legal-sized notebook out, "let's go over things I should know about. How many houses do you own? By own I mean, how many is your name in the title for?"

"Two. One in Calabasas and an apartment in New York."

"And those are also owned by Gabriel?"

"Correct."

"Have either one of you moved out of your current residence?"

"No."

The tip of his pen stopped writing, and he glanced up at me.

"Are either one of you planning on moving out any time soon?"

"I don't know."

He put the pen down and threaded his hands together as he looked at me.

"Have you discussed anything with Gabriel?"

I shook my head. "Nope."

"Why is that?"

"He's in Canada filming a movie, and I'm on set here working on one being filmed now."

"You're still doing costume design?"

I nodded, smiling that he remembered. It was the one thing keeping me sane these days. It had been for quite some time. Work and wine, maintaining sanity for unhappily married women everywhere.

"Okay. Let's go over a timeline." He slid the notebook and pen over to me. "I want you to write down your wedding date, and basically any date you remember that you think is of importance—good and bad."

I did as I was told, jotting down my wedding date and more or less the timeframe of when other things happened, though I didn't keep track of every major event of my life on my calendar. Now I kind of wished I had. When I was done, I slid the notebook and pen back to Victor.

"You were pregnant?" he asked, looking at me like I was a complete stranger. I nodded.

"Miscarried at nine weeks."

He gave a nod. "And you didn't try again?"

My heart squeezed in my chest. "It didn't work out," I whispered. We hadn't, even though I'd wanted to. Gabe then started getting major acting roles and got me a dog instead, saying we needed to wait to start a family. Wait until he could actually be there for his kids, and I couldn't argue that. I cleared my throat and spoke louder. "Why is that important?"

"Is it one of the reasons your marriage didn't work out?"

"No," I said, even though I'd often wondered if we'd had the baby, if things would have worked out between us. Would things with him have been different? I refused to put the blame of our downfall on that, though. We married each other, not the idea of having a child together.

"You sure? It took you a while to come to that conclusion."

I closed my eyes and huffed out a breath. "I'm positive. Can we move on now?"

Victor paused, his eyes searching my face. "I'm not trying to be a dick about this. I just need to know everything so I know what we're dealing with. I've had cases where the spouse came back and threw things like this in our faces in the middle of court and I wasn't prepared for it, so I try to cover all my bases. This is going to get personal. Are you okay with that?"

I took a deep breath and gave him a nod to continue.

"You put here that you got married in 2010 and you basically knew it was over by late 2013, early 2014. What happened at that point?"

I looked outside again, wishing so badly I was in that ocean and not sitting in this conference room talking about this.

"Being that I filed with the notion irreconcilable differences, can I just say he wasn't the same person I met and married?"

His eyes searched my face for so long, I was sure he was going to find the answers to all his questions written all over it. I shifted under his scrutiny before he finally cleared his throat and gave me a sharp nod, moving along to the next point I'd written.

"You want to keep the house?"

"Not really, but I want to kind of stick it to him and he loves that house."

Victor chuckled, the sound so sexy I had to contain the sigh that threatened to escape my lips. "People never cease to amaze me. You want to keep an eight-million-dollar house with six bedrooms to live in all by yourself just to 'stick it to him'?"

I shrugged. "What do you suggest I do?"

"Well, being that the eight-million-dollar house comes with an equally hefty insurance payment, I'd move the hell out of there, ask for more alimony, and buy a smaller house somewhere I'd love to live."

For the first time since I'd been there, I felt myself relax a little. I leaned back in my chair and set my elbows on the table.

"I like that idea. Let's do that."

His smile stayed intact as we went through the rest of the list. He even surprised me by laughing at the point about my dog.

"You want shared custody of the dog?"

"Yeah. Harlow Edwards just got a divorce and she has shared custody with her ex."

Victor closed his eyes and shook his head. "I should get a bonus for ridiculous requests."

"Yeah, well, I'm sure a bonus can be arranged," I said. *Shit.* I didn't mean for my voice to sound the way it did, raspy and needy, but that was the way the words came out.

His gaze heated and held. I could feel myself unraveling, could feel the pull between us in the suddenly too-hot-for-me office and wished so badly I could stand, hike my dress up, and ride him right there. I groaned at the thought.

I watched his Adam's apple bob as he swallowed. "We're going to have to end this meeting and pick up another day."

I blinked away from him and swallowed back the lurid and very dirty things I wanted to say. *What the hell was wrong with me?* I was there to organize my divorce. Never mind that we'd been living in separate quarters of the infamous eight-million-dollar house for a year and a half. Never mind that he'd been screwing half of Hollywood and acting like it was okay, while I stayed at home or enjoyed quiet nights with friends. *Me*. The one-time wild child staying quietly at home while *he*, the once good boy from a small town went out and screwed around. Regardless of the eighteen months of disappointment and hurt I had been through, lusting after Victor was still inappropriate.

He stood first, and I followed his lead, walking beside him to the door. I expected him to open it and get out of Dodge right away, but instead he held the knob in his hand and turned to look at me. I tilted my head to meet his gaze, which was serious, but not any less fiery than it had been before.

"This thing between us," he said, making the words slow so I understood each and every one of them, "is over. It never happened. You are my client. I am your attorney. There are laws against things happening between us, and I could lose my license if I break them. Do you understand that?"

I swallowed thickly and nodded, my eyes not wavering from his, my heart thumping loudly.

"Say 'yes, Victor, I understand that.'"

The man was completely serious. The problem was, being this close to him again, if I moved just a fraction, I could lean in and kiss him. His smell was intoxicating. His lips had always been so soft and fucking kissable. Damn him. I wasn't going to let him get away with making me feel this way, like I was the only one affected by our exchange. I let out a laugh.

"I understand, and I'm sorry to break it to you, but I'm not looking to hook up with you. Been there, done that, bought the shirt."

He scoffed. "That's a shirt I'd love to see."

"I'll show it to you sometime. It says, 'It wasn't a big deal.'"

His lips curled into a slow, full grin. "I'm sure the word big is definitely in there, but I highly doubt that's what the shirt says. Otherwise, why did you come back for seconds, thirds, fourths, and call me drunkenly on nights out with your girlfriends?"

My eyes widened. I took a step back. "I did not."

"Did too, and texted. I have those saved."

My mouth dropped. "Why would you . . . even if I did do that, which I'm pretty sure I didn't . . . why would you save them?"

"You're my boss's daughter. God forbid you decided on one of your rampages that you were going to bury me and say that, I don't know, I raped you or some crazy shit. I needed to have proof I was the one being pursued."

"You pursued me too in the past. Or do you think looking at me like you wanted to eat me for dinner didn't count?"

"Unless it's in print, it doesn't count."

I glared at him. "You are such a dick."

"I just want to be clear that nothing can happen here, so don't make those 'Victor, please fuck me' eyes at me anymore when we're talking about your divorce."

"I didn't do that, but okay. Now if you'll excuse me, I have someone in the lobby that I may actually be interested in."

He opened the door for me and followed me down the hall. I didn't bother looking for my father. I just wanted to get out of there. I knew I'd see him for dinner the following night anyway, so I kept walking until I reached the lobby where Marcus was waiting for me with his phone in hand. He put it away as soon as he saw me.

"Let's go, Marcus, I have a lot of pent-up tension I need to get rid of," I said. I looked over my shoulder to where Victor was standing. He looked at me, looked at Marcus, back at me, and if I didn't know him at all I wouldn't have noticed the way his eyes narrowed, or the way his jaw tightened. But I did know him.

"We'll be in touch. There are other things I'll need to ask you. I'll let you know when this is filed," he said, extending his hand for me to shake. I took it. "I look forward to working with you."

His grip tightened a little when he said that, making my heart gallop. I had instant flashbacks: arguing over insignificant topics, me walking around his desk and pushing his legs apart so I could stand between them, his fingers tantalizingly slow as they inched up my skirt, his hand gripping my ass as he thrust inside me, his mouth on my throat telling me to shut the fuck up so we wouldn't get caught.

God.

I'd be lying if I said there hadn't been times after I starting going out with Gabe that I didn't think about those moments, wondered *who* Victor was doing that to. I sighed as I walked out of the building and back into the commotion of the paparazzi. I knew Victor's warning was real. Five years ago, he'd been very clear. *I need to focus on my career.* Obviously, he'd done that. And done it well. Was I wrong to wonder if he would be tempted to dance along the line of attraction again? He'd turned me away then. He'd probably do the same now. Sadly, my body wasn't getting the memo. I couldn't help but wonder how far he would go without breaking the rules.

Chapter Three

Victor

ONE OF THE perks of having the beach in your backyard was being able to wake up, roll out of bed and catch waves. Unfortunately, today was not that day. I missed my alarm clock and showed up to breakfast at my parents' an hour late.

"You look like shit," my best friend, Oliver, said from across the table. I flashed him my middle finger. I didn't have enough energy to comment.

"What did you do last night?" my sister, Estelle, asked as she served herself orange juice for the third time.

"Nothing," I mumbled.

I'd stayed up until five "researching" Nicole and Gabriel. My associates often asked me if my extensive research was necessary and my answer was always a solid yes. Normally, I had my assistant Corinne do my research, but this thing with Nicole . . . it felt personal. I told myself it was because I'd seen how badly some of my high-profile clients treated their spouses in a divorce, and if what I'd heard about Gabriel had any truth to it, I was sure she wasn't doing well personally, but it was more. There was a sadness in her eyes and stance in those photos.

I hadn't seen Nicole since before she married, hadn't thought about her much after I found out she had, but seeing her again . . . it did something to me. I wasn't going to lie to myself about that. I just knew I had to keep it business. All business. The problem was that while my office was normally a second home to me, now it reminded me of her. I wasn't sure why after so many years it was happening, but it was. And after reading the abundance of damning gossip in the tabloids, about his affairs and his partying ways, I couldn't understand why she had married that guy. She said he'd changed. I had to take her word for it. Maybe she'd changed too. Maybe she wasn't the funny Nicole I used to know. The girl with the wicked smile and enough bite to make me want to settle down . . . just not enough to actually do it. Not then, anyway. Not now, either, for that matter. While all of my friends had married I'd stayed focused on my career. Truth of the matter was, I hadn't found a girl that sparked my interest enough to want to settle down.

"Let me get you more pancakes," my mom said, snapping me out of my thoughts as she reached for my plate. I stopped her before she could take it.

"Thanks, Ma. I can get it, though."

I needed a break from Oliver and my sister's questioning gazes. Ever since they'd married, they'd started acting like I was a little lost boy when they were around me for too long. I guess at one point they must have gotten sick of learning a new woman's name every time I brought somebody around, so they made it their mission to try and set me up with somebody they felt would gain my attention. That basically meant they were trying to set me up with every breathing female they came in close quarters with, which was what my mother had been trying to do since I graduated from law school, and having three fucking matchmakers breathing down my neck was something I could only handle in small doses. I was in the kitchen, smearing my pancakes with butter when Oliver walked in with his plate.

"What's the deal? I haven't seen you this tired in a while."

"Work. I stayed up late looking into a new client."

He frowned. "Doesn't your assistant do that stuff for you?"

I put the butter down and picked up the syrup.

"Your plate looks like a heart attack waiting to happen," he said. I looked at him as I poured the syrup.

"Oh, yeah? Did Dr. Oz teach you that?" I asked.

Much to his annoyance, I always joked and said his obsession with Dr. Oz rivaled my mom's with Oprah. He made a face of disapproval, but didn't bother to tell me he didn't care for Dr. Oz, the way he normally did. Instead he moved on to serve his measly oatmeal.

"Prisoners eat more food than you," I said, nodding at his plate.

He chuckled, pushing all that girly hair off his face before taking a spoonful into his mouth.

"I'm not even going to start a debate about prison food right now because I know how much you hate to lose. I'm just saying, you're not twenty-one anymore. You need to watch the shit you eat."

I sighed. "I'm tired and I only eat like this on weekends. You know this and you still give me this little speech every fucking week. I already told you, it's been proven that if you eat shitty food one day a week it speeds up your metabolism."

He scoffed. "Keep getting your information from those steroid-injecting wannabe nutritionists on Instagram and see where that gets you."

I smiled around a mouthful of pancake. I didn't even have an Instagram account. He knew this. My life wasn't exciting enough for me to document in photographs. We were eating in silence for a bit before he spoke up again.

"Do you want to go to a charity gold tournament next weekend?"

"Not particularly," I said. "I'll donate, though. What's the cause?"

"Childhood obesity."

"I'll donate."

"You sure you don't want to come? Lots of single women in those country clubs," he said in a voice that sounded like something he would use to tease a child.

Again with the trying to set me up with somebody. I resisted the urge to groan, but shot him an annoyed look nonetheless.

"Positive. You of all people should know I don't need help in that category."

"That's the problem. You only meet women who are looking for a good time. These women are looking to settle down."

"Which is the same thing I want," I scoffed. "Those country club women are looking for their next sugar daddy."

"No," he said, drawing out the word. "They're looking for men who have drive and know what they want. No shame in that."

"No," I said, mimicking him. "They're looking for money. Money and power."

As I'd looked at the pictures of Nicole and Gabriel that was the only thing I could come up with. Apparently that's what women wanted—money and power. It was unsettling though, because Nicole had both without him. Maybe she just liked that he was famous. Still, the Nicole I knew wouldn't have married a guy for any of those things. Or maybe the Nicole I *thought* I knew was a more accurate assessment. The Nicole I *thought* I knew didn't even want to get married. I wasn't sure what had changed, or where it did, but the thought that she had sex with me and accepted a proposal a few weeks later was just . . . mind-boggling.

"You listening to me?" Oliver asked. I blinked a few times and turned to set my empty plate in the sink.

"Sorry. I zoned out. What?"

"I asked if you want to talk about the case you're doing dirty work for."

I tore my gaze away from his and ran a hand through my hair. It wasn't that Nicole had been my dirty secret or anything, because in a moment of weakness I'd told Oliver and our other friend Jensen about her, but I didn't like talking about her. She was mine. *Mine.* That didn't seem accurate, though, since she wasn't mine and never had been. It still didn't help the sensation I got in the pit of my stomach when I thought about her. When I thought about the sex and the phone calls, and the way they'd all stopped after I broke things off. *All of it.* I was used to women lingering for a while after breaking things off with them. That didn't happen with Nicole. She didn't linger. She just moved on.

She just moved on.

"Vic?" Oliver said, snapping me out of my thoughts. *Again.*

"What?" My eyes snapped to his again. He was frowning, looking almost concerned.

"You wanna talk about it?"

"No, Dr. Phil, I don't."

He chuckled. "You're such a dick when you're stressed."

Stressed. I was used to feeling stressed. This was something else. This was the fear of the unknown—the unchartered—and I hated being faced with things I couldn't build a game plan for. I wasn't sure what it was, but I knew I needed to keep my head in the game and thoughts of being between Nicole's legs out of my head. Can't say that didn't cross my mind yesterday when she walked in looking like the queen she deserved to be. Stunning. Sexy. Yet, when I'd seen her sink into her father's arms, I knew she was hiding behind a well-preserved façade. I had told her she needed to keep her shit together around me, but it went both ways. I would not succumb to her provocative allure. *Could not.*

My sister opened the door and walked in with her hands on her hips before I could formulate a response to Oliver, and I was grateful for the interruption. These were people who could see right through me—read me like a book—and I couldn't deal with that right now. Not when I wasn't sure what language the words were even written in, and I needed to actually go see the person who had me feeling this way.

"This isn't Bean and Vic bonding time. You can do that tomorrow," Estelle said.

"You get more annoying with age. You know that, right?" I said, smiling at her when she stuck her tongue out at me.

"It was pointed out to me recently," she said, glaring at Oliver, who chuckled in response. "Anyway, I wanted to tell you that while you guys are cooped up in your living room all day tomorrow I'll be at an orphanage."

"Doing what?" I asked as we walked to the living room.

"Painting. I'm donating supplies and stuff."

"And her services," Oliver added with that love-struck smile he always had around my sister. How the hell I didn't realize they were together, or had been together, before I caught them was beyond my comprehension now I was exposed to their corny shit all the time.

"That's cool. And you're telling me this because?" I asked, plopping down on the loveseat.

"Because I haven't had a chance to make the stupid bean dip or anything else, so you're going to have to make your own or go grocery shopping."

"That's fine," I said, closing my eyes as I leaned back. I fell asleep to the sound of my sister and Oliver talking about groceries and my mom asking if she should make the dip for us. Despite the noise, I managed to sleep, and dreamed of Nicole Alessi and the sexy way she carried herself.

It was just sex. It was. Really good sex, but I could have really good sex with a lot of women. I hadn't planned on exchanging phone numbers with her after it was over, but then she adjusted her dress and laughed at the sight of her torn-up underwear and I wanted a repeat. I couldn't explain why. I just knew I did. I didn't expect to call her and end up staying on the phone when she turned down my invitation for the repeat. I didn't expect her to walk into the office two weeks after I'd gotten a job there, and I sure as hell didn't expect her last name to be Alessi.

So many wrong things.

So many illicit thoughts.

So many reasons why the repeat wouldn't happen.

But then she knocked on my door. Mouth ajar, blue eyes widened in shock.

"You're the new guy?" she asked.

In that moment, I didn't know whether to accept the shock I felt or call security because she was obviously stalking me. Even the rational part of my brain was on full alert.

"Yeah," I said, uncomfortably eyeing the door she closed behind her. "What are you doing here?"

Please don't say you work here. Please don't say you work here. Maybe she was just passing along a message for somebody. Maybe she was a florist making a delivery. Maybe she was also fucking one of my colleagues. At that I cringed. That would mean we definitely couldn't have another go.

"I'm . . . my dad . . ." She sighed, not waiting for an invitation

before sitting down in one of the chairs across from me.

Under normal circumstances, that would have bothered me, but I was quickly realizing that things with "Nicole from the night-club" weren't normal. She hadn't even called me back after turning me down. She'd sent me a few text messages, but that was it, and my text messaging skills were poor to say the least. I hated it. I hated the idea of her being able to show her friends what we talked about. I hated the idea of anybody knowing what our plans were. I didn't know why. There was no plausible explanation for me feeling that way. None. But now she was sitting across from me, I was starting to believe it was the right move.

"Your dad," I asked, "is getting a divorce?"

"Uh . . . no," she said, licking her full lips nervously. The same lips I'd kissed a couple weeks ago. The same lips I kept envisioning around my cock. "Will is my dad."

I blinked hard, away from her lips. "What?"

"He's . . . my dad," she said, her voice small, her eyes apologetic. Good. So she knew this couldn't happen anymore. But what the ever-loving fuck? This was definitely payback for me fucking my fraternity brother's girlfriend back in college. Definitely. Fuck my fucking life.

"Your dad," I said flatly. She nodded, tugging her bottom lip into her mouth with her teeth. The sight of it made something inside me ricochet.

"Yep," she said with a pop. She looked at me for a moment, just looked at me, her eyes scanning my face, dropping to my chest, and back up. "You look really good in a suit."

"Nicole," I said, a warning.

She smiled. "Yep."

"Stop looking at me like that."

"Okay." She shrugged, but kept smiling, taunting. "So, divorce law, huh?"

I kept my eyes on hers. "Yes."

"Are your parents divorced?"

"No."

She frowned a bit, looking pensive. "Interesting. Are they happy?"

"Yes," I said, feeling my lips tilt into a smile. "Are you a psychology major?"

"No," she said, eyes wide, drawing out the word as if that was a ridiculous thought.

"What are you studying? Assuming you're in school," I added.

"Costume design. I graduate next week actually."

"Costume design," I repeated, letting my eyes drift down her body.

She was wearing a skintight dress with huge colorful flowers. It covered her entirely, with small sleeves and a neckline that didn't show much cleavage, but the way it fit her left little to the imagination. I could see the outline of her perfect tits—handful size—her tiny waist, and curvy hips. When I looked back at her face she was back to giving me a coquettish smile that I felt everywhere. And when she stood and gave me a perfect back view of her round ass and went to lock the door, I gulped and started to breathe a little heavier. And when she turned around and walked around my desk in long, slow strides I had to close my eyes.

I'd just gotten this job. My eyes snapped open. Surely she wasn't considering doing what I thought she was planning to do. Fuck. No.

"Nicole, I just got this job," I said, my words going from firm to low as she swiveled my chair and kneeled down in front of me.

"My dad left," she said, looking at me through her long, dark lashes.

I swallowed. "We shouldn't do this."

"We shouldn't do a lot of things."

"I . . . this can't . . ." I started, but she was already unbuckling my belt.

"Do you have a girlfriend?" she asked, her fingers stopping. "Shit. I should have asked that before. Do you?"

I frowned. "Fuck, no."

She leaned back on her heels, hands still on my pants, and looked up at me. "Is that a fuck no because you're opposed to having a girlfriend, or a fuck no because you would never do this to your girlfriend if you had one? I can't tell."

I put a hand over hers to stop her from moving because I was getting harder by the millisecond. "Both."

She raised an eyebrow. "Opposed to having a girlfriend, really? You're a player."

"Not," I said, my word strangled when she moved a hand to cup me over my pants. "Not a player."

"You just crush a lot?" she asked with a smirk.

"Fuck a lot. Yes."

"But you don't want to fuck me because I'm your boss's daughter," she said rather than asked. I swallowed again and nodded. "Doesn't that make it more exciting? We can be quiet."

I shook my head, but fuck, it did make it a little exciting. One more time and I was done. Definitely. After this I'd break it off, erase her phone number, and just . . . be done.

"It'll be the last time," she said. "You wanted to do it last week when you sent me that text. I've just been busy with final projects."

Our gazes met, both hot, both ready to pounce. My only response was to uncover my hand from hers and my fuck no turned into an instant fuck yes.

Chapter Four

Nicole

LIVING IN CLOSE quarters with my estranged husband wasn't necessarily the smartest thing I'd done, especially when he suddenly came back from Canada where he'd been shooting, went out with his cast, brought the after-after party back to our place, and proceeded to invite me to join the fun when I woke up, looking for the source of the commotion. Being half-past drunk and fooling around with the husband I was in the process of divorcing, was an even dumber idea. Not for the first time since I woke up, I rubbed my eyes and groaned. It's not like Gabe and I hadn't hooked up since we decided to end things, but we'd steered far away from each other since making things official. I blamed my lapse of judgment on not getting laid in a year, the two bottles of wine I drank before he got there, and that one fleeting moment when he smiled at me when I thought that maybe, just maybe, this marriage could still work.

But that was before a woman barged into his bedroom, where were were almost naked, and asked him where he put the cocaine they'd just purchased. The words, their actions, the fact she knew where his room was *and* he didn't kick her out at first glance, kicked my senses into overdrive. I hopped out of bed, fixed my clothes, and went back to what we'd dubbed my side of the house.

I didn't acknowledge him when he asked me to come back. He never even got out of bed or came down the hall to stop me. Yet there I was, in our kitchen, picking up his mess as I'd done a million times before. I was half-tempted to call our housekeeper, Amelia, and have her come in on her day off, but I didn't want any more people suffering this divorce.

Our gate bell rang shortly after I was on my hands and knees, scrubbing off things I was sure you couldn't even find on floors of college frat houses to make my house presentable when Victor came over this afternoon. I pressed the open button on the gate without even checking to see who it was. I rarely did that, but I figured because of the time it had to be UPS or some other courier. Without giving it a second thought, I went back to scrubbing.

This was not how I envisioned this week panning out. Not at all. Not that I'd ever envisioned myself on my knees in this kitchen for any other reason than Gabriel standing in front of me. I sighed and pushed the thought away. That was over. Over. Never again, and I didn't want it again, especially after last night's rude reminder. I went back to cleaning whatever disgusting, sticky particle was on my floor at the moment. The loud knocks on my door snapped me out of what was becoming a pattern: scrub, cringe, scrub, cringe, repeat. I let go of the scrubber and stood with a sigh, taking off my yellow gloves and throwing them into the empty bucket. I washed my hands quickly before making my way to the front door.

To my complete surprise, Gabe was walking to the door at the same time. I would have sworn he'd sleep until this evening and only get up to eat and have a do-over of his drug-and-alcohol-infused night. I shivered at the thought. This man once made me shiver for completely different reasons. He still had that effect on women, with his toned body, striking features, and invented smile.

"You expecting company?" he asked, already looking through the peephole.

"Not until later today," I said slowly, looking around as if the white walls were going to tell me the time. A thought struck me as I picked up the pace and stood beside Gabe. "Oh, shit. What time is it?"

"Do you know this guy?" he asked as we reached the door.

I unlocked the door and opened it, ignoring his question. Victor stood on the other side of the threshold with a confused look on his face as his eyes bounced from Gabe to me, me to Gabe, and finally me again.

"Come in," I said, and moved toward Gabe so he had no choice but to take a step back and make room for Victor to enter.

I closed the door behind him and stood there as the two of them greeted each other.

"We'll be out back. Finish cleaning up your mess," I called out over my shoulder as I walked toward the living room, knowing Victor would follow.

I walked until I reached the back doors and opened them so we could sit out on the porch, where I found a single silver stiletto.

"Who the hell leaves one shoe behind at a party?" I muttered, picking it up by the strap and tossing it aside.

"Cinderella?" Victor said behind me as he closed the French doors.

I felt myself smile. He'd always been funny. Strange and intense and funny. He was the kind of guy that could have you pinned against the wall one second and kick you out of his office the next but not let you think he was kicking you out. He'd let you think you came up with the decision to leave on your own. I hadn't seen it then as manipulation, but now that I looked back on it . . . Either way, I always appreciated the short time we had together, especially the night I'd called him due to a flat tire and he'd bolted out of the bar he was in to come help me. I'd never forget the way he shook his head as he looked at me through angry eyes.

"You can't be going out at night dressed like that," he'd said, and I could tell he was trying not to look at me.

After he fixed my tire and followed me home, I'd wondered if he'd go inside with me, but he hadn't. A part of me knew he wouldn't, of course. I'd been living in my father's guest house. What would Dad have thought if he'd seen the new attorney he'd just hired walk into his daughter's quarters at midnight? A bigger part of me had wished we hadn't been in that situation at all. That I was just a girl, and he was just a hot guy who was okay with taking chances. But we hadn't been those people.

I pushed the memory aside and sat on one of the chairs, watching as he sat across from me. He was dressed down today, which apparently for Victor meant jeans, a checkered button-up, and Oxfords. His normally playful eyes looked tired and the rough scruff on his face suggested he hadn't shaved in days. He ran a hand through his hair and brushed it back in a way that made me try to fix my own and redo my ponytail.

"Rough night?" he asked, his eyes roaming over me.

"You can say that."

I fidgeted with my hair again, even though I knew there was no use. I suddenly felt completely aware of what I looked like in my black sports bra, matching yoga pants, and make-up-less face. He'd seen me in a form-fitting navy dress and sky-high heels a couple days ago. In fact, most of the times he'd seen me I had been dressed to impress, and even when we'd had sex, we'd both remained mostly dressed. I wondered what a naked Victor looked like. It was a fleeting thought, but it was one that made me flush. I swallowed when our gazes locked, feeling like I'd been caught in my sexual fantasy.

"Nicole," he said, a warning, but he kept that tempestuous gaze locked on mine and I knew he felt the same electric prickle I felt all over.

"Isn't it weird for you?" I asked, my voice a whisper.

Victor appraised me for a long moment, tilting his head as his inquisitive eyes scanned my face. I would have killed to know what he was thinking. I would have killed to ask. But I couldn't. I sat there, *wondering*, hoping he'd answer, waiting on bated breath for it. I leaned in a little, and he mimicked my movement, putting his elbows on his knees, letting his hands dangle between them.

"It's weirder than I thought it would be," he admitted, his gaze searing into mine. "I keep reminding myself that the Nicole I once knew isn't the same one sitting in front of me."

"What makes you say that?"

He leaned back in his chair and looked at the house, the pool, and back at me. "All this. The Nicole I knew didn't need the big house *or* the husband."

My heart skipped. The Nicole he knew was a damn liar. Another thing I wanted to say, but didn't. Instead I took a different approach.

"Maybe the Nicole you knew wanted you to ask her out on a real date."

"Maybe the Nicole I knew should have asked me on a date herself." His lip curled up into a sly smile. "She didn't have a problem asking for other things."

My cheeks blazed. "I didn't think you wanted to date."

His gaze softened, but his words still slapped me. "I didn't."
Yeah. That stung.

Thankfully, Gabe chose that moment to open the door beside us and we both whipped our heads toward it.

"So this is your attorney?" Gabe asked, raising his eyebrows when neither one of us answered. "Okay, then, I just wanted to let you know that I'm leaving, but the pool guy is coming today. He lost the key to the gate so he might ring. Thanks for helping me pick up." He tucked his head in, but then brought it back out as if he'd forgotten to say something. "And thanks for last night. It was really, *really* good."

What the fuck? Had he forgotten how that went down? Or rather how it didn't go down? *Perhaps the woman had stayed after I'd left. Bastard.* Nonetheless, there was no way to miss his innuendo, not with the way his voice dropped and he winked as he looked at my mouth. He shut the door and I watched as he walked off. Victor didn't comment, instead he opened up his briefcase to hand me some papers. I practically hid my face behind the papers.

"I need you to sign these," he said, going back to business mode. "There's an X on each page I need you to look at. It indicates you're moving forward with the motion and asking for alimony."

"What happens if I just poison him?" I asked quietly, still hiding my face as my eyes scanned the words on the page.

"Then I'd have to hook you up with a criminal attorney because I could no longer represent you."

I glanced up at him and found that his lips were curled into a smile, the sight of it doing things to me, and making me smile back. He had one leg folded on top of his knee at the ankle, athletic frame pressed back into the chair, sultry eyes on mine. *Just . . . wow.*

"Once this is over you can go on with your life . . . pretend this never happened," he said, signaling toward the house with his chin.

I looked inside. It was so big and empty. It always had been, I realized, but what once felt cozy and warm, now felt cold, the spaces wider, room for more problems. I couldn't afford to kick myself down over it anymore. Like my friends said, I'd kicked myself hard enough over things that weren't solely my fault while he'd continued to thrive and make a name for himself.

"I just feel like I failed, you know? I'm sure you get that a lot, but I just don't do well with failure."

"You didn't fail. Divorce doesn't have to mean failure, and it's certainly not one person's failure." He paused, scratching his chin as his eyes wandered over my shoulder, toward the pool. "How long ago did you decide it was over?"

"A year ago," I said. I'd already told him that the other day. Victor shook his head.

"I mean, you personally. When did you know it was over for you?"

I scooted back in my chair and lifted my legs, hugging them toward my chest. "A long time ago."

"Why did you wait so long?"

"Because I'm not a quitter," I whispered, tears filling my eyes as I said the words.

"Is that why you're still living here? With him?" There was bite to his words that matched the sudden anger in his eyes.

"I guess."

I wiped my eyes and went back to the papers in front of me. He continued to stare at me. The words kept blurring, so I didn't get very far into the document. I signed where it said I should and initialed the rest. I figured I couldn't be giving up any more than I already had, and my dad was Victor's boss, so he couldn't be screwing me. I looked up at him again. He could totally be screwing me. I shook my head, looking down at the paper again, and tried to bite back a laugh. Something was terribly wrong with me if the thoughts *screwing me over* were being misconstrued in my own mind. Massively, irrevocably wrong with me. I'd said the been there, done that thing to him the other day as an out because the longer I looked at him the less I believed myself.

"What's so funny?" he asked as I handed back the papers and pen he'd given me.

"Nothing. Thinking about a shirt I have."

His brows crinkled in confusion for a second before he got it and smiled.

"You must really like that shirt."

"You should see how it fits me," I said with a wink.

The way his eyes flared, I could tell my words evoked some kind of image in his mind. He didn't say anything like he would have in the past. That had been our thing all those years ago. I'd pull the string until he bit and caved to me. Not this Victor, though. He cleared his throat and stood up, offering me his hand to shake. I took it, and ignored the way my insides rocked when he touched me. We walked back through the house to the front door, and he commented on the electric fireplace and color of the dark wood floors. When I touched the door handle, he placed his hand over mine, covering it. My heart jumped at the sensation of his hand warming mine, his long fingers digging into my flesh just slightly, just enough. My eyes snapped to his.

"For the record, I would love to see how your shirt fits," he said in a low voice, lowering his face to mine so we were almost nose to nose, eye to eye. "Maybe once this is over, if the offer still stands, I'll take you up on it."

My breath hitched a little. I licked my lips. "That'll take

months."

"It can take a year," he said. He was breathing a little louder now. I wondered what he would do if I leaned in and pressed my lips against his.

"We both know if I want it to happen, it'll happen," I whispered.

"It won't. It can't."

He straightened, turned my hand on the knob, then walked out to his black Jaguar without a backward glimpse. My heart was still rattling as his car purred to life. Our gazes caught momentarily as he waited for the gate to open behind him, and all I could do was stare. I was sure my gaze reflected my neediness. I hated the vulnerability I felt when I was near this man. I was living with last year's Sexiest Man of the Year, yet there I was, feeling things I hadn't felt in over a year. For Victor Reuben, of all people. I was so screwed.

Chapter Five

Nicole

"I DON'T KNOW what's wrong with me," I said to my friend Talon as I continued to sew the eighteenth-century-style dress I was working on.

Talon had been the one who convinced me to work on this movie. Partially because she wanted to keep an eye on me with the separation and another because we always had fun when we worked on the same set, something we hadn't done in over a year. She was the makeup artist to the stars, while I was the costume designer. Completely different jobs with similar lunch breaks.

She sighed and pinned back the tight ringlets of dark brown curls falling into her face. "I don't know what to say, sweetie. You've been through a rough couple of years and now you're stuck with this guy you had a major crush on when you were younger. I just don't know what to say."

"I'm not stuck with him," I said, frowning. She shot me a look. "What? I'm not. I can hire another divorce lawyer. He just happens to be the best."

"At that and other things, if I remember correctly." A sly smile appeared on her face as she said it, and I couldn't help but laugh.

"This is a real problem. I'm around hot guys all the time. I mean, hello," I said, pointing at the poster for the movie we were working on. The poster had a partially naked Eric Austin dressed as Tarzan. "Yet for some reason I'm around this guy for two seconds and I become a fifteen-year-old girl at a One Direction concert."

Talon gasped. "I am thirty-two, thank you very much, and Harry is hot."

"So is Victor." Very, very hot.

"I know." She paused. "But you guys have history."

"We don't," I said, interrupting her. We didn't. We had a short-lived fling if you could even call it that. Late night phone calls, quick sex in an office, a bathroom . . . those things didn't constitute a fling. Right?

"Well, sexual history," she said. "And you clearly still want to jump into bed with him."

"I never jumped into bed with him," I said. True and pointless reminder.

"You know what I mean."

I shrugged.

"What happened with Gabriel? Was he weird after your almost hookup the other night?"

I groaned. "Weird? No. Annoying? Yes. He brought it up in front of Victor. I can't believe I almost did that . . ." I felt a little ill, not because I was disgusted, but because I was appalled at myself. If my dad found out about that he'd kill me. Anything that made this divorce more difficult would not be okay with him.

"That was the wine," Talon said. "We shouldn't have drunk so much, and I did push that second bottle on you, so it's technically my fault."

I laughed. "Thanks for that, but you're not going down for it, despite the fact it did almost cost me the embarrassment of a lifetime."

"Yeah, well, alcohol is normally served with a side of embarrassment. My point is, you didn't even want to touch Gabriel last year."

"That's because his nose was always powdered."

She rolled her eyes. "Save the saint story for someone who buys it. You've done your share of drugs. Don't act like cocaine isn't equivalent to a shot of tequila around here."

I slumped back in my chair. She was right. The difference was that when Gabriel did it, he became a different person. Aggressive and downright mean. I'd never told anybody, not even Talon, about the times I'd slept in the guest room out back because I knew if I went to a hotel I'd be photographed and rumors would start.

"Why is he here anyway?" Talon asked, snapping me out of my thoughts.

"Who?" I asked, looking around.

"Gabriel. I thought he was in Canada."

"Oh. Yeah. He said he was on a shooting break. I need to find out how long this break will last. I'm not sure I can actually stay there if he'll be doing that every night."

"Oh? So you actually might leave your humble abode?"

I sighed. "I didn't want to, but I don't think I can handle seeing him go to shit. That was what started this whole thing in the first place, and he's really not going to change. I see that now."

Talon took a seat in the chair beside me and took my hands in hers, her green eyes filled with concern. "You can stay with me. Mike won't mind at all. We have the room. The kids would love to have Auntie Nicky there."

I shook my head slowly. "Thank you. I can always stay at my dad's for a while. Or get my own place. I'll have to do that eventually anyway."

Her eyes widened. "So you're going to let him keep the house?"

"I don't know. Maybe. I'm tired of holding this grudge."

Talon nodded and gave my hands a squeeze before letting go and standing. "I have to get to work, but whatever you need, you know I'm here. And be careful with the hot lawyer."

"I don't have to be," I said, laughing. "He's already reminded me twice that we can't happen again."

"Well, he reminded you about that before and look how that turned out," she said with a wink before walking away.

Yeah, it turned out with him breaking it off just when I thought we were reaching a new level. A new, bullshit level that I conjured up in my head because that's all it was—bullshit. What bothered me most when he broke it off was that I didn't listen to him when he said he wasn't interested in a relationship. I didn't listen to him when he said we couldn't do what we were doing. I learned, though. I learned when people show you who they are, you should listen. And he showed me who he was the entire time. He never hid behind false promises or pretty words. He did what he said he would do, and I hadn't faulted him for that. I couldn't.

I didn't come to appreciate Victor's honesty until I realized the man I shared a life with had lied to me. *Continually.* And then I found out he'd lied *and* cheated. When I threatened divorce, he threw a hissy fit and started trash-talking me to anybody in the industry who would listen. In *my* industry. He'd been so conniving about it, too, only talking to people I didn't know but only hoped to work with. Shortly after a business friend of mine gave me a heads-up, the tabloids were talking about our divorce and how heartbroken he'd been. They stated his affairs began when *I* said I was leaving him. The sad part is that at first I thought the rumors were false. That there was no way he was already with another woman, but I quickly realized there was usually some truth to the stories printed.

If I were a different person, like Harlow Winters, I'd call in a favor and spread rumors about Gabe that made him look worse than Ben Affleck cheating on Jennifer. That wasn't me, though, and ultimately, underneath all of the shit that had smeared his character and our marriage, I still believed in the nice guy from the middle of nowhere that I'd fallen in love with.

Chapter Six

Nicole

I DIDN'T HESITATE in saying yes when my best friend, Chrissy, called me to meet her for dinner at a new hot spot. I called Marcus, who was more than a little surprised at my request for him to be ready at nine o'clock. It's not that I hadn't gone out since the separation, but I'd been very low-key about it, opting to go to friends' houses and get drunk there instead of out in public where anybody could take my picture and make a fool out of me. Not that I needed help making a fool out of myself when I was drunk. No, I did that all on my own, but I didn't need it all over the tabloids.

I'd agreed to meet Chrissy at nine thirty, and when Marcus knocked on my door a second time, telling me it was nine twenty and I was still trying to figure out what shoes I was going to wear, I knew I'd be late.

"Fashionably late," I said to him as we walked to the car.

"That's one way to put it," he responded. I smiled, feeling the excitement of my night out coursing through me. "Are we taking the Porsche?"

I nodded as he pressed the clicker to the garage. The white

florescent lights flickered on and we walked toward the white Cayenne. I wasn't sure where Gabe stood on the cars situation and who would keep what, and I wasn't a big car person. Most days I drove my Prius, but if I had the chance to, I was totally keeping the Cayenne. We made it to the restaurant at the same time Chrissy did, both of us getting out of our cars at the same time. The few paparazzi standing outside ran toward her to get a picture. I started walking to the front of the restaurant, figuring I'd meet her inside to avoid the attention, but she squealed out my name and I had to turn around to acknowledge her.

"You look so good," she said as she ran over to hug me.

She smelled of flowers and Burberry perfume. The scent of our adolescence, when our only worries had been how late we could sleep and whether or not our parents would be home in the morning after we'd had a wild night out on the town.

"So do you," I said, bringing my hand up and touching the tips of her short, wavy blonde hair. "Love the new hair."

"I had it done today. Still getting used to it. The fam sends their love, by the way." She smiled big as she stepped aside for us to walk into the restaurant. I smiled at the mention of them. We used to be attached at the hip when we were kids and then in college. I don't think I had one memory that Chrissy wasn't in. I practically lived in her house during high school, probably because I didn't have any siblings and when I was there it was like I had three sisters. Some days, when life got shitty, I yearned for her and her sisters and this was definitely one of those times.

We were seated as promptly as you can expect to be seated when you're in the presence of a reality star. One of the reasons I hadn't seen her in a few months was because she was busy filming her show. Between her filming schedule and my work schedule, our free time rarely coincided.

"I see you still have all of your fingers," she said, taking a sip of her margarita. I smiled as I took a sip of mine.

"What makes you think I'm going to chop off my fingers? You need to get over that."

"I've seen how fast you work on those patterns. How's the set of the new movie? How's Austin?" she asked, her light brows rising provocatively. I laughed.

"If you're asking me if he's as hot as ever, the answer is yes. If you're asking me if anything has happened between us, the answer is never has and never will."

"Boring. Is it because of everything that went down with Gabe? Do you think you're swearing off actors from now on?"

"Are you swearing off athletes?" I asked, raising an eyebrow. Her past three boyfriends had been athletes, and all three had been cheating pigs.

"Touché."

We talked some more, ate some edamame, and clinked our glasses in a cheer before she dropped the, "Let's go to a club tonight!" and I was feeling tipsy enough to agree. We spent the rest of the time catching up and talking the way you can only talk to an old friend—loudly with obnoxious laughter and lots of pointing at each other whenever we remembered an old inside joke.

"That's your new security detail?" Chrissy asked when Marcus walked around the car and handed the valet a tip.

"That's him."

"Maybe I should ride with you," she said in a loud whisper. I laughed.

"Do it. Tell Frederick to follow us."

She turned around and told her bodyguard to follow us as he shielded us from the cameras snapping pictures of us climbing into the car.

"How's the filming going? Are you on break?" I asked.

"Yes. Thank God. My family is driving me absolutely crazy already," she groaned. I laughed. Only Chrissy could make a reality TV show that paid her hundreds of thousands of dollars an episode sound as grueling as hard labor.

"Poor you," I said, smirking.

"Seriously, Nicole. You look fucking awesome. Are you dieting?" she asked, giving me a once-over as we sat beside each other.

"It's called the divorce diet. You should try it. It works wonders, apparently."

She scoffed. "That would require me getting married."

"Although if he's on the table, I may reconsider," she said, nodding toward Marcus with a salacious grin on her face.

"Stop embarrassing him," I said, trying to keep the laughter out of my voice.

"Marcus, who have you worked for?" Chrissy asked, ignoring me.

"That's classified, ma'am," he said, eyes flickering to the rearview. I couldn't see his face, but I could tell he was smiling.

"Ex-military. Those are the only ones who always tell me their previous employers are classified, as if I can't just make a few calls and find out," Chrissy said, rolling her eyes. She tilted her head to look at me. "Those are always hot in bed, though. Marcus, we're going to Lure."

I laughed, feeling the alcohol swimming in my head. "You told him that."

"Oh. That's right. Have you been lately?"

"Nope. I've been staying out of the limelight, as per Dad's orders."

"We're going to have so much fun," she squealed.

By the time we got to Lure, there was a line circling the side of the building.

"Holy crap," I said, eyes wide. Truthfully, I hadn't been to a club in ages, so I'd forgotten about long lines and ID checks. That, and the last time I had gone was with Gabe and lines and ID checks didn't exist when you were with an A-list celebrity.

"Drive to the back," Chrissy instructed.

Marcus kept driving until we reached the corner, where he turned into the alley and slowed down when the mob of paparazzi perked up and spotted a newcomer. If we had any doubt as to where the back door was, we'd just found it.

"Oh God," I muttered.

Even in my tipsy state I knew it meant our outing would be all over tonight's TMZ, but then, any outing with Chrissy meant that, and I was okay with the dinner portion being in the tabloids. It was this part of the night that terrified me. I took a deep breath, perked my boobs up in my dress, and did a little mantra in my head to remind myself to suck in my stomach.

"You ready?" Chrissy asked when the car stopped in front of the mob of cameras, which had now turned toward us.

"I guess so."

Her security opened the door for us, assisting us in climbing out of the car without flashing anybody and instantly, the questions started.

"Nicole, did you know Gabriel would be here tonight?"

Holy shit. Thank God the club was huge.

"Did you set up to meet him here?"

Breathe. Suck in your stomach. Smile. No. Don't smile.

"Are you guys getting back together?"

Fuck. I smiled. Shit.

"Is the divorce off?"

Poker face.

"How do you feel about him dating his co-star?"

Poker face. Poker face. Poker face. If I said it enough I'd

keep it, or become Lady Gaga. Either way was good with me.

Even though all I wanted was to scream all the answers, I kept my head down, because that's what you do when you're being bombarded with personal questions you have no answers to. The bouncer took one look at each of us and let us in without hesitation. That was another perk to having Chrissy in your squad. She had a face anybody from a tween to a geezer recognized. Because of the headlines, I was sure he recognized me as well, but I definitely wasn't the reason he let me in, especially not if Gabe was really in there. We walked down a dark hallway toward the loud house music playing, but before we reached the dance floor, we were met by a waitress, wearing what looked like a bikini top and boy shorts.

"Chrissy, nice to see you again. We didn't get a heads-up, so I don't have everything ready for you, but we can get that taken care of quickly. Do you want your usual spot?" she asked.

"Yes, please," Chrissy said, then shook her head, thinking better of it. "Actually, is Gabriel Lane up there?"

The woman's eyes jumped to me. "Yes, but not on that side. You will need to walk by his table, though. If that'll be a problem I can try to get you in through the employee stairwell."

Both of them looked at me. "I don't care. I don't need special attention. I just need a shot of Fireball and I'm good."

Chrissy laughed. "I love you."

We followed the busty blonde up the stairs to the VIP area, where people were dancing along to a new Fetty Wap song. The dance area was smaller and much emptier than the one downstairs, but just as lively. Even though it was dark, I tried to look for Gabe. Not because I needed to see him, but because I wanted to know what area to stay away from. I didn't see him, so I kept walking and figured I'd do the smart thing and not get out of my designated area unless I needed to break the seal, which I hoped wouldn't happen soon.

"Did you see him?" Chrissy asked as soon as we reached the cozy corner she apparently frequented.

"Nope. You?"

She shook her head and ran a hand through her hair. "Can we get some Fireball shots, please? And a bottle of champagne?"

The blonde nodded and scurried off.

"You don't have to stay," Chrissy said to her security guy, who was still in tow. "You can go hang out with Marcus, and I'll text you when I'm ready to go."

The way this pint-sized girl ordered such big males around was always amusing to me.

"I'm trying to see if my sister's here," Chrissy said, typing into her phone. Her sisters were as popular as she was, especially in these settings.

"She's right there," I said, looking across from us. Chrissy laughed.

"How did we not see her? Let's go say hi."

We joined their friends, catching up on whatever loud club music would allow us to talk about. Work, boyfriend, etcetera, until the inevitable subject came up. Gabe.

I shrugged. "Don't care. Honestly, I'd rather not talk about it. It's fine. I'm fine."

And surprisingly, I was. I always wondered what I would feel like if and when I actually saw him with another woman. I wondered if I'd be angry or jealous, but I felt neither. I felt nothing. It'd been so long, and I felt nothing. I started to laugh. It was a small laugh that became louder and then stopped altogether.

"I'm a little tipsy; I'm having a moment," I said. "And I need to pee."

Chrissy laughed and hooked her arm around mine. "Let's go."

We brushed past the crowd, and saw Gabe walking toward the exit with a blonde on his arm. Chrissy looked at me, her eyes wide and comforting.

"I'm sorry."

I blamed the alcohol running through me for the tears that burned my eyes. I wasn't a public crier and was definitely not going to cry over him. I was done with that. We weren't together anymore. We hadn't been for a long time, yet it felt weird to see him walk out with someone else. *Had he ever been faithful?* Between the woman walking into his room and the clear way in which he depicted that he'd moved on, I had to wonder. Had I been blind or had he been the man I thought he was? I sighed, and shook my head slowly. It was something only Gabe knew. And I wasn't hurting, just . . . taken aback by it.

"It's fine. I'm glad I saw it," I said, clearing my throat.

"I hope he gets herpes," she said. We laughed, holding on to the rails to keep from tumbling down the steps. "Oh crap. We're blocking," she said. "Sorry. We're blocking. Oh . . . wow."

I looked up and saw the *oh wow* in question. He was tall, and lean, with a pair of hazel eyes currently burning holes through me.

"Holy fuck," I breathed.

Chrissy got right into flirt mode. "Where are you going?"

"The question is, where are *you* going?" Victor asked, his attention fully on me, eyes roaming down my body slowly before making their way back to my face. I swallowed back the urge to launch myself at him and erase the past ten minutes from my mind. The shots had certainly done a number on me because I felt like I was totally ready and willing to do that.

"To pee."

Chrissy laughed. "She means to the ladies' room." She grabbed my arm and shot me a pointed look. "He's hot. Saying you have to pee is frowned upon."

I couldn't help but laugh. "*He's* my lawyer."

The look on her face was priceless as she looked between the two of us. Victor was two steps beneath us and at eyelevel to us.

"Well, then. I'm going to . . ." She pointed toward the door of the bathroom a few steps down. Before she walked away, she leaned into my ear and whispered, "He works for your dad?" I nodded. "He's the one you . . . you know . . ."

I tugged at my bottom lip, my eyes still on Victor, and nodded at Chrissy who let out a harsh breath on my shoulder before walking away. She glanced back to give me two thumbs up, and I found myself laughing again.

"Hey," I said once she'd walked away. My voice was drowned out when the music picked up again. Victor leaned forward, the scruff on his face brushing my right cheek as he reached up to speak into my ear.

"Hey," he said in a low voice that made me shiver.

"I see you still frequent night clubs," I said, pulling back a little to look at him.

His eyes heated, lips curled into a smile that told me he was remembering the same thing I was. *Us rushing to the bathroom of a crowded club, him tugging the birthday tiara out of my hair, ripping my panties off before putting on a condom and thrusting inside me with a force I'd never experienced.* Because of where he was standing, I could feel his breath on my face, smell the hint of alcohol that lingered. The pull I felt was indescribable. It was as if in that small space everything vanished, including all rational thought.

Especially rational thought.

Because when he opened his mouth to say something, surely his next warning, I pressed my lips against his, and when he moved back slightly to steady himself, my body moved with his. He broke the kiss quickly, but not before sliding his tongue into my mouth once, curving in a deep full circle around mine, and *thankfully*, not before grabbing a fistful of my hair and groaning against my lips. Suddenly it wasn't the bass of the music thumping through my veins, but the feel of Victor pressed up against me, holding me, and then just like that, with the same quickness in which it had started, he pulled back.

"Nicole," he said, a warning. I opened my eyes and looked at him.

"Yeah?" I whispered.

"Follow me."

He turned around and walked down the stairs, and I trailed behind him, rounding the corner of the dimly lit hallway until we reached a door he pushed open. I blinked rapidly, looking around, at the desk, the glass walls beside us that overlooked the club, as my eyes adjusted to the red glow of the office.

"Who's office is this?" I asked.

"The owner."

"How do you know the owner?"

Victor tilted his head slightly, stepping closer to me so I had to crane my neck to look into his eyes. My heart lurched at what I saw in them.

"Is that really what you want to discuss?" he asked, his voice low.

"What do you want to discuss?" I whispered.

"You kissed me. In public, Nicole," he said sternly.

I blinked and blinked again to clear my head of some of the alcohol. "You kissed me back."

He closed his eyes, letting out a huffing breath. "That was a mistake. This whole thing was a mistake."

"You mean me? I was a mistake?" I asked, heart rocking a

little.

I tried to gather my bearings, but it was a tough night. First I had to watch my soon-to-be ex-husband leave with another woman, and now I was going to have to stand here and listen to the reminder of why Victor and I hadn't worked out in the past. *A mistake.* My self-esteem was definitely taking a hit.

"Yes," he said.

Unable to stand there and listen to him berate me, and knowing that if I left the office and ran to the bathroom it would be to cry, I turned and walked toward the glass, placing my hand against it, feeling the vibrations of the muted house music on the other side, watching the colorful laser lights as they pointed in every which direction. I felt him, rather than heard him come up behind me. It was as if he couldn't just give me the space I needed. As if he got off on telling me to stay away but also needed to pull me closer. I closed my eyes.

"You weren't a mistake," he said, his voice dark and smooth. "Kissing in public was definitely a mistake."

"We were in a dark stairwell," I said. "And you know the owner, so even if we were caught on camera you can have the footage erased."

Victor chuckled behind me and my eyes popped open. I turned around, resting my back against the cold surface behind me, closing my eyes for a beat when I felt the massage of the bass.

"You'd make a decent criminal."

I smiled, meeting his gaze. "I know how to keep secrets."

"Nic."

"Hmm?" I asked, inching closer to him. *I wonder what if would feel like to fuck against this window.*

From the way he pulled away from me, I'd either said the words aloud, or he'd read them on my face. He started to pace around the office, running a hand through his hair as he muttered things I couldn't hear under his breath.

"This isn't going to work," he said finally, turning to face me as he stood behind the desk.

"What?"

"This. Us. Me on this case. It's not going to work."

"Because you want to fuck me against the window," I said.

He gripped the top of the chair tightly and dropped his head, but didn't comment on what I'd said. "Maybe we should just see each other when we have to . . . for the divorce," he said.

I let out a laugh. "I didn't plan to come here tonight, let alone run into you."

"You're right," he said, meeting my gaze. "You're right, but we should still stick to that plan."

"As my lawyer, I don't think you should let me make rash decisions when I'm drunk," I said. He looked down again, but I saw his smile before he tried to hide it.

"I'm serious, Nicole."

"That's fine, Victor. I get it. Is that it? I was talking to a really cute guy upstairs, and I still need to use the restroom. Maybe I'll take him with me." Even in my current state, I could see the way his eyes darkened at my suggestion.

"You just said you were drunk," he growled, gripping the chair harder.

"Not *that* drunk." I paused to search his face. "Would that upset you? If I hooked up with that guy in the bathroom? I kind of like bathroom hookups."

"Nicole," he said, his tone hard, his eyes searing into mine.

"You know, you're actually the only guy I've done that with," I admitted. "But it was so hot. You kept saying all these dirty things in my ear, remember?"

"I remember," he said, voice grating.

"You were doing that," I said, pointing at his fingers, which were digging into the top of the chair. "Gripping my ass. I had marks the next day, the soreness. So hot."

"Nicole," he growled.

"It's too bad you're all business, otherwise we could have had a little fun," I said, pivoting to face the door and walking toward it. "We done here?"

Before I could even turn the knob, Victor was at my back, his hand covering mine over the doorknob.

"Why are you making this so difficult?" he asked, his voice a deep murmur in my ear. I didn't know. I honestly didn't know. It was him. I blamed him for clouding my judgment every time he was around. I closed my eyes. I wanted to lean my head back, give him access to my neck for him to suck on. I wanted to get lost in the feel of him thrusting inside me. I really, really needed to get laid. *And my body really, really wanted Victor Reuben to satisfy that urge.*

"Why would you bring me into a dark office to talk to me about not kissing you in public? You could have told me that in the hall," I said, opening my eyes. His hand gripped mine so I couldn't move.

"I can't seem to think straight around you," he said, his breath on my neck.

He turned the doorknob and put his hand on the small of my back to lead me out of there and back to the VIP section. I shivered at the feel of his touch. I looked at him over my shoulder and locked eyes, wondering if he felt this pull too. His nostrils flared. When we reached the dark corner, where the hallway had three options: exit, bathrooms, or stairs to VIP, we stopped walking and I turned to face him. His hand ran from my lower back, to my side, and my abdomen before he dropped it.

"I guess we're sort of on the same page after all," I said.

"If that's the case, we need to get on different chapters fast," he responded, tearing his gaze away from mine and looking toward the exit.

"You're really leaving?"

He looked at me again. "It's best if I do."

"Because I'm tempting you," I said, my mouth dropping slightly open when he nodded.

"Nothing good happens after twelve," he said. "It would be wise for you to do the same."

"You just don't want me hooking up with anybody."

He smiled and reached behind me, grabbed a fistful of my hair and tugged it gently. It was something he used to do before and just like then, I felt the notion to the tips of my toes.

"You already said I was the only guy you'd done that with. I don't expect you to break the mold in one night." He winked at me as he let go of my hair.

"You know me, I like being spontaneous," I said. His jaw twitched as he tore his gaze away from mine momentarily.

"Be careful, Nicole. Please don't do anything stupid," he added, leaning in to brush his lips against my cheek before walking away and out the door.

It simply wasn't fair. The man was too sexy. Too enticing. Too desirable. *I wanted him. My body wanted him.* Although, after that encounter, I was fairly sure my heart wouldn't survive a repeat with Victor Reuben.

Chapter Seven

Nicole

I SPENT MY morning off, nursing a hangover and dodging calls from both Gabe's manager and Victor's assistant. Around three o'clock, I got cozy on the sofa in my room, eating my cup of cereal and watching Peaky Blinders on Netflix. It was a perfect afternoon until the pounding on my door started. I closed my eyes, begging for Cillian Murphy to be the one on the other side of the door. Knowing I was about to be highly disappointed as soon as I stood to open it. I sighed, threw my blanket off, and unlocked the door. Gabe and his manager were standing on the opposite side. I closed my eyes and counted to three before opening them again. Darryl looked like someone's dad, with his salt and pepper hair, thick glasses, and round belly. Someone's dad or someone with an underage porn fetish. I was always crept out by him to the point that I may or may not have had him photoshopped from some of our wedding photos. But the guy could talk his way in and out of anything, and he was as ruthless as they came, which was a gift in this industry.

"I feel like I must have done something horribly wrong in my past life."

"Nice to see you again too, Nicole," Darryl said, flashing his megawatt fake-ass smile at me.

"What do you want?" I asked, looking at Gabe, who had his hands tucked into the front pockets of his jeans and his head down.

He looked like a sullen school boy, and the fact he looked that way and was standing beside his manager could only mean one thing. One really, *really* bad thing. My heart dropped.

"What?" I said, trying to ignore the way my heart spiked.

"We have a proposition for you. A very big one, one that will benefit you immensely if you agree to it," Darryl said. Despite the mistrust I felt for him, I knew he always had his client's interest at hand. My brows rose.

"Let's hear it."

We sat down at our long dining room table. The one we'd only used a handful of times to entertain guests on holidays or to talk about the laughable proposition, because that's what it ended up being. Absolutely ridiculous and laughable. They basically wanted me to pretend that maybe, just maybe I wasn't going to divorce Gabe after all.

"We haven't been seen out together in almost a year," I pointed out. "And in that time he has been seen with multiple women. All of whom weren't me."

"He's been traveling for work. You've been busy with your own career. He's back temporarily and is finally realizing how good he has it and he wants to save his marriage," Darryl said.

My heart sunk again. Did he not realize how much this hurt? Listening to this with my estranged husband, whom I had longed to patch things up with, sitting across from me? Yes, I was over him. Yes, I wanted to move on, but his manager pointing out that Gabe would never feel the way he just described, still hurt. I swallowed my emotions and tilted my chin up.

"What I'm hearing is 'Gabe wins again.' I still haven't heard the part where Nicole gets something out of this," I said.

Gabe cleared his throat, clasping his hands in front of him. "Maybe it's true. Maybe I want to try."

My jaw dropped. I blinked, blinked, blinked. "You can't be serious," I said, once I finally found my voice. The way he said he wanted to try made me think of the time he took me to my favorite sushi restaurant because he wanted to do something nice for me, but instead we ended up in the ER because he was allergic to the crab he'd ordered. It was sweet when I told him we could never go back there again and he looked at me, big puffy red eyes and said, *"Maybe I want to try again. For you."*

He shrugged those broad shoulders of his and I blinked out of my memory. "Why not?" he asked.

"What the . . ." I paused, trying to rein in my anger before it got the best of me. I took a deep breath in order to regroup. "Gabe. I just filed for divorce."

"Forget about that," Darryl said. "Let's leave emotions out of this. We don't need to complicate something simple. If you want to discuss your marriage, that's fine, even though I think we can all agree it's probably not working out for a reason." He raised his dark eyebrows over the frames of his glasses and shot Gabe and me a knowing look.

"Bastard," I said.

Gabe sighed.

Darryl shrugged. "The proposition is this. Go with him to the movie premiere this week, and give the media some comments about your relationship. Positive comments. Keep them guessing. Wear your wedding ring once in a while. Gabe will keep his on and just play the part."

"What's the point of that? The divorce has been filed. The papers were leaked. This whole thing will look stupid, and I still haven't heard the part where this benefits me." I looked at Gabe, who was watching me with a look I wanted to slap off his face. It was almost an admirable look, as if he was impressed with me.

"We talk to all of the production companies and tell them that I acted out of spite when I said I wouldn't work with them if they hired you as their costume designer," Gabe said. I clenched my jaw and stabbed him in my thoughts. Repeatedly. I put my hands under the table and sat on them when I felt them begin to shake.

"You guys think you're so fucking cute playing with my career. You think that just because you're Gabriel Lane, Hollywood's sweetheart, that I can't end you?" I asked. "You forget whose hometown this is, Gabriel Rogers. Or is your birth name something you've forgotten too? Maybe you should lay off the fucking drugs once in a while." My chair screeched against the marble floor as I stood up.

"I'll give you the condo in New York," Gabe said as I turned to walk back to my room. My heart lurched at the mention of my beloved condo. I stopped walking and turned around.

"Just like that?"

"I've fucked up, Nic. I know I have, but with all of my . . . partying and other things, my image is looking really bad right now and I have two movies coming out in the span of four months. I need to fix it," he said, blue eyes pleading as he stood and put his hands as if he was about to say a prayer. "Please. You're the only one who can help me. I swear I'll stop making things difficult for you."

I let that sink in for a moment as I looked into his apologetic blue eyes, eyes that could very well be lying to me. Eyes that had lied to me so many times in the past. He ran his hands down his newly shaven face and looked at me again. He was so damn handsome. Handsome, charming, great in bed, and he'd once been mine. Sadly, in this moment as I looked at him, trying to figure out whether or not he was just putting on an act, I couldn't even remember the good moments.

"I want this on paper," I said finally. "On paper and I want both of your signatures on it."

"I'll have Phil draw up a contract right now," Darryl said.

"Fuck Phil. I'll have my dad do it."

"Thank you, Nic. So much. I know I have no right—"

I put my hand up. "Shut up. If I'm doing this, you need to just shut up. I'll play along because for whatever stupid fucked-up reason I still care about you, but I can't promise anything more, and if during our mediation in a couple of weeks you say one negative thing, I'll do something crazy. Don't tempt me."

My dad was outraged. I knew he would be.

"What does Victor say about this?" he asked.

"I'm not telling him about this. I don't know. I wasn't thinking of telling him. I just need a simple paper stating my demands."

"These are things you need to discuss with your lawyer, Nicole. Why do you think I appointed you one?"

I could tell he was at his wit's end, and even though I was on the phone with him and I wasn't a six-year-old climbing kitchen cabinets, I felt the crack of the belt.

"Papi," I whispered. "Por favor."

He sighed loudly on the other end of the line, and I closed my eyes, letting out a breath.

"Fine, but you'll have to come to the Newport house to get it."

My mouth popped open. "Why? Just email it to me."

"No. We haven't seen you, you've been here a handful of times in the past year, and I'm having a barbeque. Tomorrow. Come early. Bring clothes," he said, his voice leaving no room for discussion. Leave it up to my dad to make a day at the beach house sound like punishment.

"Okay. I'll see you tomorrow."

Chapter Eight

Victor

WHEN WILL CALLED me last night and invited me to his beach house, I'd been tempted to come up with an excuse as to why I wouldn't make it, but then I remembered the isolated private beach and the silence, and I agreed. I'd stayed in the seven-bedroom house in the past and had a good time, so why not now? I hadn't expected his first words over brunch to be, "We need to talk about Nicole." And I hadn't expected the way my heart launched into my throat at the sound of those words. Immediately, I thought of Friday night when I'd seen her at the nightclub. The kiss we shared, the way I asked to speak to her in private and spent the entire time trying not to lock the door, push her against the door and hike up her dress. I made an effort to keep my features as blank as I could.

"What about Nicole?" I asked, smiling as Meire, Will's wife, walked in with a tray and set cups of coffee on the table for us.

"Where's Maya?" Will asked her.

"I sent her to buy some groceries. We didn't have anything in the fridge, but I think I'll tell her to go home early if it's only going to be us," she replied as she walked off with the tray again.

"You're not going to join us?" Will called out.

"I want to make sure Maya prepared the room for Victor," she called out from the kitchen.

Will shook his head as he took a sip of coffee, and as much as I didn't mind delaying the Nicole conversation about whatever it was he wanted to discuss, I was on edge.

"So, Nicole?" I prompted.

"Right," he said, putting the cup down. "Let's start from the beginning," he said, and I groaned inwardly.

Will loved to make lengthy stories out of things he could have said in under two minutes. At least we weren't at the office and I didn't have a million files to get through. As long as my ass was sitting in his swanky twelve-seat dining room in his huge beach house, I had to suck up the story.

"When she told me she was getting married I was shocked," he said. *You and me both,* I wanted to say, but couldn't. "Not because I didn't think she wanted to get married. I think between her and her mother her wedding had been planned since she was six. They love that stuff." Definitely a surprise to me. "An aunt of hers gave her a Bride Barbie when she was small and two days later Nicole wanted a Barbie Dream House to go with it. Anyway, I was shocked because she'd known the guy for two seconds before she agreed to marriage."

I nodded, lifting the cup of coffee to my mouth and taking a sip.

"I tried to talk her out of it, but she wouldn't listen, and now she's getting a divorce and I can't help but feel responsible," he sighed. "My little girl deserves better."

"I agree," I said.

"She deserves somebody who gives her more than she gives," he added. I nodded in agreement again, not that I knew shit about what that meant. "She passed up jobs for Gabriel just so she could travel to where he was on set. Can you believe he turned her away one day when she showed up?"

I felt my mouth drop. Will nodded, eyebrows raised. "She flew to Canada to see him and he never made an effort to see her. His manager told her to leave."

"What an asshole," I said, feeling my blood start to boil. How could anybody do that to *her*? To his own wife?

"Complete asshole. And now he's trying to get her to—" Will stopped talking when the doorbell rang loudly, his eyes widened. "We'll talk about this later."

I wanted to press the matter, but then I heard Meire say hi to somebody and footsteps coming up behind me and saw the grin on Will's face. Before I saw her, I smelled her, the sweet floral scent I knew covered her entirely. When I looked over and she smiled at me, I felt the air squeeze out of me. She was wearing a long orange dress that fit her loosely, her dark hair was down and wet from a recent shower, her blue eyes vibrant as she looked at me. I smiled back and my eyes made their way down her body and zoned in on the overnight bag in her hand.

Oh no.

Oh shit.

Were we both staying here tonight?

"Hi, Victor," Nicole said, her voice soft, her cheeks pink as she dropped her gaze from mine.

I frowned. A shy Nicole was a first for me. Maybe it was because we were in front of her dad and stepmom. Maybe it was because she was remembering what happened between us the other night. I needed to keep reminding her not to do that. I needed to keep distancing myself *in that way*. She was too tempting. I had to keep thinking: forbidden fruit equals death. It would have helped if I would have actually paid attention during Bible study when I was a kid.

"Nicole," I said in greeting.

"Join us. We were just talking about you," Will said.

"I'll take your bag upstairs. I was going to put towels in there anyway," Meire said, taking the bag in Nicole's hand and excusing herself again.

"What were you talking about?" Nicole asked, taking a seat next to me.

Why next to me? It could've been because that was her regular seat, and as creatures of habit we were forced to always pick the same seat at the dinner table. It could've been because there was a setting on the table. It could've been because it was closest to the pancakes. It could've been many things, but the only one I wanted it to be was that she wanted to be near me. Beside me. And the thought that it mattered to me, because I wanted her to be as affected by me as I was by her, was fucked up. I'd ended things the first time and this time I couldn't afford to entertain the things circulating my thoughts half the time when she was around. I just couldn't. She was off limits. But then she was next to me, and her scent made me want to lean in closer, and I just didn't care. She infiltrated my thoughts in that moment, and I just didn't care. In that moment, if her father wasn't sitting across from us, I would have said something I wasn't supposed to.

"I was about to tell Victor about the contract you want me to draft."

I blinked, the pull of her presence replaced by curiosity. "What kind of contract?"

"It's simple," she said, keeping her voice quiet, in an almost whisper. "I agree to go with Gabe to some events, have some pictures taken, say good things about him and our marriage possibly working out to the media and he gives me the condo in New York. In addition, he will retract the lies he told the production companies I wanted to work with, stating he had been in a bad place."

I pivoted in my seat to look at her. She wasn't looking at me. Her face was cast down, her attention on her hands, but I knew she could feel my gaze. I knew because her cheeks were filling with a deep shade of pink, and I could tell I was making her uncomfortable. Making her feel that way wasn't my intention, but I was indescribably uncomfortable with that request. So uncomfortable that I wanted to yank her out of her chair and take her away from the attentive eyes of her father. I swallowed back my annoyance and the arguments that lay on the tip of my tongue.

"And you're okay with that?" I asked.

Finally, after what seemed like an eternity, her head turned and her eyes met mine. She nodded. "I am."

Our gazes stayed locked for a beat, or two, enough time for me to lose my train of thought as I looked into her deep-blue eyes. Enough time for me to recount the way her lips felt on mine, and the way she'd offered herself up to me. Will huffed from the other side of the table and both our heads whipped toward him. Spell broken.

"I don't think it's a good idea," Will said, looking at Nicole. "I think if you give in to these demands, you're going to find that spending time with him may make you re-think the divorce."

That thought alone made my heart squeeze in my chest. What the hell did I care? *Why* the hell did I care? I didn't have an answer to that, but it was clear I didn't want her going back and forth with a guy that treated her poorly.

"There's nothing to think about, Dad. I wouldn't have signed the papers if I even had an ounce of hope that this marriage would work," she said.

I stayed quiet until Will addressed me and told me to draft up the agreement for her, then I excused myself from the table, took my plate to the kitchen, and went upstairs to the room

Meire had put me in. It was a damn big room, with a king-sized bed and a balcony that overlooked the pool and the ocean. I stood there, thinking about the wording I would use. I'd drafted agreements for celebrities left and right without second thought. This one was going to make me lose my mind. I was startled when I heard a sniffle beside me. My head turned in the direction of the sound, but I didn't see anybody. When I heard it again, I frowned, leaning forward in the balcony I was standing in and looking over to the one beside me. Nicole was sitting in one of the chairs with her legs propped up, her arms wrapped around her knees and her head tucked down. Was she *crying?*

I pushed off from where I was standing. I didn't want to intrude on her private moment. I didn't know how to handle her private moment. I could jump over and hug her, but that would be weird. I could knock on her door and ask her if she was okay . . . but that would be weird. I could just pretend I hadn't heard her, but something about that option made me feel like shit. I cracked my neck, shook my arms and measured how close the balconies were. They were made so close to each other that my body wouldn't fit in between them so I didn't have to worry about a fall. I just had to worry about where Will and Meire were and whether or not they would see me jumping over. Fuck. What a thought. It was almost enough to stop me from doing it. *Almost.*

Nicole shrieked when I landed beside her, her head snapping up, her hands wiping her bewildered, tear-stricken eyes.

"What the hell are you doing?"

I looked at her for a beat before stepping in front of her. "I'm telling you up front. I don't know how to deal with emotional women, and if you don't want me here, tell me, and I'll jump back over to my corner and pretend I never saw you."

She opened her mouth to say something, and closed it

again, a slight frown on her face. "I don't."

Okay. Easy enough. I turned back around and just as I was about to climb on the balcony, she held my hand to stop me. I closed my eyes at the jolt. I felt her touch everywhere. What was up with that? Had it always been that way? It'd been so long, and I'd been so young and stupid, I couldn't even remember.

"Don't leave," she whispered. I opened my eyes and turned around, my hand still in hers as our eyes met.

"You said you didn't want me here," I whispered back, stepping closer. What I wanted was to scoop her up and put her on my lap. I wouldn't, though. *Couldn't.*

"Stay anyway," she said. "You could have broken your neck trying to get over here. I don't want your efforts to be in vain."

I chuckled, dropping my hand from hers as I walked to the chair beside her, taking a seat there. "You wanna talk about it?"

She sighed. "Not really. It's bad enough you saw me crying, and really, it's nothing. It's stupid."

I resisted the urge to reach over and cover her hand with mine in an attempt to comfort her. Instead, I scooted my chair closer to hers, so we were both facing the ocean.

"It's not stupid if you're emotional over it," I said, my eyes on the ocean, on the waves that splashed and disappeared out in the far distance, on the sailboats beyond them. I didn't do well with comforting emotional women, but having Estelle for a sister had taught me enough on how to deal with them, and I knew it wasn't wise to dismiss her current state.

"I don't want to talk to the media at all," she said after a few long beats. I looked over at her; she was looking out into the distance, so I had a chance to study her soft features, her small nose, and the apples of her cheeks.

"So don't."

She sighed. "It's not that simple. They ask. They always ask.

This morning I got a call from a magazine that wants to run a story. I'm sure they got my number from Gabe's manager since he was the one who suggested it, but the thing is, there is no story here."

"They always find a story."

She shook her head, turning it to meet my gaze. "I would never give them a juicy one. I would never sell him out like that."

Her words shouldn't have made me feel anything, but I felt pride in her and annoyance in myself—in my old self—the one who'd thought she would have been responsible for us getting caught. The one who thought she'd throw me under the bus if the day ever came where she had to pick between the two of us, and my career would go out the window.

"You're a good person, Nic," I said. "And Gabriel is an idiot."

"Men usually are," she said, her lips curling into a small smile.

I looked at her mouth for a moment, desperate to lean into her. I'd had her lips on mine a few days ago, and I wanted them there again, but I couldn't do it, and I definitely wouldn't be the one making the move. Maybe it was unfair of me to want something this badly and not be willing to work for it. But I knew if I did work for it—if I did go after her—I'd go all the way, and I couldn't afford to do that.

"We are," I replied. "We're complete idiots. You should remember that."

"My eyes are wide open, Victor. I know you think they're not, but they always have been. This thing between us," she shook her head, exhaling, "it was good, and I know why you ended it when you did. I get it, but I don't think either one of us used the other. I think we were what we needed to be for each other at the time, and it's okay."

"Even if you did want it to be more, which I'm assuming

you did," I said, hoping she understood I was referring to her marriage.

I didn't want to bring that up and tie it to me in any way, but I really wanted to fucking know why she jumped into such a serious relationship so quickly. I needed to know if I pushed her to it. She laughed.

"I guess we'll never know," she said, her eyes twinkling as she said the words. I scowled and she laughed again, but that was cut short by a loud knock on her door, and we both looked at each other, wide-eyed. "Stay here," she whispered.

I stood up and hid behind the French door, hoping whoever it was wouldn't walk inside. I felt sixteen again, my heart thumping in my chest as I listened to her talk with who I assumed was Meire. Instead of waiting around, I jumped back over to my balcony and sat in one of the chairs, my heart still pounding. Nicole walked back out onto her balcony shortly after, her head whipping over to me. She smiled.

"Got scared?"

"Fuck, yeah," I said honestly. She rolled her eyes, walking over to the part closest to me. I did the same, meeting her there. We both put our elbows on the balconies.

"You used to fuck me in your office, but you can't be caught in my room," she said, raising an eyebrow. My heart jumped at the mention of that. My dick was already halfway to hard at the mere mention of us fucking. I closed my eyes, tried not to picture it, but ended up with a mental image of Nicole's face between my legs, her eyes looking into mine as she sucked my cock. I groaned.

"Happy thoughts?" she said, her voice flirty. My eyes popped open.

"I was an idiot."

"So I've heard." She paused. "How long will it take you to

draft up the contract?"

"About an hour, maybe less. Why?"

"You told me once that you tried to go surfing every day," she said. "You still do that?"

"Almost every morning," I said, smiling at the fact she remembered.

"I want you to teach me. Or try to. I can paddleboard, it shouldn't be that different, right?"

I chuckled. "Oh, Nicole, you have a lot to learn."

"Well, then, I'm glad I picked a capable teacher," she said with a wink as she turned around. "I'm going to put on my bathing suit. Meet you downstairs in an hour?"

"You're . . ." I shook my head. "Yeah, an hour."

I spent the next forty minutes drafting up a contract and trying not to picture her getting naked in the room beside mine. *Naked*. In the room beside mine. *Fuck*. How was I going to sleep there? Maybe I should head home early. Maybe I should just say fuck it and get out of there as soon as I prepared the contract. I was good at coming up with excuses. But then I remembered how emotional she'd been on that balcony, and I decided to stay. An hour later, I'd sent her the contract, put on my swimming trunks, and headed downstairs to meet her by the beach. I saw Will on my way over and updated him on everything. When I reached the end of their backyard, and my feet touched the warm sand, I saw her. She was wearing the smallest bikini I'd ever seen, and I was grateful when I saw the wetsuit in her hand that she was about to put on.

"Need help?" I asked as I walked over, when I saw her struggling to stay balanced on one foot. Her head snapped up, lips spread into a smile that promised the kind of trouble I enjoyed getting involved in.

"Considering I just fell on my ass," she said, pivoting a little to show a back covered in sand. "Yes."

I chuckled at the sight and gave *not* checking her out my best effort. When I reached her, she craned her head to look up at me as I extended my arm for her to hold on to as she pushed her foot into one leg of the suit. Our gazes held as she did it, and I was glad for the loud waves feet away from us. Otherwise, she would have heard my loud breathing, and I was sure I would have heard hers. As it was, the heated glances we were giving each other spoke volumes. I couldn't have her touch me and not think about my hands on hers, her lips on mine. When she finished putting on her suit and zipping it, I thought I'd be out of the woods, since her skin wouldn't be showing, but the way that thing fit her . . . fuck. I cleared my throat, looking out into the water.

"The waves aren't that good today," I said. "Paddleboarding may be the only option we have right now."

"That's fine," she said, following my gaze. "I think I like that option better anyway."

We walked over and picked up the boards set against the house and pulled them toward the shore. I jogged back and got the sticks, and on my way back all I could do was look at Nicole and notice the way she seemed contemplative today, not the spunky woman I was used to. We both settled on our boards, but instead of standing, we sat in the water, our legs on either side of each of our boards.

"Can I ask you something?" I asked, clearing my throat as we both faced the endless ocean, our backs toward the houses. She glanced at me momentarily and nodded. "You said the other day that I was the only one you'd ever . . ." I couldn't bring myself to finish the sentence.

"Had sex with in a bathroom?" she asked, smiling, her eyes assessing me. I nodded. "You are."

"I know you don't need a reason to do anything," I said. "You act on instinct more than anything, but I'm surprised."

"You think I'm a slut," she said, but her smile didn't falter. "It's a fair assessment. I'm not, but coming from you it's a fair assessment."

"I don't like labels," I responded. I didn't. Slut, whore, promiscuous. Those were all labels I'd never understood for men or women. As far as I was concerned, what you did with your body was nobody's business.

"I know you don't," she said, "Mr. I Don't Want a Girlfriend Ever."

"That's not the kind of label I was taking about. I don't have a problem having a girlfriend."

She raised an eyebrow and looked away from me, back to the ocean. "Maybe people do change, after all."

We were silent for a moment, the water moving us in small waves. We watched as a few families played in the shore with their kids, some joggers passed by, birds cawed.

"I've never just hooked up with a guy," she said finally, filling in the comfortable silence we had going. I looked at her. She was looking at me, but I could tell it was taking effort for her to keep her eyes on mine. "In college I used to make out with strangers, but that was as far as I got. Actually hooking up with strangers, though? Never."

"Why me then?" I asked, suddenly feeling a jolt of confidence. I felt like I needed to pat myself on the back for that achievement. She shrugged.

"If I told you, you'd think I'm crazy, or knowing the way you are, it will send you running the other way," she said, tearing her eyes away from mine again. My heart began pounding a little louder. Something about the way she said that. Fuck. Maybe I would want to run the other way, but I still wanted to know.

"The good news is, you're kind of stuck with me for a little while, so it doesn't really matter what you tell me. I won't run the other way," I said, smiling, trying to lighten the mood, but when she looked at me she wasn't smiling at all. The look on her face was a mixture of forlorn and uncertainty. "Just tell me," I said, my voice almost a whisper.

"I felt something when I looked at you. Something weird. Something . . . not normal. I don't know how to explain it other than maybe my soul recognized something in you. And I know you didn't feel the same. I knew what we were," she said, giving me a pointed look. "Or what we weren't, since you said yourself we were nothing. But I felt it every time we were together."

Her words were claws that seeped into me and gripped the protective shell surrounding my heart. I couldn't explain it any other way. That's what it felt like when she said them. I swallowed past those unwanted feelings.

"Why didn't you say anything? Why didn't you tell me?"

She let out a single laugh. "What difference would it have made? If anything you would've ended things sooner." She paused, getting serious again. "I'm not saying I was in love with you, Victor. I'm just saying that a part of me felt like something bigger than what we actually had was there. At least the possibility was there." She shrugged. "Doesn't matter."

"You got engaged and married a few weeks later," I said, frowning.

Anger threatened to replace the feeling of confusion and wonderment I felt. I broke it off, but she got married. Who did that? A crazy person, obviously, but Nicole didn't seem like she was legitimately crazy, aside from her spontaneity.

"That should tell you what kind of state I was in. I guess I was a needy twenty-two-year-old," she said, shrugging. "I'm not saying I regret it, because I don't."

"Even now? With the divorce?"

She looked away, her words were low when she spoke again. "Even now. I loved him. In a sense, I still do. I don't want to be with him. I *can't* be with him, but I'm grateful for our time together."

The way her words made me feel bothered me, though I didn't let it show. Instead, I cut the conversation there and paddled to put a little distance between us. I wasn't sure I could handle any more revelations from her, whatever it was I was feeling, from this moment. I slept like shit that night, tossing and turning as her words replayed in my head, tossing and turning thinking about her sleeping in the room beside me, wondering what she wore to bed, wondering what she looked like completely naked. I needed to get a handle on myself before shit hit the fan.

Chapter Nine

Victor

MAYBE I WAS being selfish, but I really didn't want her living in that house with Gabriel Lane. Especially not after the day we had on the beach, with her confessions and my fucked-up emotions. The worst revelation I got was the sight of what life could be like with her, away from the press and the confinement of my office. I actually felt . . . something. Which meant trouble. Big fucking trouble. Nonetheless, as her attorney, I wanted her out of the house. As her friend, or whatever I was, I *needed* her out of the fucking house. Last night as I went to sleep, I caught myself thinking about her being in the house with that guy, and him sneaking into her room in the middle of the night, the way I wanted to do when I'd slept beside the room she'd been in. It drove me batshit crazy.

On top of that, my other client at the moment, Sam Weaver, had the same thing going, except in his case he was the Gabriel and his estranged wife was the Nicole. He'd been making living with him nothing short of hell for the woman.

We'd been to court once already, and she'd cried through the entire hearing, not because her children weren't getting the attention they deserved, but because she was being treated like shit in front of them. It was moments like those that made it difficult for me to represent "the bad guy," because Sam was most certainly the "bad guy." His ex had made her share of mistakes, most of which we'd uncovered throughout the divorce proceedings.

I knew I wouldn't be able to talk sense into Nicole. I could barely talk to her at all, which made my job insanely difficult to get through. Every time I saw her, though, I thought about the way her face looked at the peak of ecstasy and my concentration went to shit. I knocked on the door and waited. I needed to talk to Will before he left town.

"Come in," Will shouted. I stepped into his office slowly, taking in the dim lights and candles lit on the corner. "Meire's idea of relaxation hour. She says it's either this or I quit smoking cold turkey, so here I am." He sighed heavily and pressed a button to turn the lights back on. "What's going on?"

"I wanted to talk to you about Nicole," I said, undoing the button on my suit as I took a seat across from him. I put a hand up to keep him from jumping in. "I think she should move out of that house."

Will frowned. "The minute she moves out, she loses it."

"Not necessarily, Will, and she's fucking losing herself by staying there," I said.

"Explain."

"I went over there to take some papers for her to sign and apparently Gabriel had a party the night before. The only reason the place wasn't trashed was because Nicole had already cleaned up half the mess. His mess, while he walked around without a care in the fucking world, and the other day in Newport, she was upset over things with him. I just don't think it's good for her to stay there." My voice and fists shook as I said the words. I hadn't realized how pissed off that made me until I said it aloud. Will noticed, his brows rose as he appraised me. He stayed silent for a little while.

"Should I be concerned about this?" he asked, signaling at me. "I'm glad you've taken such an interest with Nicole and her case, but I've seen you lose your cool in here and keep it contained in court, and I want to make sure that's what's happening here. Because you know if you lose it out there, they'll have a field day with you, her, and this firm, and I can't make you partner if you have a shitshow surrounding your name."

I took a nice, calming deep breath. "I'm fine. I have court in a few hours with Sam Weaver's case and that has me riled up."

"How's that coming along?"

"Good. I think we'll be done with it today. He's giving her everything she's asking for, so I don't see why we wouldn't."

Will nodded. "Focus on that, in the meantime, I'll see what I can do about Nicole."

I looked at the man across from me one last time and nodded as I stood and walked out. I packed up my briefcase and left to pick up Sam before we headed to the courthouse. Nicole's issues would have to sit on the backburner for now. When I pulled up to the Beverly Hills mansion, I lowered my window, pressed the bell and waited until the two massive iron structures in front of me opened. I drove in, going around the ornate water fountain with the bronze mermaid in the middle, and parked in front of the steps that led to the house. I put my car in park and checked my email while I waited, and after sending out a few replies, I realized Sam hadn't come outside yet. I called his cell phone, which he answered on the first ring.

"I'm outside," I said.

"Going right now."

He was saying the last word when he stepped out of the

house and closed the door behind him before jogging down the steps to the car. I was glad he was wearing a suit, even if it was orange as fuck and made him look like a Starburst.

"I thought you were gonna get out of the car," he said as he opened the passenger door and adjusted the seat so it was basically lying all the way back. I looked at it questioningly, but didn't comment.

"I'm your lawyer, not your prom date," I said, and started driving. Sam chuckled, rubbing his hands together nervously.

"Damn. I can't believe we're finally getting this done with."

"Let's hope so. We had to pull in a lot of fucking favors to get this done on a Saturday."

Sam exhaled. "I'm just glad this bitch will be out of my life forever."

I shot him a sideways glance as we reached a red light. "Not really. You have two kids with her, so you'll be stuck with her for life."

"But I'll only have to deal with her during birthdays."

I shook my head and started driving when the light turned green again. No use in bringing up school functions, sports activities, or basically any other life event that would technically include him. I didn't know what his goals or plans were for his family, and quite frankly I would rather keep it that way. One thing I learned about this job was not to get emotionally attached to anybody involved, and shit got complicated when minors were at stake.

We reached the courthouse with just enough time to spare, and when the media started huddling around my car, I was glad for that. I knew it would take us at least ten minutes to get from the parking lot to the front of the building if Sam stopped to chat as much as he liked to.

"Don't say anything negative about the divorce," I coached.

"Don't say anything negative at all. Keep it positive. You're co-parenting. You're getting along. You're looking forward to sharing custody of the children."

Sam nodded and put on his megawatt smile and straightened his suit as he faced the first photographer. As expected, they started asking him questions about the divorce, his alleged affair, how he allegedly kicked his ex out of the house, and Sam answered everything like a pro. We walked with the cameras alongside us and took turns answering questions. When we got to the front of the building, we turned around and Sam said his final statement of gratitude that he'd surely practiced in front of the mirror.

"I'm so thankful to you guys, to my fans, to the team for standing behind me. I'm glad to put this behind me, and I'm looking forward to a good year on the field."

The cameras snapped, snapped, snapped.

"One last question," one of the reporters shouted. I squinted to see at the guy in the middle of the crowd.

"Last one," I said, glancing at my watch. We had five minutes to spare.

"Mr. Reuben, what can you tell us about Gabriel and Nicole getting back together?"

That made me stall. I was caught off guard, not only by the question, but by the way my chest tightened in response. My first thought was, "she wouldn't do that," and that scared me ten times more than the one that quickly followed which was, "I hate when clients don't keep me informed with the decisions they make."

In the end, I dreaded that my two seconds of silence would be misconstrued and used against that case, but I was able to compose myself. "I'm not here to comment on that case. I'm here representing Mr. Weaver. Thank you."

My phone rang the second we walked in, and seeing Corinne's name on my screen has never made me feel more anxious and relieved at once. Unfortunately, I had to put it on the dish and walk through the metal detector before calling her back.

"Why are these fuckers asking me about Nicole and Gabriel?" I said when she answered the call.

Her silence was telling. My heart sunk a little more.

"Don't tell me," I said when she started to speak. "I'll call you back when I get out of court. I can't deal with unfortunate news right now. Handle whatever you can handle without me." I hung up the phone before she could say a damn word. It must be the premiere. It had to be. There was no other explanation for it. Fuck if I liked the sound of it, regardless of the situation.

Chapter Ten

Victor

PICTURES. PILES OF pictures sat on top of my desk. In magazines, in newspapers, in print from what my buddy in the gossip industry was able to gather for me. Images of Nicole and Gabriel kissing on the carpet for the premiere of his newest blockbuster. Images of them gazing lovingly into each other's eyes. Images of her laughing at whatever he was telling the interviewers from major networkers. Was it an act? Was it real? If it was an act, she had a real future in Hollywood and it had nothing to do with costume design. I hated those pictures. I hated the way he looked at her. I hated that she looked at him—*period*. I wasn't a jealous man, but damn did that shit fester inside me.

"At least she only agreed to a premiere," my secretary said as she walked into my office with her laptop in hand.

"What do you mean?"

Corinne sat in the seat across from me, setting her computer on my desk. She turned it over and pointed at the headline of a popular gossip blog.

Gabriel Lane vows to work on his marriage.

"It's gossip," I muttered, running my hands over my face, feeling the exhaustion take hold of me.

"I know, but still. They look pretty freaking happy," she said, turning her computer to look at it again.

"Do you need anything else?" I asked. Corinne's eyes widened.

"No. You told me to show you whatever was being talked about, so that's what I came to do. I think this is it, though."

I nodded. "Thank you. Can you bring me coffee please? I feel like I'm about to pass out on my desk."

She stood. "Sure. You want me to hold your calls for an hour?"

I closed my eyes. That would be nice. An hour powernap on my couch. My eyes popped open, trained on the couch across from my desk, and suddenly all I could do was picture me sitting there and Nicole riding me. *Fuck.* I shook my head.

"No."

"Okay. I'll be back with the coffee," Corinne said in a singsong voice as she walked out.

I wasn't sure why I was suddenly picturing Nicole and me all over my office, but ever since she came in that day and I was assigned her divorce, she was all I saw. Originally, it had taken months to stop seeing her everywhere when I walked in. Back then, for concentration purposes, I'd had half a mind to trade offices with Bobby, but he had a shit view of the parking lot and the street, and I had the ocean, so I sucked it up and stayed. Now I wish I would've traded. I'd rather see grout than deal with thoughts of fucking my client. My beautiful, spirited, off-limits client.

Chapter Eleven

Victor

THE SECOND TO last thing I needed was to see the news that Nicole was staying with Gabriel everywhere. Everywhere. Every magazine, every news outlet, even the major ones that were supposed to report *real* news were talking about it. Apparently they'd become the *it* thing to talk about since Nicole was being painted as the fan who caught the star. Bullshit. It was all bullshit. He wasn't a star when she met and married him, but I guess they'd forgotten that bit, or they didn't care since this sold more stories. I waited the week out. They'd gone to the premiere on Wednesday night and I'd been dealing with the gossip since, but I had more important things to do like finish up my other case, and it was like Corinne said, she'd only agreed to a couple of things, one being the premiere. As her attorney, I had no *right* to be upset about it. That didn't mean it stopped the feelings of annoyance and discomfort from spreading and sticking, though.

I liked to think I was pretty good about leaving my work in the office, unless I had something major pending, but this thing with Nicole felt like it was taking over my life outside of work. On Sunday, while I was straightening up my house, it was all I could think about. As if on cue, my phone vibrated in the pocket of my sweat pants. I stopped washing the plate in my hand and switched off the water when I saw Corinne's name on the screen. She rarely ever called me on weekends. If we had things to say to each other, it all went through email. I answered it quickly.

"Umm . . ." she said. "Are you watching the red carpet by any chance?"

It took me a moment to understand what she was saying. I didn't remember what was on tonight, but I reached for the control and switched on the TV nonetheless.

"No. What am I looking for?" I asked as I flipped through channels.

"Golden Globes," she said. I stopped on what I assumed was the event when I saw a woman wearing a fancy black dress holding a microphone and smiling. My heart dropped into the pit of my stomach when she held that microphone up to Gabriel Lane, who was standing beside her, looking larger than life, and then Nicole, who was standing beside him, wearing a red dress that hugged all her fucking curves, looking like she belonged in my bed.

"What the fuck?" I growled. The Globes wasn't part of the agreement.

"I wasn't sure if this was added to the original addendum," Corinne said.

"Fuck no, it wasn't."

"Okay. Well, I'll let you go. I just wanted you to see it just in case." She paused. "Do you think they're maybe getting back together and she's unsure?"

I swallowed back my impending growl as I looked back at the screen, back at Nicole, who was now holding Gabriel's hand as he looked down at her with a smile. I was going to kill her. I was going to fuck her and then kill her. What the fuck was she thinking? What the fuck did I want her to be thinking? I didn't even know anymore. I couldn't be sure. But the thought of those red lips on anybody else but me was enough to drive me fucking crazy.

"I don't know. I'll get to the bottom of it," I said.

"May I make a suggestion?" she asked just as I was hanging up.

"What?" I said, my impatience clear in my voice.

"Maybe ask William?"

"What a great idea, Corinne. Let me call her father, who happens to be my boss, and ask him if he knows what the fuck is going on with my client. I'm sure that will bode well with the whole 'maybe you can become partner when this shit is over, Victor' thing." I paused to take a breath. "I'll handle it."

I closed my eyes and started counting backward from ten. I felt like any moment a vein would pop out of my forehead, or my neck, or my fucking arm with the amount of force I was using on my remote control.

I called my sister to see if she was watching. Maybe I should watch this with other people present so I wouldn't end up trashing my entire fucking house.

"Mia and Jensen are here," my sister said upon answering the phone.

Shit. I'd forgotten our friends were coming into town.

"Are they there right now?" I asked.

"Yeah, they didn't bring the kids, though. We're watching the Globes. Want to come over?"

"Yeah, I'll be there soon."

I'd picked up the keys, a bottle of wine, and started walking to my car before we'd ended the call. When I got to my sister's house the front door was slightly open, so I knocked loudly and stepped in, closing and locking it behind me.

"In here," Estelle yelled.

"Oh God," her best friend Mia groaned, and then caught sight of the bottle in my hands and perked up. "Oh. He brought wine."

I scoffed as I leaned over to kiss her cheek, and my sister's. "Now we know the way to Mia's heart isn't corny love stories, after all," I said, referring to her husband, and my other best friend, who was a writer and had made it his life goal to write stories about Mia, even when they weren't together. Fucking pansy. "Where is Jensen anyway?"

"Out back with Oliver, smoking a cigar."

My eyes nearly bulged out their sockets. "Oliver is smoking?"

"No. Jensen is. Oliver's probably lecturing him on how bad it is."

I chuckled, handed over the wine, and headed that way, but stopped when I got to the door and turned back around. "What do you guys know about Nicole Alessi and Gabriel Lane?"

Mia's smile widened. She tucked her short blonde hair behind both ears and sat up straight. "Well, aside from the fact that he's so hot," she said, and as soon as the words left her mouth Jensen opened the door behind me.

He looked at me and smiled, greeting me with our usual handshake and hug before looking at her again.

"I know I'm hot, babe, but you really need to stop telling everybody you see."

She rolled her eyes. "I'm talking about Gabriel Lane. He's so fucking dreamy." "He is. Did you see the pictures of his vacation in Mexico a few months ago? Holy shit. I mean, if his swimming trunks—" Estelle said.

"Would have gone a little lower. I know," Mia finished with a half shriek, half laugh.

I shook my head, making a distasteful face. "This is what you're married to?"

"We all have our vices," Jensen said with a shrug and a laugh.

"Hey," Oliver said, walking in. He frowned when he saw me. "I didn't hear the bell."

"That's because you psychos left the door unlocked and open again. I don't understand how you live. This isn't 1920, and you don't live in the middle of nowhere. Didn't you get the email about all the burglaries?"

"Oliver installed a camera system," Estelle said as she poured herself and Mia each a glass of wine. She paused. "Who else wants wine?"

"We need something stronger than wine to watch this shit," I said.

"So we save the cigar I brought you for later?" Jensen asked.

"When does this start?"

"Officially? In thirty minutes," Mia said.

I looked at Jensen. We had thirty minutes to spare. Once we were outside, we closed the door and sat on the chairs out in the porch. He handed me my cigar and the lighter.

"How's work?" he asked, blowing out smoke from his cigar.

"I need my drink, or something with a more calming effect than this for me to talk about it right now," I said, holding up the cigar. He laughed.

"I was going to stop at a shop on the way here, but Mia thought Bean would have a heart attack."

"Nah," I said, laughing because none of us had done anything like that since college, but loved to joke about it now that it was legal in California. "That shit is natural. He's good with the natural stuff."

"Noted."

"How's the book doing?" I asked.

"Pretty well," he said, putting his cigar down and swatting the air away, which meant he was basically blowing it all in my face. I put mine down as well and put it out slowly. I'd finish it another time. "How's the single life? Still not bored?"

I smirked. "How's married life? Insanely boring?"

"Fuck, no," he said, laughing. "Being with someone every day doesn't make it boring."

"We were once on the same page about that."

He shook his head. "We were once young and stupid. Some of us grew up."

"I grew up," I said defensively, taking the bait. He knew how much I hated when people put things like getting married and being a grown-up in the same box. "I have a house under my name. I have a car under my name. I'm hopefully about to make partner, if my client doesn't fuck it up for me."

Jensen's eyebrows rose, his eyes appraising me momentarily, dropping to my curled fists and back up to my face. He smiled. "Did I hit a nerve?"

I exhaled loudly and slumped back in my seat, looking out to the horizon. I focused on the water that was just a few feet away from us. Not that I could see it, but I focused on the sound of the waves crashing.

"I'm representing my boss's daughter in her divorce," I said. I looked at Jensen from the corner of my eye after a beat and caught his mouth hanging open.

"The one that you—"

"Yeah."

"The one you basically told things would never work out between the two of you?"

"Yes," I said, my voice growing more impatient.

I wasn't one to kiss and tell, but I'd told him and Oliver about our first wild encounter because even I'd had a hard time believing it had happened. This hot girl walking into my office and locking the door behind her to seduce me, and actually achieving just that. I just couldn't wrap my head around the way she went from having a regular conversation about the office to asking me if I'd ever fucked anyone on my desk and settling herself between my legs. And inching up her skirt . . . and licking her lips as she placed her legs on either side of me . . . and saying, *"Do you want it, Mr. Reuben?"* in that sultry tone of hers. Fuck. Me.

"Damn. Well, at least it only happened that one time, right?" Jensen said, cutting my thoughts short. I swallowed, suddenly feeling the need to drink a gallon of water. Or the wine I'd brought.

"Yeah, at least," I said, though my mind went to the second and third time she'd come by to visit, and then the last time.

That last time haunted me after I'd found out she'd gotten engaged. Will had told me she'd only known him a few weeks; that he asked her to marry him overnight and she'd agreed; that she was head over heels in love with him, and every single one of those things bothered me. At first I thought it was just weird for anybody, especially her, to agree to marry somebody that quickly. Then, I wondered if it had anything to do with me and the way I'd dismissed her. But she'd seemed so nonchalant about it, smiling and saying she knew it was just a good time and she'd enjoyed it as well. A part of me expected her to come back again, and when she didn't, and then I'd heard she'd gotten engaged, it dawned on me that it was really our last time together. And all I could do was hope she didn't visit me, thinking we could be just friends, because I really didn't know how to argue with her and not have it end in sex. And now that I knew she possibly felt more for me, I wasn't sure what I felt for her. This version of me felt like he was ready for that. For something more. For something *real*. And as stupid as it fucking was, I thought maybe I could have it with Nicole. Maybe in another life. A different time. Our timing was complete shit. I sighed and looked over my shoulder, where Mia was waving at us to come back inside.

"I guess the show's starting," I said, standing up.

"So you're representing her?" Jensen asked. "In the divorce." I nodded.

"You don't look too happy about it. Is it a tough case?"

"It's surprisingly easy, at least it was, but as usual women complicate the shit out of my life. We'll see."

Jensen laughed as we walked inside and sat around the television. I took out my phone to check my emails while the show started, but put it away when somebody turned up the volume.

"Oh my God! There he is. Isn't he hot? Like for real," Mia said. I looked at the screen and saw Gabriel as he spoke to another actor on the carpet. I didn't see Nicole anywhere.

"He looks gay," I commented.

The guys laughed. The girls scowled.

"You're just saying that because you're his wife's divorce lawyer," Estelle said. "Wait. What's going to happen now? Does all the work you did go out the window because they're back together?"

That was the question of the century, wasn't it? Nicole was on the screen shortly after, looking so fucking beautiful that the only thought in my head was that I wouldn't mind having her as a psycho ex-girlfriend. The thought surprised me. I tried to push it down.

"I'm saying it because he's an asshole, and they're not back together," I said. I wasn't sure if I added that bit for them or myself, but it felt like it needed to be voiced. Both Mia and Estelle shared a look before looking at me. "That's all I'm going to say about it."

"He doesn't seem like he's an asshole," Mia said. "Nicole is beautiful. Is she that pretty in person?"

I nodded, swallowing, trying not to think about just how beautiful she was. Just how good she felt.

"That's his mom," Mia said, pointing at the woman walking beside Nicole.

Gabriel's mom? Jesus fucking Christ. What a happy family. And that was just about when I decided to send Nicole a text message. If she wasn't going to answer my calls from the office or Corinne's calls and voicemails, I was going to start hounding her via text. And I hated anything that could be used in a court of law as evidence, which included text messages, but fuck it. Desperate times and shit, like my sister and Mia liked to say.

If I had to sit here all night watching them on screen, I was going to make sure her discomfort matched mine.

Chapter Twelve

Nicole

IT WAS BAD enough that I was stuck in this award show, and much worse that I'd given myself strict orders of staying one hundred percent sober throughout. The only good thing about the entire thing was that Gabe would most likely win the award he was nominated for, and it was for a movie filmed during a time when things were still . . . okay between us. Maybe they hadn't been okay then, but I still had hope. I guess that was the difference. Forgiveness always feels like a possibility in the presence of hope. Hope of which we had none now. Not enough, anyway.

The second good thing about this experience was that as I walked the red carpet with him and he joked around about the cameras flashing—the way he'd done when we'd attended our first red carpet event together—I realized I hadn't seen him as more than a friend or stranger for a long time. I think we lost that magic somewhere between picking up his vomit, dealing with his incoherent insults, and suspecting his infidelity. Despite all of that, I wished him well. I wished this guy, the one walking with me tonight—the sober and unassuming one—to have a good life.

His mom, Deborah, was with us tonight, so while Gabe went off to do his rounds talking to people, she and I found our seats. He joined us soon after, settling in the seat beside me, closer to his male costar in the movie he was being recognized for. Deborah kept pointing out the different celebrities that kept walking by, and when she wasn't doing that, she was begging me to stay with her son. It was such an uncomfortable conversation to have with someone who loved a person the way only a mother could.

She didn't know about the drugs, and that was something I couldn't bring to light. But she knew about the women, or at least as much as anybody could know about the women, which was that they were definitely around. If the tabloids had it right half of the time, he'd been sleeping around with more women than I could name. How he found the time to do it, I would never understand. How the women hadn't cared that he was married was intolerable. To Deborah, that didn't matter, because to her marriage meant standing by your man, even when he was off screwing everybody with a vagina.

I understood her standpoint, I really did, but it was something I understood the way I understood statistics in college. I got it, but didn't apply it in my life. *It shouldn't have to.* I grew up in a time when women didn't need men. We didn't need somebody to make money for us, or give us orgasms, or even impregnate us. We had the ability to make our own money, buy our own dildos, and go to a clinic. And fuck anybody who thought we needed to put up with the bullshit a man brought into our lives without questioning it. I was thankful when my phone vibrated in my purse and I was able to excuse myself from the conversation as I pulled it out.

I frowned at my screen when I saw an unknown number,

and then a message that read: *We need to talk. - V*

My heart started to race. I shoved it back into my clutch before anybody around could catch the words. Who the hell would send me that? I looked at Gabe, who was being overly *friendly* with his co-star, Lina. It wasn't him. I thought about the people in my life, men and women, who would have been watching me, and looked around. Nobody seemed to be looking at me. My phone vibrated again.

323 8374949: *Anything I should know about? –V*

I typed back, *Victor?*

323 8374949: *. . . I asked you a question.*

Me: *And I can't answer that if I don't know who I'm answering.*

3238374949: *There's a reason I don't have conversations via text.*

I smiled, shaking my head. Definitely Victor. I saved his number under V since that was what he kept sending me messages under.

Me: *I've been busy.*

V: *Clearly.*

Me: *We can talk tomorrow.*

V: *Because you're planning to stay busy tonight?*

I held my phone in my hands as I thought of a response for that. Did he mean busy with Gabe? I was sure that's what he meant. I pictured him sitting at home looking all upset over that possibility and nearly laughed.

Me: *Depends on who's keeping me busy.*

V: *. . . . .*

Me: *What the hell does ". . . ." mean?*

V: *It means I don't know how to answer that.*

Me: *Which means you're thinking you should be the one keeping me busy?*

When he didn't respond for a couple beats and I didn't see the little cloud with dots that said he was responding, I put the phone on my lap and went back to looking around at the stars, so many of which I'd dressed. I said hi and caught up with some of them as they walked by and introduced them to Deborah, who was the ultimate fan, which I loved. The magic was still shiny in her eyes. Not that it wasn't in mine. It was hard not to be affected by the atmosphere at an event like this, no matter how many times you'd been.

My phone buzzed again, and I jolted a little, turning it over.

V: *Stop tempting me.*

I smiled.

Me: *I didn't realize you were tempted. You seem to be practicing control rather well.*

V: *Control? You're succeeding in breaking me down.*

Me: *Good ;-)*

V: *Are you wearing anything under that dress?*

The words made me shiver. I closed my eyes momentarily, picturing his deep-hazel eyes looking into mine as he said those words.

Me: *Are you trying to sext with me? I'm sober. I don't sober sext.*

V: *I don't sext at all. I'd much rather spend my energy fucking.*

I swallowed and took a sip of water, suddenly feeling very thirsty, and very hot.

"Hey, did you see Macie?" Gabe asked. I jumped at the sound of his voice and the mention of his current film director, and hid my phone again. He gave me a questioning look, but didn't comment. Macie was his current producer. "She said she's gotten good comments about us being together at the premiere the other day."

"Good. That's what I'm here for," I said, setting my glass of water back down.

"Thanks for doing this," he said, reaching for my hand over the table.

Trying to play the part, I smiled, though it was small, sad, and fleeting. My phone vibrated on my lap again, but I ignored it. I would have to ignore it for the rest of the night if I was going to stay sane, then I would read all the texts and kick Victor's ass for thinking it was a smart idea to send them in the first place. If this was how he wanted to get a response from me, I was already starting to miss un-communicative Victor.

Gabe's hand squeezed mine tightly and snapped me out of my thoughts. I glanced up at him and realized we were about to be the butt of the joke the host was telling.

"I mean, if a divorce is how I'm going to get my wife to screw me again, I'm going to go file tomorrow," the host said. The crowd made all sorts of sounds and shook their heads. I was sure the camera was zooming in on Gabe's and my faces, so I fake-smiled and fake-laughed, when all I really wanted to do was hide my face inside Gabe's jacket. The evening continued on, champagne was poured, beer and wine were served. I touched nothing. Gabe touched my hand, my thigh. I wanted to punch his perfect veneers.

"Please stop touching me," I said through my teeth.

"I'm not drinking tonight, so my nerves are shot. I need something to touch so I don't lose it," he said with a laugh as he leaned into me.

"I swear to God, Gabriel, if you don't stop, I will lose it. I will go to the bathroom and pull a Britney in the middle of your acceptance speech."

He reared back a little, but left his hand on top of the fist I'd made with mine. "You really think I'll win?"

I sighed, shaking my head, my lips curling into a small, albeit real smile. "I know you will."

The first category was announced and we had to clap for the nominees and the winner. Again and again it continued until it was Best Performance by an Actor in a Supporting Role. I held my breath as Hannah, the presenting actress, read each nominee's name. Gabe was sitting beside me, looking like he wasn't fazed by any of it, but I knew he was freaking out. *I* was freaking the hell out.

"Oh my word," his mom said beside me when Gabe's name was read. I smiled, glancing at her with an *I know* smile on my face.

"The Golden Globe goes to . . ." talk about dramatic pause as she opened the envelope. I leaned forward in my seat. Gabe leaned forward in his seat. Everybody in our table was seemingly holding their breath. "Gabriel Lane in The Man Who Could Not Speak."

There was no way to contain my happiness for him. There was no way to mask the pride I felt. Everybody in our table stood as we clapped for him, and as he stood he turned to me, grabbed my face with both hands, and kissed me. He kissed me the way he kissed me on our wedding day. My heart did a little jump, but as he let go of my face and turned to kiss his mother on the cheek, and hug his costars, I remembered where we stood, and I wouldn't waver. Still, it was his moment. It felt like *our* moment. Like that gold statue should have shared custody. I'd been there for him when he filmed that movie. I'd been the one holding his head out of the toilet and cleaning up his mess. I'd been the one putting up with his rage the nights he came home when takes hadn't gone the way he'd wanted. I'd been the one who'd agreed to help fund the film when they'd thought they wouldn't be able to finish it.

Of course nobody would know any of that. It was our secret

and ours alone, and I was okay with that. I'd never been in our relationship for the limelight.

He walked to the stage and smiled as everybody cheered, and he started thanking people. He thanked me for being there for him, and believing in the film, his mother for everything, yadda yadda yadda. The longer I watched him, the less I wanted to be there. It was as if the reel became focused on the screen in my head and suddenly I saw the full, clear picture. I realized that he was an actor, and I was just another observer in his life. When it hit me, I reached into my purse and took out my phone. The last text message Victor had sent said to meet him in his office at seven o'clock sharp. I frowned, but put my phone away and willed for the rest of the show to be over. When it was, Gabriel was as busy as I knew he would be.

"Are you sure you want to skip the after-party?" he asked before being escorted away for the third time.

"Positive. Thanks for the invite, though."

He walked toward me and leaned his face in. I thought he was going to kiss me again, but instead his lips pressed against my cheek.

"Thank you for coming. I'm really glad I was able to share that with you."

I nodded and swallowed, holding back the tears that welled in my eyes. This felt like goodbye. A real one. Like it was the last time we would share something like this. I thought of the good memories we'd shared, and a part of me felt like I didn't want to let go. It was hard, being with him like this, acting like he cared and believing once he actually had. I'd mourned our separation. I didn't want to mourn the loss again. I wanted to move on. I wanted to get it over with. But having him in front of me—this man I genuinely cared for—seeing him win so big . . . I remembered the conversations we'd had about it because I'd always believed he would be big. It felt like too much for me. And that's why when he wrapped his arms around me, I let myself feel the power in his hug. I let myself feel that he, too, was sad about us not working.

"I wish things would have been different," he whispered into my hair.

"Me too," I said, and stepped back to let go. I gave him one last smile before walking to where Marcus waited for me, leaving the glitz and glamour behind. And I would mourn this too. Not the lights and cameras, but the role of supporter, a role I felt I had done a fucking incredible job at.

"Home, right?" Marcus said once we got into the Escalade. I nodded, but suddenly hearing the word *home* and associating it with the life I once I had with Gabriel pained me, and I knew I needed to get out of there.

Chapter Thirteen

Nicole

IT WAS STILL dark out when I got to the office, and Victor had to buzz me in. There weren't any paparazzi around this time, which was a plus, but Marcus stayed waited by the car in case they'd been tipped off and showed up. I assumed nobody would be in the office at that ungodly hour, unless my dad was there. On court days he also met people pretty early. During the elevator ride up, I fixed my messy hair and used the mirrored wall to check my reflection. When the elevator doors opened, my hands froze mid-finger comb as my gaze caught Victor waiting for me with his arms crossed. He wasn't wearing a suit like I expected. Instead he wore a pair of grey sweatpants, running shoes, and a white T-shirt that showed me just enough of his defined body to make my breath stop short. His hair was brushed back, but wet, and the expression on his face gave me a hint of just how much anger he was containing.

"Hi," I whispered as his eyes raked down my body slowly, sensually just once before returning to my face, and he gestured for me to step out of the elevator.

I blinked as I did so and tried not to visibly show how affected I was. I walked forward and followed him as he started down the hall. The light was off, but the light from the lobby illuminated it just enough. We stepped into the same conference room we'd met in before and he closed the door behind us. The blinds were drawn and the lights were off, so we were in the dark. A flutter of nervousness made its way through me.

"Are you going to turn the lights on?" I asked.

"Did you have a good time last night?" he asked, his voice low and close behind me.

I was afraid to turn around. I was afraid to move. Instead, I put my hands forward and held on to the top of the chair in front of me.

"I can explain that," I said, my voice as firm as my grip on the chair.

I blinked, letting my eyes adjust to the light of the projector in front of us as it switched on, giving the room a dim, orange glow. I turned around to face Victor, who was leaning against the wall across from me with his arms crossed. My eyes dropped to his defined arms and I felt my heart stumble on its own beats. I'd seen him in swimming trunks the other day, but he'd been wearing a wetsuit shirt, and while it showcased the toned ridges and definition I was already sure he had, I hadn't seen him completely naked. Now all I could do was stand there and wonder.

My imagination conjured images of myself clawing off that cotton shirt and tossing it aside as I went down on him. I shook my head and blinked rapidly to rid myself of my thoughts. What was it about being near this guy that made me so needy for him? I'd just been at a stupid award show with my hot ex, yet it was this man I lusted after. Always. It had always been that way. From the moment I met him, I'd known I'd wanted him. And now, standing in front of me with that darkened gaze trained on me—as if he could see the dirty film in my head that he was about to star in—I wanted him again, and again, but unlike the previous time we'd been together, I felt fragile. Like I could sense that I would get hurt. Maybe it was the sensitive state I was in. Maybe it was because when I spent time with him at my dad's beach house he was so different, so attentive, and I realized that underneath all that pissed-off exterior I knew there was a caring man, one who would comfort me even when I didn't want to be comforted. One that knew when to hold my hand and just shut up. I sighed.

"Nicole," he said, closing his eyes briefly and breathing out as if he was doing some kind of yoga meditation. "I am this close," he said, opening his eyes and demonstrating an inch of space with his long fingers. Long and skilled fingers. I blinked again. He exhaled again, this time pushing himself off the wall and walking toward me until he was inches away from me and I had to tilt my head to look at his face.

"I'm this close to losing my job, my license, and everything I've worked so fucking hard for," he said, his voice rough and low, and way too close to my mouth.

"Because you want me," I said, rather than asked.

"Because you keep looking at me like you want me," he said.

I pushed his chest with both hands, and he took a step back.

"You have to be the most self-assured person on planet Earth. You're the one calling meetings at crazy hours."

"And you're the one who's coming, no questions asked."

"That's how I usually like to come. No questions asked," I said with a smirk. He took in a deep breath, let it out slowly, heavily, loudly.

"Fine. Yes, I want you," he said.

His admission shocked me into silence. We both looked at each other, stared at each other, and I was sure my heart was bound to leap out of my throat and into his if he didn't break the silence. He didn't, so I finally swallowed and spoke.

"Why did you need to see me?" I whispered.

With the way he still looked at me, I was starting to feel really hot, like lava pent-up in a volcano dormant for too long, and I was afraid that at any minute this thing between us would make me completely explode. God knew it had been a while. For me, at least.

"What were you doing at the award show?" he asked. I could tell he was practicing restraint in keeping his voice reserved, and the thought of the way he held his ground and practiced control made me tremble.

"He asked me to go and I agreed," I said.

"That wasn't part of the agreement," he growled.

"I know," I said, my voice low as I tore my eyes from his and looked at the ground between us. "I'm sorry I didn't tell you. I thought you would try to talk me out of it."

"I would have."

"I know." My eyes snapped to his. "Why does it bother you so much?"

His eyes narrowed. "Because it does. And I want you out of that fucking house."

"Really? Out of my house?" My eyebrows rose at his tone. I'd already decided to get out of there, but having him demand it pissed me off. "And where would you suggest I go, Mr. Know-It-All?"

"Anywhere. Anywhere is better than living under the same roof as him. If I wasn't your attorney, which I swear to Christ I'm close to being just that, I'd haul your ass out of there and make you move into my house temporarily."

"Oh, temporarily," I said, narrowing my eyes as I took a slight step forward. "Until you got sick of me and moved on to someone new? Isn't that your MO?"

"My MO?" he asked. His voice suddenly dropped to a quiet seethe that made my heart drop into my stomach. "I'm not the one who fucks people and then goes off and gets engaged a few weeks later."

Oh my God. I wanted to strangle him. For a second I thought I could try, but then I would have to hop on a chair so we could be at eye level and that would tip him off. I took a breath and counted to five, then took another deep breath for good measure.

"In case you forgot our conversation the other day, you were the only one I did that with."

"That doesn't make me feel any better, Nicole."

"What does it make you feel?" I asked, tilting my face in challenge. "We had sex. Great sex. You broke it off, and I went and married another guy, one who wanted something more with me. Something more than just fucking me. Fucking sue me."

"I just might."

I laughed. "Oh. This is good. On what grounds?"

"Obliterating my fucking ego. Temporary insanity. Sucker punching my . . . my . . ."

"Your heart?" I asked in a whisper, and waited on bated breath for his response.

Damn him for thawing the shell I'd managed to start rebuilding around my heart with three simple, stupid incomplete sentences. His eyes widened slightly, as though he'd never even considered his heart in this, and I almost smiled. I'd never seen him look puzzled. Or unsure. It was endearing.

"Maybe," he said, frowning.

Sort of endearing.

"I don't think you realize how much I stand to lose here, Nicole. You keep making these jokes and—" I inched closer, pressing my chest against his. He sucked in a breath. "And doing this."

He stepped back again and searched my face. I hated it when he looked at me that way, like he was rummaging around in my thoughts, kicking shit around until he found something he could use against me. He licked his bottom lip, and I did the same, forcing his gaze to drop to my own lips.

"You can keep tempting me, but it won't work. Not after I saw you acting like everything was fine in paradise. Not after I saw you making out with your supposed soon to be ex-husband," he said.

"What do you want, Victor? You're like that goddamn Katy Perry song. I never know what I'm going to get with you. We talk, we argue, we fuck, and then you dismiss me because you have a client to tend to."

He shot me a glare. "Don't bring that up anymore. How the fuck was I supposed to know you wanted more? You were the one trashing marriage, bashing relationships left and right, saying you didn't want anything long-term."

"I said those things because I thought that's what you wanted to hear."

"What I wanted to hear? What happened to telling the goddamn truth? If it was a relationship you wanted, you should've said so."

"And you would have given that to me? You would have taken things to another level? Last I remembered you were married to this job."

He stepped forward so quickly, I almost lost my balance, but he held my hip to keep me from stumbling.

"Are you staying with him?"

I blinked. "What?"

"Are you going to stay with your husband?"

"Who's asking?" I whispered. "My lawyer or Victor?"

He closed his eyes briefly once more, and when they opened I knew where this was headed. "I can't represent you anymore, Nicole. I feel like I'm going fucking crazy over here."

"Why?"

"Because I want you," he said. I gasped as his fingers dug into my flesh. "I want you and I can't have you if I keep working for you."

"Says who?" I asked, surprised my voice was loud enough for him to hear me.

"I've worked so fucking hard and this case is going to blow it all to shit," he said, inching his face closer to mine. I stopped breathing. "All because I need this more than I've needed any-thing else in my fucking life."

His lips were so close to mine that I was sure he would kiss me. Was he expecting me to kiss him? Would he break the vow he made to the court over me? Was it fair for me to test his lim-its? He closed his eyes and leaned his forehead against mine, his minty breath hitting me as he exhaled. His hands were still on my hips. I was sure he could feel the rapid vibration of my heart there. I felt it everywhere.

"Have me," I said finally, unable to have him this close to me and not do anything about it. "Just . . . take me. You've done it before. You know I can keep a secret."

He shook his head, his forehead brushing back and forth against mine. "It's not that simple, Nicole."

"It was never that simple," I whispered.

One of his hands made its way up my back, stopping on my shoulder, then moving slowly, tentatively to my neck, my collarbone. My breath was becoming ragged, uneven, desperate for something, anything. I wanted to kiss him, touch him, fuck him, but more than anything I wanted him to want to do it. I wanted him to be the one to make the first move.

"You're right. It was never that simple." The way he said it made me wonder if maybe he'd felt something more than lust. "When this is over," he said, rearing back slightly to look at me, "when it's over, I'll have you."

"What if we see each other in private?" I asked.

"You want to sneak around?" he asked, his lip twitching into a smile. He shook his head and dropped his hands, stepping away from me. "Is that what you want?"

"Maybe."

He raised an eyebrow. "That isn't a maybe kind of question, Nicole. It's yes or no."

"Yes. I want to sneak around."

"Are the paparazzi still following you?" he asked, his voice serious.

"No," I said, and corrected myself when he shot me a look that said he didn't believe me. "Not as much."

"Let's see how it goes with them the next few days."

"And then we can sneak around?"

He looked down to try to hide his smile, but I saw it. "I never said that."

"Okay. Do you need anything else from me?" I asked, my eyes raking down his body to the half hard-on he was sporting.

"I need a lot of things," he said, eyes blazing.

"I would help you out," I said, pointedly looking at his hooded pants as I licked my lips before unlocking the door and holding the handle. "But you refuse to cater to my needs."

He slapped his hand on the door to keep me from opening it and pressed his hard chest against my back. I closed my eyes and tried to control my body to keep it from quivering at the feel of his breath on my ear.

"I don't want a time limit the next time I fuck you. I don't want a quick fuck where clothes don't even have time to come off. I want you naked and in my bed, and trust me," he said, lowering his voice as he pressed his lips against my neck, right under my ear, "I will cater to every one of your needs."

I had absolutely nothing to say to that, so when he put his hand over mine and opened the door, I stood off to the side and waited for him to brush past me. The light of the hallway had been switched on. Victor and I looked at each other, wide-eyed.

"Hey," Grace said, looking confused as she walked into the lobby with a big pot of coffee in her hand. "I didn't know you had an early meeting scheduled today."

I wasn't sure if she was talking to me or Victor, but he responded before I could.

"Yeah, I had to squeeze this in between my run and court," he said. "I'm going to get dressed. If anybody calls for me before it's time for me to leave, take a message and give it to Corinne when she gets here."

"Okay," Grace said, then turned to me. "Want coffee?"

"I've been wondering when somebody around here would offer me something worthwhile," I said, unable to hide my smile. Victor scowled as he turned and walked into his office.

Grace and I made small talk while I drank my coffee and she switched on the computer and did whatever she had to do to set up for the day.

"Well, I have to go. It's going to be a long day."

"What time do you go in today?" she asked. Grace was always interested in my job. It didn't matter how insignificant it was, she wanted to know about it.

"Today's a late night. Eight to eight."

"Wow, and you're here? I would be sleeping."

I smiled. "Yeah, that's where I'm headed." I paused and looked at the door to Victor's office. "Shit. I just remembered I had to give him something. I'll be right back."

She didn't even look up from the computer screen as I disappeared into Victor's office. My blood roared in my ears as I took off my sneakers, peeled off my yoga pants, slid off my panties, and quickly redressed. I walked over to his desk and stuffed them into his briefcase. I could only hope he looked inside it before he went to court. Of course, knowing Victor he probably emptied it and organized it more than I did when I switched handbags. I ran out of there before he could come out of the bathroom and catch me.

"Did you leave what you needed to leave?" Grace asked as I waved her goodbye and got into the elevator.

"I did," I said with a wide smile.

Chapter Fourteen

Victor

MY MISOPHONIA WAS out of control. I knew this, yet I couldn't help the cringe that came every time Corinne took a bite of her sandwich. My skin crawled with every chew. I sighed and stood up to pace the conference room to distract myself from my agony. I fucking hated lunch meetings. Food had no place in the conference room. None. The only reason I'd even called a lunch meeting was because we had no time to waste and I was supposed to meet with Nicole in the afternoon to give her some papers.

"Everything's in here?" I asked, going back to the file Corinne had set on top of the table. She nodded slowly. "Did you file the paper I sent you? The last one?"

"The Golden Globe thing in the agreement she made with her ex? Yes."

I nodded sharply. I needed to keep that paper out of any file I gave her back, in case it fell into the wrong hands. The fact that it had been drafted and emailed was already making me paranoid. I hated the Internet. I started leafing through the pages, making sure each page was initialed and that the ones needed signing were marked for her. As long as Gabriel agreed to this, the divorce could be sped up. Normally I tried to make these cases as painless as possible for my clients, because I could only imagine how badly they must want closure, but with Nicole I wished I could jump through hoops and just get this shit done immediately.

I wanted her out of the house she shared with Gabriel Lane. I wanted him out of her life for good. I wanted her in my bed. It was quite simple, really. I wasn't an idiot. I knew the girl was a catch, and it would only be a matter of time before somebody else caught her. If she wanted to be caught, I wanted her to have the freedom to make that choice. But first, I'd have her. Maybe I was a fucking idiot, because every time the thought crossed my mind all I could do was imagine me catching her. Me being the one she stayed with. I tried to picture what my life would have been like if I'd been the one to catch her five years ago and not the guy she was divorcing. Would I have fucked things up? Would I have let her go? I had a difficult time believing I would have done the latter. Fuck things up, maybe. I'd been young and had more drive than I knew what to do with. While my friends were busy chasing skirts and getting married, I worked my ass off. I didn't regret it. I didn't wish I could turn back time and make more out of what Nicole and I had. The way I saw it, everything happened for a reason, and we just weren't meant to happen then.

How much had I changed during those years, though? Jensen seemed set on reminding me that I would be turning thirty-one soon, as if that meant I might as well start planning my funeral.

"Victor?" Corinne asked. I looked up from the papers.

"What?"

She shifted uncomfortably in her seat. "I was wondering

how you felt about me taking time off next month?"

My gaze stayed on hers as I processed her request. When was the last time she'd taken time off? Had it already been a year? I flipped through my mental calendar, trying to remember what I had next month. There would be very little to do with Nicole's divorce by then. I would make sure of that. I had a meeting scheduled for later in the week with a well-known romance author, who was divorcing his wife, to see if they could settle out-of-court, so that shouldn't run over to the next month. I realized I was still staring at Corinne and blinked rapidly. I was in the habit of staring people down when I was lost in thought. I cleared my throat.

"Sure. Just put it on the Outlook Calendar so we can plan for it," I said finally.

Her shoulders sagged a little.

"Anything else I should know about?" I asked.

She shook her head, but I knew there was something she wanted to tell me. Women were so fucking annoying. Why couldn't they just spit it out? They would be a lot easier to deal with if they just voiced their thoughts instead of making us go on a goddamn scavenger hunt. I shook my head and went back to the papers in front of me. I didn't have time for that shit.

"It's just," she said quietly. I let out a breath. Of course she was going to start talking again when I was already trying to focus on something else. "I think my boyfriend is going to propose to me when we go on vacation."

I raised my eyebrows. "Well, that's good, right?" I asked slowly. One could never be too sure when he was going to hit a nerve when it came to women and these sensitive subjects.

"I guess," she said, shrugging. I rubbed my temple and looked at my watch. I had an hour to spare before I had to bolt to meet with Nicole, so I took a seat where I'd been before Corinne decided to turn into Bugs Bunny with her chewing.

"What's the problem? Haven't you been together for a while now?" I asked.

She started chipping at her nail polish. "Eight months."

Oh, wow. Her boyfriend really jumped into that one. I didn't comment, because nothing good would come out of my mouth. It wasn't worse than Gabriel Lane and Nicole. Fucking Nicole. Instead, I nodded for her to continue. She glanced up at me, her eyes welling with unshed tears. Jesus, fuck. I didn't do well with emotional females. How did I get myself into this mess?

"I just don't know if he's the one, you know? I don't know if he's my forever," she whispered, still chipping at her nails.

"Have you told him this? Maybe you should."

"He's a great guy. He makes me laugh, gets along with my parents, has a good job," she continued, ignoring me. "He has his own place, and he wants kids."

I tilted my head. So far I'd heard nothing but good. Throw in a vintage black Mustang, and I was about to marry the guy. I looked at my watch again.

"I'm assuming you're going to get to the bad part soon?"

She wiped her tears. "I don't know. I was with my ex-boy-friend for six years. I've only been with Daniel eight months. I feel like, I don't know." She shrugged. "Maybe I don't even know him, you know?"

"Corinne, as I'm sure you know, I am not equipped to give relationship advice." I paused and added, "At all."

She nodded and sniffled. "I know, but you date a lot. How do you know they're not the woman you want to marry?"

I let out a long breath and leaned back in my seat. That was a good question. How did I know? I frowned.

"I don't," I said with a shrug. She looked puzzled, so I con-tinued. "I've never cared enough to continue any of those relationships, so I just assume they're not the one." She continued to stare at me at a loss for words, which made me keep talking. "I'll let you in on a little secret: none of us know what we're doing. We're all winging it. Your boyfriend? He's winging it. He's proposing to you because he hopes you're his forever. Maybe he believes it, I guess he must if he's taking the plunge, but if you're not willing to take it with him, you should probably pull him off that cliff before he does it, not when he does it."

She nodded. "You're right. Maybe I'm just having second thoughts because of all of these damn divorce cases we go through."

I laughed. "I'm pretty sure that was in the job description when you applied."

"People change," she said with a smile.

Right. *That* again. I shrugged.

"You don't think somebody will come along and change you?" she asked, frowning. I thought about that for a moment, my mind instantly going to Nicole. Again. I sighed, running a hand through my hair.

"I think the right person for me will want to keep me just the way I am."

Corinne seemed to be satisfied with my answer. I gathered the papers and put them back in the folder.

"Are you done having your moment?" I asked. "Because I really have somewhere to be."

Corinne laughed. "I think I'm done having my moment."

Picking up the folder, I stood and walked toward the door. I patted her back as I passed her. "Don't believe the hype, Corinne. Being single is overrated, especially when you think you've found someone you can stand to be with continuously."

The drive to the address in Manhattan Beach was brutal. The traffic was insane. Apparently there was some kind of street market being set up, which closed off the major street I needed to take, and further pissed me off. Who in their right mind would willingly shut down all of those neighborhoods so they could sell shit? By the time I got to the house, I was barely containing my rage. I used the street parking four blocks away, left my jacket and tie in the car, and rolled up my sleeves. There was no way I was going to walk through the pits of hell in a suit. Fuck that noise.

I walked down the steep street and used the folder in my hand to shield my eyes from the sun when I got to the house. Through the window, I could see Nicole, wearing a tight flower-print dress. Her dark hair cascaded down her back in loose curls that she must have had done earlier that day. I admired her from afar, her curves, the way her toned tan legs looked in the heels she wore, and I took a second to imagine how she'd look out of that dress, out of those heels, legs wrapped around me. I took a long, deep breath and walked up the steps.

I could hear her laughing at whatever the person she was talking to was saying, and I smiled at the sound of it. She had a good laugh, not high-pitched or low, or snorty, or crazy. It was just right. A guy opened the door, and I instantly tensed. He had straight, long blond hair that reached his shoulders and was wearing a suit. I could tell he worked out. I could tell he felt I was interrupting something special going on between him and my girl. My *CLIENT.* Not my girl. Not my anything. My eyes landed on her when I looked over his shoulder, and she smiled. She had this small, tentative smile she used sometimes. One that didn't give you the slightest inkling as to how fierce she was beneath it. She could claw her way into and out of anybody's life and leave you with the afterthought that it'd all started because of that one smile.

"Hey. Rick, this is my . . ." she said, pausing for a beat, the tentative soft smile blooming into a wider one, a little wicked, a lot sexy, "my attorney."

"Oh," Rick said, stepping out of the way with a frown on his face. "I didn't realize you were bringing your attorney."

Nicole laughed. "Not for this. He has some things to give me, but now that he's here, he might as well make himself useful and help me look at the place. Unless you have somewhere to be," she added, looking at me with those big blue eyes. If I hadn't already been convinced by that look alone, the way her realtor huffed under his breath at the mention of this sealed it for me.

"Sure. I had my schedule cleared since I thought we were actually going to be discussing this anyway. Lead the way," I said, firing off a text message to Corinne so she could clear my fucking schedule for the next two hours. I didn't have a face-to-face meeting scheduled with anybody, but I did have to be back at the office for a conference call. So they'd have to wait a little while longer for me to call them back. Big deal.

Rick pivoted and walked down the hall. Nicole winked at me before turning to follow him, and between that wink and the way her ass moved from side to side in that dress I was already regretting the decision to stay. Thank God I'd taken off my jacket and tie. Rick went over the specs of the house, the kitchen, the living room, the laundry room, the dining room, his eyes were on her the entire time. Every time she turned around, his eyes were on her ass. When she spoke to him, his eyes made their way down her body. Nicole had to notice it, she'd be an idiot not to, but she didn't goad him, and I was grateful for that because for some reason I wasn't sure how I'd react to it. I'd never been the jealous type. The competitive type? Yes. But jealousy was foreign to me. I didn't have anything to be jealous of. With Nicole it was a little different, though. Maybe it was because I wanted her so much. Maybe it was because I couldn't have her, though if I was being honest with myself, I knew it wasn't just that.

"Let me show you the master bedroom," Rick said, giving Nicole a very pointed look as he said it. They started walking toward the stairs as I trailed behind. He looked over his shoulder to look at me for a second before lowering his head to her and saying, "The bed is still in there, but we have company, which is very unfortunate."

My heart picked up speed in my chest, but my feet stopped moving. Who the hell was this guy? Nicole looked over her shoulder to look at me with a coy smile on her face. She didn't comment, didn't laugh, didn't say anything at all to him. I made a face at her, nodding sharply toward the back of his head. She shrugged and kept walking.

"The steps are a little steep," he said. "But don't worry, I'm here to catch you if you fall."

I wanted to pull his ass down and toss him behind me. I exhaled and shook my head instead. I was forward when it came to telling women what I wanted, but I usually did that in a different setting.

"Is the master to the left or right?" she asked when she made it to the top of the stairs.

"Left," he said. "Or on top, whatever you'd prefer."

At that, Nicole laughed. Even I found myself letting out a laugh, though it was only because I couldn't believe what a fucking loser this guy was. I shook my head again. Thankfully, the douche got a phone call and excused himself, holding one finger up and saying it was an important client. Moron. Nicole opened the door to the balcony in the master bedroom and stepped out.

"This is nice," I said, joining her. The sand was on the other side of the sidewalk. It was a perfect beach house. "So did you finally decide to move out of your eight-million-dollar Hollywood Hills home and trade it in for this humble abode?"

She lifted her face to look at me, smiling. "It's half the price."

I chuckled. "You have expensive taste."

"I have good taste."

"I agree," I said, placing my forearms on the top of the balcony. My eyes made their way down her body. She really needed to stop wearing those dresses around me. She needed to stop wearing anything around me. She inched closer, moving so her forearm was against mine, her hip touching mine, and tilted her head back slightly so she could still look into my eyes.

"Wouldn't it be nice, though? For me to move in here. You can come over for wine night," she said, her voice quiet.

We were at eye level now, our faces so close I could smell her breath. She smelled like watermelon, like that pink marker in the scented pack my mom used to buy my sister and me when we were kids. So fucking good. Delectable. My gaze dropped to her mouth, which she licked.

"Yeah? When's wine night?" I asked, feeling myself gravitating toward her. It was unstoppable, this thing.

"Any night you pick."

My lungs squeezed a little, the air stifling at the pull I felt.

"You know," she said, beckoning my eyes to move up to hers again, "I called this guy because I remember him from a friend's wedding. He was hot and really, really knew how to move his pelvis, and you know what they say about guys who can move like that." She paused.

I felt everything inside my body begin to tighten. This burn began to form. It started in my ringing ears and made its way down to my toes. What the fuck was that feeling?

"So I called him up because I heard he was a good realtor and he liked to hook up, and I figured I'd get a two for one. Good house to rent and a hot fuck since I'm trying to maybe break the record of my one and only hot fuck being with you," she continued. The way she said it made my heart squeeze and made my dick hard at the same time. I didn't want her to break that record. Ever. Unless it was with me again. Only with me again.

"But then you showed up and I thought, damn." Her face was now even closer to mine. "That's a guy who definitely knows how to fuck, and I thought maybe I should forget about this realtor guy. Maybe I should go with the sure bet, you know?" she asked, a whisper against my lips.

For a second I didn't move. I let the wheels in my head turn some more. Pussy has ruined the career of a lot of highly successful men. I never thought I'd be on that list. Never thought I'd be anywhere near it, but there I was, headed down that path. The crazy part was that even as I thought it, I moved. I stood upright, pushing off the rail as I pulled her back inside by her wrist, and crashed my lips against hers. I kissed her with the desperation I felt for her, relinquishing all control, and she returned it equally as enthusiastically. Her hands flew to the buttons of my shirt, mine went around to her ass and squeezed.

"I want you so much," she said, pushing me back against the wall. I grabbed her ass harder and pulled her so she could feel just how bad I wanted her. She gasped against my lips, then pulled back to look at me. "Please, Victor. Don't make me wait."

I closed my eyes and loosened my grip on her, giving us a little bit of space, and let out a harsh breathy laugh. "I like to think that I'm good at practicing control, but when you're around . . ."

I didn't finish the sentence. I couldn't because her lips were on mine again, but even if they weren't I didn't have an adequate way of explaining what I felt, and it didn't matter. I could kiss her, I could fuck her once to get it out of my system, but I knew

I would want more. And I couldn't have more. Not when my career was on the line, so fucking her out of my system was the only solution we had available, and even that one could be disastrous. In the end, I broke the kiss and gathered my wits. This was going to happen, but it wouldn't happen when a douchebag named Rick could walk in on us at any given moment. I needed to go home, figure out how much longer I had to exert self-control, regroup, and probably jack off, not necessarily in that order.

Chapter Fifteen

Nicole

THAT KISS. I couldn't stop thinking about it. I thought about it as I signed the lease. I thought about it as I held the keys in my hands. And I thought about it when I called Victor to tell him it was final. He'd agreed it was a good price and great location. He also went over the contract for me and approved it since it was a standard lease and didn't lock me in for more than six months at a time. It was something I definitely needed, because I wasn't sure where I would be in six months. Our conversation took a downward spiral when it went from my new place to the scheduled date I had with Gabe. At the mention of it, his mood changed, his responses became clipped and even though we were on the phone, I could practically see him running a hand through his hair roughly. I wondered what he must have been feeling. Whether or not my pretend being with Gabe affected him as much as he made it seem.

The ice cream shop we'd agreed to go to was one we'd frequented while dating, not as much once we finally married, but that made the story even juicier, apparently. His manager tipped off the paparazzi of our outing, so I dressed in sweats and a T-shirt, and he wore basketball shorts and a T-shirt, so it looked like we were having a completely "relaxed afternoon." It was such a strategic outing, that when I didn't have time to make it home, Gabe asked me to have Marcus drive me to the mall so I could jump in his car and go with him to the place.

He was on the phone with his assistant the entire ride to the shop.

"Lee says hi," he said, in reference to his assistant, when he finally hung up the phone. I looked out the window and stayed silent because Lee was on my eternal shit list, along with Darryl. "Did you hear me?" he asked.

"I heard you."

He let out a sigh. "Just because we're getting a divorce doesn't mean you have to push away our mutual friends, you know?"

"Mutual friends," I said with a scoff. "Lee is the last person I'd consider a friend."

"Wow." He shook his head as he drove down Hollywood Boulevard.

"Wow what, Gabe? In case you didn't know, the moment we separated Lee made it crystal clear he wanted nothing to do with me. Whenever I called you when you were on set . . ." I stopped talking and shook my head. "It doesn't matter."

"No, tell me," he said, his voice soft. He looked over at me when we reached the ice cream shop. The paps were already running toward us and we'd only been parked for a second. I ignored them and continued to look at Gabe, the way I always did when they were around, because I couldn't bear to look at that lens and the one-sided story it told.

"It really doesn't matter. Nine months ago this conversation would have made sense, but you were too busy getting high and screwing every girl in Hollywood."

He lay his hand over mine on my lap, his blue eyes searching mine. "I'm sorry."

A knot formed in my throat, because for the first time his apology felt genuine. I tore my gaze away from his and instantly regretted it when I looked out the window and into five different flashing lights.

"Let's just get this over with," I said, clearing my throat.

When he turned off the car and went around it to open the door for me, smiling for the cameras and laughing at one of their jokes, I closed my eyes and for the millionth time wondered if everything about him had been an act. I hated to belittle what we'd had. I hated to see it as if it were nothing more than a puppet show inside of a light box, especially when my feelings for him had been so real, but it was all I could think when he played the part so well. The sound of the door handle made my eyes pop open. I took his hand as he helped me out of the car and walked beside him, both of us with our heads down as we entered the ice cream shop.

"That wasn't too bad," he said, putting his arm around my shoulders. *Which part?* I wanted to ask? *The part where you pretended to care about me? The one where you made me fall in love with you, only to leave me high and dry when you decided you missed the single life?* I didn't voice any of it. I knew if I did I would go off on him and the entire charade would blow up in our faces. *New York*, I reminded myself. *Smooth mediation. Painless divorce.*

I smiled at Veronica when we got to the front of the line, but instead of smiling back, she kept looking at Gabe while he looked up at the menu. The way she looked at him and ignored me made an uncomfortable feeling settle in the pit of my stomach. That sixth sense women have was as much of a blessing as it was a curse in times like these. My mom used to tell me that men were like puppies. If you didn't keep them entertained long enough, they'd move on to the next toy. I never liked that idea.

I felt like we made far too many excuses for them just because they had dicks between their legs and we had vaginas, and really, if it's about anatomy, wouldn't the channel that they're birthed from be superior? But alas, women like my mom and Gabe's mom gave men the okay to be cheaters, and liars, and showed them that it was okay and that they could get away with it. All that aside, I remember when I was little and my parents were married, my mom had a private investigator tail my dad because she needed to know what he was up to when he left work. I didn't work that way. I always felt like you had to be willing to give a person enough trust to let them make their own choices. What they did with it was a different story.

"Do you want your usual?" Veronica asked, finally looking at me with an uneasy smile.

Gabe looked down at me, flashing me that wide grin that got me to agree to go out with him in the first place. "Cookies 'n' Cream?"

I nodded and smiled after a beat, when I remembered to. "In a waffle bowl."

"Got it," he said, still looking at me like I was something to be cherished. I hated him for it. I hated myself for even feeling anything at all, though what I felt wasn't the unrequited love I'd once felt. When he looked at the girl to order, he paused momentarily. A flirt smile bloomed on her face.

"You never called me back," she said.

I tried to swallow, but it turned into a cough, and soon after, I was slapping my chest and coughing. Gabe patted me in the back, but I jerked out of his touch. She spoke to him as if she had no idea who I was. As if she didn't know I was married to him. As if I wasn't wearing the gigantic rock on my finger that he'd given me five years ago. It wasn't her I was mad at, though. It wasn't her I'd given my trust to.

My skin began to prickle with a heated rage I hadn't felt since the day Gabe hit me with an onslaught of insults in the midst of his drug-induced state. I turned around and began to walk away. My idea was to sit down while he waited for the ice cream I could no longer eat, and breathe it out, but Gabe's hand on my arm stopped me.

"That was a long time ago," he said.

I kept facing forward, toward the doors, where the paparazzi were still standing, aiming their cameras right at us, capturing the moment. I prided myself in being calm, cool, and collected when I wanted to be. I prided myself in being able to control everything that left my mouth, in being able to reel myself in when I was going too far, but I couldn't. I couldn't. *That was a long time ago? THAT was his excuse?*

"It was a long time ago?" I said, seething as I turned to face him. I pushed his hand off me with my other hand. "Long time ago when, Gabriel? When we were fucking married?"

"Don't make a scene, Nicole."

"Don't make a scene? Are you serious right now?"

"It was nothing serious," he said, lowering his voice and softening his gaze as if his sudden concern was going to be enough to keep me there.

I pushed back on his chest with both hands and turned around again. "Go fuck yourself."

He grabbed me by the wrist, hard, and pulled me back against his chest. His mouth was near my ear. "All we have to do is get out of here with smiles on our faces. That's all we have to do. I fucked up. I was a terrible husband. I'm sorry. I am, but doing this isn't going to solve anything."

I closed my eyes, surprised by the sudden need to cry. I felt sick. It wasn't surprising. It wasn't. I'd heard he was having sex with other women. This wasn't breaking news, but the heavy and unwanted feeling still settled in the pit of my stomach. I felt myself soften in his hold as I let out a long, deep breath.

"I have to go to the bathroom," I whispered. He let go. I didn't look at him at all, or in Veronica's direction as I disappeared down the hall and pulled out my cell phone.

"Hello?"

"I need you," I said, my voice hoarse with unshed tears.

"Are you crying?" he demanded. "Where are you?"

"I'm not crying," I said, even though it was clear I was about to. "Cold Stone in Hollywood."

"I'll be there in two minutes." He paused. "Four minutes. Fucking traffic," he yelled, then softened his voice. "Are the cameras still there?"

"Yes," I whispered, wiping my face. I hated crying. Hated it, and I had an aversion to crying in front of people, so I needed to calm down before he got there.

"Can you go out through the back?"

"Yes. I just have to tell Gabe first." There was a long silence. "Victor?"

"Yeah, I'm here. Okay. I'm at the light. I'll pull up to the back door," he said.

I thanked him, but realized he'd hung up the phone. I put it in my purse and looked at myself in the mirror. I looked normal, and it reminded me of how little we let people see of us. When I walked out of the bathroom, Gabe was standing in the hallway with our ice creams in his hands. He held mine out to me, and I took it.

"I'm leaving."

He flinched slightly, frowning. "Okay. I'll take you home."

I shook my head. "No. I'm leaving. Without you."

I could tell I caught him off guard when he lowered the hand he was holding his ice cream in and sagged his shoulders.

"Really, Nicole?" he asked, sighing. "It was a mistake. I was an idiot. It was one time—"

"I don't care. I don't care," I added slowly, sternly. "I haven't cared for a long time, Gabriel. I haven't, but for you to bring me here? How fucking insensitive can you be? And I'm here to do you a favor. I can't fucking believe—"

"You signed an addendum."

"And because I signed an addendum I'm supposed to stick around while somebody disrespects me and you *let* them?"

"I didn't realize you needed saving, Nicole. I didn't realize you were a damsel in distress."

He was *such* a bastard.

"I don't need saving. The only damsel in distress in this situation is you. And I'm sick of being your knight in shining armor," I said, pointing a finger at his chest before turning to walk toward the back door. I stopped when I reached it, hand on the handle as I tossed the ice cream cone into the waste basket next to me. "P.S. Fuck your addendum."

Victor's sleek black two-door Jaguar was parked right outside the door. I pulled the door open and got in. I hid my face in my hands momentarily before I even got a chance to look at him. Thankfully, he took that as a sign to start driving. As we reached the curb, the paparazzi started running toward the car with their cameras in tow. I hid my face, but I was sure they'd caught me in their photos.

"Where am I going?" he asked.

"Anywhere."

His fingers peeled away one of my hands from my face. I still didn't look at him, but I let him take my hand down with his and left it in his grasp when he threaded our fingers together.

"Having second thoughts on that stupid paper you signed yet?" he asked after a beat, squeezing my hand so I couldn't move it away when I tried.

"Something like that."

"What happened back there?" he asked, taking my hand with him as he shifted the gear.

I sighed. "Nothing out of the ordinary. We agreed to go for ice cream, and it was fine until the cashier, who I used to think was nice, basically told me she'd fucked him."

From my peripheral I saw him nod and mutter *he's an asshole.* He exhaled sharply and continued to drive down Pacific Coast Highway. Neither one of us said anything until we got to a house on the beach, where he parked his car right outside the garage. I swallowed, thinking about how quickly things could escalate as soon as I walked in the door. I'd wanted him for so long, but now that the moment was finally here . . .

"You brought me to your house?" I asked as he switched off the engine. He looked at me and smiled.

"Not my house. This is my sister's. I told her I'd come by to help her put up a TV. She wants to surprise her husband before he gets home from work."

I blinked. "Oh. Okay."

He reached out for my hand again and placed it over his open palm, looking at it as if he were measuring it.

"I've never seen you wearing this," he said, turning the bottom of my wedding ring in his fingers.

"Cameras," I said as way of explanation. There was turmoil in his eyes that made my stomach flip. "Does it bother you?"

He stayed silent for so long, just staring at me, reaching deep within me for something unknown to me, that I thought he wouldn't answer. I watched as his Adam's apple bobbed when he swallowed, and finally he nodded slowly.

"It does. A lot," he said, threading his fingers through mine and bringing his free hand up to my face. He used it to brush back some of the hair that had fallen out of my ponytail and caressed my jaw with his knuckles, those deep hazel eyes still on mine. I couldn't close my eyes even if I wanted to, and my heart felt like it was at the point of no return, kicking into overdrive as his hand continued to move down to my neck, my collarbone.

"I want to take you to dinner," he said, voice low. The only thing I could do was nod. I would have agreed to just about anything. "Somewhere public, where I don't feel like ripping your clothes off, but you know how the media will get if we do that."

I smiled at the thought. "And let's be honest, regardless of where we are, you'd still want to rip my clothes off."

His eyes darkened. "Who wouldn't?"

My smile dropped momentarily thinking of Gabriel. He obviously wouldn't. Not that it mattered. Not that I cared at this point. But, God, how many women could a man have sex with in order to stay satisfied? Wasn't one enough? I tried to lift my lips back into a smile before I gave my thoughts away, but Victor noticed. He brought my hand up to his mouth and kissed the back of it, his soft lips moving down to my wrist, over my pulse as he kept his eyes on me.

"If you were a cockatoo, your flock would've killed you already," he said, lowering my hand, but keeping it in his. I frowned, shaking my head as a laugh escaped me. I was glad for the distraction, so I went along with it.

"Random. Why's that?"

"They try to hide their ailments, but the flock usually notices, because they feel it, and they gang up on them and kill them off."

"That's harsh," I said, raising my eyebrows. "And you feel something? In me?"

He chuckled. "I can make a million jokes about that statement, but I won't. And yes, Nicole, I feel something, in you, for you. I thought that was clear."

His admission was so natural, so nonchalant, but my veins thundered at the words nonetheless. He picked up my hand and kissed it once more before turning to get out of the car. "But the flock still would've killed you."

I got out and walked beside him down the side of the house. I inhaled the smell of the ocean.

"You would let them?" I asked as I walked behind him. "The flock, I mean. You would let them kill me?"

"It would be one against a flock of birds, because you'd probably be crying in a corner."

"So you would let them kill me."

He shook his head and stopped walking. I could sense him smiling before he turned to look at me. "I wouldn't."

"Do you do this much for all of your clients?" I asked, trying to lighten the mood with a smile. I half expected him to joke about how much they pay him, but instead he brought a hand down and held the side of my face, dipping his closer. I felt like I was going to seriously combust right there if he set his lips against mine. He didn't, though. Instead he kissed my cheek, then the corner of my mouth before moving on to the other. He backed away from me slightly, gazing into my eyes with an intensity that made my heart flip.

"I think you know I don't," he whispered, still holding my face. "And I think you know this has passed the client boundary by now." He paused, dropping his hands from my face. "All jokes aside, I'd do anything to make sure you were safe, Nicole."

I felt his words roll through me as he turned around. It took me a second to get my feet to move and follow him down the side of the house, toward the door.

Chapter Sixteen

Victor

MY SISTER'S HOUSE was a mess. I should've called ahead of time and let her know I was bringing someone with me, but I didn't have any time to process the fact I was bringing someone with me. When Nicole called me I had just left the courthouse. I didn't have time to do anything other than haul ass to the ice cream shop and pick her up. Once I got there and saw the impending breakdown written all over her face, I thought she'd be a sobbing mess, but she wasn't. It surprised me and disappointed me, which caught me off guard. I hated dealing with emotions and shit. Why the hell did I feel so desperate for hers? Probably because she didn't give them to me.

"Estelle?" I called out, picking up the sweater by the door. I turned to Nicole, who was standing behind me, looking nervous. "Sorry. This place is a mess today." And almost every day since Oliver went back to work, really. I couldn't even imagine what it would be like when they started having kids. A shiver ran through me and I shook it off. Nicole laughed.

"Did you see something that creeped you out?" she asked.

"Hey," Estelle said, appearing in the hallway. "I didn't hear you."

I didn't say anything, I let my eyes do the talking as I looked at every surface of her crazy house. She rolled her eyes.

"Don't start with your shit, Victor," she said. "I need your help to set this up so I can pick up before Bean gets home."

"What you need is to hire somebody to help you pick up this insanity," I said, walking in all the way. "Oh, this is Nicole. Nicole, this is my messy little sister, Estelle. She's an artist," I said by way of explanation. It seemed like most artists were messy. Then it hit me. Shit. Nicole was in the fashion business. Was she this messy?

"Oh," Estelle said, her eyes widening as she looked from me to Nicole and back to me. "That's fine. Sorry about the mess."

"Totally fine," Nicole said, waving her words away. "This is my house on a good day."

My head whipped to her. *What?* She shrugged in response, a little smile forming on her face. I sighed and looked back at Estelle, who was still studying the hell out of Nicole.

"She's—" I was going to explain to her who she was when I remembered my sister seemed to know more about Nicole than I did.

"I know who she is," Estelle said. I held my breath, waiting for her to start freaking out. "You're on TMZ right now, you know? I literally just saw you and Gabriel in an ice cream shop." She paused and frowned, looking at me momentarily. "Was all of that an act? Wait. Don't answer that. I don't want to know. Sorry. I'm sure you're sick of people asking you about him and stuff. Make yourself at home."

All I could do was stare. My sister was an idiot. Nicole surprised me by laughing.

"You'd be surprised how many regular people don't ask me

about it. I only get questions from the paparazzi."

"Oh. That must suck so bad, being followed like that," Estelle said, walking over to the kitchen. "Do you want wine? Is it too early for you? Do you even drink? Sorry, I kind of assume everybody drinks."

"She does," I said. "She assumes a lot of things. Forgive her. I'm starting to think maybe my thirteen-year-old self had been right about her being adopted."

Nicole laughed. "I drink, and it's never too early for wine."

Estelle came back with two glasses and handed one to Nicole with a smile. "I hope you like Riesling."

"I do. I have a hard time discriminating when it comes to alcohol."

Estelle laughed. She looked at me, and I already knew what she was thinking. I glared at her so she would take that out of her mind, but she smiled wider.

"So, you're a costume designer, right? That sounds like such a cool job. How did you get into that?" Estelle asked.

"Umm . . . where's my drink?" I asked, raising an eyebrow. She shot me a look.

"You know where the kitchen is."

I shook my head and headed over there. Either way I was going to change my clothes before I started this process. I went to the guest room, where I kept some just-in-case clothes, for late nights drinking when I didn't feel like driving home, and changed into a pair of basketball shorts and the first shirt in the drawer, which happened to be a Born Sinner shirt from the J. Cole concert Jensen and I went to a couple years ago.

"I think my room is the neatest place in this entire house," I said, walking back to the living room, where Estelle and Nicole were sitting facing each other like old high school girlfriends reuniting.

The sight made me smile. It was like she'd been here count-less times. My sister had met all of my past girlfriends, and some girls I dated briefly. I liked bringing them around her before I took them anywhere near my parents. I couldn't remember the last time she acted so comfortable around one, not that I was dating Nicole, but then again, my definition of dating differed from the rest of America it seemed.

"If you're so concerned about the mess, then pick it up," Estelle said. I caught Nicole's smile before she hid it behind her glass of wine. I held back my comment because talking about somebody's mouth on you in front of people was inappropriate, but there were a million things I wanted to do with that mouth of hers. *Stop thinking about her mouth. Stop thinking about her tongue and the way it feels against yours, and her soft skin be-neath your grip.* Deep breath. I turned around quickly.

"Where's the box?"

"Right there beside the table."

I sighed, putting my hands over my head. This fucking girl. I let them continue to have their conversation about elastic and glass hearts and started to pick up everything in my way from a pair of flip-flops to a box of canvases. Once I was finished I realized it really wasn't as much as I originally thought. It just looked like a mess when it was in the way. I would keep that to myself, though. I took the TV mount out of the box and all the screws and stood up to get the drill out of the garage.

"You know I'm going to need your help after I'm done with this part, right?" I asked when I saw my sister serving more wine as I walked back to the living room with the drill in my hand.

"I know," she said, smiling. She blew me a kiss as she walked back to the kitchen with the bottle of wine, which I assumed was empty. "I love you, brother."

I made a face as I sat back down on the floor. Of course she loved me *now*. I heard Nicole get up from the couch, but didn't look up from the instruction booklet in my hands. She kneeled down beside me.

"You look hot with a drill in your hands," she said in a whisper.

My heart jumped. I tilted my face to look at her. Her cheeks were flushed from the wine, and her hair was falling out of her ponytail again. I reached out and pulled on her hair tie, letting it flow down her shoulders. I kept my hand at the nape of her neck. It was a beautiful sight. So beautiful that all I could do was picture all that hair splayed over my pillowcase.

"I always look hot. It's a curse I've had to live with all my life," I said. She smiled, a small laugh leaving her lips as she tilted her head to better meet my gaze.

"Are you going to help me set up my TV?" she asked, leaning forward, brushing her breasts on my arm.

I inhaled sharply, gripping her hair a little. Her eyes widened, darkened, her lids lowering at the move. It didn't help the situation in my pants. None of it did. I dropped my hand and stopped breathing for a moment, stopped inhaling her sweet scent. Maybe if I didn't breathe I could cut off some of my blood supply and I wouldn't get hard.

"I'll help with whatever you need," I said, swallowing thickly.

My eyes were on her breasts, which were covered in that stupid Mowgli's shirt she wore. I was a fan of the band, but not when I couldn't make out whether or not she was wearing a bra, though I'm pretty sure she was. I looked back into her blue eyes; they were soft and light, the color of a cloudless sunny day. Fucking perfect, like she was.

"Do you guys want something to eat? I have leftovers from last night," Estelle called out from the kitchen.

I cleared my throat. Nicole sighed and stood up. She leaned down and her hair cascaded over both sides of my face as she placed a kiss on the left side of my neck. I closed my eyes, wishing I was free to pull her onto my lap and kiss her.

"That depends," I said loudly so Estelle could hear me. "What did you eat last night?"

"Black bean burgers," she said.

"On bread?" I asked. Oliver had a thing about bread. They normally didn't keep any in their house.

"Lettuce."

I rolled my eyes, pivoting my torso to look at Nicole, who was typing on her phone.

"You want black bean burgers on lettuce?" I asked. She looked up, blinking. I repeated the question, and she nodded.

"Sure. That sounds great."

"We'll have some," I shouted as I went back to work. I stood up with the measuring tape and started to mark the wall.

"Okay, it's ready."

I set the pencil and tape measure on the floor. We walked to the kitchen together, playfully bumping at each other like high school crushes on their way to their next period. Before we reached the open doorframe that led to the kitchen, I put my arm around her shoulder and pulled her to kiss her temple. It was a quick move. I dropped my arm as quickly as I'd pulled her to me. She stopped walking, though. And I stopped walking. Her lips were parted as if she had something on the tip of her tongue, but instead she shook her head, blinked it away, and smiled as she stepped into the kitchen. I wanted to pull her against me and ask her what she was about to say. I wanted to slither my way into every single crevice of her mind and dig until I found her deepest thoughts, her darkest flaws. I couldn't, though. I couldn't, so instead, I followed her into the kitchen and sat beside her at the small wooden table in Estelle's kitchen.

Estelle and Nicole talked about food and wine as I ate and watched the animated way Nicole moved her hands when she spoke. I had to make a conscious effort to look away from her. I looked at my empty plate instead, but when Estelle brought up the subject of the media, my eyes found their way back on Nicole's face. I couldn't help but notice the way her smile dropped, and the light in her eyes dimmed. She shot a quick glance my way before giving a slight shrug and a little smile that upturned the side of her mouth just slightly.

"I don't think they'll follow me around anymore. I'm not that interesting. They only really follow me when I'm with Gabe anyway," she replied.

It was stupid that it bothered me when she called him that, right? She'd been with him for a long time. She could call him babe and I shouldn't care. But I did. And it irked me. Why the fuck did I care? It was a nickname. Then again, even if she called him by his full name at this point it would bother me. Maybe I wouldn't care if he was being amicable, but to get a call from her and know she'd been crying . . . I wasn't okay with that shit. We spent the rest of our time eating and talking about Nicole's new place on the beach. She took down Estelle's number and promised to invite her over. I excused myself from the table when I finished because I really needed to drop by the office to pick up some files before I went home for the night, and that had to wait until after I finished putting the TV up and dropped off Nicole.

I was almost finished drilling the stand when I heard footsteps approach. I glanced over my shoulder and looked at my sister, who had her arms crossed as she watched me. She came closer. I looked around but Nicole was nowhere in sight, and for a fleeting moment I panicked and thought she'd left.

"She's in the bathroom," Estelle said.

I swallowed and nodded.

"You look at her funny."

"Funny how?" I asked, lowering my arms.

She shrugged. "Just funny. Like how you used to look at Jenny Doherty."

I felt my lips twitch at the mention of Jenny. She'd been the only girl I'd dated for well over a year. I wasn't a player. Maybe back in high school I had been, but I'd had long-term girlfriends. It was just that my definition of long-term and my sister's definition of long-term differed. Jenny had been a catch, though. She'd been top of our class and once we graduated and I went to law school, she'd done the same in Connecticut. And then she'd met another guy and married him and started a family. We'd been broken up for years by then, but I still had fond memories of her.

I always thought if I settled down it would have to be with somebody like that. Not somebody who was as smart or as pretty, but somebody who cared about something other than her appearance or the amount of money in my bank account. Somebody who had a balance. That seemed like a simple request, but it wasn't. Not these days anyway, when everything was about Instagram follows and Facebook likes, and who thought you were pretty and who didn't. I would say that only extended to LA, but Jensen was in New York and had the same experience when he was dating, and I had clients who had more money than God and were in the same predicament.

"Vic?" my sister asked, frowning. I shook my head.

"Yeah. No. I'm her lawyer, and I care about her and want what's best for her, but she's not a Jenny." She was *better* than Jenny. I knew it because while I had loved Jenny, she hadn't made me feel like I was burning up inside. Nicole was a flame. And she wasn't going out anytime soon. I knew that. I knew that, but I felt so lost in this, in the way she made me feel and the way I couldn't control my feelings for her, and that scared me. She was my client first and foremost. I felt the need to reiterate that to myself when she wasn't around, because when we were in the same room, I could feel myself getting too comfortable for my own good.

Estelle patted me on the back and snapped me to again. "Whatever you say, Vic." She paused. "Thanks again for doing this."

"Sure. I just need to drill this right here just for extra support and then I'll need your help putting up the TV."

"Okay. I'm going to finish putting this shit away so you can stop glaring at every surface of my messy house," she said as she walked away.

Thank God for that. I went back to the drill.

"You look really good when you're doing housework," Nicole said. I smiled.

"I believe you."

She laughed. I could picture her rolling her eyes behind me, but then I felt the warmth of her breath on the back of my right shoulder and I stilled, gripping the drill a little tighter.

"Maybe I'll make an honest man out of you and you can quit your job and stay home while I go to work," she said in a low voice. I could tell she was having a hard time not laughing as she said the words.

I scoffed. "Fat chance."

"What? You wouldn't be a stay-at-home husband?"

My shoulders shook with laugher as I lowered my arms from the wall and turned around to face her. We were standing so close that if my sister walked in this very moment, she'd have a lot of I *told you so's*. Nicole had a huge smile on her face, her cheeks a deep pink from the wine, or her laughter, or a mix of both. Either way, she looked gorgeous.

"Are you proposing? Because in the state of California one needs to finalize one's divorce before jumping into another marriage," I said, raising an eyebrow. Her smile dropped a little, just momentarily before she rolled her eyes and smirked at me.

"If only you'd be so lucky," she said, backing away a little, her gaze lingering on my face, my eyes, and making their way down my body. She licked her lips as she appraised me, and my heart jumped. Thank God I could control my dick in situations like these, even though it was getting semi-hard from that look alone. I gripped the drill tighter in my right hand, but the only thing I could do was think about pushing her against the wall and drilling my dick into her.

"Yeah," I said, but I didn't even know what I was responding to anymore. I didn't care. Her eyes widened slightly. We looked at each other for a long moment. Too long for comfort. Too long for my lips not to be on hers and her legs not to be wrapped around my waist.

"When is the mediation thing again?" she whispered thickly.

"Not soon enough," I said, my heart hammering.

"God. I can't wait for this to be over. I just . . ." She sighed. "I really wish you had no morals."

I chuckled. If she only knew. "When it comes to you, my morals are very questionable, Nicole."

She looked wicked when she smiled and turned back to sit on the couch. She stopped walking suddenly, frowning when she turned around again.

"Don't you need help mounting?"

"I can assure you I do not need any help mounting," I said, my eyes raking down her body. She crossed her arms and laughed.

"The TV."

"What?" I paused. "Oh. Yeah. I need your help mounting that."

Nicole was still laughing when Estelle walked back into the room. She didn't bother asking and I was glad for that because the last thing I needed was another mental image fucking Nicole.

Chapter Seventeen

Victor

DAYS LEADING UP to the mediation, I caught the flu. I was sick, pissed, and panicked. I'd never called out of work, but between the way I couldn't keep one pair of clothes on without sweating right through it, my eyes not staying open for more than two minutes at a time, and the pain in my throat, I had no choice. Thankfully Corinne passed by with the files I needed and I was able to call Nicole and speak to her on the phone about the mediation so she knew what to expect. I was in the bathroom, blowing my nose for the tenth time, when the doorbell rang. I really fucking hoped it was my mom. Fuck any man who can't admit that when they're sick they want their fucking mom. I opened the door and had to shield my eyes from the sun, and then blink to make sure my meds weren't playing tricks on me and it was really Nicole standing in front of me.

"Didn't we just talk on the phone?" I said. Fuck, it hurt to talk.

"Yes, and I brought you soup," she said, holding up a white plastic bag.

"Those words have never sounded sexier," I said, getting

out of the way for her to walk into the house. "How'd you find my address?"

"I asked your sister for it."

I nodded. That's right. They'd exchanged phone numbers the day of the ice cream parlor drama. Nicole followed me into the kitchen and looked around.

"I was a little shocked when Corrine called me to cancel our meeting today, and I didn't like the idea of my lawyer not being on his A game in a few days, so . . ." She shrugged and held up the bag again as she set it down on the kitchen counter.

"That was nice of you," I said, my voice a croaked whisper. It was really fucking nice of her.

"Where are your bowls?" she asked. I pointed at the cupboard behind her. "And your spoons?" I pointed at the drawer beside me. "And," she glanced around once more, "I found your napkins." She smiled at me. "Okay, your majesty, go lie down. I'll be right there."

I groaned and did as I was told, going back to my living room and putting my feet up. I covered myself with the Chargers blanket Estelle and Oliver had gifted me for my birthday last year and let my eyes drift shut. I jumped a little when I felt a cold cloth on my forehead, and my eyes popped open to find Nicole's concerned eyes right beside my face.

"That feels good," I said, groaning. I tried to smile but I wasn't sure my lips were working.

"Your soup is getting cold," she whispered. I tried to sit up, but kept failing, and then I felt her hands reach under me and heard her groan as she pulled me up.

"You're strong," I said, and felt myself smile when she laughed.

"I try." She leaned down to pick up the bowl of soup and sat beside me. "Open your mouth."

"You're going to feed me?" I don't know why I was so taken aback by her gesture.

"You don't look like you're in any condition to feed yourself. Unless you want me to call your brother-in-law and have him put in an IV?"

My eyes widened. Did she know I hated needles? Had I told her that before? I frowned and asked her. She laughed.

"I didn't, but I'm glad I know now."

"Don't get any ideas," I said, opening my mouth to drink some soup. I closed my eyes. It was so good. "Did you make this?"

"Is it good?"

My gaze met hers. "Did you make it or not?"

She smiled and fed me another spoonful. "That really depends on whether or not it's good."

"It's better than good."

"Well, I didn't make it," she said, laughing. "My old housekeeper, Amelia, did."

I nodded, swallowing the soup in my mouth. "Well, tell Amelia I may want to marry her."

Nicole scowled, blinking away, her eyes trained on the soup. "I'm not sure I like the sound of that," she said.

"Why?" I asked, opening my mouth for another spoon.

"I thought you didn't believe in marriage."

I frowned. "I never said that."

She looked at me, one brow raised in a challenge.

"Okay, so maybe I said that, but I was a twenty-five-year-old idiot. People change."

"Not that much," she whispered.

"You did," I said. "But you're right, not that much. You were still willing to let me mount you the other day at my sister's."

She smiled. "Even if I had been willing to let you do that

there, which I wasn't, you wouldn't have done it." She paused. "So I guess people do change after all. Twenty-five-year-old Victor would've done that anywhere I asked him to."

"Like I said, twenty-five-year-old Victor was a fucking idiot."

"You were pretty hot, though."

"Still am," I said.

She shook her head. "I think that fever is really getting to you."

I laughed, but stopped short because it hurt. I closed my eyes as Nicole stood and got the plate of soup, taking it to the kitchen. I heard the water behind me, but couldn't even tell her not to wash the plate. When I felt her presence near again, I opened my eyes. She had a glass of orange juice in her hand.

"You have to drink this," she said. "And then you're going to get up and shower."

I groaned. "Is this your way of telling me I stink?"

"No."

"Is this your way of getting me naked?"

She tried to stifle a laugh by pressing her lips together. "No."

"Is this your way of getting me in the shower and having your way with me because you'd have to give me a bath since I'm so weak right now?"

She laughed. "No."

I glanced up at her. She was so fucking beautiful. I hadn't really paid attention to the red dress she was wearing, or the way it curved out at her hips to accentuate her small waistline. I hadn't noticed she'd worn her hair loose or the way it draped over her shoulders and covered her tits.

"You're so fucking beautiful," I said before I could stop myself. Her eyes widened slightly. She took a seat across from me, placing the cup on her lap. From the way the orange liquid moved in the glass, I could tell her hands were shaking.

"Thank you," she whispered.

"I don't tell you that enough, but you are. I never told you that enough," I said. "Before, I mean. Before I pushed you away and you married that fucking asshole. I should have told you how beautiful you were."

"Victor," she whispered, "just . . . drink this."

My head felt light, as if at any moment I'd pass out again. It was definitely the Nyquil.

"This isn't me telling you these things because I'm drugged," I said. "I'm not him." Not that I knew what he was like when he was drugged, but I felt the need to add that. "I liked you, Nicole. I really did."

"Before?" she asked in a low voice. I nodded. Before, during, after. I really fucking liked her.

"But your dad was my boss, and I couldn't . . ." I yawned. "I couldn't take that chance."

"I know. Priorities," she said and smiled.

She didn't seem upset about the admission. I didn't really expect her to be. Nicole never saw me as her long-lost lover. She'd been whole before I found her at the club, and whole after I left her at the office.

"I had no idea you wanted to get married," I said, yawning again.

"You wouldn't have settled down even if you had known," she replied, shrugging.

"It had nothing to do with you. That was all me," I said. She sighed.

"That was a long time ago. A lot has happened since." She stood from her seat and leaned down to place her hand on my forehead. I closed my eyes at the feel of it, tried to inhale the fresh scent she carried with her. "Do you just want to go to sleep then? Not shower? You should still drink this."

She brought the cup to my lips and I took a sip, cringing as the cold liquid hit my sore throat. When I was finished, she stepped away and put the cup down.

"I should probably—" she started, and I realized, to my horror, that she may be about to leave me here by myself, and I really wanted her to stay. I wasn't sure which one of those things was worse.

"Stay," I said. "Stay with me."

She let out a sigh and sat down beside me, and without a second thought, I put my head on her lap. She started running her fingers through my hair so softly, sleep didn't stand a chance.

"I have some designs to work on," she said. "Do you mind if I get my sketch book and do that here?"

"Please do. I want to see them," I said, looking into her eyes. She nodded and gave me a small smile as she continued to touch my hair. "I always liked watching you sketch." That was the last thing I remember saying before I fell asleep.

Chapter Eighteen

Nicole

VICTOR AND I had been talking on the phone for the past few days. Ever since I left his house after taking him soup, he'd been calling me. It was mostly talk about the mediation and him apologizing for canceling our meeting, which led to him thanking me profusely for bringing him soup. Bringing him soup, which I wasn't sure was key word for a new page we turned or just literally bringing soup. It felt like a new page to me, though. With the late-night calls and the movie talk, and bowling challenges, and promises of surfing lessons, it felt like maybe we were becoming something. Something else. Something I wasn't sure either of us knew or wanted to label. But all of that was gathered in just a few days, and I'd married a man I barely knew within just a few weeks once before and look at how that turned out. The reminder left a bitter taste in my mouth. I washed it down with the cup of coffee in my hand, gulping it until it was all gone.

Victor called me at six thirty in the morning to wake me up and make sure I'd be ready on time. The meeting was scheduled for eleven thirty. Who the hell calls somebody at six thirty in the morning? Ever since the girl from the ice cream shop ended up on the tabloids with a tell-all about Gabe and her, Victor had been on edge, trying to figure out how we could really stick it to him during the mediation. My dad had been livid. Chrissy and Talon were furious. *"My wild night with Gabriel Lane"* was the title on the tabloids. It was definitely catchy, and if I was being completely honest with myself, I didn't care anymore. I was just . . . done.

Victor wanted to meet with me beforehand just in case I had any questions. I told him I didn't. He insisted I had to as way of apology for the missed meeting and I agreed just so I could get him off the phone. At nine thirty there was loud knock on my door. Thankfully, I'd gotten dressed already and had just finished drying my hair. I walked downstairs and opened the door just as he was putting his hand up to knock again.

"You have absolutely no patience," I said, gawking at him. He was dressed in a dark navy suit today, looking way too good to be my off-limits attorney. He gave me a quick, but thorough, once-over. I felt his gaze to the tips of my toes.

"You're not ready." He brushed past me and walked inside.

"I just need my shoes."

I closed the door and locked it, turning around to find him looking up at the ceiling with his eyes closed and his hands in his pockets.

"What's wrong?"

"Did you know there were photographers outside?" he asked, walking toward my kitchen.

"No." I paused, looking out the open windows in the front of the house. "Right now?"

"I was bombarded with flashing cameras on the walk from my car."

I rounded the counter and set up the coffee machine again

before facing him, butt against the counter arms crossed. "Is that why you stormed in here like you were being chased by a White Walker?"

"A white what?"

"From Game of Thrones, you know?" I paused. "Didn't we talk about this last night?"

"Yes, and I told you I don't watch it."

I shook my head. "Have you tried to watch it and you just didn't like it? Because, I mean, this could very well be the moment I fall out of like with you, or whatever."

His eyes roamed over my face, a slow tease of a smile splaying on his face. "Fall out of *like* with me? Did I miss the middle school memo?"

"I'm just saying." I turned around when the coffee finished pouring in the first cup and replaced it with another. I held the cup in my hand as I walked over to him and extended it for him to take. "If I could go on any set for a day, it would be that one. Too bad I have no connections there."

Victor took the cup from my hand with one of his and picked out something in my hair before looking back into my eyes. "Have you tried applying for a job there?"

"Have I tried?" I scoffed. "Of course I've tried. They have the best costume designers ever, though. I mean, Michele Clapton is a freaking genius. That's like if Prada hired Kanye West or something."

Victor chuckled, taking a sip of coffee. "So now you're throwing Yeezy under the bus too?"

I smiled, trying not to laugh along. "I'm just saying. I'm good at what I do, but I'm not her."

"I think you're good," he said, and added, "Really good."

His words were serious, though the crinkles around his eyes were still present from his smile. I was tempted to run the tips of my fingers along each line. I loved it when he smiled like this, as if he were giving me a private showing of the Victor not many were allowed to see.

"I think you're pretty good too," I replied, smiling. "And for the record, I would have hated you in middle school. And also, I like Kanye's music, I just think that when it comes to fashion, he thinks he's better than he actually is."

"Well, it doesn't matter what you think. You don't have the answers, Sway," he said. I started laughing. Hard. And he joined in, setting his mug down in front of him.

"You know, for somebody who's all business, and thinks his job is the most important thing ever, you can be pretty fun sometimes."

He appraised me for a moment, his eyes dropping to my chest. "I'm fun a lot of times."

"Sometimes," I said, my voice beckoning his attention back to my face. "And you haven't been much fun in that sense."

"With good reason. Let's try to get today out of the way."

"And then you'll be more fun?"

"Considering I'm just about ready to explode every time I hear your voice, let alone see you, I'd say that's a possibility," he said, his gaze heating the longer we looked at each other.

"Hmm." My heart did a series of wild pitter-patters as I put my mug in the sink and walked around the counter. We stood face to face, one of his hands gripping the side of the counter and the other in his pocket. I placed my hand flat on his hard chest and trailed it down to his stomach, stopping above his belt. His breath hitched. "A big possibility," I said.

"A very big possibility," he said, swallowing, eyes blazing.

I smiled and dropped my hand, stepping away just slightly. "I should probably go put my shoes on."

"You definitely should." From the way he was looking at me,

the last thing I wanted was to put more clothes on. "You should probably go do that now," he added, stepping a little closer and bringing his thumb to my face to wipe at the side of my mouth.

My lips parted slightly, I felt my breath coming in tiny spurts as we looked at each other. His gaze held a promise, but more than that, there was a soft curiosity that hadn't been there before, and as his hazel eyes brewed and studied mine, I went completely still, my body anchored by his. An earthquake could have shaken, my door could have been pounded down by a million paparazzi, and I still wouldn't have moved, because his hand on my face and that gaze was the only thing I felt I needed.

We both blinked at the same time, his hand dropping as he cleared his throat.

"Yeah, let me . . . go get my shoes," I said again, and disappeared into the hall. By the time I reached the top of the stairs, I wasn't sure if my heart was galloping because of the steps I took two at a time or what had just happened in the kitchen. I didn't know what was happening, but I knew I needed to get to that courthouse and make this go away once and for all so I could at least explore the realm of possibilities between us.

When we got outside, Victor positioned himself on the side the paparazzi were standing and put his arm on my shoulder as he led me down the sidewalk. When the cameras started flashing, I was glad I had my sunglasses on.

"Nicole, what happened the other day at the ice cream shop?"

"Is the divorce back on? Is that why you moved here?"

"Are you still working on your marriage?"

I kept my head down, my eyes on my black Jimmy Choos, and kept it moving. The questions continued until we got to the car, and even after our doors shut, the flashes continued.

"I don't understand how anybody could live like that. It's like living inside a fishbowl," Victor said.

"With no water," I replied.

He glanced at me as he stopped at the red light. "Do you get used to it?"

"I guess in a sense it becomes the new normal, which is insane to admit. Once this whole thing is over I can go back to living life, though."

"You mean go back to partying without worrying about them trailing behind you?"

"Goals," I said with a sigh. I paused to think on that for a beat, though, and it didn't accurately portray what I wanted out of life. "As lame as it probably sounds, I kind of just want to be able to pump gas without being followed around and asked about Gabe. I'm assuming once it's over they won't feel the need to mention every woman he's seen out with."

Victor didn't take his eyes off the road, but nodded. "Does it bother you? Hearing about him and other women?"

"I think what bothers me is their need to throw it out there just to get a good picture of whatever face I make. The knowledge of the women . . . doesn't bother me anymore."

Once I saw him leave the club with the blonde, and survived, I knew that ship had sailed, and even though it had hurt a little, I realized rather quickly I was completely fine without him. I'd been without him for so long anyway.

"Do you read the tabloids?"

"Of course I do."

I was just as guilty as everybody else in Hollywood who *didn't read the tabloids*. I'd rather find out what they were saying about me firsthand. Victor didn't respond to that, instead he hit the steering wheel with his palm when we hit a wall of traffic.

"Fuck you, Los Angeles. Fuck you," he said. I couldn't help but laugh, and when he shot me a glare, I laughed harder.

"We're on time," I said.

He sighed. "I guess we are. Sorry. Court days make me crazy."

"Oh. Court days make you crazy. What's your excuse every other day of the week?" I asked, smiling. I could tell he was having a difficult time keeping a serious look on his face. He looked at me, his eyes dead set on mine.

"You."

My stomach flipped. "Me? How do you figure that?"

"You make me crazy every other day of the week."

"How?" I asked, hyper aware of the way my heart was pounding in my ears.

His hand reached out to grab mine. He put it on the shift and covered it with his as he moved it to another gear.

"Well, you're occupying my mind every day of the week, so my deduction is that you're the reason I'm completely crazy."

I swallowed. "Do all of your clients occupy your mind as much as I do?"

When we stopped at the next red light and he set the gear in neutral, he looked at me, and from the way his expression intensified, I was sure he was going to kiss me. Ravish me. I shivered slightly, and put my hand out to adjust the air vent so it wasn't hitting me directly. Victor smirked knowingly.

"Fuck, no," he said. "They don't, and that terrifies me."

I reared back slightly, taken aback by the sincerity in his tone. My heart was pounding so loudly now, I wasn't sure I could even say what I wanted to say.

"Why does it terrify you? Because of your job?" I asked in a whisper. He ran his thumb along the seams of my fingers.

"Not because of my job."

Our gazes were locked on each other. I wanted to ask so many things.

Because you like me more than you care to admit?

But I didn't want to ruin the moment. If he said yes to either of those things, I would be thrilled, but I still had to be mindful of his promotion. I wouldn't get in the way of him getting it. Yes, I wanted him. Yes, I thought sleeping with him again would douse this flame, but I knew we had to be careful. And the reality was that I liked him. A lot. He started driving again and I sat back in my seat. How messed up was it that I was feeling these things for another man? For the man who was helping me divorce my husband? If I was being honest with myself, I didn't really care how messed up it was. As far as I was concerned I hadn't been married for a long time, because even though we were on paper, the things that happened in that relationship over the past two years were things no respectful relationship should have to endure. I didn't blame Gabe on the matter, either. It was both of us. He changed. I grew. *Apart.*

When we reached the parking lot of the courthouse, he looked over at me.

"You ready?"

I gave him a small smile. "I think so."

He turned slightly in his seat with a serious look on his face. "No. You are. There is no think. There's only know. You're a hellion. Fuck what they say. Fuck what they want. This is about what you want, and whatever you want, we'll get."

His words filled me with a sense of serenity. I'd told Gabe I didn't need a knight in shining armor, and I didn't. I didn't need Gabe. I didn't need Victor, but it felt good to have somebody like him on my team. Fighting for me. Fighting *with* me. I told him as much, and caught a glimpse of a more tender Victor, one I'd seen more often than not lately. He looked at me for a long beat, with those beautiful eyes and just said one word. One drawn out, gravelly, deep voiced word that threatened to make my toes curl in my heels.

"*Nicole.*"

He gave my hand one tight squeeze before switching off the ignition. I took one last long breath before we got out of the car and headed toward the building.

Chapter Nineteen

Victor

I SHOULD BE awarded a medal for dealing with imbeciles. First, the metal detector kept going off and I kept having to go back through it, even though Jean was the one securing the place and had seen me walk through these doors a million times. I wanted to say, "I'm pretty sure I left my shotgun at home this time, Jean." But with all of the mass shootings I couldn't really make a joke out of it. I told Nicole as much as I put my jacket back on and she laughed.

"That and your temper," she said.

"You're the only one who thinks I have a temper," I said, picking up my briefcase and glancing at my watch.

Nicole scoffed. "Maybe I'm the only one who *tells* you that you have a temper."

I waved at my friend Ezra as he walked by going the opposite direction with his client.

"Golf this Sunday?" he asked.

"And miss the Lakers game?" I shot back. He laughed, shaking his head.

"Maybe sometime next week then. I have a case I want to

discuss with you."

I nodded and continued walking. "See? People like me."

We stopped outside the doors and I propped my briefcase on the piece of crown molding on the wall so I could look for the file I needed. As my fingers sorted through the tabs, I chuckled, thinking about the day I found Nicole's panties inside. We hadn't talked about it at all, mainly because there hadn't been a good time to bring it up. If I asked her about it when we were alone, we'd be charting troubled water. As it was, things were choppy, lines were blurring, if they'd even been there in the first place. When I found the file I was looking for, I took it out and shut my briefcase.

"Maybe it's because you only let them see one side of you," Nicole said. I frowned. What the hell was she talking about? I looked at her.

"Are you talking to me?"

She shot me a look. "No shit. Who else is standing here?"

I looked around, and sure enough, we were the only ones in the hall. I shook my head. "What are you talking about now? Your voice box hasn't taken a break all day."

She laughed and pointed at me. "You see? So grouchy. Like Oscar."

I rolled my eyes and put the file under my armpit. "Be an adult, Nicole. Stop talking about cartoons and fantasy shows for a moment."

"Oh yeah, let me just sit here and quote rappers so you can keep up with me."

I sighed. She wasn't going to shut up. Maybe it was her nerves. Everybody had a coping mechanism. As long as hers wasn't open-mouthed chewing, we'd be all right. Hell, as long as her mouth was on me, we'd be all right. I shook my head and blinked out of my thoughts.

"Nic," I said.

"Hmm?" She tilted her head slightly to look at me.

"Can you please be quiet for a little while? I need to think and I can't if you make me keep looking at your lips."

She smiled and put her hands up. "I won't even make a joke out of that."

I wanted to take her face in my hands and kiss that smirk off right there in the middle of the courthouse that was practically my second home. Instead, I walked until I reached the room and opened the door. Lewis was sitting at the conference table with the phone to his ear, taking notes of something. He looked up and nodded in greeting.

"I'll have to call you back. Okay. Sure." He hung up and stood, offering his hand for me to shake. "Good to see you again." He looked at Nicole and did the same. "Unfortunate circumstances, but good to see you."

We sat down across from him.

"Where's the prince of Hollywood?" I asked.

"Running a little behind. Thanks for agreeing to meet me here. I have a case ten minutes after this one and there was just no way I'd make it here with the traffic."

"The fucking traffic is unbearable. Is it me or is it getting worse?" I asked.

"It's getting worse," Nicole said.

Lewis smiled slightly. "We'll try to do this as fast as possible. Gabriel said you're amicable."

She scoffed. "Did he? We seem to have a difference of opinion in more things than I realized."

I looked at her. "This is off the record right now, but when he walks in here and we start our meeting, I can't have you jumping in when he says anything."

"So I just stay quiet?"

"If you can," I said, hoping she understood it was for the best.

I got along with Lewis, until we were put on a case against each other. Then the gloves were off, mainly because he was damn good at his job and I took no chances.

The doors opened and Gabriel walked in with a little kick to his step, looking like a man who was ready to be single. It gave me a vote of confidence because we'd be closing this sooner than expected, which meant soon I'd have his ex-wife in my bed. I'd always heard the saying, "One man's trash is another man's treasure" and took it at face value, but it was the first thing that came to mind. The problem was, now I was in the situation, I realized that in reality it wasn't one man's trash. Women weren't things you could discard. Much less a woman like Nicole.

"Sorry I'm late," he said, looking around the room. I didn't miss the way his eyes stayed on Nicole. A man walked in behind him. At first I thought it was the mediator, but I knew all of the mediators and I'd never seen him.

"Who's this?" I asked when the man took a seat beside Gabriel.

"I'm his manager, Darryl Cusack."

"And you're here because?"

"You're about to find out," he said, smiling smugly. He looked like a fucking caricature, his head not proportioned with his body.

Soon after, Marvin Harrison walked in. I could have leaped from happiness. From the smile on his face, I could tell Lewis was having the same reaction. Out of all the mediators, Marvin was the easiest one to work with. He was clear, to the point, and most importantly, fair. I rubbed my hands together as he took a seat. When I glanced over at Nicole she was giving me a funny look. *What?* I asked with a frown and a shrug. She shook her head, looking away from me.

Marvin started talking, and I shut all personal thoughts about Nicole out. He asked if they were both sure they wanted the divorce. They both said yes, though with the way he was looking at her, Gabriel didn't look like a man who was done. I looked away. We went down a checklist of things, the King Charles named Bonnie that Gabriel had kept (for now), the Hollywood Hills home, the Escalade, the Prius, the Porsche, the Bentley, the farm in Idaho, the stocks in a production company, and the New York condo. Darryl perked up at the mention of the condo. I kept the expression on my face impassive. Nicole made it clear that she no longer wanted the house in The Hills, but she did want to be compensated for the money she put into remodeling the kitchen and the guest house.

"The dog?" Marvin asked, looking at Nicole first.

"He can keep it."

"So there will no longer be a need to share it?" he asked.

From the corner of my eye I caught the way her hands gripped her thighs. I looked at her. "You sure about this?"

She nodded, her eyes watering. "I just want it to be over. I don't want to share anything that ties me to him," she whispered.

Across from us, Gabriel cleared his throat. "You can take her."

Nicole's gaze tore from mine and flew to his. She didn't speak, though.

"You can take her. It's fine. I'm barely home anyway," he said.

She blinked rapidly and cleared her throat before smiling. "Thank you."

"Of course."

I kept my face impassive, but couldn't bear to look at the moment they were sharing any longer, so I looked back at Marvin.

"Cars," he said.

"I want the Prius," Nicole told me.

I looked at Gabriel, who nodded. Lewis spoke up. "Done."

"And the Cayenne," she added. Gabriel's brows hitched, but he nodded.

"Done."

"The house in Idaho?" Marvin prompted, looking at Nicole again.

"It's his."

"Done."

"The condo in New York," he said.

"My client and Gabriel came to an agreement on this," I said, sliding over the contract they'd signed. Marvin picked it up and read it quickly.

"Objection. She didn't uphold her end of the bargain," Darryl said. I could tell he was having way too much fun with this.

"She went to two events with Mr. Lane, er, Rogers," I said, unsure of which last name to use for somebody who evidentially acted like Dr. Jekyll and Mr. Hyde. "The contract doesn't state how many events she was to attend, so to the best of our knowledge she upheld her end of the bargain."

"The best of your knowledge isn't enough," Darryl said, slamming a hand on the table. I shot Lewis a look. His face was so red, I thought he was going to explode right there.

"Please let me handle my client, Mr. Cusack," Lewis said.

"Then do something about this, because she still needs to go to at least one more red carpet event with him after the scene she caused during their ice cream outing the other day."

I grit my teeth together. I took a deep breath. I clasped my hands together on the table in front of me.

"My client needs to process and think about it before she

makes a decision. Is that all?" I asked. My patience was running thin, so for Darryl's sake it was best he kept his mouth shut.

"No, that's not all." But of course he didn't know when to shut the fuck up. "She needs to attend this event with him and we need to schedule another candid appearance."

I drummed my fingers on the table, and looked at Lewis again. He heaved out a heavy breath. "I'm going to have to ask you to leave, Mr. Cusack. We both want what's best for our client, and what's best for him right now is for you to wait outside."

He huffed and puffed, but did as instructed.

"As far as the appearances go, I'll speak to my client in private as well," Lewis said.

Marvin nodded and stacked up the papers in front of him. "Well, I guess we just need to come to an agreement on this and we should be able to put it behind us."

We stood with the condition that we'd figure it out by the end of the week. I shook Lewis's hand, then Gabriel's, and then stood off to the side with Marvin and Lewis as Gabriel and Nicole spoke. They were being very quiet, and I kept finding myself looking over to them frequently as Marv tried to set up a game of golf. Golf was a sport I didn't even like, but had learned to play because many successful business meetings tended to happen over a game.

The last time I looked over, Gabriel had his hand on Nicole's shoulder and she was nodding at something he said. A wave of jealousy crashed through me, and I didn't even know why. They were getting a divorce. They'd been married. They had history together. Maybe that last bit was what bothered me. She had history with him. That, and to my horror I realized, I wanted her to only have eyes for me. I glanced at my watch and excused myself from the conversation. I had a meeting in my office scheduled in an hour and I still needed to take her home.

"Excuse me," I said, walking up to where she stood with Gabriel. "I have a meeting scheduled soon."

"Oh," she said. "Oh. Crap. I'd forgotten we came in the same car. Will you be able to drop me off?"

"Sure, it's on my way," I said. It wasn't on my way at all, but I didn't want to give Gabriel the chance of offering.

"I can take you," he said anyway.

Nicole looked at me for a long moment, searching for something. I wished she would just ask me for it so I could give it to her. Then she tore her gaze away and looked at Gabriel. For as long as I could remember, even when I was back in elementary school, I'd always be the first to get picked for things. Soccer matches, kickball team, softball, basketball. You name it, I had been picked first. I'd never understood what the other kids felt like until this moment. That feeling of your heart dropping into the pit of your stomach and your gut filling with uncertainty? I was in my thirties, for God's sake. That wasn't a feeling I wanted to experience at this point in my life. But as with everything that came to Nicole, there I was, experiencing uncomfortable shit.

"It's fine. Victor can take me. Thanks anyway. I'll see you soon though, as I have to go pick up Bonnie," she said after what felt like an eternity.

Gabriel returned the smile she gave him, and for a fleeting moment I felt another pang in my chest as I caught a glimpse of what their life must have been like when they were good together—the laughter, the dreams they must have shared, the heartaches they'd endured. They were over, though. That seemed to dull the pain just enough for me to smile and shake his hand as I walked away with her.

Chapter Twenty

Nicole

I'D PICKED UP Bonnie from the house I shared with Gabe and he'd asked me to stay awhile. Initially I said no, but he kept talking to Bonnie and scratching behind her ear, and I knew he'd miss her almost as much as I would have had he kept her instead of me, so I stayed. I was comfortable with it, until I wasn't, because as usual, we ended up back at: *where did we go wrong? What happened to us?* Those were topics I no longer cared to address. I told him as much, and he agreed it was unfair of him to revert back to them, but I could tell the thoughts lingered even as he stood by the door and watched me walk to my car with Bonnie.

"Are you still going out with Chrissy tonight?" Talon asked as she came into my work area. She was dusting off one of her makeup brushes against a towel as she watched me sew the black corset in my hands. "To celebrate?"

"Yeah," I said, smiling. "I feel like a celebration is in order in the form of getting intoxicated and dancing wildly."

Talon laughed. "That's a good way to celebrate. I would join you, but the girls are sick."

"Sucks," I said. "I won't even try to convince you then. Moms are the best medicine."

"Speaking of which, when are you going to go visit yours?"

I sighed, pushing away from the sewing table and running my hands down my face. I was dying to go see her, but with this whole ordeal, I hadn't even looked at flights.

"I don't know, but hopefully soon. She's finally done telling me the divorce was a mistake, and I really want to just go over there and lay low for a while."

"Is your dad still on his cruise?"

"Yeah, they come back next week. Meire emailed me pictures and said he was itching to get back to the office. I can only imagine what a pain in the ass he's being."

"These attorneys," Tal said, shaking her head. "That's probably why you like Victor so much."

I couldn't keep the smile that spread over my face. I rarely spoke to him during the day unless he had something to tell me about the case, which at this point he said would be white noise until we got the finalized papers, but our late-night calls continued and those were much more interesting than law talk. He'd told me about his first girlfriend. I'd told him about my first boyfriend. We spoke about our longest relationships and shortest, and weirdest, and sometimes we'd throw in things from our past together and laugh at the fact we still remembered.

"You really like him," Talon said. I shrugged a noncommittal answer, though I didn't make an attempt to deny it. I *definitely* really liked him. I always had, but this time it seemed like I liked him more. Like we were connecting on another level. As if we were becoming friends first. *Had that been what we'd missed the first time around?* I tried not to psyche myself out over it though. I knew him and his priorities were still intact.

On my way home, I called Marcus. He'd asked for time off

to see his sick aunt a few days before the mediation. He said he hoped there was still a job for him when he got back, but he understood if I needed somebody else immediately. I told him he wasn't getting rid of me that easily. I'd gotten used to having him around. When Marcus didn't answer the phone on the second ring, I hung up and called Victor.

"Hey," he said. My veins thundered at the sound of his masculine voice. "Can I call you back? I just got to a restaurant where I'm meeting with a client."

"A woman client?" I asked. He chuckled.

"Hmm. No answer. Interesting," I said.

He paused for a beat. "Are you jealous?"

"Is she hot?"

"Not hotter than you," he said, his voice firm, but I could also feel a hint of amusement in it.

"Whatever," I mumbled. The entire time I'd been his client, I hadn't gotten the *let's go to a restaurant and discuss your case there* treatment.

He sighed. "Nicole, please don't be jealous. I can assure you that you have no reason to be."

"I'm not jealous," I said, and I wasn't. I just wished things would have been different. I wished we could go out and do things while we got to know each other instead of hiding our conversations behind late-night calls and stupid meetings, where our personal conversations were overshadowed by my past with Gabe.

"Good. I really have to go. I'll call you when I get out of here."

I mumbled a goodbye I wasn't even sure he heard before hanging up. I was stuck in traffic for twenty minutes before Marcus called back. After asking him how the ailing aunt he went home to visit was doing, I gave him the overview of what tonight would be like: club, girls, drinking, partying.

When I got home, Bonnie trotted to the door to greet me, her floppy ears dangling as she tilted her head for me to scratch. I did and picked her up as soon as I set down my bag, keys, and kicked off my heels. I held Bonnie on my hip and sorted through the bottles of wine I had placed on the wooden bottle holder on the wall and set her on the floor and poured some into a glass before putting on a pair of sneakers, and headed out back with her. I let her roam a bit while I sipped on my wine and took in the ocean breeze, watching her to make sure she didn't number two without my knowledge. There were few things I hated more than stepping on the shit an irresponsible dog owner left behind.

"Is that a cocker spaniel?"

My head snapped up to the shirtless guy slowing down from his jog. Perks of living on Manhattan Beach—hot shirtless guys jogging.

"Nope. King Charles."

He smiled, crouching down to meet Bonnie's excited little hop. "She's beautiful."

"Thank you." I smiled.

"She looks like you."

I felt my face heat up a little as I smiled. "Thank you."

"I've never seen you around here."

"I just moved from . . ." I paused. He obviously didn't know me as Gabriel Lane's wife, so he wouldn't know where I'd lived. It was the first time I realized I was starting from scratch. I was just Nicole Alessi again, and unless you were into digging into people's past and saw my socialite, wild child days, very few people knew who I was. "I just moved over here," I said, correcting myself.

"Oh. Where did you move from?"

"Like twenty minutes away."

"Oh. I moved here from Georgia a few months ago." He paused. "I'm Brent, by the way."

"Nicole," I said, bumping the fist he extended for me.

"My hands are sweaty," he said as way of explanation.

I heard my phone ringing inside and jerked out of my seat. When I looked at Bonnie again, I noticed she'd chosen that exact moment to take a crap. "Sorry," I said sheepishly. "I have to get that. Enjoy your run. I'm sure I'll see you around again."

"I hope so," he said, taking off again. I watched him leave for a second before Bonnie tugged at her leash, and I sighed, coming back to reality.

"What have I told you about using the bathroom in front of people?" I whispered, crouching down with the baggie in my hand. "So disgusting, Bonnie. So disgusting."

When I walked back in the house, I noticed the missed call was from Victor. I debated not calling him back, but I didn't want him to think I was being childish or jealous because he was out with a female client, so I called back.

"How was your lunch date?" I asked. The harsh breath he exhaled into the phone line made me shiver as if his face was on me.

"Meeting, Nicole. It was a meeting."

"Same difference."

"Not the same difference. I don't sleep with my clients."

I bit back a smile, tried to mask it from my voice. "That's too bad. I heard you have a client who was just about to touch herself thinking about that possibility."

"Fuck, Nicole," he groaned.

"Hmm?"

"You're killing me," he said, voice gruff. Butterflies ignited deep in my belly.

"What kills you more, Victor? Knowing you can have me and passing it up or thinking about me going out tonight and finding another man to satisfy this urge?"

He was quiet, but I knew he was there because I could hear his labored breath in my ear. I stayed quiet. I was never one to shy away, but I was afraid maybe I'd pushed the envelope and in turn pushed him farther away.

"I've been sitting outside, staring at the office building trying to get rid of the hard-on you've managed to give me, and now that's looking like it won't be going away any time soon, which means I'm going to be late to a fucking meeting I arrived twenty minutes early to," he said, pausing. I smiled. "To answer your question, both of those options fucking kill me, but when I fuck you again, and I will have you again, it's my name you're going to be screaming."

"We'll see," I said, trying not to sound as affected as I felt.

"Yeah, we will see." He let out a breath. "I have to let you go so I can see what to do about my . . . problem."

I laughed. "Sorry. Sort of. Good luck in your meeting."

"Thanks. I'll call you tonight."

"Oh. I won't be home," I said. His silence told me he was expecting me to expand on that, but I didn't. I wanted him to be the one to ask.

"Where are you going?" he asked finally.

"Out with Chrissy."

"Chrissy . . . the friend you go club-hopping with?"

I laughed at the fact that he knew Chrissy as the club-hopper. "We don't club-hop. We're not twenty-one. We just go to one."

"Still sounds like trouble," he said, but I could hear the smile in his voice as he said it.

"You know me, always up to something."

"I do, and I like that. I'll call you when I get home. Maybe I'll catch you before you head out."

After I hung up with him, I drank two more glasses, soaked in a bath, ordered sushi, got dressed and put on my makeup before Marcus knocked on my door. I opened it and welcomed him inside while I walked around making sure I'd blown out all the candles I'd lit during my hour of relaxation. Rather than her picking me up, I promised Chrissy I'd meet her at the club.

"Let's go, Marky Mark. If I don't leave now, my buzz will be gone by the time I get there and I won't be brave enough to walk into the club by myself."

"Didn't you just tell your friend to put me on the list so I could escort you in?"

"You know what I mean."

"I don't, but it's okay, I don't want to know."

It took us a bit to get to the club, and then a little longer to park in the back. Marcus suggested valet, but I said no. There was no way I was letting a valet drive my Cayenne. And there was no way I was getting out of the car with the paparazzi around. I wanted to wait for at least some of them to scurry out. Once they did, we got out of the car and walked to the back door. We got inside with no hassle at all. The bouncer looked at me and let me go in, and then did the same to Marcus.

"I'm surprised they didn't card you," I said loudly, over the music.

"Why?"

"Baby face," I said, raising a hand and slapping him playfully. He shook his head.

We made our way upstairs, where Chrissy was waiting with Cass and a few other friends again. The minute she saw me, she bolted out of the chair and pulled me into a hug. But the moment she saw Marcus she let go and gave him all her attention. I couldn't stop laughing at the look on his face. He came over and told me he was going to stand by the foot of the stairs just in case I needed anything. I was sure he was doing it to get away from Chrissy and her forwardness.

I joined Chrissy and let her pour me a drink from the bottle she'd ordered.

"How's the hot lawyer?" she asked.

"He's . . . there. Being hot," I said as I took a sip of champagne. I really didn't want to get into it, especially not at a loud club.

"I'm pretty sure I saw him here," she said, looking around. "I mean, it's dark, but I could swear it was the same guy."

My stomach dipped. Victor. *Here?* I looked around and did a double, then triple take when my eyes landed on Victor. Even though his upper body was facing away from me as he spoke to the people beside him, my heart raced. And when he turned toward me, as if he were looking for me in the crowd, and his eyes met mine, unblinking, I felt the breath whoosh out of me. He stood, and even though it was too dark to see his eyes, I could read the lines of his face and followed suit.

"I'll be back," I said to Chrissy, who was now enthralled in conversation with one of the girls sitting in our table.

Victor turned and started walking in the direction I'd come from, and I followed. I saw Marcus when I got there and told him I would be right back. He saw Victor, looked at me, and nodded.

"I'll be right here," he said as I walked away.

Victor didn't stop walking or go outside like I half expected. He didn't go toward the bathrooms either. Instead, he walked to the right, toward the huge dance floor. My head was pounding with the music, my heart with excitement, trepidation. He stopped walking and stepped off to the side, toward a dark corner where nobody could bump us, and pulled me with him. He leaned back against the side of the bar, his forearm on it so the drink in his hand was dangling.

"What are you doing here?" I asked, stepping forward and speaking up so he could hear me over the music.

His eyes made their way down my body slowly, he licked his lips as they made their way back up and suddenly, despite the vodka in my system, I felt parched. I swallowed and reached out for the drink in his hand, taking a sip of it and making a face at the unexpected bite of alcohol. Victor's lips bloomed into an amused smile. When he extended his arm, I thought it was to take the drink back from me, but instead it went around my body and pulled me close to him so we were almost chest to chest and the heat of his gaze wasn't the only thing warming me.

"Isn't that obvious?" he said, his breath tickling my ear. I shivered and shook my head. His chuckled vibrated into me. "What are you doing here?"

"Dancing," I said, tilting my face slightly so my nose brushed against his light beard.

"So dance," he responded, setting his hands on my hips. I leaned forward, brushing my chest against his arm as I set the drink down behind him, smiling when I felt his grip tighten a little. I started to move my hips side to side, quirking a smile at the way his gaze smoldered on mine.

"Well, I'm not going to stand here and give you a private show," I said, raising an eyebrow. "I charge for those."

His grin was dark and full of mischief as he pushed himself off the bar and began to move with me, his hips in perfect tune with mine. "I'd pay a fuck ton of money to see it."

I smiled, running a hand through my hair to push it away from my face. I tilted my head slightly with the movement, and gasped when his lips came down and sucked me there.

"Did you find what you were looking for?" he asked, his lips making their way up my neck, to my chin, my cheek, my earlobe.

"Did *you*?" I asked breathily, still moving along with him.

He reared back, cupping the side of my face as he gazed down on me with those dark, lust-filled eyes. He nodded.

I stopped breathing.

Stopped moving.

I looked at him, eyes wide. "What?"

"Come home with me," he said, his mouth brushing the edge of mine. "I'm sick of playing games. Come home with me, Nicole."

"Why now?" I asked. I tried to swallow that thought before I vocalized it, but it was no use. I had to know. I had to know he wasn't the one playing games with me.

"Because I want you too fucking much. Because the thought of you coming to this place and hooking up with some other asshole is just too much for me to bear."

I felt myself smile. "So you want to be the asshole that takes me home?"

"More than anything."

More than anything. I didn't dare question him further. There was no point. I could see the resolve in his eyes, and that alone assured me that this was happening. I could've just brought up the reasons he'd been turning this idea down, but I wanted it more than anything, so instead, I went for light.

"No bathroom sex?" I asked, gazing up at him. His smile was slow, wide, and sensual as he shook his head as he brought his face close to mine again.

"Fuck. No. Definitely no bathroom sex, unless it's one of our bathrooms," he said, his mouth near my neck. He dropped a kiss there. "People change."

All I could do was nod and turn around, ready to bolt out the door, but suddenly his arms were around me body, pulling me back to him, and I gasped at the feel of his hard body pressed up against mine. God. It'd been so long.

"Do you remember where I live? Have Marcus drop you off there," he said into my ear before nipping the tip of my earlobe. I rocked against him. "We need to be careful until everything is finalized."

I nodded and stumbled a bit when I felt his mouth on my neck again. *What I would do for him to just fuck me right there on that dance floor. In that stairwell. In the club bathroom.* I was past the point of caring. He let go of me and walked at a normal distance once we reached the top of the stairs and into the VIP section. I introduced him to Chrissy, formally. They already knew each other from the first club experience Victor and I had, and then from the whole *the guy I fucked in the bathroom on my birthday works for my father! What are the chances?* fiasco.

"I saw you on TV when you represented Harlow Winters in her divorce. You look hotter in person," she said. Victor gave her a *tell me something I don't know* smile.

"Let me go tell Bobby I'm leaving," he said after I told Chrissy I was leaving. At the mention of my Bobby's name, I paused. Victor shot me a confused look, so I pulled down on the sleeve of his suit jacket so he could lower his head.

"Isn't it going to look weird if we both say bye to him and leave together?"

He straightened and looked at me for a long moment. I could practically hear the wheels in his head turning, trying to think of a solution. Finally, he nodded in agreement. I walked back to where Marcus was instead, and left while Victor went back to his table. When we opened the back door to go outside, the paparazzi snapped pictures, probably hoping to catch their newest juicy story, but stopped quickly when they saw it was only me, though they did ask their usual questions. *What are you doing now that Gabriel is filming in Canada? Do you miss him? Will you visit him on set?*

I let out a relieved breath once I got into the passenger seat.

"They are so fucking annoying," I huffed when Marcus got into the driver seat.

"Where to now?" he asked. I hated when he ignored my remarks. *Didn't he understand that I wanted to rant?*

I pulled up Victor's address from the text message Estelle had sent me the day he was sick and instructed Marcus to drive me there.

"Drop you off?" he asked when I said that.

"Yes." I leaned back into my seat as I sent a quick reply telling Victor I'd be there. "I'll get a ride home."

Marcus looked at me for a beat. I didn't acknowledge it, but I felt his stare on the side of my face before he sighed and started driving. I kept quiet the entire time. My hands on my lap shaking slightly. My nerves making it difficult to breathe calmly. I'd done this before. I'd done it often, but I couldn't escape the fact that I'd never completely planned for it. The ride was long enough for me to have no choice but to think about the decision I'd made. I wondered if he'd purposely sent me there in a different car for that reason, to see if I chickened out and decided I couldn't follow through with it. I took a breath and let it out slowly when the car slowed into a stop as we reached the quaint two-story beach house that I'd fallen in love with the day I came to visit.

"I'll wait here," Marcus said when he put the gear in park behind Victor's Jaguar.

I swallowed. I could have him wait there. It would be the perfect scapegoat. But I didn't want a scapegoat. I didn't want a way to leave. If he wanted me to stay, I'd stay, and if he pissed me off, I'd Uber home. I took a deep breath.

"No. Just go home. I'll call you when I need you to come pick me up." I put my hand on the door handle and looked at him. I could tell he was still having a difficult time with the idea of just dropping me off. "I know I don't have to say this because you signed non-disclosures, but—"

He put a hand up, and I stopped talking. He didn't say anything, but his clear-blue eyes were sharp and serious, and I knew I was understood. I got out of the car, made my way up the gravel driveway and the few steps to the door. My hand went up in a fist to knock, but the door opened before I could. Victor didn't peek out, he just opened it wide enough for me to step in and closed it right behind me. The house was dark, only the glow of the kitchen light seeping through.

"Hi," I whispered, suddenly feeling shy as I tilted my face to his.

"Hi," he whispered back, grasping my wrist with one hand and pulling me a little closer, until his minty breath was over my face, and bringing his other hand up to the side of my face in a slow caress.

"I don't know if I already told you this, but I really love your house," I said.

I could barely make out his smile, but I knew it was there. In this kind of lighting I could barely make out his face, but I knew his features so well it didn't matter. If I went blind in that instance, I could perfectly describe him for a sketch.

"Wait until you see my bed," he said, his voice still quiet as if he were afraid to burst the bubble we were in. I smiled.

"Were you followed?" he asked, bringing his lips down to my jaw. "I don't want the media assuming things about you." His mouth worked its way up to my ear and back down slowly.

I sighed against him.

"You mean about us," I said. He pulled back slightly, his hand still on the side of my face, the other making its way down to my ass.

"I wish I cared about that. I should, but I want this to happen too much to let that stop me," he said squeezing my ass. "I don't know if you were serious about finding another man to satisfy your needs, or just saying it to push me over the edge, but fuck that idea, Nicole. Fuck that idea. I need you. I want you, and I always get what I want."

"So spoiled," I whispered, leaning into him and tipping my face a little more until our lips brushed against each other's.

"Hard working," he replied as his hand slid to the back of my neck and his lips molded against mine.

They were soft and tentative, tasting, his teeth teasing as he tugged on my bottom lip, his hands making their way down my body and inching my dress up slowly. So slowly. I started undoing the buttons of his dress shirt quickly, and he chuckled against me, the sound vibrating through me and making me shiver.

"We're not rushing this, Nicole," he said, a whisper against my lips. I felt like I was on fire, burning for him, desperate for anything he'd give me, my breath fast and erratic.

"A quickie is fine by me," I said when he successfully pulled the dress over my head. His gaze alone made me feel like I was off balance. The way he looked my body up and down, slowly, as if savoring me. He shook his head.

"No quickie."

I reached for his shirt again, tugging it open and planting my palms on his hard chest, making my way to his shoulders and down his sculpted arms, taking the shirt off with my touch. My heart was beating wildly as I studied the sight in front of me, his lean frame, the six-pack I had no idea he had beneath his work clothes. I swallowed thickly as my gaze made its way back up to his eyes. The fire in them made my stomach flip. He took his shoes off, kicking them off to the side before stripping out of his socks, then he pulled me back to him and took my mouth in his again, his hands groping my ass, my waist, my breasts. His hands went around and unclasped my bra, tugging it down quickly and throwing it to the side. His hands cradled my face as he gazed down at me and my heart began to thunder inside my chest. He opened his mouth like he was about to say something, but didn't, instead lowering his mouth to mine once more.

He walked backward, bringing me with him as he held me by the waist, his mouth all over me—my mouth, my neck, my shoulder, my collarbone. I held on to his strong forearms so I wouldn't trip over my feet or his. He pushed a door open and I gripped on to him when I opened my eyes and realized I was standing inside Victor's bedroom. The young version of me did a backflip. Never in a million years did I ever think my life would take me there, to his intimate lair. And never in a million years would I have thought it would be so normal, so cozy, unintimidating. It was a very manly room, from what I could see—large bed, dark sheets, dark décor. He pulled me toward the bed and pushed me down so I landed on my back, the plush mattress catching me and springing me up slightly.

I laughed as I looked up at him, towering over me, looking all serious wearing only his slacks.

"You look like you're about to punish me," I said.

"Be careful what you wish for."

His gaze made its way down my body as he said the words, licking his lips in the process. I shivered against the soft sheets beneath me. He came closer, putting a knee between my legs to push my legs farther apart. In only a black silk thong and matching pumps, I was exposed. I would have felt shy, had it not been for the way he looked at me, like I was the most incredible thing he'd ever seen. I opened my legs farther as he stood up straight and started working on taking off his belt. As he unbuttoned his pants, I fondled my breasts, and he groaned at the sight. My hands trailed over my stomach. I laid them flat against my abdomen, tucking them into my panties.

"Fuck. Yes, Nicole," he said, his voice raw as he stripped out of his pants, taking his boxer briefs with them. My heart stopped for a second as I looked at his erection and just how ready he was for me. His hand closed over it as he pumped and watched me. I moaned, slipping my fingers along my folds, remembering what he felt like inside me.

"You look so fucking beautiful right now," he said. "I wish you could see yourself."

"You look so fucking beautiful right now," I said, biting my lip to stifle another moan. "I wish you would touch me instead of yourself."

His jaw clenched as he stepped toward me. It was as if his self-control snapped in that instance.

His hands gripped my panties and pulled, the thong biting into my ass as he ripped them off me.

He brought his face down to my chest, making his way to one of my nipples and licking, biting, tugging before sucking the entire thing into his mouth. My hands flew to his hair and pulled.

"Holy shit," I said, feeling the sensation everywhere. "Victor."

"Yes," he said against my other nipple. "Keep saying my name. Tell me how much you want this."

"I want this so much," I said, a gasp when he made his way down my stomach, licking, biting, dragging his teeth all the way to my clit and sucking it into his mouth. "Oh my God." He licked the seam, up and down, not leaving any bit of it untouched by his tongue, before focusing on my clit again.

"Tell me, Nicole," he said, tugging at my lips. "Tell me how much you missed this."

I groaned, my pelvis jumping at how good his mouth felt on me.

"Tell me how much you need this," he continued as he groaned, putting more pressure on that spot. I felt my eyes rolling to the back of my head, my toes curling, a burn gradually moving from the tips of my toes to the top of my head as an orgasm began to wash over me. He kept licking me, sucking me, even after I screamed out his name. I shook my head, pulling at his head.

"I can't," I said in a whimper. He kissed the inside of my thighs and replaced his mouth with his fingers as he made his way up my body, his eyes right in front of mine. "Victor," I cried out again when he pushed his fingers inside me. He didn't do it slowly. He didn't let my body acclimate to anything.

He wanted me to feel it.

And I did.

Everywhere.

"I am going to fuck you so hard," he said, lowering his face to suck on the side of my neck.

"I thought you said no quick—" I said, gasping loudly when his fingers began to move against my clit and inside me all at once.

"Does this feel like a quickie?" he asked as the tips of his fingers stroked my clit, bringing another orgasm out of me. I cried out again and again.

"No," I said, my voice barely containing the shrill behind it. He took his fingers out and licked them one by one as he looked down at me. My head was still clouded with what had just happened, but the sight of him licking his fingers, and knowing it was me he was tasting—*savoring*—with a look of ecstasy on his face that made my core tighten more than it already was. Victor didn't let me take breaks. He didn't give me time to sit up and try to please him. Instead, he propped a hand on either side of my head and pushed himself inside me. I screamed, my back arching off the bed. He was so big. I felt so. Fucking. Full.

He paused his movements. I shot him a confused look.

"You okay?" he asked. I nodded wildly.

"More than okay."

"You sure? You look like you stopped breathing there for a while."

"I don't need to breathe. I just need you to fuck me."

"Yeah?" he asked, his mouth coming down to my ear. "How would you like to be fucked? You want me to go slow?" He pushed in and pulled out slowly. So. Slowly. In and out. In and out.

"Fuck," I said. "Fuck." It was the only thing I could make out. It was the only word I could even think.

"You like this?" he asked, his hips moving in and out in a slow, long tempo that had me searching for my next breath.

"Fast." I gasped. "Hard."

He groaned, pulling out of me completely, and flipped me over. "Get on your knees." I did, and shrieked when he slapped my ass hard. "You like that?" he asked, his voice raw. "You like it when I slap your ass like that?"

I whimpered. It's not that I hadn't had someone slap my ass before, but the way he did it, the things he said while he did it? I felt like I was going to come right there. I pushed my hips back, wordlessly begging him to fuck me. He grabbed my hips and pounded into me. I shrieked again. This time, he didn't go slow. He fucked me hard, pumping inside me hard, reaching for my hair and tying it to his hand as he pulled me up. The bite of it felt good. Everything felt so good. I couldn't even remember what my sex life had been like before that instance. I couldn't remember how another man felt inside me.

"I'm going to make you come again. And again. And again," he said as he pulled my hair harder, until my ear was by his mouth. "You're never going to be able to forget who makes you feel like this."

"Oh God," I said, feeling myself tighten around him, feeling the familiar burn of another orgasm forming. "I'm going to come, Victor."

"You're fucking mine, Nicole," he said, thrusting harder.

I groaned, nodding as I tightened around him. "Yes."

"Say it."

"My . . ." I gasped when he slapped my ass again. Hard.

"Say. It," he said through his teeth, slapping my other ass cheek. "Your ass is mine. Your pussy is mine. Your tits are mine. Fucking say it."

I did, though my voice was hoarse and my words were quiet. I couldn't remember him pulling out, or the way he pulled my back to his chest once he came back from throwing the condom away. I couldn't remember how we fell asleep or what he said to me, but I remembered those words, because I felt him inside me when I woke up before the sun came up and called Marcus to pick me up.

Chapter Twenty-One

Nicole

MARCUS'S SILENCE ON the ride home made me uneasy. I could only imagine what a straight-laced guy like him was thinking, and I wasn't sure I wanted to know, but of course I asked.

"You think I'm a slut," I said finally, unable to stand the discomfort any longer.

He didn't respond, not even when I looked over at him and caught him glancing at me quickly.

"You think I'm a slut because I didn't even wait to finalize my divorce before hooking up with another man."

At that, I saw the corner of his mouth tilt. "I don't think that."

"Why are you so quiet then?"

"I'm always quiet, ma'am."

"No, you're not, and you never call me ma'am."

"Okay. Miss Alessi."

I glared at him. He didn't acknowledge me. "Just Nicole, please, unless you've decided to go back to being all proper because you think I'm a slut." Again, no answer. Finally, as we were getting close to my house, he sighed.

"What you do is your business. I don't think anything less of you."

"So you're not mad that I called you before the sun came up?"

He laughed. "That's my job."

"Okay." I nodded. "Thank you, and thank you for not judging."

"That's also my job."

I shook my head and smiled as I climbed out of the car. I practically stumbled into my house. My legs were tired, my thighs were burning, my vagina felt like it had been pounded . . . which, it had been, but I hadn't expected to feel it as much as I did. I hadn't done the walk of shame in a long time, and I felt a little excited, like I was back in the game. Along with giving me the best sex of my freaking life, Victor had also made me feel desired. I hadn't felt that way in so long, I'd forgotten the power it held. I stripped off my clothes, showered, and slept like the dead. The only reason I woke was because of Bonnie's whimpers.

"I know. I know," I said as I got out of bed and wiped my face. Back to the bathroom I went to brush my teeth and make myself semi-presentable for my new neighbors before I went outside with Bonnie.

I was holding on to her leash with my eyes closed, face tilted to the sun, when a shadow suddenly set over my face. My heart jumped as I sat upright.

"You scared me," I said. Victor's face was serious as he looked at me. He turned his face toward Bonnie, who was now trotting toward him. Without saying a word to me, he crouched down and started to pet her. He took her nametag in his fingers and smiled.

"You left," he said, still looking at my dog. "I wanted to take you to breakfast."

"I left because I didn't think it would be smart for me to be there and do the walk of shame in front of photographers."

He appraised me for a moment. I wondered if he was thinking about what we'd done last night. My stomach clenched at the memory: his mouth on mine, his head between my thighs, thrusting his dick inside me like he was afraid it would never happen again. I felt a blush creep over my face and had to look away.

"That is smart," he said, finally.

"I thought you'd appreciate it."

He opened his mouth to say something, and closed it again.

"I had a good time last night," I said.

Understatement of the century. I wanted to tell him that it was a night so memorable, I'd be sure to have fantasies about it continuously. I wanted to tell him how much my ass hurt when I sat down and how I kept smiling at the recollection of why. I wanted to ask him what his possessive chants meant. *You're mine.* Was that just something he said during sex or was it something he said during sex with *me*? The thought made a flush creep into my face. I ducked my face to hide it.

"I wasn't sure you did," he said, "with you leaving before I woke up and everything."

"Was that a first for you?" I asked, smiling at his handsome, serious face. He smiled slightly.

"You could say that."

"How are we supposed to go to breakfast without it looking like something is going on?"

He was dressed in jeans and a button-up shirt, looking hot as fuck, especially now that I knew what was beneath his clothes. Despite the burn in my inner thighs, I wanted to strip him and climb him again.

He looked thoughtful for a moment and sighed, running a hand through his hair. "You're right."

"I'm beginning to sense a theme here," I said, smirking. "Me leaving, me being right . . ." His scowl encouraged me to continue. "You know what's funny? The world seems to think that women are the chasers after a one-night stand. That we go along with it and then are all broken-hearted when the guy doesn't call, because God forbid we use what's between our legs to have fun the way guys do." I paused to smile. His ears were red, which made me smile harder. "So I think it's funny that you, Mr. *I Have Work to Do* came over here to chase me down."

He was quiet for a beat before reaching down to pick up Bonnie and going inside my house. I followed, confused, but still feeling like I had the upper hand, until I shut the door and curtain and turned around to find Victor taking long strides toward me. I took a step back, my heart rate spiking at the sight of his narrowed eyes on mine, his head slightly tilted as he appraised me. When he reached me and placed both arms on either side of me, caging me in, I swallowed as I looked up at him.

"Like I said, people change. Besides, that's how it works in nature," he said, his eyes on mine. "Most of the time, males chase until the woman is forced to cave."

"And that's what you're trying to do? Force me to cave?" I asked in a whisper.

"I'll do whatever it takes if it makes you cave to this," he said, lowering his voice.

"You're not afraid of the consequences anymore?" I asked.

"I am." He paused, his eyes searching mine. "I think you might be worth it, though."

Even if my galloping heart would have let me speak, I had no response for that. This careful man who cared about his job more than anything else had taken a chance and chased me down, and it thrilled me.

"Come to breakfast with me," he said. "I'll leave through the back. We'll take separate cars, but come."

I nodded, in awe of what was happening, and when he lowered his face and brushed his lips against mine, I reached out and pulled him closer into me, taking his mouth in mine, and kissing him deeply. He groaned against my lips before pulling away.

"I'll text you the address."

"Okay," I whispered.

I fed Bonnie before I walked to my car. On my way there, I sidestepped a jogger, almost losing balance because I was looking down at my phone screen.

"Nicole," he said. My head snapped up from my phone, where I was typing a response to Victor, letting him know I was on my way.

"Hey," I said, smiling at the hot jogger I'd met the other day. I couldn't for the life of me remember his name. It must have been apparent from the face I made because he chuckled and said.

"Brent."

I smiled. "Brent. Sorry. How are you?"

"Better now," he said, eyes glimmering as he gave me a once-over. "I'm assuming you're not headed to the beach."

"Not today. I still haven't been able to enjoy the perks of living here." I sighed. "I work all day tomorrow, so that's not looking promising either."

"On a Sunday? Tough job."

"You can say that." I looked up and down the sidewalk. "It was nice seeing you again."

"Maybe Monday?" he said. I looked at him with a frown.

"The beach?"

"Oh." I thought about it. "Maybe."

He smiled. "I'm going on my run at noon. It's the perfect time to catch rays."

"Maybe I'll see you then," I said with a smile.

I watched him jog away. He was really freaking hot. Twelve months of zero interaction by any straight male and suddenly I had their attention. Unfortunately for the rest of them, my heart was set on one. I shook my head and sighed as I walked toward my car.

Chapter Twenty-Two

Victor

I GOT TO my parents' house earlier than usual and dropped the bomb about Nicole coming over. My dad didn't say anything, only raised his eyebrows. My mom, on the other hand, gasped and covered her mouth as if I was announcing my engagement.

"She's just a friend, Mom," I said. "A friend who I also happen to be representing in her divorce."

"Oh. Dammit, Victor. I thought you were bringing a girl-friend," she said, sighing. "Maybe she has friends."

"Please don't talk about my love life, Mom."

"What love life?" she asked. "You have no love life. Even your friends are somehow involved in your work."

I groaned. I really wished I could just be straight and tell her how I felt about Nicole, but *I* didn't even know how I felt about Nicole. I felt this overwhelming sense of needing to see her again after last night. So overwhelming that I panicked when I realized she'd left. Panicked and chased her down. I had to. And then she'd tried to treat it like a one-night stand, as if I would jeopardize my job for a fucking one-night stand. I wanted to tell her to pack a bag and go away with me, but she'd mentioned that she had to work Sunday, so I knew she wouldn't do it. Restaurants were out of the question because they were so public and I really wanted to touch her. I wanted to talk to her and look at her openly.

My phone rang in my pocket, pulling me out of my thoughts. I looked at it and frowned at Quinn's name. Quinn was the founder of one of the biggest gossip blogs in the world, so big they'd turned it into a television series. He only called me on a weekend when something important was going on.

"What's up, Q?" I asked upon answering.

"Dude. I was going to call last night, but then I got busy. How's everything?"

"Everything was good until I saw your name on my phone screen."

He laughed. "Yeah. Well. Yeah."

I raised an eyebrow. My parents were watching me, so I put a hand up and excused myself, walking outside. "What's up?"

"Somebody has been contacting one of my photographers and having him follow Nicole Lane."

"Alessi. She never changed her name," I said, my blood simmering at the mention of her name. "We knew she was being watched."

"Hmm."

"What?"

"I'm going to text message you some pictures right now. Look at them while we're on the phone."

At the sound of the vibrate, I pulled my phone down and looked at the text. It was a picture of Nicole and me on her balcony. I recognized it as the day she was inspecting it. In the photo we were standing very close to each other, looking into each other's eyes. To an outsider it looked like we were about to kiss.

The next picture was more of the same. Close. Almost kissing. My heart hammered. The way she was looking at me in those pictures was so fucking intimate. From the look in her eyes . . . from the look in *my* eyes, there was more than just lust going on there. We looked like we were . . . *holy shit*. I couldn't even bring myself to admit that, even though for the first time in a long time I wanted to explore the possibility. Under different circumstances, I would have. *Could have.*

"Your photographer took this?" I demanded.

"That's the thing, Vic, he didn't take these. These were brought to me. The ones he's taken of her have been just her doing everyday things."

"Who brought these to you? What did they say?"

"You know I can't give you my source. I'm showing these to you because you're my friend and I'm not going to put them out there, but I can't promise you that other blogs will extend the same courtesy."

Fuck. I sighed and closed my eyes. We were just talking. Just talking, but I knew they could potentially turn it into something more.

"I have more coming in tomorrow morning. I'll call you if I feel like it's anything you need to see."

"Call me if it's anything with her at all."

"Will do."

"Thanks, Q."

"Of course."

As we hung up, my parents' gate opened. I watched Oliver's black Cadillac pull up and Nicole's white Prius follow behind him. I felt a pang in my heart at the sight of her. She was so beautiful. I thought about the images on my phone. I remembered the very moment they were taken. I remembered my desperation and how badly I'd wanted to kiss her, touch her, hold her, fuck her. Make her mine. I'd gotten just a taste that day. Just a hint of what her lips felt like against mine. Our fate was set that day. Maybe even before then. Maybe it'd been set the day she stepped into that goddamn conference room wearing that tight-fitting dress and looking at me with her *fuck me* eyes. Whatever the case was, I would take care of this. I wouldn't tell her about the pictures. Not yet. Not until I had more information. The last thing I needed was a worried Nicole.

"Hey Chicken," I said as my sister walked over to me. She rolled her eyes and gave me a hug.

"Hey Vic. I see you invited Nicole."

"She can't go out to breakfast without being hounded. It was the least I could do," I said. Estelle shot me a look that said she didn't buy my story. I shrugged.

"Who's the girl?" Oliver asked as he greeted me.

"Nicole."

"The one married to that guy?"

"The one who *was* married to that guy," I said, at the same time as Nicole walked up and smiled at my words. She looked so fucking good in that long black dress she wore. I wanted to peel it off her and discover what she had underneath.

"Oliver," he said, offering his hand for her to shake. I wanted to kick his ass when he smiled at her like he was trying to flirt with her. "I hear I owe you a thank you for helping my wife and brother-in-law install my TV."

Nicole laughed. "Victor did most of the work. I just sat back and watched him *mount* it and drank the wine Estelle offered."

My heart hopped when she looked over at me with that flirty gleam in her eyes as she said it. Fuck. This girl did things to me. She did things to me and I realized something.

The woman I would have to let go of if I wanted to keep my career was the same woman I didn't want to live without.

How's that for life issues? I was half tempted to write a letter to Jensen Talks and see what my friend had to say about this fucked-up situation in the newspaper column he wrote. Oliver went inside and Estelle followed after she exchanged a tight hug with Nicole.

"Where did you bring me?" she asked, looking at the house.

"My parents' house."

From the look of sheer panic that crossed her face, I thought for a second time that maybe bringing her here was a bad idea. It was a good idea before I'd gotten that call, but now I knew what was to happen, I felt every part of me breaking down slowly, like a car running out of gas. I hated that feeling, and when Nicole's smile dropped and she frowned, I felt it punch me in the gut.

"You really need to come with a warning label," she said as she stepped in front of me. "A serious warning label. Are you regretting your decision? I can still leave." She brought her hand up to me face. She was so fucking sweet, thinking of my feelings before her own. Comforting me even though she had no clue what I was thinking. I closed my eyes and leaned into her touch; it was so soft, warm and inviting. I never wanted to leave. I never wanted to let go of this moment. I cleared my throat and straightened. What the fuck was going on with me?

"I'm fine," I said with a smile. "Come meet the people responsible for making the hottest man you've ever laid eyes on."

Nicole laughed beside me. "Oh my God."

I shrugged. Before I could say anything else, my mother walked toward us with a huge smile on her face, light eyes trained on Nicole.

"Hi. I'm Hannah, Victor's mom. It's so nice to meet you, Nicole," she said, walking up to her and giving her a hug. Nicole smiled, a little blush on her cheeks when she pulled back. She gave me an embarrassed glance that I'd never seen and wish I could record and watch forever.

"It's nice to meet you. Thank you for having me over," she said.

"Of course. Make yourself at home. Thomas. We have a guest," my mom shouted, taking Nicole by the hand and dragging her forward.

"Mom, she's not going to run away, you know," I said.

My mom looked over her shoulder and shot me a pointed look, mouthing the words "shut up." I couldn't help the laugh that escaped me. I mouthed the word "client" as a reminder, and she shrugged. I walked behind them and into the kitchen, where my dad also greeted Nicole with a hug.

"Where are you from?" he asked.

"Argentina," she said, smiling.

"Argentina. Beautiful place. Hannah and I have been there a couple of times. Great people. I'm Puerto Rican, and when I lived back home I made some connections in Argentina," he said as way of explanation.

"Oh, that's so cool. What do you do?" Nicole asked.

"I'm an orthodontist. It was cooler before I decided to slow down and stop traveling." He laughed when my mom nudged him in the ribs. "But of course that means I get to spend more time with my lovely wife," he said, pulling my mom into a side hug.

"You guys are gross," Estelle said. "Also, I set the table."

"Let's eat," my mom said.

We sat around the table, Oliver and Estelle on one side, me in my usual seat across from them, and Nicole in the normally empty seat beside me, while my dad sat at the head and my mom at the other end.

"I hope you eat carbs," my mom said, bringing out the first dish: waffles. Estelle stood and went to help her.

"I eat everything. Do you need help?" Nicole replied.

"No, no. Stay right there. I don't want Victor to have an early heart attack because we made one of his girl . . . friends work the first day he brought her over," my mom said.

I tucked my hand under the table and reached for Nicole's hand over her lap. She jumped at the notion, and I ran my thumb over her soft hand. I wanted to pull her close and kiss the hell out of her. Our fingers threaded around each other as if on autopilot, as if we held hands every day. It felt . . . right. It reminded me of what I had told Corinne about why I had never settled down. I couldn't deny that the ease I felt with Nicole by my side, with my family, *felt* right.

"What time do you have to be at work tomorrow?" I asked.

"Eight in the morning. It's supposed to be a twelve-hour day," she said. I leaned closer to her.

"Would you mind leaving your car here today and picking it up tomorrow after work?" I whispered in her ear. Her eyes widened as I backed away. She shook her head, then leaned in and whispered in mine.

"I don't have extra clothes, though."

"Neither do I. We can stop somewhere along the way."

She smiled, a big, happy smile. "Okay."

Breakfast was great. Oliver talked about the kids at work. I tried not to talk about work at all, which brought on a conversation about what a workaholic I was. Nicole talked about her job, which had Estelle and my mom enraptured. My mom practically begged her to design a dress for a friend's daughter's wedding.

"She's been looking everywhere for somebody. Don't you think this is the perfect solution?" she asked when I told her to please stop.

"That's not what Nicole does," I said defensively.

"I can," Nicole said. I looked at her, trying to read her and

make sure that she was okay with it. She didn't know how annoying my mom could get about things she wanted to get done.

"She can be difficult to work with," I said, squeezing her
hand a little. "You have a lot on your plate."

"I can handle everything on my plate."

That smile accompanying the words with made me want to
be everything on that goddamn plate. Once we were done eating, my mom, Nicole, and Estelle went off to the office room to
talk about the dress, and my dad, Oliver, and I went to the living
room to watch college football.

"Are we on for tomorrow?" Oliver asked every weekend
and every weekend for over ten years I'd always responded a
solid yes. This time, I hesitated. Sure, I'd have Nicole back in
time for work, but I also had to meet with Quinn, and that was
a priority to me.

"I'll have to let you know in the morning," I said. Oliver
balked.

"You're . . . kidding."

"I have work to do tomorrow."

His eyes widened. He looked around, at my dad, who was
dozing off on the recliner, the television, as if Lee Corso had the
answers to whatever question he had, and finally he looked at
me again, jaw still dropped.

"I've known you most of me life, Vic. We've been through
some real shit together," he said, pausing. "And I . . ." he sighed,
shaking his head, "I'm not going to say anything. I'm not going
to get involved. I just hope you're thinking this through."

"Nothing is going on," I said. He shot me a *don't give me
that shit* look.

"Tell that to someone who doesn't know you. Actually, forget it. Even a goddamn blind man can see that something is
definitely going on. You better be fucking careful."

I groaned, but didn't respond. I knew he was right.

"Like I said, be careful."

I *was* being careful. I was about to take the girl to Newport Beach so that we could be together without worrying about getting caught. How was that for careful? Though the more I thought about it the less I knew if I was being careful or just needy for wanting her this badly. But I wasn't a needy guy. Just careful. I wasn't an idiot. I knew I couldn't have both. I knew that if those pictures got out, I would have to let her go until she was no longer my client. We would be fine. We'd done it once before. *But she moved on that time.*

Thinking that made me feel sick.

She'd moved on and got married.

I'd told her she was mine—pounded that into her—as if that alone could keep her around.

From every which angle I thought about it, *I was fucked.*

Chapter Twenty-Three

Nicole

"Y OUR PARENTS ARE the sweetest people ever," I said, smiling as I waved to his mom while getting into the passenger seat of his car. "I don't know how they ended up with a grouch like you."

I inhaled, like I usually did when I was in his car. It had a new-car smell. How? I didn't know. Mine lost that smell after two weeks. Probably because I ate so many In-N-Out burgers in it. Victor didn't say anything, instead he reached for my hand and threaded his fingers through mine. My heart skipped a beat every time he did that. Every time he touched me. Every time he freaking looked at me. I felt like a ridiculous junior in high school who had a crush on the star quarterback. I just couldn't get enough of him.

Victor chuckled. "They really like you."

"I really like them."

"*I* really like you."

My heart summersaulted into my stomach and back up. Oh my God. I was going to die via sweet nothings from Victor Reuben. I really was, and damn what a beautiful death it would be.

"I like you too," I whispered. I felt my cheeks burn as I smiled and looked over at him. We were stopped at a red light that changed to green and he was just looking at me without a care in the world. He leaned in as if to kiss me and I said, "The light is green. People are honk—"

"Fuck them. Let them honk," he said, his lips grazing mine.

I forgot how to breathe, let alone how to complain. I grabbed his face and kissed him back amidst the honking behind us. He pulled back slightly, gaze tender on mine, as if he were seeing me for the first time. As if he were just now realizing his words about liking me were actually true. I smiled softly, and he mimicked it as he pulled back. Somebody else honked and Victor stuck his middle finger up.

"Idiot."

I slapped my palm on my forehead and lowered myself into the seat. "Victor."

"What? People act like they can't wait three seconds. Like they have somewhere important to be on a Saturday afternoon."

I laughed. "Maybe it's a doctor."

"Well, they should've left their house ten minutes early so they wouldn't have to deal with assholes like me."

"Oh my God. You are so fucking crazy."

Without looking away from the road he lifted my hand and brought it up to his mouth. "And you love it," he said, kissing my palm lightly before nipping it with his teeth.

I yanked it away. I really did love it, but I would never in a million years tell him that. "So, where are we going to stop to buy clothes? Target?"

"I was going to take you to Nordstrom, but if Target is good with you, let's go there."

I laughed. "Well, I'm not going to pass up Nordstrom."

"Nah, Target was your first choice."

I poked him in the ribs and he laughed, taking his hand off the gear to catch my hand and bite the tips my fingers until I yelped. He let go and shot me a look, raising a brow in challenge. I smiled and looked out the window. He turned the radio up a little and started bobbing his head to the Bryson Tiller song playing.

"I like you like this," I said after a while. He lowered the music a little.

"How?"

I shrugged. "Not cautious."

He looked over at me quickly, tilting his head a bit before looking back at the road ahead. He didn't acknowledge my statement, instead turning up the radio again and singing along. We talked and sang and scrolled through different songs on the playlist he had set up in the memory of his car. I made fun of him for having Justin Beiber on there, and he assured me that it was Estelle's doing.

"Liar," I scoffed.

He shrugged. "Maybe I like some of his new songs."

"I knew it," I said and paused as I continued scrolling. "You know, for a half Puerto Rican guy who doesn't speak Spanish, you listen to a lot of Hispanic artists."

He chuckled. "I never said I didn't speak Spanish."

"Do you?"

"Un poquito."

I smiled wide. "My mom will be pleased to hear that."

"How often do you visit her?"

"Not as often as I would like," I said, sighing. I put my hand over his on the gearshift. "I'll probably go over there in a month when we're done filming this movie."

He gave me a sharp nod, opening his fingers to hold on to mine. "I would offer to go with you, but your Spanish is completely different than mine, and I probably wouldn't understand anything you guys are saying."

I laughed. "I'll teach you."

"I'll hold you to that."

I felt my heart expand. Was he serious? Gabe never cared about any of that, though he did go with me to see my mom a couple times when we first got married. I smiled at the memory of him eating a ridiculous amount of steak and getting a stomach ache for the rest of the trip. He was so funny then. So willing to please me. I sighed, looking out the window again. There was construction in the canyon we were near and I was grateful we were driving along it during the day. I always had a fear of driving so close to the edges of the canyons, despite the barricades that were supposed to keep the car from actually falling into it.

Victor pulled into the parking lot of Target a few minutes later. I couldn't even imagine this Armani-suit-wearing man's man at Target, and I couldn't wait to experience it with him.

"Let's get what we need first, like body wash," he suggested, steering the cart to the right.

"Okay. Should we get snacks?" I asked, eyeing the chips on the way over.

"Are you planning on kidnapping me for more than a day?" he asked, looking over at me. I shook my head, smiling. *I totally should, though.*

"Then no snacks needed. We'll go to dinner at the hotel."

The hotel. Oh my God. I was going to stay at a hotel with this man. I had to bite down on the inside of my cheek to contain my giddiness. Much to Victor's amusement, I sent Talon a text message and asked her if she could watch Bonnie. *That's why I don't have pets,* he'd said. *I don't have time for more stress.* Shopping with Victor was worse than shopping with Talon or Chrissy. The guy took forever to decide what shorts he should buy: cargo or not. Then, button-up or polo. Then, socks for the shoes he had on or flip-flops? And all the while, he was acting weird, looking around, keeping his distance from where I was standing, not looking me in the eye. Somewhere between the men's underwear and the pajamas, I got sick of it.

"Why are you acting so weird?" I asked, pivoting to face him with my hands on my hips.

"What do you mean?" he asked, picking up the bottom of the oversized Batman footie pajamas in front of him. Still avoiding my eyes. "Who the hell buys this?"

"Victor."

"Really, though, who over the age of twelve months wear this?" he said, ignoring me.

"Victor," I said, raising my voice. I felt my face burning with anger. "Stop looking at the ridiculous pajamas and look at me right now."

He whipped his head to look at me, letting his hands drop to his sides. Now that I had his full attention, his eyes on mine like that, I lost my train of thought.

"What?"

"Why are you acting distant?" I asked, lowering my voice and stepping closer to him.

He let out a heavy sigh and stepped even closer, until we were toe to toe and reached his hand out to take mine.

"My mind is just . . . occupied."

"Occupied," I repeated, taking his hand and wrapping it around my body so he was holding me against his chest. He dropped his face into my hair and inhaled deeply.

"Occupied," he murmured against my ear.

"We're far enough from home that we can act like we know each other, Vic."

"I know, baby. I know," he said, dropping a kiss on my temple, and another on my cheek. "For the rest of the weekend, you're the only thing occupying my mind, okay?"

I pulled back to look at him. "Only this weekend?"

He looked at me for a beat. "Oh, Nicole. What am I going to do with you?"

He pressed his lips against my forehead as he dropped his hands and started to walk toward the T-shirts, shaking his head as he did. I smiled when I heard him rambling about how much time I occupy in his mind. He went back to looking at every piece of clothing in the men's section. What shorts should he get? Cargo or not? Khakis or denim?

"Are you kidding me, Victor?" I demanded, finally. I took the cargo shorts, the non-cargo shorts, the polo, the button-up, the socks, and the flip-flops and threw it in the cart. "You act like you can't afford all of it."

He pointed at me. "That's the kind of mentality that makes people Target's bitch."

"Yeah, well, I was put in that category a long time ago. I don't plan on getting out of there any time soon. Besides, Red Card."

He shook his head, but kept walking toward the women's section. I took two seconds while he was on the phone to get what I needed before moving to the underwear. Suddenly Victor told his caller that he "needed to go because he had something important to do." I rolled my eyes as I sorted through the bras.

"This one's nice," he said, holding up a bra a row over. I frowned.

"That's like . . . a D."

He examined it better. "Yeah, you're right. How'd you know?"

I raised my eyebrows and shook my head, going back to my

section.

"What about this one?"

"Thank God we're not in Victoria's Secret," I muttered, looking over again. He was holding up a sheer bra. I laughed. "That one's good."

"34 C, baby," he said loudly. I felt my face turn a shade of red as a woman walked by us. She shot me an amused look.

"Excuse him, he doesn't Target much," I said with a smile.

The woman laughed and walked away.

I gasped when Victor came up behind me and wrapped his arms around me. "You're having way too much fun with this," he said into my ear.

"Just a little," I said, smiling. "Did you get my bra, honey?"

"I sure did, baby."

"Let's go," I said, starting to walk. He held me tight in his hold so I couldn't move and kissed my cheek.

"You make me this way," he said. The tone of his voice made my insides rattle. I tilted my head to look up at him.

"Like what?" I whispered.

"Not cautious," he said, snuggling into my neck. "I feel free when I'm with you."

I closed my eyes and leaned into him. It felt so good to be in his arms like that, away from it all, without fear we'd get caught. He pressed his lips against the side of my temple and dropped his hands.

"Let's go. I'm only getting you underwear because you'll need them for work tomorrow. Don't even think about wearing them to bed tonight," he said, slapping my ass as he walked away. I laughed as I followed behind him.

When we got to the front of the line, the cashier tried to talk Victor into signing up for a credit card, and he started rambling about credit lines and stores that want to lock you in and keep you in debt. The woman laughed.

"All right then," she said, shaking her head as she looked at me. "Good luck with this one, hon."

"Oh, no. We're not together," I said, wrinkling my nose. "Too straight-laced for me."

Victor narrowed his eyes at me. I smiled at him and shrugged. The woman laughed again. We left and on our way to the car Victor held the bags in one hand and wrapped his free arm around me body, lifting me off the ground.

"Straight-laced, huh?" he growled. "I'll show you straight-laced."

I laughed the entire way to the car. When he set me down I reached up and kissed him. "I was just kidding."

"Too late."

I smiled. "You should let me drive."

He balked at me, pausing as he put our things in the trunk. "You've completely lost your mind."

"Why not?"

"Because it's my car and nobody drives my car."

I jutted my bottom lip out. "Please?"

His gaze dropped to my lips. "No."

"You really wouldn't let me drive your car?" I asked, putting my hands on my hips.

Victor looked at me for a long, quiet moment. He sighed. "Do you know how to drive stick?"

"I'm very good with a stick," I said with a wink. He wasn't having it.

"I'm serious."

"Yes, Victor," I said, rolling my eyes. "Give me the damn keys. I'll take care of your baby."

He wasn't happy about it, but he handed over the keys. I was sure he regretted it instantly when I jumped up and cheered, doing a little dance as I made my way over to the driver's seat.

"God help me," he said, making the sign of the cross as he sat down in the passenger seat. I laughed.

"He gives a girl his car keys and suddenly he becomes a born-again Christian."

He huffed, looking out the window. "I'm Catholic."

I laughed harder. I started the car and pushed down on the petal, clapping at the sound of the purr before I took off.

"You need to tell me where to go."

"You need to stop talking and focus on driving."

"I can drive and talk at the same time."

"I don't care."

"Why don't you go back to praying? You were much less annoying," I said, but I couldn't help my smile. He was kind of adorable when he was like this.

"Nicole," he groaned, "just . . . please stop talking. You're making me nervous."

I laughed. When I reached a stoplight, I turned the music up. "Is Selena Gomez also on your playlist?"

He sighed. "No, Nicole."

"Straight-laced."

"Wait 'til we get our room," he said. "I'm going to fuck you until you can't talk anymore."

I sighed. "Goals."

He stayed quiet for a beat. "What's up with that?"

"What?"

"Goals. You say that all the time. Why?"

I smiled. Of course Victor didn't know what that was about. "You mean you can't deduce what it may mean?"

"I can deduce it, yes. I just don't know if my deduction is correct."

"Tell me what you think it is."

"I don't know. When you like something or you want to do something, you say goals? Is it like a bucket list of sorts?"

"Yeah, I guess."

"Hmm."

I looked at him from the corner of my eyes. "Do you have any goals?"

He was quiet for a moment. I thought maybe he hadn't heard me over the music, but then he said quietly, "I do have goals." He didn't elaborate, so I didn't push him.

We got to the hotel, checked in, went to dinner, laughed our asses off as Victor came up with a story for every old man in the restaurant. I'd missed this. Fun. Laughter. Feeling carefree. I realized in the last eighteen months, I'd become a reclusive, introverted side of myself, one I couldn't entirely get used to. With Victor, I slowly felt I was getting myself back. *Finding me.*

"So basically all of their wives married them for money," I said, taking a sip of my Riesling.

He shrugged. "Basically."

"Do you ever want to get married?" I asked.

His eyes snapped to mine, and for a moment I got lost in their intensity, the greens mixing with the browns, and the blue undertones swirling around.

"Maybe . . . probably."

My eyebrows rose. "Really?"

"Yes, really. Why is that so hard to believe?"

"I don't know. I just didn't take you for the married type."

His lips twitched. "You only took me for the random hook-ups in his office type?"

"I guess so?" I smiled. "At least I didn't assume you'd hooked up with any previous clients."

His eyes dropped to the table, and my stomach went with them.

"Have you?" I asked. I wasn't sure why it bothered me. Suddenly, I felt disgusted. The way I felt when I found out Gabe had potentially cheated on me. My stomach turned at the thought of Victor with another woman, driving her away like this to not get caught. He was quiet for so long, that my mind threatened to run off into the realm of visualization. Victor with some prissy redhead, or skinny blonde, everything I wasn't. His deep chuckle cut through my thoughts.

"No, Nicole. You're my first. And last."

My heart pounded loudly at his admission, at those words and the way he said them. I narrowed my eyes at him despite the way I was feeling.

"Asshole," I said. He laughed harder, and even though I was laughing along and felt a sense of ease at his words, I wondered if he felt the same. I cleared my throat. "Would it bother you if somebody asked me out on a date?"

His laughter stopped instantly. "Why? Who asked you out? That asshole realtor?"

That made me laugh. "No. You know there are more men in the world, right?"

"Who asked you out?"

"Some guy. A neighbor of mine."

"What's his name?"

"Why do you need to know his name?" I asked, frowning. "It's not like you know my neighbors."

"You can tell a lot about a person from their name."

I laughed. "Brent."

He shot me a look. "You're going to go out with a guy named Brent?"

"What's wrong with that?"

"Everything." He stood up and folded his napkin on the table. "Ready?"

By the look in his eyes, the thought of me on a date wasn't sitting well with him. He looked . . . demanding. Intense. *Sexy.* Irresistible. I put my hand in his and stood. He brought it up to his lips and kissed it before pulling me closer and walking toward our room. I expected him to throw me against the door the moment we walked in. Instead, he'd said he was going to shower first because he needed to make a phone call to follow up with a client. I couldn't say I wasn't a little disappointed, but I took it in stride. He'd brought me here to spend time with *him,* away from prying eyes. I'd seen the desire in his eyes. I knew he wanted this as badly as I did, but I also knew work was a priority, and I wasn't going to act like a child over it.

The shower switched on as I was unpacking our things and removing the tags. I tried not to picture him naked on the other side of the door, but it was difficult not to visualize the water dripping down his hard body. I groaned, and when he walked out of the bathroom wearing a white bathrobe, I had to take a calming breath to regain composure.

"I'll only be fifteen minutes," he said, kissing the top of my head. I wanted to tuck my hands inside the robe and climb him like a fucking tree, but I nodded and brushed past him instead, taking my new underwear with me.

When I walked out of the bathroom wearing a white fluffy robe, I found Victor sitting at the edge of the bed with his phone in his hand. As soon as he sensed me come in, his head snapped up. He took in my appearance and pushed a button down on his phone, slinging it to the couch beside him. I untied the robe and parted it to show off my new lingerie.

"You like me in my sexy Target bra?" I asked, placing a hand on my hip and jutting it out as I modeled for him. He nodded, eyes hooded as they raked over my body.

"I like you in any bra. Every bra. But I prefer no bra," he

said, voice raspy, eyes darkened with desire. "Strip for me."

My stomach flip flopped at the command in his voice. *Strip. For. Me.* I swallowed and started to lower the shoulders of the robe, letting it drop and pool at my feet. My bra came next; I unclasped it and took it off slowly. Victor spread his legs farther apart. He was wearing his own robe and a devilish grin that made my knees quiver.

"What are you wearing under that?" I asked, tossing my bra aside. His eyes fell to my naked chest.

"Why don't you come find out?"

I walked forward, stopping right between his knees, close enough for him to reach out and grab me, but far enough that he couldn't put his mouth on me without pulling me to him, which was what he did, his arms circling around my waist and tugging me. He placed his mouth on my stomach, kissing me lightly. I felt the effect of his mouth everywhere.

"Are you ready for me, Nicole?" he asked against me, his mouth moving lower, to my belly button, his light beard grazing my panty line. "If I keep going down, will you be wet?"

My breath hitched. I nodded.

He glanced up, his eyes locked on mine. "Tell me."

"Yes."

"Yes what?" he asked, licking along the top of my panties. I repressed the urge to shiver, my hands shooting out to grab his hair.

"Yes. I'm wet," I said in a shaky whisper.

He groaned, letting his forehead fall against my stomach for a beat before hooking his fingers on either side of my panties and sliding them down. He grabbed my thighs and made a groaning sound in the back of this throat.

"I fucking love your legs, Nic," he said, gripping the backs of my legs and biting the front. I cried out. "Do you like that, baby?"

I whimpered out, "Yes."

"You like it when I'm rough with you?" he asked, sliding his fingers between my thighs, gliding along my folds. I pulled his hair tighter and moaned. "Do you want me to go slow?" He tilted his face to look up at me as he leaned in and sucked on my clit. My knees buckled.

"Oh my God, Victor."

He smiled against me. I couldn't see his lips on me, but I could see it in his eyes. "Say it again," he said, licking me. "Say my name, baby."

"Victor," I said, throwing my head back in a moan when he inserted his fingers into me and continued to lick my clit. "Victor." I said his name again, and again in a whispered chant. "I'm going to come."

He groaned deeply, and I felt it vibrate everywhere. "Come for me, baby. Show me how ready for me you are." His fingers worked faster inside me, his tongue lashing against me until my eyes rolled back and my knees gave out and I was only standing upright because he'd grabbed my hips. He was reaching for the condom beside him when I caught my breath and opened my eyes, and I stopped him, kneeling between his legs and parting his robe to expose his hard, thick cock. My heart skipped a beat at the sight of it. I licked my lips and looked from it to his face.

"Nicole—" he started to say, but I cut his sentence short by licking the tip of his cock and taking him into my mouth. His hand gripped a fistful of my hair as he muttered a string of curse words. "Fucking shit, that feels so fucking good. Oh my fucking God. Your mouth. Your fucking mouth." His words became unintelligible as I continued to suck, bobbing my head up and down, his dick popping in and out of my mouth loudly. His breathing was labored and loud, and I loved the look of awe on his face when my eyes met his momentarily. He pulled my hair hard and successfully popped out of my mouth and leaned down to crash his lips against mine.

"I need to fuck you," he said, reaching for the condom and sliding it on. "I need to feel you."

I nodded and stood, putting one leg over each of his and pushing his chest back so he was lying flat on his back. "I'm going to ride you," I said. "And you're not going to remember any woman you fucked before me."

His lips tilted into a slow, tantalizing smile as he gripped two handfuls of my ass, helping me climb on him and settle myself on the tip. "Show me, baby. Make me scream your name."

Oh, I would. As I placed my hands on his shoulders and lowered myself onto him slowly, I wondered if he realized how sexy those words sounded to me. I held my breath as I let myself acclimate to his girth. I was still sore from yesterday, and I remembered it as I completely sat on his lap. I cringed and gasped.

"You okay?" he asked in a quiet voice, as he sat up again, his hands pushing my hair out of my face. I nodded, though my eyes filled with unshed tears. It was too much suddenly, having his face in front of mine, his heart beating against mine, his eyes trained on mine. In that one instance, where he was looking at me like I was the only woman he'd ever really seen, I felt everything.

Everything.

This was so much more than the last time. So much more than the times before that. And it was terrifying.

"Nic, are you okay?" he asked, his voice a whisper.

I nodded, blinking rapidly. "I'm fine. Just a little sore, but this feels good. I'm fine."

He looked at me for a beat, until I started to grind against him and he threw his head back with a loud growl. "You feel so fucking good."

I kept moving, up and down, slowly at first, and then picked up the pace. I tried not to look into his eyes. I tried to focus on the shape of his muscular arms, the definition of his chest, the way he bit his bottom lip every time I clenched. He gripped my ass harder, moving me up and down with ease as if I weighed nothing. His eyes snapped open at the sound of my moan. When he lifted me, his mouth closed over my left breast, his tongue teasing, his lips grazing against me.

"You make me desperate for you, Nicole," he growled, cradling the back of my head and crashing my lips to his. "You're fucking mine."

I nodded, slowing my pace and closing my eyes to hold back tears. "Yes."

"Say it. Tell me," he said, his lips against mine, his tongue doing a slow sweep of my mouth, playing with mine, teasing, sucking. "Tell me you're mine."

"I can't," I whispered. I felt the familiar burn building inside. "I'm so close. So close."

Victor gripped my thighs, trapping me so I couldn't move. "Look at me."

I opened my eyes and my heart skipped.

"Tell. Me," he said, pumping me up and down once. I moaned.

"Please, Victor."

"Tell me." He moved again, standing up and pumping me up and down as he stood, my legs wrapping around his waist. He was so deep like this.

So deep.

So good.

I grind against him, trying to reach my resolve. "Why won't you say it?"

I grabbed the back of his head and pulled him into a kiss, making him forget for a moment. He walked and thrust deeper, walked and thrust harder, biting my bottom lip as he did it. My moan was deep and long, a mix of a growl and an *I'm yours* as I reached my climax. He thrust inside me a few times more, long and deep, growling a "fuck, yes," as he reached his own.

Chapter Twenty-Four

Victor

I KNOW WHEN a woman is falling for me. I know because I usually leave right before it happens. Right before she gets that look in her eyes that says *this could be us* when I'm fucking her. Nicole had that look tonight. I saw it. She'd had that look while we were at my parents', while we were out shopping, and as she'd handed my keys to the valet when we'd arrived at the hotel. And I couldn't fathom leaving her, even though I had to. I had to. I should. Not because I wanted to, because for once *I didn't*. For the first time that look on *her* face most likely mirrored mine. But my career was on the line as well as her reputation, and those were two things I wasn't willing to mess with. I sighed and ran my fingers through her hair. Her face was on my shoulder, her lips slightly parted as she slept peacefully. It looked like a scene right out of a goddamn romance movie. Me watching her like a total creeper while she slept peacefully.

"I think I'm falling in love with you," I whispered as she slept. "And I really don't fucking want to. You probably don't even want a serious relationship right now. You probably just want to have fun." I sighed. "But the thought of you having fun and being like this with anybody but me . . . kills me."

I stopped talking when she groaned and moved against me, leaving some drool on my shoulder as she moved her head. I chuckled. That was a first. That's what I get for letting her snuggle up on me and shit. She was so cute when she slept, though. Probably because she wasn't talking or taunting me. Most likely because she was on me, though. Nicole Alessi on top of me was my new favorite sight. Nicole Alessi anywhere near me was my new favorite sight. On me, under me, next to me . . . This was bad. Really fucking bad. I was starting to think like Oliver . . . or worse . . . Jensen. Fuck. I couldn't possibly have the same love-struck fool look on my face as those two did when they looked at their wives. I adjusted her so she was on the pillow and no longer on me, but I kept my fingers running through her hair because it was soft and doing it soothed me.

"Just . . . promise me that when I let you go you won't run into another man's arms. You're mine, Nicole. We just need to get through this. We need to sort this out and let it blow over. It's just a break. Just a short break," I said, sighing and pulling her closer to me. "Good talk."

Fuck my life. I finally had somebody I wanted to keep in my life, and she had to be the only one I couldn't have. I knew letting it get this far before finalizing everything in her divorce made me a complete idiot, but there was no stopping. And having her, kissing her, fucking her, being beside her like this made that clear. The issue now was that I wasn't sure my heart could take it if she didn't believe a short break was all it would be. I'm not sure I would believe her if she said she'd wait for me. That hadn't been the plan before, but I needed it to be this time. Fuck all of this.

The phone rang way too fucking early, but I'd set the call an hour earlier than we needed just in case, and I was glad. Nicole kept rubbing her ass on my hard-on and there was no way I wasn't going to take advantage.

"Hmm . . . that feels good," she said, moving her hips when I tucked my fingers between her legs and started strumming on her clit.

"I'm going to make you feel very good," I said against her ear as I thrust inside her. She yelped.

"Holy . . . Victor."

I chuckled, biting down on the skin between her neck and shoulder. "There's nothing holy about Victor."

I moved us so she was on her knees and I was bent over behind her, holding her hips to meet my thrusts. I wanted to slow down for her, but everything about her had me on overdrive. I couldn't be near her and not go full throttle. She pushed back onto me, and I groaned at the feel of her clenching around me. I slapped her ass.

"Fuck," she said, clenching harder. She was so wet for me. I slapped her ass again. "Victor."

I couldn't take it anymore. I reached for her hair and looped it around my hand, pulling her toward me as I pounded into her. I was sure between the two of us, we alerted everybody within a fifteen-mile radius that we were fucking, but I didn't care. My only regret was that I was wearing a condom. I wanted to feel her on me. And I would. Not today, but soon. *I hoped.*

We took a long time in the shower, because the way the soap ran down her curves and her tits as she washed her hair distracted me.

"Stop touching me," she groaned when I pushed her against the wall. "I'm going to be late."

"Fuck that job," I said, taking her lips in mine. She laughed against me.

"Would you say fuck your job and skip work tomorrow if I

asked you to?" she asked.

I pulled back, grazing the pad of my thumb over her nipple. She groaned and pushed onto me. I held her gaze.

"I would. If you asked me to, I would," I said, and I meant it. If she asked me to take a day off, I'd do it. She looked as surprised as I felt. Without another word, she lifted herself up and wrapped her legs around my waist, clinging on to me.

"I'm really sore," she whispered. "Really sore. But I want you."

I shook my head, holding her in place. "I don't want to hurt you."

Her blue eyes searched mine. "Rain check?"

I nodded with a smile. She must have sensed my uneasiness, because she narrowed her eyes.

"Promise?"

"Promise."

She looked at me for a beat longer before putting her legs down and turning around to finish washing. My heart dropped to my stomach. I felt like shit. I didn't make promises I didn't keep. Ever. And that was one I wasn't sure I could keep even if I wanted to. I tried to put it out of my mind. No use in thinking about it now. I'd deal with it when I had to. I needed to meet with Quinn before I jumped to any conclusions. We ordered breakfast and took it on the road. We were both quiet, contemplative, as if we'd been changed by our little outing. Maybe we had been. Whenever I looked over at her, she looked like she was lost in thought. In an effort not to rock the boat, I didn't say anything at all.

We kissed when I dropped her off in front of the lot, and she thanked me.

"I'll get a ride to your parents' house," she said. "I have your mom and Estelle's number, so I'll be fine if you're busy."

Why would I be busy? I wanted to ask, but didn't. Instead I nodded.

"Thank you," she whispered as she got out of the car, her back facing me.

"Thank you," I whispered back, wanting to reach out to touch her. Instead, I let her go. I wasn't sure I could watch her walk away again, so I turned my face and looked the other way. And I think we both knew it was more than just a drop off.

"Who did you piss off?" was the first thing Quinn asked upon my answering my phone the following day.

I'd heard from Nicole late last night when she was still at work and I could hear the exhaustion in her voice as we spoke, so I kept the conversation short. Short and sweet, though it didn't feel that way, because after we hung up I felt like I couldn't bear to listen to her voice again until this thing with the pictures got resolved, which was what I hoped to do today.

"I'm assuming you're going to spit it out and not make me beat it out of you," I responded. Quinn laughed.

"Are you in the area?"

"I actually am," I said as I drove past the café he and I frequented. "Usual spot?"

"Be there in five. Bring your laptop."

The call ended and my Bluetooth shut off, the sound of classical music circulating the airwave of my car again. I turned the steering wheel and made a U-turn at the light, going back to the café. We pulled up at the same time, me in my Jaguar, and Quinn in his Mercedes-Maybach S600. The guy had made a killing exploiting celebrities and reaped the benefits quite openly with his extravagant purchases. He had a different car for every day of the week and mansions in three different countries; all of them worth more money than I'd probably ever see in my lifetime. He gave his keys to the valet, walking around the back with an oomph in his step that made women's heads turn. He was a cocky motherfucker. Rightfully so. His smile was wide as I approached and he leaned in to give me a side hug.

"My man," he said.

"Just when I was starting to think the world may be a peaceful place," I said, backing out of the hug. "The devil himself calls me up."

Quinn chuckled. "Gotta keep you on your toes."

I shook my head, smiling as we walked into the café and walked toward the table in the upper right corner. We always sat at the same one. Even when I came in without him, I saw him at the same one.

"Do you lease this table?"

"Basically," he said, smiling. I could tell there was something more to his smile, but didn't ask. Quinn had a don't-tell policy, and while he'd shared private things about his life with me in the past, he tried to avoid getting personal with anyone.

"What do you have for me?" I asked after we each ordered our food and drinks.

His brows rose as he sat back in his seat, and lifted the glass of water to his mouth. "How many clients do you have right now?"

He loved playing a game of cat and mouse before handing out cheese. I ran through my mental catalogue, knowing he wouldn't meet me to give me bullshit stories about closed cases. He knew what high-profile divorces I was working on. With the media, it was impossible for anybody not to know. Something about the gleam in his eyes made me uneasy. I narrowed my eyes a bit.

"I'm not in the mood for games today. The pictures you sent me the other day were nothing."

His expression turned serious as he set the glass of water down. "How much is Nicole Lane worth to you?"

My heart dropped. I stared at him for a long moment. "Her name is Nicole Alessi, and she doesn't have a price tag." I paused, feeling at odds with the situation for once. "Are you printing a story?"

"Not yet. I knew she was yours so I wanted to bring it to you first."

Mine. Clearly he didn't know the half of it if he was so nonchalant. I intended to keep it that way. He reached into the pocket of his jacket and took out a USB, setting it on the table and sliding it across.

"What's this?" I asked.

"Compromising pictures."

My throat tightened. I swallowed past the knot sitting there. I didn't want to ask what kind of pictures they were. I took the USB from the table and put it in the pocket of my jacket. My chest burned in that spot.

"How'd you get it?"

Quinn shot me a look. "How do I get anything?"

"Who's shopping this?"

"You know I can't give you a source."

Slow, hot anger started to burn through me. "This isn't . . ." I stopped talking when the waitress came by and put the plates on our table. "I can't have somebody shopping naked pictures of her right now."

"It's not just her that's naked," he said, taking a bite of the steak he ordered while I nearly choked on mine.

"What?"

Quinn nodded slowly. "I wanted to bring it to you first."

"Who else has seen this?" I asked, taking the USB out and reaching for the laptop in my briefcase.

"No clue," he said, shrugging. "As far as I know, I'm the only one. I usually get first dibs on things like this."

I inserted the USB and waited for the items to load. Without even clicking and enlarging, I could already feel the burning anger returning. My ears felt like they were on fire. I was undoubtedly staring at a semi-naked Nicole sitting in front of Gabriel Lane. In the next picture, her head was thrown back, his mouth on her neck. I felt bile rise in my throat. I hadn't expected for it to bother me as much as it did, but the longer I stared at the image, the hotter my blood simmered. I knew it was her ex-husband. I knew she was with me now. Sort of. But fuck, it hurt seeing her with him. It hurt knowing her lips, lips that belonged to *me*, were on his just short days, maybe weeks before they were on mine.

In the next frame, she was looking at the camera with a look of shock on her face. And in the next she'd stood up and was fixing her shirt. I felt sick. Physically ill. My stomach was turning in disgust. The shots were grainy, no doubt taken on a cell phone, but it was her. It was her curvy frame and her perfect tits, and that incredible mouth of hers. I took a deep breath. I needed to stop thinking about it before I made myself sick.

The next photo was one of her and me on the balcony of her house. It was similar to the one Quinn had texted me before, but these were less grainy, sharper, and from the angle they were taken it definitely looked like we were kissing. My heart pounded as I looked at them, at the way she was looking at me in the picture. I was uneasy about the way I was looking at her. It was as though nothing else in the universe mattered but us. If anybody got hold of it, there would be no sense in denying what was going on between us. Nobody would believe it. I cleared my throat.

"I'll buy every copy of this. Every single fucking copy. And I'll throw in a bonus if you give me your source."

"Vic, you know I—"

"How long have we known each other, Q?"

He sighed, running a hand over his face. "People will want to see this. This is huge. They're supposed to be getting a divorce, and they've been popping up everywhere together and now these pictures . . . this is the type of thing that breaks the Internet."

I propped my elbows on the table and buried my face in my hands, closing my eyes to try to forget the image of her half-naked in front of another man. I needed to think of her as my client, not the woman I felt I could say anything to without second thought. Not the woman I'd had the most meaningful sex of my life with, because that's what it was. Meaningful and hot as fuck.

"What's going on with you and Nicole?" Quinn asked. My head snapped up. "Off the record."

"Off the record, I want you to give me your goddamn source and help me make these pictures go away," I said, shutting my computer. He studied me for a long moment.

"Yours or all of them?"

My eyes narrowed. "Every single one of them."

Quinn smiled. "This one's special."

"Don't start with your shit, Q. I don't have time for it."

"I'm not judging. She's beautiful," he said, raising his hands.

"Keep your fucking opinions to yourself. I'm having a hard enough time accepting that other people have seen this shit. And I don't think you want anybody to know how much you've been visiting an unnamed married woman. We should probably keep that between us," I said. "For now."

His eyes widened, but his smile stayed intact. The reason

Quinn and I got along so well is because we respected each other, and we knew not to call each other's bluff. We were both ruthless. We'd claw the shit out of anybody who stood in our way, regardless of who it was.

"I don't understand why you don't come and work with me," he said.

I chuckled at the thought, but got serious quickly. "One of us would be dead by the end of the first week. Now, give me the fucker's name, and while you're at it, I'm going to need a favor from a mutual friend of ours."

Chapter Twenty-Five

Nicole

NORMALLY I WASN'T one to dwell on reasons guys hadn't called before their three-day quota, but with Victor it was all I could think about, mainly because he wasn't the type of guy who played by any rules. I'd spoken to him just briefly after our weekend together and I'd been busy when he called, so it couldn't even be considered a conversation. Over the weekend, half of the wardrobe on the movie set had been messed up, and luckily I was insanely busy working with two seamstresses to get caught up in making everything. Still, when I got home and soaked my hands in ice-cold water because they hurt so much from sewing non-stop, all I could think about was Victor. My phone finally rang with a call from him when I got home from work that night. I was soaking my hands in iced water, stumbling and spilling it everywhere to answer it.

"Hey," he said, his voice making me lose my breath momentarily.

"You really stuck to the three-day rule," I said. He was quiet for a beat.

"Sorry. I've been busy."

"So have I."

"Yeah, my mom said you left the car there until the next morning because you'd gotten out of work too late to call," he said. "I need you to come into the office to sign the final papers so we can put this divorce behind you. Are you free tomorrow morning?" His voice was serious, all business, all Victor. I sighed.

"Sure. What time?"

"Nine?"

"I'll be there."

"Good," he said, pausing to clear his throat. "And . . . you're good? Everything is going okay?"

I made a face. He couldn't see me, but he was acting really fucking weird. I chalked it up to his fear of everything being recorded. The guy swore he was Richard Nixon or something.

"I'm fine. See you tomorrow, Victor."

"Looking forward to it, Nicole." The way he said that made me stomach flip. Maybe I was just worrying for no reason. We were good. We were fine, and he said he was looking forward to seeing me.

When I woke up the following morning, my entire body ached. My hands, my head, my throat, and I was pretty sure I had a fever. I could barely open my eyes, and when I did I realized it was eight forty and I was going to be late. Before showering, I called Marcus because there was no way I could drive like that. By the time I finished getting ready, he was standing outside, his mouth dropping when he saw me.

"You look tired."

"Thanks," I muttered. At least he found a nice way to tell me I looked like crap. "We should be quick, and the quicker we go, the quicker I get back to bed."

"Okay."

He didn't make small talk. Shocker. And for once I was completely glad for the silence in the car, which I think was a shock to him. He kept looking over, probably to make sure I was okay, but I was too busy blowing my nose and trying to keep my snot from going everywhere to care. I'm pretty sure he was completely disgusted by the time we reached Victor's office.

As soon as we got there, paparazzi swarmed my car.

"What the hell happened now?" I asked, my voice nasally in my own ears.

"Stay in the car. I'll go around," Marcus said.

I did as I was told and kept my head down as he walked me to the front door. I couldn't even make out their questions because of the pounding in my ears, but I did catch Victor's name, which further confused me.

"What were they saying?" I asked Marcus as I buried my nose in a tissue.

He frowned. "I didn't really understand them."

"Me either."

When I stepped out of the elevator, Grace looked at me with wide eyes and an open mouth. The last time she gave me that look was when rumors about my divorce began circulating. I smiled and waved at her as I walked down the hall, because even if I had time for her crap, I didn't feel like dealing with it today. Marcus stayed behind as I walked up to Victor's door and knocked. It opened and Corinne stepped out. She gave me a quick once-over and smiled.

"He's on the phone, but you can go in."

"Thanks," I said, stepping in as she stepped out.

My blood was vibrating with nervousness. I'd been there a million times, but it felt different, though I couldn't quite put a finger on why. Was it because of what we'd shared? Would things be weird now? Would he be weird toward me? Would I be awkward? We'd had sex, yes. Like in the past. But not like in the past. It felt like more. Something about what had been going on between us even before we hooked up this time felt like more. And he'd said he had the final papers. The *final* papers.

Victor straightened in his chair when he saw me. His eyes searching my face, wandering down my body and back up in a slow caress that made my breath hitch. Whatever Mr. Perfect saw now when I was makeup-less and wearing sweats was definitely good, because he was eyeing me the same way he did when I was in a skintight dress. I plopped down in the chair across from him and put my arms on the table to lay my head down, hoping to relieve the pounding in my head, because despite his very wanted attention, I felt beyond sick and very exhausted.

"I'm going to have to call you back," he said into the phone and hung up. I heard the squeak of his leather chair as he stood up and walked around his desk, and felt his hand on my hair as combed it with his fingers. I moaned a little. "What's wrong?" he asked, his voice soft as he crouched down beside me.

"I think I caught whatever you had." I sniffled and shivered.

His hand stopped moving. I lifted my head up as he stood. "You should have told me. I would have come to you."

"Maybe if you would have called," I said. I closed my eyes momentarily, trying to regain composure. *What was it about this guy that made me revert to my teenage self?* "Just . . . let's get this over with so that I can go back to bed."

He sighed and took a seat beside me instead of going back behind his desk. He was quiet for so long, I accidentally dozed off in my chair. When I woke, it was with a start, blinking rapidly.

"I'm so sorry," I said. "Please, just . . . do I need to sign something?"

"I should have called. I'm sorry. I just," he paused to take a long, deep breath, his eyes looking pained, "just this." He handed over a paper similar to one we'd gone over in the past. I signed and handed it back, when I did he held my gaze. The seriousness in his eyes made my stomach dip. "Nicole, we need to talk."

An array of possibilities crossed my mind in a split second, and if I wasn't already on the verge of crying because of how sick I felt, I would have cried over what he was insinuating. I closed my eyes. Those words were never a good sign. Flashbacks of how this had happened the first time assaulted my thoughts. *We can't do this anymore,* he'd said then. If he said that now . . . God. If he said that now I wouldn't know what to do, what to say, how to react.

"About what?" I whispered.

"This. Us," he said, his voice firm, though his eyes looked anguished, and I knew he wasn't thrilled about the talk either.

I swallowed, even though it hurt. "Are you kidding me?"

"I wish I was," he said, letting out a sigh. He reached over his desk and placed some pictures in front of me. I squinted to look at them, and gasped when I saw the one of me on Gabe's bed. It was from the drunken night when that girl had interrupted us. Bitch.

"Nothing happened," I said, looking at Victor. They were taken before we got together, so I didn't have to explain myself to him, but I still felt the urge to. "I mean, we made out, but I swear nothing else happened."

He closed his eyes momentarily and breathed out. When he opened them back up he looked as torn as he did before he took a break to think.

"It's . . . it doesn't matter. It's not about that."

He paused, reaching out and flipping to another picture.

The picture was one of him and me on my balcony. Before I signed my lease. The *day* I signed my lease. My eyes snapped up to meet his. This was the reason for the *we need to talk* speech. The sinking feeling threatened to return. It was his biggest fear come to life. We'd been caught and now anything said about him, about us, about this case, would come back and haunt him when the time came for his promotion. *His promotion.* Dammit.

"Can we make it go away?" I asked, my voice a croak.

"I'm working on it. Trust me, I'm working on it. These," he said, pointing at the ones of Gabe and me, "will never see the light of day." He pointed at the ones of us. "These, unfortunately, are already circulating. My guy couldn't stop them. I'm trying to get to the bottom of it."

My heart squeezed in my chest.

We'd had our fun.

I kept telling myself that to keep the tears at bay, because despite going through this once before, it felt different this time. It felt personal. It felt . . . *wrong.* I didn't feel just a little crushed by this. This felt like a boulder was sitting in my throat, making its way to my heart.

"We can't see each other anymore," I whispered, meeting his gaze. "I get it. This was just a fire we needed to put out. And we did that."

I wiped my nose with the tissue in my hand.

But I didn't get it. I didn't get it and I felt the intense urge to cry. I was losing him. I was losing him and there wasn't anything I could do about it because now there were pictures of us together. Proof of what was happening between us. Things that could rip apart his career and mess up my divorce. I expected to feel something when we ended it. Last time, I'd felt hurt. This was worse.

Annihilated.

I never expected to find a man so soon after Gabe. I hadn't. I'd set my mind to having fun and working on myself, which I did. But I also hadn't expected for my life to collide with Victor's again or to feel so connected to him.

"Nicole, please don't," he said, his voice quiet, his eyes pleading. "Don't belittle this."

I blinked, trying to stop impending tears. Blinked again when I felt one escape through my lashes. I wiped it quickly.

Don't belittle this.

"It's okay," I whispered, standing from my chair. I took one of the pictures with me and shoved it into my purse. "I know how this goes. I hope you know that even with these pictures, I'll deny it. You don't have to worry about me. I would never do anything to jeopardize your job."

He stood up and reached for my wrist, squeezing. I yanked my arm quickly. I couldn't bear his touch right now. Not when it hurt this much. His eyes widened, his broad shoulders sagged a bit.

"I'm sorry. Had this happened under different circumstances—"

"Stop apologizing. It's fine," I said, interrupting him. "Been there, done that, bought the shirt."

"That's not funny, Nicole," he said, his face serious. I dropped my head, unwilling to look at him anymore.

"I've learned to deflect."

Despite how weak I felt, I started walking toward the door, and he followed, holding me by the shoulders possibly when he saw me sway a little. I tilted my face to look at him, and cursed the stir in my heart when I realized our faces were so close.

"Please don't touch me," I whispered.

"I don't know how to stop," he whispered back, dropping his forehead to the back of my shoulder.

"You'll learn."

I left his office, heard him follow behind me, and when I reached Marcus, I could barely keep my legs moving. I practically threw my arms out for him to catch me. Thank God he did.

"Let's get you home," he said, looking over my shoulder.

I turned my head and saw Victor standing in the hall with his hands in his pockets looking as defeated as I'd ever seen him. I tried to smile, tried to reassure him that he was doing the right thing, but I couldn't find the energy to do it. I let Marcus lead me away, back to the car, and drive me home. On my way there, I got a call from Meire and answered straight away, which I rarely did.

"I saw the pictures," she said upon my answering. "Are you crying?"

"No," I sniffled. "I'm sick."

"Come stay over here. You shouldn't be by yourself right now."

"Okay," I said, and agreed to drive to their house later on, after I'd showered and napped on my bed. I needed to be by myself for a little while. Needed time to process everything that had happened earlier.

Later that night, when darkness had fallen over, there was loud knocking on my door that startled me awake. Fuck. Shit. I was supposed to go to my dad's. I checked my phone and saw the missed calls from Meire and Dad as I walked to the door and opened it. Victor was standing on the other side dressed in jeans, a Dodgers cap, and a black hoodie. I knew it was him because I knew him, but you could barely make out his face with that thing over his head.

"What are you doing here?" I asked, my voice a croaked whisper. It was getting worse.

He held up a bag. "Soup."

I closed my eyes and stepped back so he could walk in.

"Didn't we break up? Did I imagine that?" I asked, closing the door and following him down the hall.

Bonnie jumped on her back legs and wagged her tail when she saw him. Stupid dog. Hadn't I spent an hour crying over him to her? Why was she being nice to him?

"Get comfortable while I heat this up," he said, rounding my kitchen counter and tearing the bag open.

I looked at him for a long moment, studied his face now he'd taken the hood off: the planes of his chiseled jaw, the light scruff, the light brown hair curling under the baseball cap, those hazel eyes that made my knees go weak, his long fingers as he popped the lid on the plastic container. Each second that passed made my heart hurt a little more. I turned around and left the kitchen, opting to sit in the living room and switch on the TV. Maybe if I had a distraction I wouldn't have to think about how over we were.

Victor returned with a bowl of soup and a glass of orange juice and sat beside me. He put the juice and a napkin with two blue pills down on the coffee table and turned to face me. He was too close.

I could smell the scent of his body wash and shampoo.

So close.

I could see the lines of brown on his greenish eyes.

Too close.

I could practically taste his lips against mine. I swallowed and cringed at the pain, and when he lifted a spoonful of soup up for me to drink, my eyes widened.

"You can't feed me," I whispered. The dip in his brow, and the look in his eyes told me he was crestfallen.

"Please, Nic," he whispered, a plea. I'd never heard him plead before. It made my chest squeeze, my eyes water.

"I can't, Victor. It's all or nothing, and you know it can't be all."

The spoon clinked against the bowl as he closed his eyes. "It can be," he said, opening his eyes again, "just not right now."

"I get it."

"I really . . . this . . . it wasn't just for fun," he said.

"I know." I swallowed. "But we still have to keep our distance. You being here isn't helping anything."

He nodded slowly. "I couldn't just . . ." He sighed. "I wanted to make sure you were okay."

"I am, Victor. I'm okay. I'll be okay, but you can't be here. You can't say no to me and tell me this isn't good timing and then show up in my house with soup. I'm strong, but I still have feelings."

Feelings that were overwhelming me.

"I know. I'm sorry," he said, sighing. "I really am."

"Thank you for the soup."

"You're welcome." He paused, taking his cap off with one hand to run his hand through his hair. "I'm going to leave now."

I nodded. He glanced at me again.

"I'm going to leave because this is the responsible thing to do," he said. "If I was careless, I'd stay."

"That's . . . good to know," I said. And it was. Maybe not now, but someday there would be a future for us. Maybe someday we'd work out.

If I was careless, I'd stay.

When he left, I drank my soup, picked up Bonnie, and then headed to my dad's. Meire didn't even let me knock before she opened the door and pulled me into a hug.

"Your dad is not very happy. He's not even going to the office tomorrow."

My heart dropped. I was afraid of that. I let go of Meire and started walking toward his study, where I knew I'd find him.

"There's soup for you in the kitchen. I'll warm it up," she called out. I didn't bother to tell her I'd already had some. I could have another bowl.

"Thank you," I called out, cursing my teenage self for all the times I'd talked shit about her for marrying my dad. I wasn't one to welcome new people with open arms. I was always cautious about letting people in because I'd seen so many people get burned by loved ones, and I just never wanted that to be me. The irony.

I knocked once on my dad's office door before walking in. He was sitting behind his desk with his hand on his forehead.

"Hey, Dad."

His head snapped up. He smiled softly. "How are you feeling?"

I shrugged. "Like shit."

"Nicole."

"Like crap," I said. I never understood why crap was accepted while shit was frowned upon.

"Can you please explain these to me? I'm having a hard time understanding them," he said, waving the pictures of Victor and me around. I took a deep breath and let it out as I sat across from him.

"There's nothing to explain. It was windy and we were trying not to be loud so the realtor wouldn't hear what we were saying about the house. End of."

His brows rose. "You're sure?"

"I'm positive," I said, but the more his blue eyes searched my face, the more nervous I felt. Every time I lied to my dad I felt like I was going up against the Supreme Court justices and pleading my case. Technically I wasn't really lying. There was nothing going on between Victor and me anymore.

"Okay," he said with a sigh. "I was worried I'd have to let him go."

My heart lurched. I leaned forward in my seat, suddenly feeling all the energy come back to me at once. "Let him go? Why?"

"It doesn't look good if a lawyer is involved with his client. I'm sure I don't need to explain that to you."

I tried not to roll my eyes. He'd met Meire when she'd hired him as her estate attorney after her husband died. Not the same, but close enough, and Dad had made it very clear that their relationship didn't start until after her things were taken care of and she was no longer his client.

"I know, Dad. Like I said, nothing is going on. We are friends, though. I don't think that's against the law."

"It's not, but you need to steer clear until this blows over. Victor is very serious about his job and I don't want anything interfering with my making him partner."

"I won't."

"Are you dating somebody?" he asked suddenly.

"No," I said, and it pained me to say it. Physically pained me as I thought of Victor and his smile and his grouchiness.

"Well, find someone." He paused. "Well, that's probably a good thing to be single at this point. Probably good for you too. I'm having a company party to announce Victor's promotion in a couple weeks." He paused. "I'm not trying to pimp you out, love, but if you want to bring someone as a friend, do so. I'm just trying to make *this*," he holds up the pictures again, "go away for everybody's sake. I'm sure he will bring a date, so I won't have to worry about him. People will see you guys with other people and this will be erased."

"I hear you," I said.

And I wasn't lying. I heard him loud and clear. It still didn't help the deep cut I felt at the idea of Victor dating another woman. *Someone he didn't have to worry about being careless with.* I excused myself and left his office, not even bothering to get my bowl of soup before I went to the guest house. I face-planted onto the plush queen-sized bed and let out a single sob before I fell asleep.

Chapter Twenty-Six

Victor

"WHY WOULD YOU invite her to your birthday party?" I asked my sister, who looked at me like I was an idiot. It had been a couple weeks since I'd seen Nicole and I was doing pretty good at avoiding her as a whole. The only time I communicated with her was through Corinne, and it was solely about the divorce and the agreement she had with Gabriel to attend an event with him.

"Because I like her, and I was handing out invitations the day I met up with her to talk about Sunny's wedding dress. Or did you forget that you practically begged me to call her to see how she was feeling when she was sick?"

I blinked. That was beside the point. I couldn't call her after I took the soup to her house. I was being a pussy but I was man enough to admit that the sound of her voice would break me if I wouldn't be able to touch her or see her. Estelle waved an envelope with my name on it and jerked me out of my thoughts.

"Are you five? Is this your fifth birthday party? Who the fuck hands out paper invitations?"

She rolled her eyes and flung an envelope across the table. It hit me in the chest before I could catch it. "If you don't want to go, don't go. Nobody told you to act like an asshole to a perfectly perfect girl."

I let out a breath and shook my head, trying my best not to roll my eyes right back at her. I hadn't seen or spoken to Nicole in a couple weeks. That was nothing. It wasn't even enough time to miss a person, but there I was, missing the shit out of her and thinking about her every time I closed my damn eyes.

"When is that party your boss is throwing for you?" she asked.

I ran a hand through my hair, closing my eyes momentarily. "After he tells everyone about my promotion. When is your adult-child party?"

She glared at me. "Do you think Nicole will go to the office party?"

"I doubt it." I hoped not.

"Are you taking a date?"

I looked at my sister. "What are you getting at?"

"I'm just curious."

"I'll probably take somebody. I need to make sure people understand the pictures circulating aren't what they've made them out to be."

"Aren't they?" she asked, raising an eyebrow.

"Are you done?" I paused. "I know you're dying for me to find the love of my life and all, but some of us don't think love is the end-all be-all of life."

It was a good thing I was a good liar.

"Some of you are idiots."

"Thanks."

"You're welcome." She took a deep breath. From the way her ears were turning red, I could tell she was getting upset about this. I tried not to smile. She was so funny when she got upset.

"It doesn't matter. Even if she goes and you take someone it'll be fine. She's dating this really hot guy."

Until she wasn't so fucking funny. "What guy?"

She shrugged. "Some guy named Brent that lives by her house. It's pretty convenient, really," she said, her smile widening as she looked at me. "He's gone over a few times. She says he has an incredible body. I mean, I know he does. She showed me a picture."

I felt like there wasn't enough room in my body for the air that I needed. I clenched my jaw, trying to rein in my anger and keep all the words in, because the last thing I needed was to give her more ammunition. I thought about the cases sitting on top of my desk and looked around the coffee shop, my eyes everywhere.

"Good for her," I said when I felt like I could speak without sounding like I wanted to murder whoever the guy was.

"That's what I said," Estelle said, lifting her cup of coffee and taking a sip. My eyes focused on her paint-stained hands. I was dying to get out of that place already. "I think he's a producer or something."

I exhaled. What the fuck, Nicole? *What the fuck?* Did she completely ignore the *we just can't be together right now* part? Was she really moving on? A sense of déjà vu fell over me, when I'd asked her to leave the first time, and she had, and three weeks later she'd gotten engaged.

Fuck.

My.

Life.

"Like I said, good for her," I repeated.

Estelle smiled as she stood up. "I have a class to teach in twenty minutes. Let me know if you're going to make it to the party."

"Obviously I'm going," I said, giving her a kiss on the cheek.

I started opening the envelope as I walked away and reading the invitation, but she was too far for me to say anything to. A costume party. She was turning twenty-eight and was having a costume party for her birthday. I hated themed parties. They meant going out and looking for specific outfits and spending money on those outfits and then keeping them on at the actual event instead of just wearing whatever was already in your closet. And a fucking pirate-themed party?

"You're fucking kidding me," I muttered, putting the invitation away and tossing it to my passenger seat. Oliver wasn't going to hear the end of it when I saw him on Sunday. I'd have to buy something online. Once that was out of the way I could figure out who I was going to take as my date to the office party going on in my name. They were honoring me and I was already dreading it. Under normal circumstances I'd be glad to go and stand up there, thanking the people who'd helped me get there. But under normal circumstances, Nicole *would* be on my arm and we'd be able to walk around openly. Under normal circumstances, she wouldn't be dating producers named Brent.

A few days later, I couldn't stop thinking about it and I realized I was running out of options, and I didn't like running out of options. I wasn't the kind of man that could just sit back and take a punch. I liked to be the one punching. I knew it wasn't right, I knew it wasn't necessarily professional, but I was in the business of not giving a fuck. If Nicole wanted to go off and date other guys, I couldn't stop her. I actually appreciated it. That way the spotlight was off of me for the time being and I could take care of unfinished business.

For two weeks I had been okay showing up at the office and getting patted on the back by Will and pretending the story about his daughter and me was fabricated. It was easy enough to go in, get lost in work, meet with clients, look into their cases, go to court, defend them, and close a case. I was on autopilot. No. I was back to where I was before Nicole ambushed her way into my life. I was back to being me. The difference was that I was an unhappy version of myself. I'd tried to get in touch with the douchebag that was Darryl Cusack, who happened to be the source Quinn gave me for the "leaked" pictures, but he hadn't responded to any of my messages. The guy clearly didn't want me to find him. Gabriel Lane was my last resort, and I didn't intend to use that card at all if I could help it. My last resort was to exchange information with some of Quinn's photographers.

They'd tell me where I could find him, and I would give them a few pictures they were after. The day after I put that out, I got a call from one of them letting me know Darryl was eating at a popular Italian restaurant in West LA. I showed up there with an old friend of mine, Jessica. She was the kind of friend I used to take on group dates, one of the girls my sister couldn't stand, but she was also always down for whatever, whenever, wherever. As soon as she heard there would be paparazzi there, she agreed. She owned a hair salon, so I assumed she thought it would be good for business. I figured as soon as they got pictures of Jess and me hooking up, they'd move on and bury the story about Nicole and me. Who liked old news anyway? Jess and I played it up outside, holding hands, kissing right outside the restaurant, laughing at some stupid comment she made about possibly having gum under her shoe but not being able to bend down because of her short dress, and basically doing shit people who went on dates did. I hated every second of it. Her lips felt wrong against mine. Her hand felt wrong when I held it. It was just . . . wrong. I hadn't even thought about giving Nicole a heads-up about the photos, but I hoped she never saw them, and if she did, I hoped she had enough sense to know it was all for show and that I'd done it with her best interest in mind.

From my seat I had the perfect view of Darryl's table. He was there with a known actress and a couple of her friends. When I saw him get out of his seat and head to the bathroom, I excused myself and did the same. When I got back there, my friend Sergio, one of the waiters, handed me a pair of gloves and I asked him to block the entrance of the bathroom with a sign. I waited for the other man in there to walk out and put the gloves on before turning around and locking the door when I walked in. Darryl did a double take when he saw me.

"You know what I appreciate about you, Darryl? That you stay true to yourself," I started. I took a baseball out of the pocket of my jacket and started throwing it up and catching it softly. "I don't know if you know this, I'm sure you do because it seems you've taken a liking toward me." I raised an eyebrow. "And I'm flattered, though I don't bat for that team." I shook my head. "Before I got into divorce, I practiced criminal law. It only lasted about two years." I tilted my head as I thought about it. "But in those two years I earned the trust of a lot of criminals. People you wouldn't think I'd know. I don't have to tell you how shady people can be, and I'm sure I don't have to tell you the lengths people go through to make sure they stay out of jail." I paused for dramatic affect. His eyes were a little wider now as he looked at the ball I was throwing up.

"Where did . . . is that my . . ." he started, frowning as he looked at the ball in my hand, recognizing it from his home office, where it was taken from.

"So this is what you're going to do next," I said. He looked more concerned about the ball than he did scared, and that was fine. I didn't want him scared. Scared people went to the cops. Nervous people went to bed with their secrets.

"You're going to pull whatever photographers you have following me and Nicole, and you're going to give me their names. That's all you have to worry about. I'll make it all go away."

Darryl scoffed, pushing his oversized glasses higher on the bridge of his nose. "In exchange for what?"

"In exchange for me not having some old friends of mine who owe me some really big favors pay you a visit."

"I'm not doing anything," he said, his voice firm. I knew he was calling my bluff. I knew he was probably thinking that a clean-cut guy like me was ruthless in the courtroom, but the courtroom and real life were two completely separate things. I appreciated that seed of doubt. I kept calm until he started screaming.

"Nicole is nothing. Nobody cares about her. Fuck you. You're just mad because she's still hung up on her ex. And guess what? She will be forever because you're not a multi-million-dollar earning actor," he said, his face turning red. "And if you want juicy pictures, I can show you the ones of her and her new boyfriend. Those make your balcony pictures look like a walk in the fucking park."

I breathed one more time, but the burn of fire inside me was stronger than the breaths I took. Finally, I pitched the ball, the way I did when I played baseball with the guys the seldom times we were all free. I pitched it so that it hit the mirror beside him and shattered it, the pieces flinging off it and going in every direction. One nipped me in the side of my face. I felt the sting, but not enough to care.

"You're a fucking lunatic," he screamed, holding on to his head. "Security!"

I stood, arms crossed, waiting for the security I knew wouldn't come, as he kicked the glass on the floor, his eyes wild, glasses falling, head turning in every which direction as if he didn't know what to do with himself. Finally, his eyes landed on the ball. He gaped at it as he lifted it out of the sink.

"Where the hell—?" He looked up at me. "Is this from my house? You were in my house?" he yelled.

"I would never step foot in your personal property," I answered calmly, feeling much better after my outburst. I hadn't. I hadn't been to his house or made the call for the guys to go there. I'd been very calculated with my orders and made sure nothing could be traced back to me.

"Who the hell do you think you are?" he demanded. I smirked. I'd been waiting for that question.

"You're about to find out," I replied, and turned around to walk out.

I unlocked the door and looked over my shoulder to where he was still standing with the Babe Ruth baseball in his hand. "My professional opinion? Don't fuck with me anymore."

I walked out of there, thanked Sergio and Lazaro who was now also standing there.

"Sorry about the mess, guys. The man in there went crazy over the empty soap container," I said. Both of them looked at each other before looking at me and shrugging. I handed Sergio two wads of bills. "Please give this to Ignazio. That should cover it. The rest is for you guys."

"It's the wine, dawg. That makes these old men go crazy," Sergio said with a tsk. I smiled as I walked away. I went back to where Jessica was sitting and she gasped.

"Holy cow. What happened to your face?"

I brought my hand up and felt liquid covering my left cheek. I looked at my hand, now wet with blood.

"I think we're going to have to cut this date short."

She nodded, eyes wide. "Of course. Let's go. You probably need stitches."

As soon as we stepped outside, there were photographers

everywhere. What wasn't supposed to be a money shot, became one. Me dating a different girl wasn't news anymore. It was me dating a different girl and the blood all over my face. I doubted they'd put them up anywhere. I wasn't a celebrity.

"I hope they don't think I did that," Jessica said with a nervous laugh as we climbed into the car. "Wait. Let me drive."

I gave her a side-eyed glare. "Are you out of your . . .? You think I would let you drive my car? I'm dropping you off at home."

She protested the entire way there, saying I was an idiot— an asshole—that she didn't understand why I couldn't just be like a normal human being and let her take me to the hospital. By the time I parked outside her house, I had a migraine.

"Jess, I've had a really rough night, so I hope you don't take this the wrong way, but, get the fuck out of my car."

"What about your office party? Aren't we supposed to be taking pictures that make you look like you've found a girlfriend?"

I groaned. She was right. "Meet me there please. Just . . . meet me there. I'll pay you. I'll send a celebrity to your salon. I don't care. Just meet me there in two hours."

I drove to the hospital, got three stitches on my face, and was parked outside the office building a little past nine o'clock. My heart lurched at the familiar white car parked outside the office building. Would she be here?

Chapter Twenty-Seven

Nicole

BY THE TIME Victor walked in, looking like every sin I was ready to commit, in a black suit and navy tie, I was on my third glass of champagne. He came solo. I smiled at that, but my smile quickly faded when I saw the bandage on the side of his face. I gravitated toward him as if on autopilot, only stopping when I remembered I was supposed to keep my distance. I was furious with myself, with my dad, with the media, with Victor. I'd gone from sad and understanding to angry and bewildered, like a rabid dog on a leash wanting to attack the postmaster. I hated it. Hated him for making me yearn for him this badly. Hated me for putting myself in this situation. Hated the stupid laws in place that prevented us from being together.

"I got you an hors d'oeuvre," Brent said, walking back to me. He also looked great in a suit and tie, opposed to the running shorts I usually saw him in, but he wasn't Victor. I'd invited him as my date because sadly I had nobody else to bring, unless I brought Marcus and everybody knew he was my security detail. He wouldn't really pass as my sudden boyfriend. Well, with my track record, he might, but that would have been awkward for both of us. Brent stuck out the tomato and mozzarella skewer in his hand and brought it up to my mouth for me to take a bite. I complied and thanked him.

When I looked back up, Victor was looking right at me and I felt the air swoosh out of my lungs. I tried to look away, but I was a prisoner to his gaze, and couldn't until I felt Brent's finger on the side of my mouth and was jolted out of the moment. My eyes snapped back to Brent.

"You got some olive oil here," he said, wiping it off.

I couldn't formulate words as I watched Victor move toward us, his jaw clenched, eyes narrowed. My heart dipped into my stomach, and when he stood right in front of me, I could only swallow it all down and tilt my head to look at him.

"Hi. Congratulations," I said.

"Thank you." He paused, looking at Brent. "I don't think we've met. I'm Victor Reuben. Nicole's attorney." The way he said it, almost as if he loathed the introduction, made my heart gallop.

"Brent Thomas. Nice to meet you."

They shook hands, and all I could do was look at Victor's face and wonder what happened.

"I need to speak to you before you leave," Victor said to me, lowering his voice. "Alone. In my office."

I was sure everybody in the room could see through us, hear the promise in his statement, feel the tension we created. His eyes raked up and down my body slowly, without a care in the world, as if there weren't at least forty eyes on us. As we stood there, a tall blonde woman came up to us. At first I smiled at her, thinking she was one of the guy's wives, but then she put her red nails on Victor's face and touched his cheek, and my smile disappeared.

Victor's lips twitched at whatever expression I must have

been making, and it became clear that we were playing a game. A stupid, annoying, childish game I had no interest partaking in. My life was already a damn game with the media attention and Gabriel. I didn't need that to bleed into this part of my life. *Why the hell would he do this to me?* He knows how much I hate the games I've had to play with Gabe.

"Does it hurt?" the blonde asked. Her voice felt like nails on a chalkboard, and I knew it was just me that felt that way.

"It's fine," he said. I wanted to punch him for not moving away from her touch.

"I can't believe you didn't let me drive you," she said.

"I don't let anybody drive my car," he said. I hid my smirk behind my glass of champagne as I took a sip.

"I feel you," Brent said beside me. "It takes a real special girl for me to take things to that level."

"I feel the same. Only Marcus drives my car," I said, feeling the need to chime in.

Marcus, who I needed to call so he could take an Uber here at some point and drive me home. Unless I just took one myself. Brent laughed and draped his arm around me. The way Victor was glaring at him, I was surprised lasers weren't shooting from his eyes. Maybe this game would be fun after all.

"Maybe tonight will be my lucky night," Brent said, clinking his glass of water with my nearly empty champagne flute. I raised an eyebrow, looking at our glasses.

"Maybe you're right."

"It was nice to meet you," Brent said to Victor. "Congratulations. Nicky, aren't you going to introduce me to your father?"

"Right," I said, looking at Victor's date, who he still hadn't introduced. She was smiling at me though, so I felt obliged to return her smile as I walked away. My gaze got caught on Victor's again. "See you around."

claire contreras

While I introduced Brent to my dad, I checked my phone and veered off to the side to look at the text messages Chrissy had sent me.

CC: *Did you see this?!?!*

I opened up the message and clicked the link she'd attached, my stomach instantly dropping and curling in disgust as the pictures of Victor and the blonde girl appeared on my phone. They were holding hands, laughing, kissing, acting very together. *Today.* I felt the heat hit my ears first, and then spread quickly through my body. I'd hung out with Brent a few times outside my house, but that was all it was. Hanging out. It had never gotten to the point of kissing. He'd tried, but I'd shot him down and told him my mind was on someone else, because it was. I'd been too busy thinking about Victor, and that asshole now seemed *too* busy, actually playing the part a little *too* well.

Unless he wasn't playing the part at all.

I narrowed my eyes in his direction, and sure enough, there he was, holding hands with the blonde.

Holding. Hands. With. The. Blonde.

I glared so hard, trying to make his head explode first, then hers. One of the waitresses passed by with more champagne. I set down my empty flute and took another.

"What is that? Number four?" Brent asked, joining me. I was too mad to smile, but I nodded as I took a sip. "I would say tonight might really be my lucky night, but I'm not into taking advantage."

I looked over at Victor again, his broad back facing me, his hand on the blonde's shoulder, and something inside me snapped. I took a deep breath, walked into the dimly lit hallway, and pulled Brent by his tie. The last thing I saw before my lips crashed on his was the confused look on his face. Luckily his confusion didn't translate into his kiss. I tugged his tie a little harder, wishing he'd drop the good-guy act and kiss me. I wanted to be kissed like I was needed, but he was cautious, nice, his lips soft, his tongue coaxing. I ended the kiss and he leaned away with a huge smile on his face, his brown eyes glinting.

"That was . . . unexpected."

I smiled, trying to work up some excitement, and took another sip of champagne.

"Nicole."

I gasped at the sound of Victor's voice saying my name. Brent's smile dropped as he turned around, wiping lipstick off his mouth. Victor's eyes jumped from me to Brent and back to me.

"Am I interrupting anything?" he asked, his voice a quiet storm that made me uncomfortable.

"No, we were just . . . talking," Brent said slowly. He turned toward me again and smiled over his shoulder. I forced myself to meet his gaze and smile back, because fuck Victor. The only thing I could picture was his lips on that girl. It was driving me crazy. Why? Why was such a stupid thing driving me crazy?

"I need you to sign some papers. I won't take up too much of your time," Victor said, beckoning my attention. I cleared my throat and walked forward, brushing past Brent.

"You're going to make me snap," Victor said, his voice dangerously low as I walked beside him. I plastered on a fake smile for whoever was looking at us.

"Already beat you there," I said, continuing to walk toward his office. "Where's your girlfriend?"

"Is that what this is about?" he asked, closing the door behind us. I inhaled the smell of him. His office was coated in it. I exhaled, walking to the front of the desk as he stepped behind it.

"No, I just act like a fucking child for absolutely no reason."

"I thought you weren't jealous," he said, his voice hard.

Did he not want me to be? I looked down at the desk between us, unwilling to look at him. "I thought you weren't jealous either."

He scoffed, and at the sound, I lifted my head. Our eyes
locked. My gaze held a challenge. Daring him to let me go
home with Brent. His eyes seemed to hold the same challenge.
Or something. I didn't even know anymore. Maybe I'd had too
much champagne, but I knew that no amount of alcohol was
going to dull the fire inside me. I was burning for his touch,
for his kiss, for *him*. After a moment, he punched the top of his
desk, making me jolt.

"Apparently I fucking am," he muttered, and cleared his
throat as he slid two papers across the table.

My mouth dropped. I couldn't even respond. I just reached
for the papers and looked at them, though I couldn't even make
out the words.

"One is just finalizing the terms, the other is the agreement
that you'll go to that red carpet event with Gabriel."

I put my left hand on the paper, my right hand reaching
for the pen he offered. He held it until I acknowledged his gaze
on mine. Our faces were close. So close. Too close. My heart
jumped.

"Don't go, Nic," he said, his voice so soft I had to swallow
the lump forming in my throat.

"I saw the pictures of you and the blonde," I said, licking
my lips. His eyes dropped to my mouth momentarily before he
looked back at me.

"Nicole," he said, sighing as he ran a hand through his hair.
"You know why I'm with her."

"For the media? So that people will think we're not together? To make those pictures go away?" I posed, my voice rising
with each word I said. "Do you forget I was married to a celeb-

rity?"

His jaw clenched. My eyes shot to the Band-Aid on his face. "I can't forget you were married to a celebrity. I'm reminded of that every time I fucking turn around. You're not the only one being harassed by the paparazzi."

"Oh. I'm sorry I've made your life so difficult," I said, yanking the pen from his hand and signing both papers. I dropped the pen and glared up at him. "Is this it?"

We both stood up and looked at each other. I could tell he wanted to say a million things, but I knew he wouldn't, and I was sick of that. Despite the stupid paper I'd just signed, I was sick of men acting like *I* had to cater to their needs. I was okay with bending over backward for somebody who would return the favor, but I wasn't going to do it for somebody who wasn't willing to reciprocate.

He walked around his desk and stood in front of me. I took a step back, but didn't stop his hand from circling around my waist, or his lips from crashing down on mine. I got lost in that moment, with our lips locked and our hearts pressed against one another. It was a slow kiss, not urgent, but it held the sparks that Brent's hadn't. Victor's lips were meant to mold against mine. They were meant to push me over the edge. But they shouldn't. They couldn't. *We* couldn't. And that was the realization that made me break the kiss.

"Don't go to the premiere," he said, a hard breath against my lips.

"Are you telling me this as my attorney?"

He took a step back, raking his fingers through his hair as he looked away. I felt my heart sink as I followed his line of vision from the floor to the large window in his office. We couldn't see the ocean in the dark, but the sound of the waves was soothing enough.

"No," he said finally, his voice low.

Our eyes met again. "Are you staying with the blonde?"

"I'm not *with* the blonde."

I rolled my eyes and took out my phone, holding up the pictures Chrissy had sent me. Surely he would understand how much it had hurt me to see these. "Your tongue down her throat tells a different story."

"Jesus Christ, Nicole. It was a fucking picture. Pictures hold more lies than they do truths. You of all people should know that."

"I can't erase what I saw."

He let out a laugh and muttered, "Tell me about it."

"What's that supposed to mean?" I said, knowing he was thinking about the pictures of me and Gabe. "Those were taken before . . . before *us!*"

"And these were taken *because* of us," he shouted, pointing toward the door.

I knew he was right, but it didn't change anything. Unless it did.

"Will me not going to the premiere change anything? Between us?" I asked. He closed his eyes, and didn't open them as he shook his head slowly. I closed mine as well, trying to rein in the pain. I didn't do pain publicly. I swallowed and crushed it.

"Okay. I'll see you around, Vic," I whispered, walking out and heading to the bathroom. On my way there I let Brent know I was ready to go as soon as I got out. In there, I was hoping to calm myself, but then ran into Grace, who seemed startled to see me.

"I thought you'd left," she said. "Did you see my dad out there by any chance?"

I frowned, trying to think about when I'd spoken to my uncle. I was pretty sure it was when I was having my first glass of champagne. I'd been pretty good about going around the room and talking to everybody, introducing them to Brent, but once Victor got there it all became a blur. He seemed to have that effect on me.

"I think he left."

She sighed. "My boyfriend is picking me up here, but Dad hates him."

"Oh. Okay," I said, walking into a stall and closing it behind me.

"So, what do you think of Victor's date?"

I blinked rapidly, trying to sober up quickly. "Nothing. What am I supposed to think?"

"Corinne hates her."

I half-laughed, half-snorted as I flushed the toilet and fixed my little black dress. I looked at Grace in the mirror when I went to wash my hands.

"Corinne hates everybody that gets near Victor. I'm sure she hates me too."

Grace smiled. "I don't think anybody hates you."

She was so young and innocent, probably thinking I was the nicest person ever. I dried my hands and looked at her one last time. "Have fun tonight."

"Thanks. Are you leaving?"

"Yep. My time is up. I came, I saw, I stirred up shit." I shrugged. "Now it's time to go home."

Grace laughed as I walked out of the bathroom. Brent was standing in the hall, waiting for me.

"Ready?" he asked, offering me his arm, which I tucked mine into. Instinctively, I looked for Victor. He was off to the side, talking to the blonde. I was so not waiting to talk to him in private.

"So ready. My feet are killing me."

"I can carry you."

I smiled, but didn't say anything. Brent was hot. He had an incredible body, a great smile, a nice personality, but I was his height when in heels. Not that it meant he couldn't carry me. I was sure he could. But I didn't even want him to try. I sighed. I should probably just have sex with this guy and see if I stopped thinking about Victor. Unfortunately for me and my vagina, I was just not that kind of girl. Once I had my mind set on one guy, it was set on that guy until I was over him. Despite walking straight into Gabe's arms all those years ago, I had to move forward. I wanted to be cherished, but I wasn't that needy girl anymore. I didn't *need* a man to sweep me off my feet. Maybe I should go back to just having a little fun.

Whether Victor was over me or not, I didn't know. What I did know was that he wouldn't act on whatever he felt. I could read him enough to know that his resolve was steady again. Maybe because he got his promotion. Maybe because I gave him what he wanted of me. It hurt to admit that to myself. It hurt because I gave him more than just a hookup. I gave him me, and he didn't even know it. Or maybe he just didn't care.

I looked over at Brent again, who was there and available and willing to try to make me forget things that could be hidden but not forgotten . . .

Chapter Twenty-Eight

Victor

WHAT BOTHERED ME most about Nicole going home with the guy named Brent was that she didn't go home. I knew because I went to her house after I left the office and her car wasn't in the driveway and all her lights were off. If she wasn't there, it could only mean she was still with him. Spending the night with him. The thought made me crazy. Fucking crazy. I knew then, while I was standing outside her house, listening to the sound of the waves crashing, that I would willingly go insane for her love. It was more than just desire that I felt. It was deeper than that, more serious than that. In that instant, as I thought about her in bed with another man, the rage that ran through me was aimed toward myself for being an idiot. For not opening my eyes sooner. For not handing the case to somebody else when I should have. For not realizing the kind of woman I had and now had probably lost. No, fuck that, I hadn't lost her. Not yet. But worse than losing her, I was now sharing her. And I didn't share. Ever.

Chapter Twenty-Nine

Nicole

"YES, DAD," I said for the tenth time. I was definitely going back home. I'd stayed a week longer than anticipated because when I went to get clothes the day after the promotion event, the media frenzy outside my house had been too much for me to handle. *Why were they still on my case?* During my week at Dad's, I managed to stay away from the cameras, aside from the day I went to the premiere with Gabe, which was when he asked me if I wanted to fly to Argentina. *To visit your mom,* he'd said. *I'll pay for your flights. It's the least I can do.* And I had agreed. It was the least he could do, and I was dying to see my mom.

"I just want you to be careful over there. Are you staying with your mom?" Dad asked. He knew I would. I never went to Argentina and stayed anywhere else. I responded anyway. "Good," he said. "What time is Gabriel picking you up?"

"At four. No need to get up and ready your shotgun at such an ungodly hour," I said.

"And you're sure you won't be with Gabriel?"

"No, Dad. We're over."

I told him I wouldn't go to the actual press events with him, but I would go on the same flight. He seemed okay with that. Gabe was definitely being cautious around me. Good thing, too, because despite my agreement, I still hadn't forgotten about our ice cream shop experience, or that girl's tell-all. Despite that, I wasn't going to turn down a free trip to go see my mom.

"Okay, sweetheart. Good night. Call me when you land," Dad said.

"I will."

I gave him a hug and went out to the guest house to finish packing. I couldn't sleep, so I went online and looked through gossip sites, because I needed to see what they were saying about me now. I'd kept a very low profile since the night of Victor's promotion, so I couldn't imagine they had much to say, unless Darryl fed the media things about Gabe and me. One of these days I would wake up and not find anything posted about me, and no cameras following me. *Goals*. One day soon. I just needed to get through one last media frenzy first.

I woke up at three and got ready, and Gabriel pulled up at the gate just as I was lugging my suitcase to the front of the house. He opened the backdoor of his Escalade and jogged toward me with a smile on his face. He looked like the man I'd met all those years ago, willing to help, excited to be going on a trip with me. Excited to see *me*. He leaned down and kissed my cheek as he reached for my suitcase.

"Thanks for coming," he said.

"Thanks for inviting me," I responded. As I looked at what he was wearing, which looked very similar to what I had on, I laughed. He gave me a once-over, taking in my black sweats and white T-shirt, and did the same. My shirt was a tank I'd tied at the bottom so it fit more like a crop, and his was just a regular white tee. We were both wearing the same black Nikes. Gabe laughed.

"Great minds, huh?"

"I guess so."

On our way to the airport, we both kept yawning, and at some point I dozed off with my head on his shoulder. I was startled awake when he moved, and I felt a flash of light on my face.

"Holy crap," I said, wiping my eyes and fixing my hair. "How the fuck do they wake up so early?"

Gabe groaned. "I don't know, but I swear Darryl didn't call them."

"Where is that asshole anyway?"

"He's in Argentina," he said.

"Oh. Fun."

Gabe chuckled, but didn't reply. A mob of paparazzi surrounded us as we stepped out of the car, security in tow. They started with their usual onslaught of questions, and we ignored them, both of us keeping our heads down. Gabe pulled me into his side just as we were trying to step inside, and in that moment, I was grateful to have the bit of comfort he provided.

The moment lasted all of two seconds. Once the doors closed on the cameras, I pulled away and waited for him to hand me my ticket. I was surprised his manager wasn't traveling with us and said as much as we went up the escalator. We both slept throughout the flight, not even bothering with the food they served, and by the time we landed we were starving. My mom had offered to have food ready for us, and I felt the need to extend the invitation to him, though I was hoping he turned it down. He didn't.

"I feel like I owe it to her to see her before . . ." He let his words hang. Before the divorce is final, I guessed. Before he never sees her again, I assumed. I didn't care enough to ask, and I didn't mind him going. "You know, I've never been to a red carpet event without you," he said as we waited for the security detail to sort things out so we could exit the car.

Similar to the U.S., the paparazzi didn't stop in Argentina. Once they caught wind that we were there, they were relentless. I was sure Darryl played some part in that.

"Yeah, well, you've done a lot of other things without me," I said, shooting him a pointed look. He flinched.

"I'm sorry."

"Stop apologizing. It's fine." I paused. "It's not fine, but it's over, and I'm over it. I'm just glad the LA premiere is over with."

"I really am sorry, Nic. I feel like . . ." He sighed. "We really had something good going for us. You were the only normal thing I had in my life, and I completely fucked it up."

"You definitely did. Maybe we both did, though," I said.

He shook his head. "It was all me."

"Maybe you were right, though. I just couldn't handle sticking around when things got tough. That's on me."

"Things got tough because of me," he said. "I let this," he waved his hands around, "change me. I let it change me. I see that now. I'm sorry I realized it so late."

I shrugged. It is what it is. You can't turn back time. "I wish you well, you know that, right?"

"Same goes for you." He stayed quiet a long time. We got out of the car and were escorted to the front of the house, and he put his arm around me to shield me from the overzealous cameras that were nearly in my face. When we reached my mom's door, he sighed and turned to me. "I've been dying to ask you something. Is something really going on between you and your lawyer?"

My mouth dropped. "I'm going to pretend you didn't really just ask me that."

My mom opened the door before he could say anything

else, and my heart soared at the sight of her. People said we looked like twins, more than we did mother-daughter. I used to hate it when I was young because all the guys in school would tease me about wanting to bang my mom, but now I appreciated it. We had the same long dark hair, dead straight unless we attempted a curling iron, and the volume was always short-lived, the same blue eyes, and the same curvy body. Hers was a little fuller than mine, but she still looked incredible for her age.

"Hija," she said, throwing her arms around me. I squeezed her so hard, I was sure I cracked her back. She backed away and held my face in her hands as she looked at me. "Te vez cansada," she said.

"I am tired. I woke up at three in the morning and flew twelve hours," I said, stepping aside so she could greet Gabe.

They hugged as if we weren't waiting for the final papers of our divorce. My mom was like that, though. Forgiving, caring, always willing to give people a second chance until you fucked up again, in which case she'd put you on her shit list. With Gabe it was different though. She felt she saw him grow up, and she felt sorry for him. I also hadn't filled her in on just how many women he'd evidentially cheated with.

The three of us sat around the dinner table and chatted while being catered to by the cook and housekeepers, and I felt myself relax. Of course, that was until I saw the pictures of Victor leaving a nightclub with another woman. Then, I was raging and actually glad I'd agreed to go to the premiere with Gabe and wasn't back home in LA where these pictures would've been pushed down my throat. I needed to stop looking for things I had no interest in seeing. All I was doing was forcing the knife deeper into my heart, and I couldn't bear it anymore. I hid my pain behind a bright smile. It was the only way I knew how to cope. I hid. I hid my pain behind a bright smile. But inside, I also cried. Inside, my heart broke a little more, as if I hadn't experienced enough pain over the last two years. He was moving on. Despite that kiss in his office—our last kiss—he was really moving on.

At least I knew I was going to spend the week with my mom and not in public with Gabe. I was finally done with that life. Still, it didn't mean when Victor actually did text message me that it didn't bother me. I knew the game. I knew he was trying to make it seem like he was never with me, but those pictures, seeing them, seeing his smile, seeing him shielding the blonde with his arm so the camera's flash wouldn't get her . . . it hurt. It hurt, and I knew I couldn't talk to him. I wouldn't talk to him. Not unless he was ready to actually be with me. Not until after all of this was over. Not unless he was ready to actually be with me. I deserved better than to be somebody's dirty little secret. I deserved to be number one in somebody's life.

Chapter Thirty

Victor

"LOOK AT THIS one," Estelle said.

While we'd been watching the Golden State game, she'd been scrolling through her phone, showing Mia the latest on TMZ's update about Gabriel and Nicole. Did she not realize how sick to my stomach I was over it? Did she not comprehend to what extent the whole thing angered me? Thankfully, I was holding Greyson in my arms and it was hard to rage while you were holding such an innocent little thing. I smiled, looking down at him.

"Women suck, Grey. When you grow up all you'll hear about is how much men suck and how terrible we are, but remember, they make us this way. They drive us crazy and make us want them and then they go fuck everything up," I said in a coo while I kissed the top of his head. He smelled so fucking good.

"What are you saying to my kid?" Mia asked. I lifted my head up to look at her.

"Nothing. Guy talk."

She shot me a dissatisfied look. "I'm not sure I want you

having guy talk."

"Why not?"

"Because you're a bad influence."

"What?" I paused, frowning as I adjusted Grey in my arms. "I'm not a bad influence."

"Every time I look at this," she said, waving her phone around, "you're with a different girl. Weren't you supposed to be with Nicole?"

I groaned. "I'm not *with* any of those women."

"Yeah, good luck convincing Nicole of that," Estelle said.

"She doesn't care. Aren't you looking at pictures of her and Gabriel, looking like they're back on and about to go to the courthouse and get remarried and shit?" I asked, not caring how pissed off I sounded. Greyson cooed in my arms, and I stuck the pacifier back in his mouth with my finger.

"Can they do that?" Mia asked, gasping. "That would really suck."

"It would really fucking suck," I said. The thought alone made me feel defeated.

"Is she wearing . . . an engagement ring?" Estelle asked slowly, quietly, almost in a whisper.

I walked toward her and handed Grey over to Mia, and as I did, I caught a glimpse of the picture they were looking at. She picked him up and I took the phone from her hand. It was a video of Nicole and Gabriel. I clicked on it and brought the phone closer to my face. They were walking through a street market, and she was smiling up at him. His arm was casually draped over her shoulder. At the end of the video, the camera zoomed in on her hand and the voice-over made mention of the ring she wore. Nicole wore a lot of rings, though. She wore bracelets, and rings, and necklaces of all lengths.

"She wears a lot of rings," I said. I knew it wasn't her engagement ring because it looked much smaller. Seeing it on that finger didn't make it hurt any less.

"Let me see," Jensen said, reaching for the phone. "On that finger, though?"

I tried to shrug nonchalantly, but the lump forming in my throat spoke volumes. I looked at the television, so I wouldn't have to witness the compassionate looks they were surely giving me. I might actually break down right there in her living room. The truth was that when I told Nicole that she was mine, I'd meant it. I couldn't bear the thought of Nicole with anybody else in any capacity, much less in such a serious one. It physically pained me when I thought about it.

"When are you going to admit to yourself that you're in love with her?" Estelle asked suddenly.

Her words came at me hard, pushing a boulder of pressure against my chest. *Love.* I'd told her I thought I was falling in love with her when she'd been lying in my arms. All this time apart did nothing to diminish my feelings for her. Nothing. If anything, it made me realize how much I was missing. No late-night talks about our days. No humorous discussions. No kissing. No fucking. No . . . light. No Nicole. Fuck. And I realized Estelle was fucking right. *How did that happen?* There was no way around it. No point in denying it. I was in love with her and there was nothing I could do to stop it. I'd known it in that hotel room. I may have known it before then. Who knew? Love was a strange thing. But the more time that passed without seeing each other, and the longer she was in Argentina, the clearer it became that I'd lost her. Probably for good. Maybe I'd have to come to terms with the fact that I let go of the one woman who made me want to settle down once and for all.

"I . . ." I started, but stopped.

"Dude. She's right," Oliver added.

I closed my eyes, but it was useless, because all I could picture was Nicole's smile when she looked at me, her laugh when she made fun of me, the way her blue eyes lit up when she saw me walk near her. And fuck, I loved all of that. I loved the way she tried to hold back her emotion from the world but let me see it. I loved the way she let me see all of her, unfiltered. And my sister was right. I was in love with her.

"This is you admitting it?" Jensen asked with a laugh. I opened my eyes and looked around the room, at him, at Mia, Oliver, Estelle, and finally, at baby Grayson.

"I . . . it doesn't matter. I can't . . . it doesn't matter what I feel," I said.

"Shit. Victor stuttering and at a loss for words. This is big," Mia said.

"I fucking lost her," I said quietly. "The one girl I could stand to be near when she chewed her food and got all emotional and shit . . . and I fucking lost her." *Again*, I wanted to add, but didn't.

"You haven't lost her yet," Estelle said with a small smile.

I loved my sister. She was a pain in my ass most of the time, but she encouraged me when I needed it. I haven't lost her yet . . . but it didn't take away from the fact she was still in another country with her ex. I decided to call her. What else could I do? But her phone went straight to voicemail. Once. Twice. Three times. Finally, I sent her a simple three-worded text message in hopes she'd get it. Thankfully they hadn't pushed me for more, because there wasn't much I could offer. I wanted to fight but I had no idea how. The only thing I'd ever had to fight for was my career. My love life always sorted itself out. Fuck.

Later that week in the office, I snapped at everybody. Corinne cringed every time she walked into my office to drop off a paper, and I didn't blame her. I was sick of her, William, Grace, Bobby, and everybody else I had to see. The next time somebody knocked on my door, I growled a loud, "What?"

Bobby.

"Did your promotion come with a pissy attitude?" he asked as he stepped in.

I took a deep breath and put down my pen so I could massage my temple. When I knew I wouldn't snap, I dropped my hands and looked at him.

"What's up?"

He raised an eyebrow. "You wanna talk about it?"

"Not really," I said, letting out a breath. The last thing I needed was to talk about it. I went from being upset at myself for letting her go, to being pissed off at her for going and going with him. *Him.* The guy who had treated her like shit, cheated on her, let himself be seen in public with other women, and then there was the ice cream parlor thing . . . I just . . . I couldn't understand. I couldn't.

"Okay. You want to go watch the game, have a drink? Maybe it'll help you sort your shit out."

"I'm fine," I growled. "Nothing to sort out."

"Dude. Everyone in the office is fucking scared to talk to you right now. This has been going on for a week. You really don't think we realize you have a problem?"

My hands formed fists. I ground my teeth together to keep myself from lashing out. The moment I felt my heart tighten and thought of the heart attack scare my dad went through a couple years ago, I realized I couldn't do this anymore.

"I have to go talk to Will," I said, standing from my chair and heading toward his office. I knocked once, twice, and raised a hand to knock once more before he shouted for me to come in. He was sitting on the other side of his desk with his eyes closed, the lights dimmed down as he listened to one of those relaxation podcasts he'd been into as of late. He'd even gone as far as to email one of the links to me, which I deleted without opening.

"Hey. What can I do for you?" he asked, straightening in his chair and pushing down on his phone to shut the Zen bitch up.

I took a deep breath and sat down across from him. This man had given me the opportunity of a lifetime twice now. First, when I came to him looking for a job in divorce law and he took a chance the moment I sat down and went over the reasons why I thought I'd be a good fit in his firm. Second, when he named me partner. *Partner*. My fucking name had just been painted on the outside of the goddamn building. Alessi, Cohen, and Reuben, Esq. I wasn't ashamed to admit tears were almost shed when I saw that. And there I was, about to let it all go. Or most likely let it all go, because if he told me I needed to quit, I'd do it and start from scratch at a different firm. The thought alone made me want to throw up, but the thought of my life without Nicole in it was unacceptable.

"I'm in love with your daughter," I said, surprising myself. That wasn't the way I wanted to start the conversation, and from the way his eyes nearly bulged out of their sockets, I could tell I took him by surprise as well. He cleared his throat, blinking.

"I'm sorry, what?"

"I'm in love with your daughter," I repeated. "I'm in love with her, and I don't know when it happened, but I do know I should have passed her case along to someone else when we were well underway with it. It was wrong of me, and I'm willing to take responsibility for all of it."

Will stayed quiet for a long moment, just staring at me. He was going to ask me to pack up my shit and leave. I knew this, because he was giving me the same look he gave Roger Petit when he fired him in front of the entire staff.

"Does she know?"

I swallowed, nodding, and then shook my head. "Not . . . no. I don't know. She should know. It's obvious."

At this, his mouth twitched. "Obvious to whom?"

"Everyone, apparently," I said, shrugging.

He put a finger up as if telling me to hold on, and pressed the intercom button on the office phone. "Corinne, will you come to my office?"

I frowned. Maybe he would tell her to pack up my shit for me. At least then I wouldn't have to do all the work. That may be a good idea. But then she wouldn't know where to put what and she'd probably mix up my boxes and I'd have to work double. Fuck.

"Yes, sir," she said behind me. I didn't even turn around to acknowledge her.

She probably still had the mustard stain on her ivory top anyway, and my eyes would get glued to that and she'd think I was staring at her tits and get the wrong impression.

"Come here for a second," he said, signaling for her to come in. I finally looked up at her when she stood beside me, and sure enough, the mustard stain was still there. "Have you heard anybody say that Victor is acting a little . . . off lately?"

I examined the side of her face. Her cheeks flushed. She shot me an embarrassed look before looking at Will again. "You mean, more off than usual?"

My mouth dropped. "What the fuck is that supposed to mean?"

She shrugged, cringing. "Just . . . you've been in a bad mood."

"Says who?" I asked.

"Everyone," William answered. "Everybody here has made mention about your mood, and it started the day after your promotion went through." He looked at Corinne. "Thank you. You may go now."

She scurried off. I narrowed my eyes at the betrayer as she left the room.

"That's bullshit," I argued.

"It's not, and now you come in here telling me that you may have feelings for my daughter," he said, raising an eyebrow as if to say *what the hell am I supposed to think?*

"I don't think I have feelings for her, William. I fucking know it. If I didn't know it, I wouldn't be sitting here telling you, and if I wasn't absolutely certain I was in love with her, I wouldn't risk my job."

I decided that if I was going to get fired or demoted, I was going to go out with a fucking bang.

And that's pretty much how my two-hour meeting, later known as *The Big Debate* with William started . . .

Chapter Thirty-One

Nicole

"AND YOU JUST let him go?" I whispered, my heart and head pounding simultaneously.

"I had no choice," my dad said.

I closed my eyes, sagging down to my living room floor. Bonnie climbed on my lap and nuzzled herself between my legs.

"He was okay with that?" I asked, running my fingers through Bonnie's soft hair.

"He had no choice."

Sadly, no choice seemed to be the only choice we had.

"Okay, Dad. I have to go. I'll see you soon."

"I'm sorry, pumpkin. I love you."

"Yeah. Love you too."

I hung up and tossed the phone on the couch behind me. I felt sick to my stomach. He'd acknowledged us? To my dad. Why would he do that? Why would he even . . . I didn't understand it. Clearly he hadn't told my dad because he wanted me. He'd told him because he wanted to come clean about having supposed feelings about me. Because he couldn't live with himself, knowing it was something that was against the company policy and not telling my dad about it. But it wasn't for me. It wasn't because he wanted me.

I twisted and picked up my phone again, texting Estelle to thank her for inviting me to her party, but sending her my regrets for not being able to attend. Victor had sent me a text message while I was in Argentina. Three simple words that set my soul aflame.

I miss you.

I hadn't responded because I was shocked he'd do that, especially with his paranoia of having things traced. I hadn't called because what I wanted to say to him couldn't be said over the phone.

My phone rang a few seconds after I'd tossed it.

Estelle.

I almost didn't answer, but then figured it wouldn't be fair to her. She seemed like a planner and probably had something specific for the attendees.

"Why aren't you coming?" she asked.

"I just . . ." I sighed. I could lie, or I could just come out with it, and because I was a shit liar, I came out with it. "I think it will be awkward to see your brother. I need to see him, but I don't think your party is the right setting."

"Who cares about him? I invited you, not you and him together. You. Please come. I already made you a heart."

I closed my eyes, feeling impending tears form behind my lids. "You made a kaleidoscope heart for me?"

She made *me* a heart, made of broken glass that represents broken hearts and pain and how beautiful the brokenness we carry inside makes us. *Why did she have to be so nice? How could she have known how badly I needed something like that right now?*

"Of course. You said you liked them," she said.

I swallowed. "Okay. I'll just pass by."

"Yay. See you tomorrow. And remember, pirate."

"I remember," I said, smiling as we hung up.

I called Marcus and asked him to pick me up, not because of the media—as I hadn't seen any—but because he was still on the payroll and I didn't want to park anywhere. He showed up much sooner than expected.

"You must have been dying to see me again," I said, opening the door.

He shook his head, but smiled a little. "If Gabriel didn't pay me so well, I would have taken twenty minutes longer."

I hid my smile by turning around and locking the door. "You're getting better at jokes," I said.

"I'm not sure that's a compliment coming from you."

"It's a very big compliment coming from me. I'm the funniest person you know."

"I worked for Martin Lawrence once," he said as he turned on the car.

"Ah. So he will tell me who he's worked for in the past."

He shrugged and went back to silence while I sketched out some pirate outfits I thought I could make by tomorrow night. In the end, I decided to buy most of the materials already done, like a white frilly blouse and tall black boots. I'd figure out what I could do with the elastic, black chiffon, black lace fabric, black latex, and basically any black material I could find. After I bought what I needed and got back in the car, I started feeling nervous again. I was going to the party, and I was going to see Victor, and I hadn't even spoken to him. I'd have to call him. Right? I'd text. He'd texted, so I'd text back. Tonight. Or maybe when I got home.

"Marcus, let's say you were going to a party, and you knew a girl you used to . . . have something with was also going . . . would you take a date?"

"Maybe. Are you taking one?"

I blinked. "I'm not talking about myself."

Marcus's eyes slid toward me. "You're asking for a friend?"

I pursed my lips. "You know, I didn't ask Chrissy to come shopping with me because I thought we could use this time to do some quality bonding, but if you'd like me to call her . . ."

His eyes widened. "I wouldn't."

"She really seems to like you," I said, smiling.

"No. I mean, I wouldn't take a date," he said, frowning.

"Oh." I paused. "Well, he's been seen with a lot of blondes lately."

"You've also been seen with more than one man."

"That's different."

Marcus shrugged.

"It's different. I didn't hook up with either of them. I kissed Brent because I was tipsy and Victor was pissing me off, and then I went with Gabriel because I had to," I said defensively, and looked out the window when Marcus stayed quiet. "And I went to Argentina because I needed to get the hell away. I mean, who the fuck tells somebody's dad they have feelings for his daughter after they get a promotion? I'm not taking responsibility for his stupidity. I kept our secret."

Marcus parked in front of my house and left the car on. We stayed quiet for a long moment. It was so quiet, but all I could hear was noise. My dad's conversation kept replaying in my head, the pictures of Victor flashed in and out in between . . .

"Don't take a date," he said after a long time.

"Huh?"

"Don't take a date to the party. Go by yourself. You're a fun girl, you can party by yourself, can't you?"

"Of course I can," I scoffed. "I don't need anybody's help to have fun." I paused. "Will you go with me?"

Marcus laughed. "Definitely not."

"I'm scared," I whispered.

"That's usually a good sign."

I rolled my eyes, picked up my bags, and got out of the car. "Pick me up tomorrow at eight."

As soon as I was in the house, I went to work, but when I took a break to feed Bonnie, I felt myself gravitating toward my phone. I typed quickly, before I could change my mind. He was probably out anyway. It was Friday night, after all.

Me: *I miss you too.*

I set the phone down as if it were burning me and walked away from it before I could do anything crazy, like call him. My phone buzzed a few seconds later.

V: *Did you have a nice vacation?*

Me: *Yes.*

He didn't respond after that, and I developed a sinking feeling in the pit of my stomach. I went back to my costume and tried to ignore the phone and the way it wasn't buzzing.

Marcus knocked on my door at seven fifty, and I could tell he was having a hard time not looking at what I was wearing when I opened the door.

"It's okay, you can check me out. I look hot," I said. "Unless I look slutty, then I have to wear the other outfit."

"You look fine."

"Not slutty?"

He shrugged. "I thought you didn't care if you looked slutty?"

This guy. I shook my head, grabbed my purse, and followed him to my car. Thankfully there was still no sign of photographers, but as we were about to drive off, there was a knock on my window that startled me. I looked and saw Brent standing outside.

"Hey," I said, lowering the window.

"Hey. I haven't seen you around. Are you back with Lane?"

Evidentially, I'd used Brent as my sounding board one too many times. Thankfully I never said Victor's name, so I guess he thought my rants about men were all about Gabe. I tried not to laugh at that thought.

"No. Definitely not."

"Oh, good to know," he said with a smile. "Maybe we can have dinner one of these days."

"Sure. I'm running late though, so I'll have to get back to you."

"Of course," he said, stepping away from the car. We waved at each other and Marcus drove away.

"Good thing you didn't invite him," he said after.

"Funny."

We were quiet on our way to the party, which was at Victor's parents' house. Even that made me nervous. I'd be seeing them again, and I really, really liked them. The funny thing was that this was reminding me of a divorce in itself. A divorce where instead of the dog, I wanted shared custody of his family. The gates were open for us to drive in without ringing the bell, and we were able to pull up to the door. I stayed in the car for a while, breathing in and out.

"Call me when you need me to pick you up," Marcus said.

I took one last long breath before stepping out of the car and telling him that I would, then walked up the steps with the bottle of wine I'd brought along and rang the doorbell. My heart pounded and shook in my chest, and when Victor opened the door, I was pretty sure I was close to fainting. I swallowed, registering the look of surprise on his face, his gaze skimming over me slowly. I felt the charge everywhere, and realized that despite the time we'd been apart, nothing had managed to numb what I felt for him, let alone make it vanish.

"Hi," I managed to say, clearing the croak in my throat.

"You look beautiful," he replied. My heart leaped again. I was finding it impossible to breathe with the way he was looking at me.

"I . . . thank you. You look . . ." My eyes followed the length of his body. He was wearing a legit pirate costume.

"Ridiculous," he said. "I know."

I smiled. "I was going to say hot."

He tilted his head a bit and smiled. It was so sexy, and real, and unexpected, that it made my heart squeeze in pain. "I'm glad that wasn't lost under this ridiculousness."

I laughed as he stepped aside for me to walk in. The house was decked out in pirate paraphernalia. I felt like I was on the set of Pirates of the Caribbean. "You guys really know how to throw a party."

"Yeah, my mom and sister have no life."

"I heard that," Estelle said, appearing from where I knew the dining room was. She looked like a sexy Captain Hook, with a hook on one arm and a parrot on her shoulder. She walked over to me and pulled me into a hug. "Hi. Oh my God. I love your costume; did you make it? I'm so glad you came."

Victor's lips twitched when she said that, and I found myself smiling as my stomach flip-flopped again. I wanted to stop looking at him, but I couldn't. I knew I missed him, I guess I hadn't realized just how much until I saw him again.

"I made most of it," I said. "Pulled an all-nighter."

"Vic, can you help me get this?" a woman said, and when she walked in wearing her own sexy pirate outfit, I recognized her as the blonde in one of the pictures I'd seen of him. My smile instantly vanished and I started to feel like I couldn't breathe.

"Victor," she said again, more demanding.

"Chill out, woman. I'm coming," he responded, looking at me momentarily. "I'll . . ." He walked away without finishing his sentence, and I didn't even know what to feel. I just knew my heart felt like it was too big for my chest and would possibly climb up my throat and spill out of my mouth at any moment.

"They're planning something for me," Estelle said in a quiet voice. "They think they're slick, those two."

I tried to smile at her, but couldn't, so I just nodded. "Everything looks great."

"Thank you. My mom did most of it," she said.

"And me," the blonde said, coming back to where we were still standing. "I helped. A lot."

"You did a good job," I said, catching Victor's gaze over her shoulder.

He was looking at me with an intensity that wasn't appropriate while out in public, much less with his girlfriend standing right there. However, I felt the heat of his gaze everywhere.

"Oh my God. I'm sorry. I've been staring at you since you walked in and haven't even introduced myself. I'm Mia," she said with a huge smile.

"Nicole. Nice to meet you," I said, returning her smile, though mine was much smaller, not as excited.

"Hey, can you help me carry the drinks outside?" Estelle asked Mia.

Mia gave her a sharp look. There was an exchange in their gazes, and Mia finally seemed to get whatever it was that Estelle was trying to tell her. I felt another pang in my chest. They were really, really familiar with each other. Clearly Mia had either been a part of their life a lot longer, or really hit it off with Estelle, much more than I had.

"I'll see you later," Mia said, shooting one more smile my way before she turned around and punched Victor in the arm playfully. He rolled his eyes at her before looking at me again.

"She's really pretty," I said once they walked away.

"Not as pretty as you." He took a step toward me. I swallowed.

"You shouldn't say things like that," I whispered, tilting my face to look at him when he stood right in front of me.

"I only speak truths," he said, his voice low, making my heart stutter.

"Stop."

"Hey, is that Nicole?"

Victor groaned. "I'm in a house full of cock-blockers."

I sidestepped him until I reached his mom. She wrapped her arms around me. "Hi, Hannah."

"I've called you a couple of times so you could come over and see the dress. I can't wait to show it to you. The seamstress was very, very impressed with your design. She really wants to meet you," she said, her words fast and close together.

"Mom, she just got here," Victor said.

"I was in Argentina for a little while."

"Oh, you visited your mom? How was it? Did you have fun?" She pulled me toward the back of the house, and I was glad for the intrusion of whatever moment it was Victor and I were sharing. We couldn't have those anymore, especially now that he'd clearly moved on. I hated my dad right now. Why would he call me and tell me all those things if Victor had clearly moved on? He should have just kept his mouth shut, then I would have never known that Victor had thought about me at all.

Hannah took me around the yard, introducing me to the people there, which was interesting in and of itself. Some of the people were artsy, painters and such, others were doctors, architects, housewives, you name it, they were at the party. I'd already met Oliver, so I said hi to him, and he introduced me to some of his friends. At least there were hot guys there. Maybe they'd help me keep my eyes off Victor.

I excused myself and walked back to the drink table to pick up a glass of wine.

"I'm assuming your dad told you we spoke," Victor said, his voice making me shiver. I took a long sip of wine, hoping it would calm my nerves.

"He did."

He put his right hand over the handle of the pirate sword sticking out of its holster. I couldn't imagine how he thought he looked ridiculous. I'd never seen a sexier pirate in my life.

"What did he tell you?" he asked. I tore my gaze away from his hand, those long fingers of his, and looked back into his eyes. Big mistake.

"Are you going to cut off my tongue if I don't tell you?" I asked, smirking. His gaze heated as quickly and my breath caught in my throat.

"I can think of more than a few things I'd like to do with your tongue. Cutting it off isn't one of them," he said, bringing the hand he had on the sword up to my hair, pushing some of it behind my ear. I closed my eyes as he adjusted the bandana I had on.

"I really don't think it's nice for you to say things like that," I whispered, eyes still closed.

"Why?"

"Because you have a girlfriend, and I don't think she'd appreciate it," I said, opening my eyes to look at him. He frowned.

"What the hell are you talking about?"

"Really? You're going to the 'let me pretend I don't have a

girlfriend' route while she's here?" I paused to take another sip of wine and tipped my head a little to glare at him. "I'm not a good candidate for bullshit, Victor. I see right through it."

He balked at me. "And as you know, I'm not good at practicing patience. What the fuck are you talking about, Nicole?"

"Mia," I said, a little louder than anticipated. His face morphed from confusion, to amusement, to anger, and back to amusement as he started to laugh.

"You're fucking insane."

"Yeah, well—" I started. Before I could finish, he was pulling my hand and practically dragging me to where Mia was standing with Oliver and the hot guy crew. "Victor."

"No," he said, stopping in the middle of the yard to look back at me. "If you're going to accuse me of something, you should have the sense to get your facts straight. Do you know how fucking mad I am at you? Do you know . . .?" He stopped to take a deep breath before pulling me again. "We'll discuss that later. Just . . . come."

Oliver, Estelle's husband, turned around with a frown. He pushed his long hair out of his face and looked between Victor and me.

"Everything okay?" hot guy number two said to our right.

"Mia, why are you here?" Victor asked, his voice strong.

Mia pulled a face. "I'm not sure I'm understanding the question."

Hot guy number two, I was pretty sure his name was Jensen, hid his smile behind the bottle of beer in his hand.

"Jensen, stop fucking laughing. Tell Nicole why Mia's here," Victor said.

Jensen started laughing and shaking his head, then Oliver joined in, and the other guy they were talking to followed.

"I told you," Jensen said when he finally stopped laughing.

"No, I told you," Oliver said.

"Fuck you. I said it first." He paused, wiping his eyes and looking over at Mia. "Babe, what did I say about Victor last week?"

Babe? My eyes widened. Oh fuck. *No.*

Mia frowned. "I don't know, Jensen."

"You need to remember."

She rolled her eyes. "Are we done here? I need to go see if Grey's still sleeping."

"You have the video monitor attached to your ass. I'm pretty sure he'll alert you when he wakes up," Victor said. "Can you answer my fucking question before I punch your husband?"

Oh motherfuck. She was *not.* And she was a mom?

"Estelle's my best friend. I'm not going to miss her birthday," Mia said.

"Okay, and who did you come with?" Victor pressed.

"Jesus Christ. With this idiot," she said, pointing at Jensen, who started laughing again. "Why?"

"She thought you were my girlfriend," Victor said, his eyes cutting to me. I wasn't looking at him, but I could feel them on me.

"What?" Mia said, laughing now. "Oh my God. That's disgusting." She paused and looked at me. "No offense or anything."

I opened my mouth to say something, but there was absolutely nothing I could say.

"Don't worry, this one right here is your brand of crazy," Jensen said, pointing at Mia with his thumb. She pushed him.

"Shut up," she said, then looked at me again. "Why . . . oh. Is it because our pictures in the tabloids? I told you we were famous. I'm a huge fan of yours. Well, I was a huge fan of Gabriel, but then all that . . . stuff happened, so I'm not as big a fan as I used to be, but I still like him as an actor because he's really good."

Jensen wrapped an arm around her shoulder and pulled her to him. "Babe."

"What?"

"Your fangirl is showing."

She buried her face in her hands and took a breath before looking at me again. "I talk a lot when I'm nervous."

I smiled. "That's fine. I'm sorry for probably giving you the biggest bitch face earlier. I really didn't know you guys were just friends."

"Totally fine. Totally cool," Mia said. I smiled at her and everyone else before excusing myself once again. As I walked away, I heard Mia say, "She's officially my new best friend," and I had to laugh.

"You thought I was dating someone?" Victor asked when he caught up to me. "And you didn't even fucking think to ask?"

"How would I ask?"

"You could have called."

"You broke up with me." *And it broke my heart.*

He narrowed his eyes, jaw set. I raised an eyebrow, daring him to take a different approach. "You're going home with me."

"What?"

"Tonight. You're going home with me, and we're going to have this fucking conversation. Either you go with me, or I go with you. You pick, but I swear to God if that Brent guy shows up at your house I'll get arrested, and you'll have to bail me out of jail."

I bit my lip to keep from laughing but was unsuccessful. "You're the lawyer."

He scoffed. "If I get to keep my license."

My smile dropped. "What do you mean?"

"Your dad didn't tell you?"

I blinked and shook my head slowly.

"We're having a meeting with the associates on Monday to see if they want to keep me on board as partner."

My stomach dropped. "What?"

"What did he tell you?"

"That you told him you had feelings for me."

"He didn't tell you what we argued about?"

"No," I said, frowning. "What the did you argue about?"

"You."

"Me?" I asked. My head was spinning. I needed to sit down for this. I needed an entire bottle of wine for this.

"Come home with me," he said. "I'll tell you everything."

"Okay." I paused. "Okay, but I need to call Marcus."

Victor growled. "Always calling some guy."

"He's security detail, and a friend," I said, rolling my eyes as I took out my phone and dialed. "Marcus, you don't have to pick me up tonight."

Before I could explain anything, Victor snatched the phone from my hand. "Marcus, this is Victor. If you must know, she's coming home with me, and she's staying until, and if, I let her go. If I let her go, I'll be the one driving her home, so if she fucking calls you before five in the afternoon tomorrow, ignore the call. Thanks. Bye."

He hit the end button before handing the phone back to me and all I could do was stand here, holding my hand out to take it.

This. Fucking. Guy.

Chapter Thirty-Two

Nicole

W E STAYED AT the party long enough to sing happy birthday. Long enough for Victor's friends to tell him he was whipped and make fun of him. Long enough for him to send them all to hell. And long enough for me to witness Victor holding a baby with so much care and love, I was afraid my ovaries would explode right there. Neither one of us said a word on the drive to his house, me because I was afraid I would say the wrong thing. I wasn't sure what his silence was about, but it was making me nervous. He hadn't touched me either. Not since we were outside, when he would do the occasional drift of his fingers along my bare shoulder to call my attention. It made my stomach dip every time and even though I tried to focus on the wine, after two glasses I didn't even want any more.

His house was dark except for the porch light when we got there, and I was so worked up I was sure if he touched me I would jump out of my seat. He switched off the engine and sighed as he glanced over at me.

"Let's go."

I nodded and stepped out of the car, taking caution with my heels in the gravel of his driveway. He seemed to notice, or maybe he'd had many women in heels over, because he came over and grabbed my arm to steady me and help me inside. I thanked him and let him open the door and switch on the inside light for me. I looked around and crossed my arms as he locked the door behind me and gasped when he walked back over and dropped a kiss on my shoulder.

"I've been wanting to do that all night," he said, his voice a rasp behind my ear. I closed my eyes to savor the moment. "Turn around."

I opened my eyes, my heart pounding in my throat as I did.

"I'm so mad at you, I don't . . ." He sighed. "Maybe we should talk in the kitchen."

I felt like I was being sent to the principal's office on the first day at a new school, like everything was riding on this conversation. My nerves were shot to hell because whatever I'd done would never truly be forgiven. But I hadn't done anything wrong. Not really, anyway. I'd tried to save his job, and he was possibly being demoted anyway. We sat beside each other on the barstools after he served us each a glass of water.

"So you're meeting with my dad and the other guys on Monday," I said, figuring I'd start where he left off earlier.

"Right."

"How'd that come about?"

Victor looked down at the floor for a long time before tilting his face to lock eyes with me. "I'm not sure I want to start at that part."

"Okay," I said, lifting the glass of water to my lips to take a sip and setting it down. "Start, then."

He clasped his hands on his lap, his leg bobbing rapidly. "What's going on with you and Gabriel?"

"Nothing." I paused. "You're handling my divorce. Why don't you tell me?"

His eyes narrowed. "It wouldn't be the first time you kept something from me."

"That was different, and there's nothing I'm keeping from you. Everything's on paper," I said.

"Him holding your hand, putting his arm on your shoulder, hugging you, kissing you, that shit is on paper?" he said, his voice rising.

"He didn't kiss me," I said, but he ignored my comment and stood suddenly, the top of the chair hitting the edge of the counter with a little bang. I flinched. He started pacing, taking off the pirate sword and vest, and I watched.

"If I knew that shit was going to be part of the agreement, do you really think I would have let you sign? What else was part of the fucking agreement, Nicole? Did you fuck him too? How does one get into that kind of contract with you? Is being an asshole a requirement? Cheating on you? Being a drug addict? Treating you like shit? Tell me. Tell me because I wanna know where the fuck I'm going wrong."

I blinked. And blinked. Trying to make the stupid tears I felt forming in my eyes go away. I swallowed the lump in my throat and swung my legs to and fro to distract myself from crying, because I wouldn't do that. I wouldn't cry.

"Tell me," he seethed, walking over and placing his arms on either side of me, his face at a reachable distance from mine. I swallowed again.

"If those are the requirements, I'd say you fit at least two of those categories," I whispered. His eyes widened as he stood straight and rubbed his face with both hands. "You know what? Fuck you, Victor. Fuck you for putting this on me when you pushed me to it." I seethed, feeling hot tears burning my eyes.

"Just like I pushed you to marry him five years ago?"

I flinched again. I'd seen Victor angry. I'd seen Victor annoyed. I'd seen Victor let loose and have fun. I thought I'd seen Victor in all of his elements, but I'd never seen him like this. I wasn't sure what to do with this version of him, so I stayed silent and let him work out his issues in front of me. If this was his ugly, I wanted to see it. I wanted to see all of him. I needed to see all of him before I could decide whether I would stay or leave. He closed his eyes and took a deep breath before coming over to me again and standing in front of me, farther than before, but still close enough for me to reach out and grab him. Or slap him. I took a deep breath. Long, deep breath.

"What happened to your face?"

I hadn't asked him when I saw him last. Whatever it was looked like it was almost healed, but the scar was still there. He let out a chuckle, although it sounded anything but amused.

"I had a difference of opinion with someone."

"A difference of opinion . . . Care to expand on that, or are we here to keep harboring secrets?"

"I don't know, Nicole. You tell me. You tell me what we're harboring."

"I flew to Argentina with Gabriel because he was going and I wanted to go see my mom. I only saw him that one day. After that I spent the rest of the time with my mom. Look at the fucking pictures. We're wearing the same thing in all of them." I paused, taking a breath and letting it out, trying to calm down.

"I'm here because you asked me to come. I'm here because I want to know what happened with you and my dad and your job, because the only thing I'm guilty of is helping you keep your goddamn dream alive."

He moved closer, standing between my legs. "My dream? You don't know anything about my dreams. You never asked me what I wanted."

"You never asked me. You broke up with me. You broke things off because you were afraid you'd lose your precious career."

He closed his eyes and let out a harsh breath that caressed my face.

"You made me think that us being with other people was the right thing to do, so I went and saw other people, like you did," I added.

"I didn't see anybody else, Nicole. All I ever saw was you."

"I saw the way you kissed that blonde. Not Mia, but that other one, the one you took to the office party."

He growled. "Fuck that girl."

I tilted me head and shot him a look. "Did you?"

"No! Christ, Nicole. How could you even ask me that?"

"How could I not?" I said, my voice breaking a little. "How could I not, Victor?"

He placed his palm against my cheek and tilted my face so I could look into his eyes. "I would never do that to you. *Ever.* Did I kiss her? Yes. For pictures. That was all."

"It hurt," I said, swallowing back that damn lump of emotion. "It hurt a lot."

His gaze fell over my features, appraising me for a long moment, and during those seconds I saw his expression thaw and his posture relax. He lowered his forehead to mine.

"I'm sorry, baby," he whispered. "Seeing you with Brent at the office hurt too. So did seeing you with Gabriel fucking Lane in every news outlet available while you guys were off in Argentina visiting your mom. Did you think that would be easy for me?"

"I didn't know what to think," I whispered. He held my face with his hand.

"It was fucking brutal," he said, lowering his hand and setting it over the elastic corset I'd made. He tucked a finger underneath it and snapped at it. "I'm not this," he said. "I don't stretch. I don't mold. I don't conform, and despite what people say about my career, I'm not a liar. So when I tell you I'm in love with you, Nicole, it's because I'm in fucking love with you. And when I barge into your dad's office to tell him I'm more in love with his daughter than I'll ever be with my career, it's a big fucking deal."

My heart stopped as I processed his words, and I found that no amount of swallowing or blinking was going to keep my tears at bay. He cradled my face with both hands and wiped my tears away with his thumbs.

"You said that to my dad?" I whispered. He nodded, bringing his mouth down to mine and placing a chaste kiss on it. I leaned forward to try to get another, but he moved. "So they really might demote you because of me?"

"Not because of you, baby. It has nothing to do with you," he said.

"But you just said—"

His lips curled into a small smile. "Okay, it has everything to do with you, but it's not your fault. I made my choice. I'm surprised your dad didn't tell you when you spoke to him."

"Well," I said, eyes wide, "he asked me if there was anything going on between us and I denied it, and then he said you argued and left and . . . yeah, I don't know. He didn't make it sound very good." I paused, searching his face. "I am so sorry."

"Not your fault."

"I can talk to him."

"I have a meeting on Monday. I'll plead my case and see what they say. If they don't want me as partner, then it wasn't meant to be."

"How can you say that?"

He didn't answer me. Instead, he bent down and kissed my temple. Just once, but the gesture somehow gave me the answer I needed.

"Are you staying?" he asked. "For good?"

"What does for good mean?" I asked.

"It means for good. That you're mine and no one else's. No more fucking around."

"Are you mine and no one else's?"

He smiled, caressing my face with his thumb as he brought his lips down to mine. "Always yours. I was never anybody else's." That tone. It made me think of the time he'd begged me to scream that I was his. When he'd pounded into me with a ferocity I'd only experienced with him. Just thinking about it had my heart racing. He loved me. He was *in fucking love* with me.

"Hmm," I said, moaning when I felt his mouth on my neck, his hand crawling up my leg and under my skirt. "You mean I finally caught the untamable Victor Reuben?"

He chuckled against my chest, his other hand pulling my panties hard and ripping them off. I gasped, startling a little, and when he started moving his fingers inside me and using his thumb on my clit, I threw my head back.

"The untamable Victor Reuben," he said, nipping my cleavage. "Take your tits out and I'll show you how tame I am."

I pulled the top of my bustier down, and uttered an unintelligible "oh my God" when I felt his mouth on my left nipple as his fingers moved inside me. I was all nerve endings, all feelings, no holds barred as he played my body with his fingers, his tongue.

"I'm going to fall," I said, feeling my toes curling with an impending orgasm. "I haven't . . . oh my God . . . that's so good . . . you're so good . . . oh my God. Victor!"

"Say my name. That's right," he said, biting my other nipple.

"Fuck."

"That's right, baby."

And then, on his kitchen stool, I orgasm, eyes closed, toes curled, head thrown back. He pulled me off the stool and turned me around, pushing my torso down, my breasts on the freezing cold granite as he spread my legs. I tried to brace myself, but it was no use. When he thrust inside me I took in a huge gasp of a breath. He yanked the bandana off and threw it on the counter.

"I should use it to tie your fucking hands." His voice low and in my ear as he fucked me. Hard. "I should blindfold you." He leaned back and pulled my skirt up, his hand coming down on my ass in a hard slap. "I shouldn't even fuck you right now," he said, pulling out of me completely.

"No. No. No," I shouted, pushing myself back. "Please."

He thrust in just as quickly and hard as he pulled out, and I yelped at the feel of his girth and the slap of his hand on my other ass cheek. "I should make you fucking beg for it. If I wasn't so desperate for you, I would."

"Oh my God," I said, feeling another orgasm surfacing.

He grabbed a fistful of my hair and brought his other arm around my body to play with my clit. "You make me feel desperate for you, Nicole. I can't stop thinking about you. I can't bear the thought of you with another man."

I gasped, my eyes rolling back. "You're the only one." I gasped again, the strumming of his fingers on my clit was increasing and I knew I'd lose it in a second. "Never anybody else. I swear."

"Good," he said, pushing my face down so I was flat on the surface as he increased his pace and started to fuck me wildly. I squeezed my eyes shut and screamed when the orgasm finally ricocheted through me, and gasped at the feel of him emptying himself inside me in three slow, long thrusts. "Fuck, baby."

"Hmm," I gasped. It was the only thing I could say.

He helped me upright after a couple seconds and pulled me to his chest, holding the back of my neck. "I missed you so much."

I looked up at him. "I love you too." His smile was slow forming, but huge.

"I know."

I laughed, pushing his chest. "*You know? This* isn't Star Wars."

He shrugged. "No, but I know. I think you fell in love with me the last time I fucked you in my office, before you got married."

"That makes absolutely no sense, but let's say I did, what took you so long?" I asked. He bent his knees and lifted me into his arms, carrying me toward his room.

"I was a fucking idiot."

Chapter Thirty-Three

Victor

HAVING NICOLE IN my bed, fast asleep, for two days in a row when I woke up was perfect. I got up and headed to the bathroom to brush my teeth before putting on a pair of board shorts and heading outside. I hadn't stepped foot in the ocean since I brought her home on Friday night, and I needed to clear my mind before I headed to the office for my meeting. We'd talked, fucked, and argued the entire weekend, and I wouldn't have traded it for any amount of promotions or money in the world. I ran out with my board and caught some waves, and on my way back in, I smiled when I saw her standing outside with a cup of coffee in her hand. Bonnie was running around my grass, probably taking various shits, but that was fine. I'd deal with the dog later. At least she was potty-trained. I unzipped my wet suit and grinned when I caught Nicole licking her lips, her eyes dropping to my exposed chest. I couldn't stop fucking smiling.

I took it off and tossed it in the basket I had outside and put my board down as I ran up to her and swept her into a hug.

"Victor. You're going to get burned," she said, laughing as

she tried to balance her cup of coffee.

"I'm sure you don't have any left in there," I said, looking in. Sure enough, there was only a drop left.

"I could have just poured it," she said when I let go of her. My eyes drifted down to her white shirt, which was now completely wet and see-through. She had no bra on. She slapped me on the chest and my eyes snapped to hers.

"What?"

"Stop looking at my boobs."

I put my hands out and grabbed them, playing with her nipples over her shirt. She moaned. "You want me to stop?"

"No," she said, gasping when I pinched them. "Let's go inside."

We went inside, stripping clothes off until we were both naked. I propped her up by the wall and started closing the sliding glass door, my lips on hers. She broke the kiss and gasped out a, "Bonnie's outside."

Of course. The shitting dog.

"Bonnie. Get the fuck inside the house," I yelled. Nicole laughed until I pinned her with my stare and pushed the tip of my dick inside her, and then her laugh turned into a series of gasps and oh fucks. Those were my favorite.

"You have to leave soon," she said, moaning when I grabbed two handfuls of her ass and started driving into her. Fuck. She felt so good. She was so fucking wet. So. Fucking. Wet. I threw my head back, increasing my pace.

"I know."

"I'm going to come. Fuck. Victor. Victor," she shouted. "I'm going to . . . oh my . . ."

And then I shattered inside her. I caught my breath and let her catch hers before I helped her stay steady on her feet.

"I'm pretty sure the entire beach heard us," she said.

"Good."

She laughed and went back to the kitchen while I ran to my room and into the shower. I had thirty-five minutes to get to work. Fuck.

I was finishing putting on my tie when Nicole walked into the room.

"I brought you coffee. Do you have time to eat?"

I looked over my shoulder at the clock on the nightstand. Eighteen minutes. "Nope. I'll have Corinne get me something on her way."

"You look hot."

"Thank you."

"Really hot," she said, lowering her voice. I closed my eyes.

"This is going to be a problem," I said, looking at her.

"What?"

"Me having to go to work and wanting to stay home to fuck you instead."

She smiled, looking at the floor between us. I walked over to her and lifted her chin.

"No matter what happens today, I love you. That's not going to change, and I want you here, that's also not going to change."

She swallowed and looked at me. "I'm going to have Marcus pick me up. I should probably stay over there a couple of days. I do pay bills, you know."

I let go of her chin. I didn't like that idea at all, but I understood why she felt the need to go. I'd have to find someone to take over her lease so she could move in with me. That topic hadn't been discussed as of yet, but it would be soon, and that was a battle I'd win.

In the office, everybody greeted me a little warily since I'd been a complete ass for a few weeks. It made me wonder if they hadn't been informed of anything. When I got to the conference room, only William was there, sitting at the head of the table. He looked up from his phone when he heard me come in.

"Have a seat."

"Where's Bruce?" I asked as I unbuttoned my suit coat and sat down where I normally did, beside him. Bruce was the other partner.

"I decided not to call anybody in for this." He paused, setting his phone down. I looked at it, wondering if he'd set it to record. As if reading my thoughts, he chuckled and lit it up so I could see the home screen. "So paranoid about some things, so careless about others."

I let the jab slide. He was right.

"How's Nicole? Did you speak to her about . . . your situation?"

I tried to keep my face impassive, but my lips twitched into a smile. If he only knew how many situations his daughter and I got into over the weekend . . . "I did."

"And?"

"I already told you. I wouldn't have gone through the trouble with her if I didn't know it was the real deal."

"And how do you know it's the real deal? How do you know that in five years you won't be in this office talking about your own divorce? I know your track record."

My brows rose. Good questions. Fair questions. How did I know . . . how could I explain that?

"I don't," I said. "I have no idea what will happen in five years. I came in here thinking there was probably more than a fifty percent chance I'd get fired, or demoted, and I still haven't been able to stop fucking smiling, and that's the only way I know that. Who knows?" I shrugged. "Maybe it won't work out the way I want it to, but I sure as hell want to try, and when I think about my life five years from now, the only thing I see with sureness is Nicole."

Will tilted his head, his eyes assessing me. "When do the finalized papers get here?"

"They should be here soon. Possibly next week. I rushed Judge Matthews."

Will nodded. "You know how I feel about you as a person and as an employee. You're like a son I never had, and that's one of the reasons I'm being hard on you about this, because as much as I love you, I love my daughter more."

He picked up his phone and pushed a couple buttons, turning on the speakerphone. Three rings later Nicole's voice seeped through the room. My breath caught in my chest. I glanced up at him, and he shrugged as if to say let's see what she says about this.

"Hey, Dad," she said. My heart gripped at the sound of her voice.

"Hey, sweetheart. I have a question for you, and I need you to answer honestly."

Nicole groaned. "What now?"

"Promise?"

She stayed silent for a second. "Promise."

"Are you involved in any way with Gabriel?"

She stayed quiet again. My heart constricted. "No. Argentina was the last thing I was going to attend with him. Why?"

"I mean romantically, Nicole."

"No."

"That's a definite no? What about in Argentina?"

My heart squeezed again. I didn't want to hear this. I didn't want to know. Out of mind, out of sight. That had been my motto.

"No, Dad. Why are you asking weird questions?"

"What about Victor Reuben?"

"What about him?" she whispered.

"Last time I asked you, you said nothing was going on with you guys. Were you lying?"

She breathed into the phone.

"Promise, Nicole."

She breathed into the phone again. "Yes."

"Yes you were lying?"

"Yes."

"Why?"

"Because I thought if I told you the truth, you'd fire him," she said, and I could tell she was crying. I saw her cry the other day, but hearing her like this and knowing I wasn't there to comfort her made my heart physically ache.

"Why would I fire him?"

"Because he's my lawyer," she said, crying openly. "Please, Dad. Please don't fire him. It's my fault. I pushed him and pushed him."

I closed my eyes, burying my face in my hands. I couldn't do this. I couldn't sit there listening to her plead for me like this.

"He's not getting fired," Will said. My head snapped up.

"Oh, thank God," she said, sniffling. "Thank God."

"He said he told you he's in love with you."

"He did." She sniffled. "And I love him."

Will stayed quiet for a moment, his eyes appraising me. I kept my face neutral because I wasn't sure I wanted him reading into my relief. I didn't want him to know I felt like celebrating. He smiled after a couple beats. "Okay, sweetheart. I'll let you go now."

"Okay. Talk to you later."

He ended the call and drummed his fingers on the table. "So . . . that happened."

"Like I was saying, when I met you, I saw myself twenty years prior. I didn't have a mentor or anybody to walk me through things or help me when I fucked up, and I really wanted to be that person for you," he said. "But then I hired you, and I never really had to do that. You were like a newborn child who was already potty-trained. I've never seen anything like it. I didn't assign you to take care of my daughter's divorce so you could make partner. You were going to make partner anyway. That promotion has been yours since you stepped foot in this office." He paused.

To know I had his support for the role was incredible. While gaining Nicole in my life was a far greater reward, I couldn't deny the way hearing those words made me feel.

"I wanted you to represent her because I knew you'd do right by her, and I know you'll do right by her now as well."

I let out a breath. "Thank you. That means a lot." More than he could ever know.

"You wanna know how I know you're right for her?"

I swallowed. "How?"

"Because I don't even feel like I need to give you a warning, or tell you the things I'd do if you fuck things up, though maybe I should warn you that she can be a little difficult."

I chuckled. "I got that part."

"So then you're good," he said, smiling. "I couldn't have picked a better man for her."

"Thank you," I said, because I didn't know what else to say and fuck me, I was feeling emotional. "I'll always do right by her, Will." I took a deep, relieved breath. "Does this mean I'm not getting demoted?"

Will laughed. "Yes, but you will need to take time off until Nicole's papers come in."

"And not work?"

"And not work."

My jaw dropped. "What the fuck am I supposed to do?"

"You'll figure something out."

I sighed. I guess I would have to.

On my way out, I took a pit stop to Corinne's office to let her know. She looked at me like she wasn't sure what to do with the information.

"You're serious?"

"Yes, I'm serious. Why would I joke about that?"

"But you never take days off."

"Maybe I was waiting for my vacation to accumulate so I could take a longer break."

She frowned. "Six years later?"

"Corrine," I said, sighing. She closed her mouth when she realized she was pushing my buttons.

"Sorry. I just . . . I'm shocked. Does that mean we'll be on vacation at the same time? Does that mean I won't be able to take my vacation?"

Why did she have to get so shrilly? I let her have her moment, but instead of getting over it, she continued to look at me like I had some kind of answer written on my face. Finally, I cleared my throat.

"You put in your vacation and you'll take it. There are five other attorneys in this office, Corinne. Go get engaged, or married, or whatever," I said.

"What will you do?"

I made a face. How was that her business? "Not go get engaged or married or whatever," I responded. She smiled.

"I heard," she whispered, leaning into the desk as if she were sharing a great secret with me, "that you're in a very serious relationship."

I opened my mouth and closed it immediately. Whatever I said would be used against me for life around the office, and taking time off for what I'd done was the most lenient form of punishment for most people. Even though being without work for more than a couple days was like walking through the pits of hell, I had to be grateful it was all I got. That said, being out in the open with Nicole right now wouldn't be the smartest thing to do for either of us, and I knew that. Instead of answering her question the way I wanted—which was: I am in a very serious relationship—I just shrugged.

"If you need anything, call my cell phone," I said as I walked off. "Good luck on your vacation."

"You too."

I knew Nicole wouldn't be at my place when I got home, but it didn't keep me from missing her as I walked through the house, looking for any sign that she'd been there. The only sign was a navy blue blanket on the living room floor where the dog had slept. I'd never cared to have a dog, but I'd definitely have to get used to it being around. I looked at the blanket for a long time, debating whether or not I should pick it up. Itching to pick it up, really. In the end, I took a breath and made myself walk away. I went upstairs, changed into something comfortable, and smiled at the sight of my shower still being wet with her handwriting on the foggy mirror that read, *I love you.* I took my phone out and snapped a picture of it before I decided to call Quinn to ask him for a huge favor before heading to her house. I only hoped what I had planned would work and that she'd be able and want to go with me.

Chapter Thirty-Four

Nicole

I WAS SITTING outside with Bonnie, enjoying a cup of cereal, when Brent jogged by. As much as I appreciated the eye candy, I was seriously starting to wonder if he had a job.

"Hey, you want to grab lunch today?" he asked, stopping to catch his breath in front of my porch. I put my hand up to shield my face from the sun as I looked at him.

"Nah. I kind of—"

"Have a boyfriend," Victor said, his sudden presence making me jump an inch out of my seat.

Brent's and my head whipped toward him. My heart leaped at the sight of him, standing there in a pair of jeans and a polo. The fact he wasn't at work and had changed from his suit to this was not a good sign.

"What are you doing here?" I asked, blinking rapidly.

"Aren't you her lawyer?" Brent asked, frowning.

"Was."

My stomach dropped. *Was?*

"Yes. Was. Do you have any more questions for me or are you going to finish that run now?" Victor asked. I wanted the ground to swallow me whole.

"Maybe another time," I said to Brent, who nodded slowly.

"I'll catch you later," he said as he ran off.

"That was so mean," I said as soon as he was far enough away. I took a handful of cereal and began to chew.

Victor eyed the cup in my hand as he sat down in the chair beside me and patted Bonnie on the head. "Fuck that guy."

My eyes widened. "He's a nice guy."

"A nice guy who wants to fuck you."

I smiled, shaking my head. "Can you blame him?"

He had this wicked gleam in his eyes as he gave me a slow once-over. "Fuck, no. Doesn't mean I want to see him try, though."

"Now I know why you never have a girlfriend," I said, raising an eyebrow. He lifted my foot from the little table I had it on and placed it on his lap, massaging it. I closed my eyes and tossed my head back, putting down the cup of cereal on the floor beside me.

"What were you saying?"

"Huh?" I asked, opening my eyes to look at him. He was still smiling as he lifted my foot and bit down on my toe. "Ouch! Fuck."

He chuckled. "You were saying that you knew why I never had a girlfriend."

"Oh." I straightened a bit in my chair. "Your controlling tendencies. I don't know if women can handle that."

"Can you?" he asked, raising an eyebrow.

I looked at him for a beat, unable to keep myself from getting lost in the intense look his eyes held. The challenge. I freaking loved it. Loved *him*. I realized, as he massaged my feet, clearly not at work like he would have been if he'd worked his magic on my dad and whoever else he met with, that in a world full of

Gabriels, men like Victor came a dime a dozen.

"I think I can," I said quietly. I smiled when he dropped my feet and stood, towering over me with both hands clutching the armrests on either side of me.

"If anybody can, it's you," he said, dropping his lips to mine and kissing me deeply, his tongue delving into my mouth in a way that took my breath away. He broke the kiss and backed away slightly, still holding the armrests. "I have a surprise for you, but now that you're being so sassy, I'm not sure I want to give it to you."

"What are you going to do? Spank me?" I asked, smirking.

His gaze heated instantly. "Don't tempt me."

"Maybe I want to," I said, bringing my foot up and brushing it against his crotch, which was already hardening. He breathed out harshly.

"You love playing with fire, Nicole," he said, his voice a low rasp as he placed his forehead against mine.

"I love playing with you," I replied, pressing my lips against his.

He reached down and carried me, my chair making a screeching sound against the concrete as he lifted me and pushed it aside.

"Wait," I said as we waited for Bonnie to walk in before closing the door behind us. "Did you get fired?"

He chuckled, setting me down on the couch. "You wait until now to ask me that?"

"I was distracted."

"By how handsome and controlling I am?" he asked, grinning.

"You are so full of yourself."

"So I've been told," he said, grabbing his crotch in his hand. I nearly moaned at the sight of it.

"Did you?"

"No, I'm on leave until your divorce papers come back."

"So . . . you're still partner?" I asked quietly.

He sighed and took a seat beside me on the couch, putting an arm around me. I put my legs on his lap and scooted closer. "I am," he said, running his fingers through my hair. If he kept this up, the massages and the hair touching, I'd definitely keep him. "I was there when your dad called you."

My eyes widened, meeting his. "Did I . . . well, obviously he kept you on board so I didn't mess anything up, but . . ." I groaned. "I hate that he put me on the spot like that."

"You did great, Nic." He pulled me closer to him. "You did great, and," he let out a breath, "you were fine. It was fine. Will just doesn't want any more attention around this until it's clear the divorce is over. I really can lose my license. That's not a game."

I blinked. "We were just outside kissing. You just told Brent that you were my attorney and insinuated you were my boyfriend."

"Fuck Brent. He's not a threat."

"You don't know that."

He shot me a look. "If he becomes one, I'll take care of it."

"Like you took care of Darryl?" I asked, raising an eyebrow. I knew I'd caught him off guard because of the way his eyes widened and he reared back slightly. "I saw him in Argentina. His face was all cut up the same week you had a bandage on yours. Coincidence?"

"Probably. I'm sure a lot of people want to cut his face," he said.

"You're going to sit here and lie to me?"

He sighed, running a hand through his hair. It was telling.

"You can't just go around beating people up because of me,"

I said. "Isn't that worse than us being out together?"

Victor let out an unamused chuckle. "Not in the state of California."

"He can press charges."

"Let him try," he scoffed, then looked at me. "You don't have to worry about any of that, Nicole. Trust me."

"I do. I just don't want to be the reason you go through all this trouble and lose a great job."

His gaze held a seriousness that made my heart dip. He didn't say anything else, instead he reached for my hand and brought it to his lips. I leaned the side of my head on his shoulder, and we sat in silence for a little while, just silence. A comfortable, beautiful silence.

"I have something for you," he said, arching off the couch to pull something out of his back pocket. He handed over a folded packet, which I took as I sat up. I opened the papers and read through it, gasping, my heart beating uncontrollably. Tears started to form in my eyes before I even finished reading the entire thing.

"We're going to Iceland?" I asked in a hoarse whisper.

Victor smiled softly. "We're going to Iceland."

"You know that's where they film—" I started, but he snatched the papers from my hand and turned the page before I could finish. I screamed. Loud. And bolted out of the couch. "Oh my God! Oh my God! We're going? We're really going? But how?"

Victor laughed and pulled me onto his lap. "I know people."

"Did you tell your sister about this?" I asked after long quiet minutes, in which I read everything on the pages he'd given me.

"Hell, no. She'd kill me. We can send her a picture when we get over there. We leave in a week by the way," he said, kissing my forehead.

"A week." I paused, eyes wide. "I have to find out if we're still on shooting break."

"You are."

"How do you know?" I asked, my veins still drenched in adrenaline.

"Your friend Talon told me."

"What?" My mouth dropped. "How did you get in touch with her?"

He chuckled, pulling me so I could straddle his lap. "I already told you, I know people."

I wrapped my hands around his neck and smiled. "I really do love you."

"You better," he said. "I don't even watch that fucking show."

Chapter Thirty-Five

Victor

ICELAND WAS FUCKING freezing, but the permanent smile on Nicole's face made the trip worth it. We were on set, and even though she said she was a huge fan of the costume designer, all she did was check out the guys.

"You're drooling again," I whispered in her ear. She shivered, wrapping her arms around herself.

"I'm sorry. I know it's in bad form to check out another man in front of your boyfriend, but oh my God," she said, her teeth rattling. I laughed, wrapping my arms around her.

"I'm not worried."

She smiled, tilting her head to look up at me. "You're so sure of yourself."

I shrugged. No point in denying it. She wasn't going anywhere, and neither was I. Even if I wanted to leave her, my family would probably disown me at this point. In the week we had between our reconciliation and the trip, we'd been inseparable, which meant everywhere I went, Nicole was there and vice versa. One of those days, we'd gone over to my parents' house for dinner, where Mia, Jensen, Oliver, and Estelle joined us. Whenever Nicole wasn't in the room all I heard was, "put a ring on it" and "you better marry that girl." Every time I reminded them her divorce wasn't even officially final, they shook their heads as if it was somehow my fault. But when I admitted I would marry her someday, Jensen and Oliver didn't shut the fuck up about me being in love.

I let them have their fun because every time the subject was brought up they ended up arguing about who won whatever bet they had going. It was amusing to watch.

"I'm glad you've taken such an interest in my personal life," I said when we were sitting outside having a drink.

"We bet five hundred dollars and this asshole won't admit he was wrong," Jensen said, nodding at Oliver. I gaped at them. Five hundred dollars?

"What the fuck was the bet?"

"That you were involved with a client," Oliver said.

"No. That you would become involved with a client and actually fall for her," Jensen corrected.

"No. He only had to fuck one of his clients, and he told you he was representing Nicole before we made the bet, so it should be thrown out the window," Oliver said, raising an eyebrow.

"You should have bet for Jensen to get a tattoo on his ass and for you to cut your fucking hair," I said.

They scoffed.

"All I'm saying is I won," Oliver said. "Did you or did you not fuck her before you became her attorney?"

My jaw twitched. I didn't want to talk about my sex life with Nicole, and I couldn't even throw anything back at him about his because I really didn't want to talk about his sex life with my sister. I took a gulp of Jameson and looked at him over my glass. "Fuck you, Rapunzel."

Jensen laughed loudly. "You do need a haircut."

"Fuck you both," Oliver said, running a hand through his hair. "The kids like it."

They probably did. I'd heard from a friend of a friend that the pediatrics office where he worked boomed after he'd gotten a job there. My sister seemed to be amused by the whole hot doctor thing he had going on at work. I shook my head.

"Both of you are assholes," I said, standing and stretching. "Now let me go get ready. I have a long flight and I hear Game of Thrones shoot is pretty epic, so I don't want to be tired when I get there."

That shut both of them up for all of three seconds before they started with an onslaught of insults. *You bastard! I can't believe you're going! I hope they hire you as an extra and kill you off!*

I chuckled and raised my middle finger up as I walked away from them. "They only kill Muggles."

"That's not even the right series," they screamed.

"Keep betting against me. You'll never win," I shouted back.

"You're an asshole. Send pictures."

"I'll think about it."

Now we were here and I realized just how impressive the set actually was, I'd sent short of a thousand pictures. Nicole was just in awe of everything, the way I probably would have been if I'd actually watched it on television. I'd always avoided things when my clients worked on shows I enjoyed because I thought they'd take away from the fantasy of what I liked watching on screen, but this was the real deal. The set was Iceland, and Iceland was breathtaking. And I'd probably never set foot back here again, so I tried to enjoy every second of it and openly being with Nicole.

My phone buzzed in my pocket and I took it out. Nicole rolled her eyes.

"I thought you were off work. You check your phone every

two seconds."

"Some of us need to stay employed, baby," I said, scrolling through my email. My heart stopped when I saw it was from Will and had a smiley face on the subject line. A fucking smiley face from Will could only mean one thing. I opened it up and noticed the attachment. Above it, the email said, *Good to have you back, partner.*

My heart leaped, soared, in a way that only rivaled what Nicole made me feel when she looked at me.

"Your hands are shaking. You need better gloves," Nicole said beside me. I shook my head.

"No. I'm not cold," I said, and meant it. As I opened the attachment on the email, all I felt was warmth. I let out a long, relieved, icy breath. "Thank. Fucking. God."

"What?" she asked. I turned the phone so she could see, and smiled when she gasped. She stayed quiet for so long, that I had to look at her. I noticed she had tears in her eyes. Tears that would probably freeze before they fell onto her face. I pulled her head and crashed it onto my beating heart. "It's over," she whispered. "It's really over."

I wasn't sure if she was sad, happy, relieved, and I didn't know if I had it in me to ask. I faced things head-on, but if she told me she was sad about her divorce finally being completely over, I wasn't sure how I'd feel. Probably broken-hearted. Probably crushed. I decided I need to man up and took a deep breath, rearing back slightly and tilting her face to look into her eyes.

"You okay?"

She nodded, blinking slowly. "I am." Her smile was slow, but wide. "I think . . . I really am." She let out a smoky breath. "I feel . . . free."

I smiled, bringing my lips to hers in a soft, chaste kiss. "Sorry to break it to you, but you're kind of stuck with me."

She laughed. "I'm okay with that."

"You better be, or I'll go tell that guy with the black feather cape to lend me his weapon," I said. Her eyes got huge and she completely froze for a beat.

"Is he behind us?"

I looked over her head. "Not right behind us, but yeah."

"Oh my God. I think I'm going to faint."

I laughed. "You haven't even seen him. He's not that big a deal."

If possible, her eyes widened more. "Jon. Snow. Is. A. Huge. Deal."

I groaned, remembering Mia and Estelle and everybody else I knew talking about him. "That's the fucking famous Jon Snow?"

Nicole turned around and let out a little silent excited shriek. "Yes."

I wrapped an arm around her and pulled her to me. We were on top of a little hill as we watched him walk with a heavy-set guy. He was not a big deal. He looked short. I was sure his hair made Oliver jealous, though, so I snapped a picture of him and sent it, knowing I wouldn't get a response until later on.

"Are you happy?" I asked, my mouth near her ear. She nodded.

"So happy," she said, turning in my hold and wrapping her hands around my neck. "I really, really, really fucking love you, Victor Reuben. Despite your aversion to marriage."

I grinned. She was so clueless. "I don't have an aversion to marriage."

"I heard you talking to your parents the other day." She paused, her blue eyes searching my face. "I'm okay with that. I don't need to get married again. Been there, done that, bought the shirt."

"Fuck that shirt."

"You say that about everything that has nothing to do with you," she said, laughing. "I'm just saying, you have a really great life. I'm not here to disrupt your organized, meticulous lifestyle. I just want to be part of it."

I sighed and bent my knees, pulling her down to the warm blanket we'd been given when we got here. I held her gaze as I spoke to make sure there was nothing I said that would escape her realm of comprehension.

"You once said this was a goal for you," I said, waving a hand around the set around us. "My goals were always career-driven, and when I attained those, I realized my goals had changed a little and that somewhere along the way you became my goal. I'm in love with you. I've achieved a lot in my thirty-one years, and I'm proud of those accomplishments, but none of them make me feel the way you do. When we go back home, my next goal will be to get you to move in with me, and later on down the line it'll be to get you to agree to marry me, because I love you and I never want to be without you."

It took a moment for my words to sink in, and when they did, she blinked, and blinked, and the tears forming in her eyes began to fall. I caught them as they did, brushing them away.

"*I'm* goals?" she whispered, smiling.

"You are *every* goal I never knew I wanted."

Our lips met in a slow, sensual, long kiss that made me want to run back to the hotel and fuck her in our hot tub. When we broke apart, we smiled at each other.

"You know, this is the second time you've proposed to me," I said. "That's a record for somebody who says she doesn't care to get married again and just finalized a divorce."

She blushed, looking away. "I never said I was against marriage just because it didn't work out for me before."

I caught her chin and made her look at me again. "Good, because I'm going to marry you."

"You say that as if you know I'll say yes."

"Haven't you learned by now?" I asked, pulling her bottom lip into my mouth and letting it go with a pop. "I always get what I want."

She was it for me. I'd never in my thirty-one years wanted anything the way I wanted my beautiful, feisty, and sexy Nicole Alessi, and I knew I never would.

Epilogue

Nicole

Two years later

"YOU SHOULD JUST quit your job and design wedding dresses for a living," Talon said as she did my makeup.

"Maybe one day I will," I said, looking up as she applied eyeliner.

"You're going to look incredible. Victor is going to wish he'd asked you to marry him eight years ago."

I smiled. "I wasn't ready for him then."

"He is pretty intimidating," she said, smiling.

"A little." I paused. "Are the girls ready?"

"If by ready you mean dressed, yes. Mike said they're picking up all the flowers they scattered during their practice session, though."

I laughed.

"Stop moving."

"Sorry."

There was a knock on the door, followed by the loud voices

of Hannah, my mom, Mia, Estelle, and Chrissy. Mia and Chrissy hadn't stopped talking since they met at the bachelorette party last week. They were highly entertaining to be around. I think all of us agreed on that. All of us except Victor, who groaned every time they walked into a room together.

"I *so* hope you guys have daughters," Estelle said. I smiled and reached to touch her pregnant belly when she stood beside me.

"So your brother can have a heart attack by the age of forty?" I asked.

Estelle laughed.

"He'll be a great dad," Hannah said. I completely agreed with that sentiment.

"He would be, and they'd make beautiful babies," my mom agreed. When I first told her that instead of moving into another place when my lease ended, I was moving in with Victor, she flipped out, but then she came to the U.S. and met him, and they instantly hit it off.

"I completely agree, and so will you," Meire added as she walked into the room.

Mom's head whipped around quickly. We'd all gone out to dinner numerous times through this process and it had given Mom and Meire a chance to get to know each other. I doubted Mom would approve of anybody Dad married, but she seemed to have a lot of respect for Meire.

"You look incredible," Chrissy said.

"I know, right? I wanna marry you right now," Mia added.

I laughed. I was already feeling overjoyed, but having these people in my life, on this day, took my excitement to another level. I didn't want a big wedding this time around, but once we started adding up our family members and friends, we ended up with two hundred people on our list. I put eloping on the table, but Victor turned it down as quickly as I said it. He didn't say it in so many words, but I knew he didn't want me to compare this wedding with Gabe's and mine. Not that I ever would. Victor made me feel stable, and cherished, and loved, and even though I could make a million comparisons and give a million reasons as to why this marriage was a one hundred percent sure thing, I didn't. It wouldn't have been fair for me to diminish *the good* I'd once had with Gabe just because we hadn't worked out.

I'd seen him a couple times when he'd met up with me at the dog park to see Bonnie. Something the paparazzi loved to speculate about, much to Victor's annoyance, but he was okay with us maintaining a friendly relationship.

"I don't expect you not to be friends with somebody you were with for that long, but it doesn't mean I like the attention it gets," he'd said. *"And I still think he's an asshole."*

He did appreciate Gabriel sending him a box of Cuban cigars and a bottle of Blue Label as a congratulatory gift for our wedding, though.

"That was a nice thing to do. He owed me for keeping you from me all those years," he'd said when Marcus dropped off the present at his house, which we'd been sharing since we came back from our trip to Iceland.

Marcus no longer drove me around. Well, not all the time. I definitely didn't need security anymore, but we'd kept in touch and now he had to deal with Victor's and my rants. He seemed to be totally okay with both, but preferred Victor's, probably because the rants usually happened over basketball, baseball, or football games, which were a thing in our house. I hated sports, so how I ended up marrying somebody who was so obsessed with them was just . . . crazy. I loved it, though. I loved having a house full of people.

He'd brought up marriage a few times, but I never imagined

him getting down on one knee. I never imagined him pulling me into his arms one night as I'd walked through the door after a long day at work and holding me for the longest moment. Just holding me and breathing into my hair. When he leaned away from me just slightly and wordlessly searched my face, I began to worry. I was going to ask what was wrong, what had happened, when he dropped down on one knee and took a little black box out of his pocket as he looked up at me.

"I've had this ring for a few months, but there hasn't been a right time for me to ask, with work, and everything else we've had going on. There's never a right time because that's how life is. It's always chaotic, it's always hectic, and work will never stop, and I love sharing that with you. I love being able to come home and have you as my sanctuary. You've built that for me, with me, and I want us to have it forever. I don't want to imagine a life without you, Nicole Alessi. Marry me."

I still got teary-eyed thinking about it. Estelle saw the look on my face and slapped my arm playfully, snapping me out of my thoughts.

"Stop it. You can't cry," she said.

"I know. I was just thinking about Victor."

"Ugh. Yeah, I'd be crying too," Mia said, making us laugh.

"Are you ready?" my mom asked.

I nodded. "Yes." And I had been.

My dad's eyes widened when he saw me, a huge smile spreading over his face. I remembered the last time we'd done this and how serious he'd looked. Today he looked carefree, happy, as if he'd been waiting to give me away his entire life instead of wanting to grab me and lock me in my room forever. I asked him what changed, and he chuckled.

"I don't know. Maybe the fact that you've already done this?" he mused, and locked eyes with me. "Or maybe it's the man you're marrying. I see the way his eyes light up when he hears your name, and the way he takes care of you and puts you over everything. Not many things can drive him out of the office, you know? You did good, Nic. He's one of the good ones."

I smiled, feeling myself tear up again. Shit. I needed to stop doing that. "I know."

When the church doors opened, our friends stood up along the aisle, but the only man I saw was Victor, who looked fucking edible in his sharp tux. Victor, who didn't look at me like I was the end of something, but rather, the *beginning* of everything. I loved that man. So much. When I reached him and he shook hands with my dad, I felt my heart nearly jump out of my chest. This is what it felt like to be complete. This is what a fairy tale was like. This feeling right here. *This* was goals. This moment.

We looked at each other for a long, quiet moment, one filled with endless possibilities, the way our future together felt.

"You look beautiful," he whispered as the priest started the mass.

"So do you," I replied. His lips curved up.

"I know."

I shook my head, rolling my eyes.

"You already signed the paperwork, Nicole Reuben. No going back now," he said, his eyes twinkling.

He was so keen to mention that every five minutes since the day we'd gone to the courthouse. His face had been priceless when I'd reached for the name-change form and filled it out. I'd not taken Gabe's last name. I didn't really want to change mine, as I loved the name Alessi, but I knew how much it meant to Victor, and the more I thought about it, the more I liked it. Nicole Reuben had quite a nice ring to it.

"I would never," I said.

"Not even if I was richer?" he asked. "Not even if I was famous?"

"No way. Been there, done that, bought the shirt."

His eyes darkened. "I tore that shit up."

"Victor," I whisper-shouted, giving him a pointed look. We were at church.

"I'm just saying, my shirt's better," he whispered with a shrug, then smiled. "And much bigger."

Note from Claire:

Thank you so, so much for reading!

The characters in this series will forever have a part of my heart. They've been there for me when I needed to focus on the lighter things in life and believe in love so powerful, it could pull you out of any funk life wants to bury you under. I hope they did the same for you!

If you can take a minute to write a quick review, I would be incredibly grateful!

Also, if you'd like to receive a bonus scene from Victor and Nicole, fill out this form:
http://goo.gl/forms/aWqhuRGhxz

Xo,
Claire

Acknowledgements

I'm not going to name everybody because publishing a book takes a village, and my village has so many wonderful people in it that I'm afraid I'll forget to name some of them, like the bloggers who share my things, the authors who support me, and the readers who continuously tell their friends to buy my books. You're the ones who matter most, so thank you, from the bottom of my heart.

To my SQUAD. I love you. #SQUADGOALS

MY FYW girls. I'd be lost without you.

B.B.F.T. & the incredible girls in my FB group-- YOU ROCK.

Willow A., Jenn W., Rachel K., Yvette V., Tiffany C., Michelle K., Lisa C., Julie V., Clarissa L., Sandra C., Priscilla P., Jen G., Jessica S., Katie R., Bridget P., Toski C, Karinna B., Anabelle, Diana, Barbie, Mimi, and the list goes on and on! --- you guys are incredible and deserve a medal for putting up with me.

Every single blog who has shared my cover, read my books, reviewed them, and spread the word--- I appreciate you more than words can say.

TRSOR- THANK YOU for putting together my tours.

Sarah at Okay Creations- thank you for putting up with my anxiety and designing the most amazing covers on my shelf.

Marion Making Manuscripts & Karen Lawson- The dynamic duo! I love your eyes.

Stacey Blake- you're a queen. I love you.

Printed in Great Britain
by Amazon

49650169R00203